HARRY BOWLING
Conner Street's War

First published in 1987 by
HEADLINE BOOK PUBLISHING PLC

This edition published in paperback in 2015 by
HEADLINE PUBLISHING GROUP

1

ISBN 978 0 7553 4034 7

Typeset in Times by Avon DataSet Ltd,
Bidford-on-Avon, Warwickshire

Printed and bound in Great Britain by
CPI Group (UK) Ltd, Croydon, CR0 4YY

Headline's policy is to use papers that are natural, renewable and recyclable
products and made from wood grown in well-managed forests and other
controlled sources. The logging and manufacturing processes are expected to
conform to the environmental regulations of the country of origin.

HEADLINE PUBLISHING GROUP
An Hachette UK Company
Carmelite House
50 Victoria Embankment
London EC4Y 0DZ

www.headline.co.uk
www.hachette.co.uk

Harry Bowling was born in Bermondsey, London, and left school at fourteen to supplement the family income as an office boy in a riverside provisions' merchant. He was called up for National Service in the 1950s. Before becoming a writer, he was variously employed as a lorry driver, milkman, meat cutter, carpenter and decorator, and community worker. He lived with his wife and family, dividing his time between Lancashire and Deptford before his death in 1999.

To Shirley, Stephen, Sharon and Sally

Prologue

An old man walked slowly past the shuttered shops that spread along the base of the building on the Riverside Estate, and took the walkway to Conner Point. The wind caught the door of the high-rise building as he opened it and slammed it behind him as he crossed the hall. As he waited for the lift, the door again creaked open and slammed behind a woman carrying a bulging shopping bag. She put it down and pulled up her coat collar against the cold wind that whistled through the glassless window panel beside the door. A plastic sheet had been crudely nailed to the frame and it flapped fiercely. The woman held a hand to the middle of her back. ''Ello Mr Bowman,' she said, glancing up at the light above the lift which had remained on above number ten. 'It's them kids wot do it. They press all the buttons.'

Bob Bowman looked at her and grunted.

She stabbed at the lift button impatiently. 'I keeps on tellin' the porter, though a fat lot o' good 'e is.'

The old man nodded and looked up at the light that had now started to move along the numbers. At last there was a clunk and the lift door slid open. The two entered the lift and the woman's face screwed up as she noticed the puddle at the rear. 'Bloody kids. They don't even live on the Estate. 'Arf of 'em are gyppos' kids.'

Bob Bowman was getting irritated. He pressed the button marked fifteen and the woman reached across and pressed the button above. Bob noticed that she had a tic. Her eyes blinked and her nose twitched like a rabbit's. A grin ghosted over Bob's hawkish features and his pale blue eyes twinkled. 'Coffins,' he said, and the lift stopped at the eleventh. He pressed the correct button and the lift moved up.

The woman looked at him blankly.

'That's right yer know. These lifts were made ter take coffins. Saves slidin' 'em down the apples.' The woman's nose twitched. 'Well, coffins an' stretchers,' he added as the lift stopped on the fifteenth. He alighted grinning, aware of her stern gaze boring into the back of his head.

There was a numbered door at each corner of the hallway. He made for the one to his right and put his evening paper under his arm as he started to search for his key. The door opened suddenly and Brenda his daughter stood in the doorway. 'I heard the lift, Dad. We were getting worried.'

The lights below spread out into the distance. They twinkled, a myriad earthbound stars. A twin row of lights arced away, tracing the path of the Old Kent Road. Eastwards, a square of lights lit the railway station. A commuter train slid along towards the dark hills of suburbia, its carriages coughing out blue flashes. Immediately below, the grassed area looked clean and deserted in the light from the tall concrete lamp-posts.

Brenda sat in an easy chair, a sewing basket at her feet. She held a needle and cotton out at arm's length, her eyes squinting as she sought to thread the needle. On her lap lay a pair of torn trousers. Her husband Joe sat facing her, his back to the window. He had the evening paper spread out over his crossed legs as he tried to interest himself in the news. Right then sleep seemed to be the better proposition, and his eyes started to close.

Bob Bowman sat by the window. The curtains remained open, for as his daughter often remarked, 'only the birds can look in'. The young woman studied her father's face as he sat hunched in the high-backed chair. Concern showed in her eyes. She had noticed the change in him since he had moved in with her and Joe just over a year ago. His shoulders sagged more of late, and his sure stride had become slower, more deliberate. His eyes were now growing glassy and faded. Worse still, he had started to mumble to himself on occasions. He was doing it now. Brenda thought about their impending move down to Sevenoaks. Her father had flatly refused to leave dockland. ''Ere I was born, an' 'ere I'll die,' he'd said.

The council had promised her father a bedsit in the old people's dwellings near the river, and the old boy was looking forward to it, but as yet there was nothing definite. Brenda hoped that once he got away from the tower block and among people he knew, her father's health would improve. Brenda felt helpless. Her husband's firm was moving, and there were houses made available for the staff. If only she did not feel so worried about her father. She turned to Joe but her husband was lost to sleep. His head hung to one side, his mouth gaping open.

Down below a car turned into the estate, its headlights scything a path before it. The car revved along the road and the muffled sound of its engine was lost on the old man. He had heard a different sound, the deep, throaty sound of a river boat as it dragged its charge towards the Pool. The tug belched again; a long hoot, then a shorter one. The familiar sound stirred his memories. He was back once more amongst the river men: stevedores, dockers, cranemen, like himself, and lightermen. He could almost taste the river, with its pungent-smelling, greyish mud, its sudden fogs that crept up from the Estuary and spread inshore, swirling over the quayside and into the narrow, cobbled dockside streets. He remembered the muffled sounds of the chugging workhorses of the Thames, the tugs that sat low in the oily swell and hauled and fussed at the complexities of moorings. He remembered the dangerous climb up the cold iron ladder that took him high above the quay, up into a space above the sheds, where he was powerful, where he lorded it over the men below, yet was attentive to their every signal and gesture. Up here he pulled and pushed the levers that moved the monstrous crane jib and arm, which hoisted, swung, lowered, and set down rope-slung cargoes gently onto the quay. Up here the smells drifted, smells of sweating wine casks, ripening fruit, and sour mud.

There were other sights that the old man's memories surveyed. He saw Tower Bridge rising and he sighed deeply. He saw again the cantilevers rise and sink, the slender part reaching high for the bridge towers, the bulk sinking into the giant stone bastions. He heard the warning bell and saw the large vessel as it slipped slowly and silently out from the Pool of London, towards the Estuary and the oceans beyond. He saw once more the scene down river, the rotting boatyards where ships were once made of stout English oak. He saw the riverside taverns, where long ago corsairs hung to rot, their popping, sightless eyes meat for the crows, and a terrible warning to returning mariners.

Bob Bowman raised his shoulders and let them sag again. The river ache was in his bones and he looked down below. The scene changed. He saw the little backstreet and felt its heartbeat. There was the iron lamppost, its light spreading over the cobbled stones. A looped rope hung from the ladder support and at the bottom of the rope a coat was folded to make a seat. A young girl occupied the seat. She swung slowly, her feet scraping over the cobbles. Above her the hiss of the damaged mantle sounded and the escaping flame burned blue in the cold evening air. A small boy stood inside the lighted area, his face stained with the juice of the half orange that he held in his dirty grasp. Bob Bowman looked down into the dark backyard. A door opened and a shaft of light caught the rusting wringer with its dry wooden rollers that had started to split. He saw the long bathtub and the dartboard hanging from the whitewashed wall. The door shut and the darkness reclaimed its secrets.

Iron wheels sounded on the cobbles as the horse-cart rounded the turn. A carman sat, his shoulders drooping in fatigue, while his eager horse was struggling home to its hay-filled stall. Bob Bowman, sitting by his window in the sky, saw the lights all go out. A terrifying wail reached his ears as the generator on the police station roof started up. As the scream of the siren died so another familiar sound reached him. It came from the dark sky, and Bob stiffened in his chair. He watched as the pencils of light danced about the heavens and then converged on a tiny silver object floating in the light. The object drifted on. There was a loud swish and a louder roar as mortar and bricks flew skywards and the rush of flames engulfed the wharf. A whole wall toppled into the Thames and the water burned. The old man's head was held sideways, his ears straining for the sound. It floated up to him, 'There's an old mill by the stream.' Softly, then more loudly, 'Nellie Dean,' it said, and he looked down, his eyes searching for the place. There it was, the mound of earth, like some prehistoric barrow. From the bricked vents on top of the mound, the voices were now loud and clear. The song went on, 'Where I used to sit and dream.'

Another roar, and the urgent shout of 'Oil bomb on the factory!' Burning contents from the building spewed over the mound and the earth burned. Gun flashes lit up the street and the running feet as the men raced to the shelter. They dived down into the gutter for safety, then jumped up and ran faster. One man stayed still, his life-blood draining out and down into the sewer.

There was a shout 'The warden, get the warden!'

He was running; steel helmet held down by the tight strap under his chin. His hands were blackened and cut. His chest was heaving and his coat scorched and torn. He saw the faces; grey, dust-caked and pleading, ''Elp us, Bob! . . . Don't leave us, Bob! . . . Gawd bless yer, Bob.' Bob Bowman shuddered and sank back into his chair, his eyes closed.

A voice, nearer and louder, came to him. 'Dad. Dad.' He felt the hand on his shoulder. 'There's your tea, Dad. Was you dreaming?'

Bob sat up, shook his head and clasped the mug of steaming tea. 'Sorry girl, must've dozed orf.'

His daughter looked out of the window at the full yellow orb floating in the night sky. 'It's a full moon,' she said.

'Bomber's moon we used ter call it, once upon a time.'

Chapter One

The early morning light had filtered very rapidly into the velvet sky, and caused the elevated signal box at Bermondsey Crossing to stand out in sharp relief. The white painted weatherboards around the four sides of the cabin had lost some of the grime after the night storm, and the water had run down on to the six feet high bricked base, which had absorbed the moisture like a sponge. The storm had laid the dust and the air was crystal. The rows of track glistened, and seemed to forge into a silver strip away into the distance. Westwards, the track bent, a long arc that reached the London Bridge terminal. One track split from the sweep and took an opposing curve into the goods depot, a half mile from the station.

Inside the cabin Joe Harper yawned and stretched his aching back. The first of the morning trains was due, the Kent milk train.

A bell sounded; a shrill ring that told the signalman the 'milkman' was on time and he responded by throwing over the heavy lever that controlled the bisection of the track. He then pulled on an adjacent lever that dropped the signal-arm into the 'clear' position. Joe glanced down the track to check that the green light showed, then wiped his hands on a piece of cotton waste. The kettle rattled as the blue gas flame licked around its sides. A steam ring popped from the spout and enlarged as it floated upwards. Joe carefully counted out four heaped spoonfuls of tea leaf from a battered canister into a brown enamel teapot. A minute later the milk train clattered past and the cabin became enveloped in steam. Rivulets of the condensed vapour ran down the windows and the cabin shook. The kettle started to boil and Joe Harper filled the teapot to the brim, stirring the brew thoughtfully. Fred Harris, the day man, was due soon and, as was the custom, the shift always started and ended with a strong brew.

Joe put the filled teapot under a ragged looking cover and stretched again, his fingers reaching around for the offending ache. There was a stained mirror taped onto the wall and Joe Harper looked at his reflection. The wide spaced eyes, grey-green and tired, stared back at him. He studied the thick dark hair that had started to recede and the square chin that had sprouted a black stubble. He looked at his broad nose and noticed how the skin was becoming loose around his neck. He sighed and pulled a face at his reflection, then walked over to the window facing down the track. He grinned to himself as he saw Fred Harris limping towards the cabin. The day man carried a canvas bag that was slung over his shoulder, his thumb crooked around the strap. Fred's limp was the result of a shell splinter, obtained on the Somme in '15. Pieces of the metal had been removed by doctors, and by Fred himself over the years, as tiny pieces worked their way to the surface of his leg. Fred was convinced that the steel portion still embedded was going rusty. 'Stan's to reason, don't it? Wiv all the rain we get.'

The two men were lifelong pals. They had run the streets as boys, and marched out of those backwaters to fight in France. They took the 'King's Shilling' and suffered the mud and slush of the trenches, and they both returned. Fred Harris limped back on crutches and his pal returned with his lungs blistered and scarred from the evil vapours of the mustard gas.

Fred Harris climbed the wooden steps up to the cabin and walked in. 'Mornin' mate, quiet night?'

'Not too bad, Fred, got two extra early on. One looked like a troop train.'

Fred sat down and rubbed his leg. 'It's the bloody rain, bin givin' me 'ell all night,' he complained. Joe grinned, handed a mug filled with red-coloured tea to Fred, and sat down on a tall stool. 'That'll oil your rusty leg, me ole mate.'

Fred sipped the hot tea noisily. 'Rained all night, so my little woman tells me.'

Joe nodded and he took a swig at his tea. 'Left off around four this mornin'. 'Eavy too.'

Fred Harris rubbed a large hand over his eyes. 'My Sara woke me up just about then. Said she could 'ear the water drippin' in. I said to 'er, wadja s'pect me to do, shin up the drainpipe wiv a load o' slates? Go back to sleep I told 'er.'

Joe laughed and finished his tea. He collected Fred's empty mug and washed them both under the running tap. There was a large calendar hanging on the wall which depicted a young lady in tennis clothes and sporting a large green eyeshade. She smiled down into the room. Joe tore the date slip off to expose the new date. It read Sunday 3rd September, 1939.

'Well I'm away 'ome, mate, take it easy.'

'See you, Joe,' Fred replied.

The night man paused by the door. 'I'm goin' to stay up for the speech, it looks bad.'

Fred nodded. 'Don't see no way out now, wot wiv the Czechs, an' now the Poles.'

Joe opened the door of the cabin. 'Gawd 'elp us if it does start. Be a sight worse than the last lot.'

*

9

A flock of pigeons flew over the pickle factory as Joe Harper walked along the empty street. Birds were singing and the sun had started its journey into the sky. Joe was feeling a sense of uneasiness as he walked on. The sound of iron wheels on cobbles reached his ears, and from around the corner Taffy Davies appeared, struggling to get his heavy milk-cart on an even course as the wheels slithered over the cobbles. The empty milk bottles on top of the cart rattled in their containers and two small metal churns swung together on the side rail. Taffy leaned forward against the weight, his head down and his neck muscles straining. Joe nodded a greeting but the Welshman ignored him. Joe stood for a moment watching as the cart resumed a straight course, then he turned into Tanners Alley, a cobbled pathway that led to Conner Street. The alley was flanked on one side by the high wall of the leather factory, and on the other by a row of pretty little cottages. The local kids had named the place 'Door Knocker Alley' – and for good reason. On every door there were the most hideous-looking door knockers. One was of a lion's head, snarling; another, the grinning face of the devil. A mailed fist warned from one door, and many other leering, threatening monstrosities confronted the passer-by.

It was as though someone had looked at the pretty cottages, with their ivy-covered walls, their colourful flower-boxes that hung below the shuttered windows, and had decided to exact a penance. This someone had looked at the front doors that opened onto the cobbled path and maliciously concluded that a reminder would hang there. Beauty had no place in such an area; for how could any tranquillity exist with the grimy wharves and warehouses, the noisy grind of the leather factories, the belt-driven machines and the steam presses that thrashed and thumped, the ugly arches and cold iron bridges that carried the railway, and the run-down streets and tenement blocks, stained and covered with sulphur and carbon. Why should there be such a place in the morass that was dockland?

The knockers were fitted, and the perpetrator stood back to ponder. He was not pleased, for the ugliness of his work was partly concealed, subdued by the flowering beauty that grew from the window boxes, and from the wall-rooted vines. Yellow primrose, and bright red geranium calmed the ashen iron. Shades of begonia and pansy and the white of the doorsteps soothed the trepidation of the passer-by and he breathed more easily. Young children walked the alley without fear as they leered back at the faces, and they gave the place its name.

Joe Harper heard the gurgle of rain water running beneath the drain grill as he walked along the path and into Conner Street. At the point where the alley opened into the Street was an iron hitching post. It stood upright and embedded in the path. The post was once the barrel of a Crimean war cannon. But now its muzzle was plugged and faced the sky. Joe touched the cold, smooth surface as he passed by and thought it strange that he had never really recognised the significance of the harmless looking piece of ironmongery, until this morning. But then this particular morning was different.

The signalman turned left, and strolled along the quiet street towards number 22. As he passed the Flannagan's house at number 30, he heard the new baby yelling, the loud shout from Patrick, then the soothing voice of Bridie as she no doubt satisfied the belly pains of the child. The Flannagans were a large brood. Bridie fussed over them all like a mother hen over her chicks. She also kept a firm hold over her huge husband, although she barely reached his shoulder. Patrick worshipped them all, but there were times when the strain, and the din, would force him to seek the peace and quiet of the Eagle, a little pub on the corner of Conner Street.

Joe reached his house and pulled on the door string. He

walked into the dark passage and entered the tiny parlour. His lodger, a wizened looking old man, followed him in and stood waiting as Joe sat down heavily into his favourite chair.

'Like a cuppa, Joe?'

'I could do, Skip,' replied the younger man.

The old man blew his nose on his large red handkerchief.

Joe started to take off his boots. 'Is Rosie awake?'

The old man poked the handkerchief into his back pocket. 'I took 'er up a cup, gone back to kip,' he answered.

'You're up early this mornin', Skipper.'

'Couldn't sleep for the rain, and that wind. Reminded me of those storms we used to get at sea.'

Joe licked his lips and grinned. 'I'd really like a cuppa, Skip.'

The lodger pointed his long boney finger at him. 'Comin' up.'

Joe Harper knew the man well. If he allowed the old seaman to get started on a subject concerned with the sea, then the chances of a quick cuppa would evaporate. There were nights, when the wind howled and the fire burned bright, when Joe and Rosie listened with interest as the old seafarer spun his yarns from the oceans. On this particular morning, however, and at this early hour, he was not inclined to listen.

Skipper was in his mid-seventies, a dapper little man, with a full mane of snow-white hair that hung over his coat collar, and defied the comb. He had spent his youth walking the piers of the world and sailing the oceans under canvas; in the coal-fired tramps, from Yokohama to Lisbon, from Valparaiso to San Francisco. He'd weathered the storms and suffered the food, until the pains in his bones and the hardships became more than he could bear. He had said goodbye to the feel of the wind and spray and settled for the lodging room near the docks. That way, he could still walk near the ships, and meet the like of himself, men that smelt of the sea and talked of the ships. For a time the old seaman moved around, then he found the Harpers and he loved them like his own. They were a real family, and they cared for his needs. He'd seen the girls grow into women and marry. He'd been around when the eldest's two were born. Yes, this was his home, his family.

Joe sat back in his chair and lit a cigarette. Skipper came in with the tea. ''Ere we are, son,' he said.

'Thanks, Skip,' Joe answered, looking quizzically at the other's fluffy white hair. 'Wot you been doin' to your barnet?'

The old man ran his fingers through his mane. 'Rosie got on to me to get it washed, said I was goin' lousy, so I used some of them there Lux flakes.'

Joe smiled. 'Looks like a pile of candyfloss, mate.'

Skipper growled and sat down.

Rosie came into the room. She had her dressing gown wrapped tightly around her ample figure.

'Mornin', luv, busy night?' she asked.

'Not so bad, bit of extra traffic.' he replied. 'Did you sleep okay?'

'Didn't 'ear a thing, I was that tired out.'

Joe puffed a cloud of cigarette smoke ceilingwards. Rosie started to remove the wire pipe-cleaners which served as curlers from her hair. 'I'll get you some breakfast,' she said.

'No rush, luv, I'm staying up for the news anyway.'

Rosie looked into his pale eyes. 'Bad ain't it?'

'Yeah, it is, an' there's no use sayin' otherwise. There's goin' to be a war, my love, an' it's goin' to be a nasty one.'

Rosie pulled up a chair and sat down at the table. She placed a small mirror in front of her and started to comb out her hair.

Skipper took out his pipe and greasy tobacco pouch then proceeded to fill the blackened bowl. When he'd packed the 'Nosegay' strands down tight, he struck a match and drew on the stem. Sparks flew onto his dirty waistcoat and he quickly brushed them off. Rosie gave him a cold stare. 'One of these days you're goin' to set yourself alight.'

The street was coming to life. Footsteps sounded as folk went for their Sunday papers and their usual weekend supply of winkles and shrimps. Near Tanners Alley, the old rag-and-bone man leaned on his battered barrow and called out his unintelligible cry. On the pavements, the children played at hopscotch and with their coloured glass marbles along the kerbsides. They cracked their whips and sent the wooden tops skidding along pavements and in amongst the cobbles.

Two girls slowly turned a skipping-rope as a smaller girl hopped in and out of range of the thudding cord, singing a ditty as she went. The sun shone down from a cloudless sky, and at the end of the street the ice-cream man fixed the canopy above his stall.

Skipper had gone for the morning papers and Joe sat with Rosie in their tiny parlour. The woman looked up at the framed photograph sitting on the mantelshelf. 'I'm worried over 'em, Joe, what with them children bein' so young. I've told Josie to try an' get out of London, get 'em into the country somewhere.'

Joe looked at her. 'Listen Rosie, Josie nor Brian would let them kids be evacuated. Brian will be called up soon and as for Mary an' Bob, well, Bob's bin mobilised now, an' Mary's workin' at the 'ospital. It's goin' to be difficult.'

Rosie looked down at her hands and studied her nails. 'Mary's takin' it well, but young Josie seems upset,' she said.

'I've noticed 'ow our Josie's got lately, seems jumpy with the kids,' replied Joe.

Rosie's eyes filled with tears and her husband leaned forward, taking her hands in his own and gently squeezing them as he planted a kiss on her forehead. Rosie dabbed at her eyes and stood up. 'I'd better get those breakfast things washed up,' she said.

The door latch slid over against the pull of the string and Skipper came into the parlour and dropped the papers onto the table. He had his clay pipe held in the corner of his mouth. Joe ignored the papers and lit another cigarette. Skipper sat down by the empty firegrate and reached for a pipe-cleaner. 'Rosie looks upset, Joe.'

'Yeah, it's the girls, an' the two little ones. Rosie wants 'em to try an' get away from London.'

Skipper threaded the pipe-cleaner along the stem of his stained pipe and worked it back and forth. He then tapped the bowl gently against his foot and blew hard down the stem. 'If it does start we're goin' to get a pastin' aroun' this area. Stan's to reason, there's the docks, an' railways. The bastards are gonna get them sort of places.'

Joe stood up. 'I'm goin' for a breath of air.'

The signalman leaned against the door post, his gaze wandering up and down the street. A large woman was having an argument with the ragman, 'You want to get that there contraption fixed. It must come to more than that,' she exploded.

'I've 'ad this spring balance for donkeys' years, it's right to the penny,' the man said with conviction.

'Looks like it could do wiv a drop of oil,' she replied, not wishing to be outdone.

The ragman counted out a few copper coins and dropped them into the woman's hand. She turned without another word and marched off. The man tucked the spring scale into his belt and threw the bundle of old rags onto the near-empty barrow.

Joe's gaze took in the row of terraced houses opposite. The sulphur and black carbon stains on the bricks were somewhat toned down by the white-laced curtains and the clean white-stoned front door steps. The grey slated roofs sloped down to meet drooping gutters and above, perched precariously, were the brick stacks, supporting red earthenware chimneypots.

Almost directly across from the Harpers' house was a newly erected structure. The design was of a hump-shaped tunnel with a thick wall placed down the centre to divide the space into two separate caverns. The roof was at ground level, and to get inside a path had been provided that sloped down to the entrance. The whole thing was covered by a thick layer of rubble and earth, making it invisible from the air. The path was flanked by metal railings and a gate closed the entrance. Just inside the iron gate there stood a wooden post set into the ground. A square board was nailed on top of the post and the square was painted a dull green. Beneath the painted part a sign was hung which said: 'In the event of a GAS ATTACK the paint will change colour'. What the notice did not say was which colour the board would take, nor did the sign inform the curious that, should they wait around to see the miracle happen, they also would change colour.

Joe looked over at the shelter and noticed that the padlock was missing and the gate ajar. He pondered over this and went into his house. The loud ticking clock on his parlour mantel-shelf said ten forty-five.

A few miles away, in a room overlooking the quiet Westminster street, last minute preparations were taking place for the broadcast that was to change the lives of the folk of Conner Street. In fact it would never be the same again for millions of people throughout the whole world.

Chapter Two

The long, wide Tower Road stretched from the wharves and docks to a junction, and from that junction main arteries led away to tidy suburbia, to large homes and to well kept gardens. The arteries led away to open green areas and to places with large smart shops. Tower Road had shops, but they were not smart, and the only greenery in Tower Road poked out from the boxes and bloomed from the barrows and stalls in the market. The dockland market was famous, for it was said that if an item could not be purchased there, then it wasn't made.

The Conner Street folk were proud of their market, and when they walked up the street, and dodged across the busy road between the clattering trams, they found themselves right in the middle of the kerbside trading.

The bone-shaking trams squealed to a stop at the beginning of the market and disgorged stern-faced, basket-carrying women who hurried into the trading place. The trams also transported idlers, who came to be part of the bustling scene and who strolled along the line of stalls at a leisurely pace.

Early each weekday morning a number 68 tram brought Stanley Nathan to Tower Road market. Stanley walked through the area at a brisk pace, for he had a business to attend to and by nature he was punctual and conscientious. The stall-holders acknowledged him as he passed by and Stanley returned their salutations with a nod and a grin. Stanley Nathan was well-liked and a respected member of the market fraternity. He had been a 'market man' for as long as he cared to remember, as his father had before him. The bustling scene and the smell of the place never failed to stimulate him and as he walked to his particular place of trading his face took on a cherubic expression. Stanley had had his share of sadness, however, and sometimes he dwelt upon it, but this was his home and he experienced a feeling of contentment when he looked about him.

Fruit and vegetables were piled high on the stalls, and there were barrows stacked with odd clothes, salads and toiletries. There was a fish barrow, and a live eel stall, where the children peered into the galvanised tanks to watch the squirming, sliding snakes of the sea. There was a 'Cheap-Jack' stall, where cards of buttons, thimbles, needles and pins, and blocks of coloured dyes were heaped together with cough mixture, soap and soda. When the pile started to diminish, Cheap-Jack would tip another box of mysteries onto the heap. One day, Mrs Wallace stopped to search for some shirt buttons and, delving into the pile, she discovered a bottle of patent cough cure. The label was dirty and stained, but she was able to read about the miraculous qualities of the tar-black contents. As her husband had a racking cough, Mrs Wallace took the bottle home.

It didn't cure her husband's cough, but it did turn the spoon green and a small drop burned a hole in her only tablecloth.

Spaced about the market were solemn-faced hawkers, who stood over their open suitcases displaying bundles of boot and shoelaces, cards of collar studs, and razor blades. They sold dusters, handkerchiefs and cheap brooches, little celluloid dolls and rubber ducks. The hawkers stood in the gaps between the stalls, alongside the traders, their backs no more than a couple of feet from the passing trams.

One character stood between the eel stall and a salad barrow. He wore a dirty, faded raincoat with a row of campaign medals pinned to the lapel. A strap slung around his neck supported a tray, which contained matches and shoelaces. A ginger-tinged moustache grew down over his lower lip. The man never, ever, spoke, nor did he ever seem to move his eyes. He stared ahead, like a sentry, protecting the space between the stalls. Even when a passing baby, held over the mother's shoulder, grasped a packet of laces the man's eyes remained perfectly still.

The smells of the ripened fruit and the fresh fish hung in the air, and were carried on the wind into the little backstreets, so that the inhabitants became aware of the market the moment they opened their front doors. The sounds too carried into the backwaters, above the noise of the clattering, rocking trams.

The market had shops that faced the stalls and barrows, and if an item was not available at the kerbside then it could more than likely be found in one of the shops.

The fame of Tower Road market spread afar, so that one day a lady in a moth-eaten fur coat came to the market to buy a parrot. She went away with a fine specimen, a talking parrot in a tall round cage. It was Cheap-Jack who told the story when he'd attracted an audience around his stall: 'True as I'm standin' 'ere,' he said. 'This 'ere lady takes this lovely parrot 'ome, an' stan's it on 'er sideboard. Well the bleedin' parrot won't say a word. So back she comes an' gives ole Silas an earful. Anyway, the ole man knows what's wrong, an' 'e sells the lady a little mirror. It turns out that parrots like to see 'emselves, it perks 'em up. "That'll make the cow-son talk," 'e says. Anyway, next week, back come this 'ere moth-eaten lady. "That bleedin' parrot's not said a word yet." "P'raps the thing's short-sighted," 'e says. 'E sells 'er a little silver bell, an' 'e says that when the parrot 'ears the tinkle it'll answer.' Cheap-Jack cleared his throat and a customer who had just stopped at the stall asked him how much was a packet of collar studs. 'Just a minute lady, I'm tellin' 'em about this parrot. Anyway, the lady goes away an' sure enough, back she comes the next week an' gives ole Silas a right mouthful. "The bleedin' parrot's dead," she says. Silas can't understand it. "Didn't it say anythin'?" 'e asked 'er. "Well", this lady said, "it did try to mumble a few words before it croaked it . . ." "Well, go on," Silas almost shouts at'er. The lady dabs 'er eyes cos she's a bit upset. "It sounded like it tried to say food . . . food."'

The customers erupted in laughter, and the woman holding the card of collar studs asked him again about the price.

'Just a minute, lady, I'm nearly finished. Ole Silas went berserk. "You mean to stan' there an' tell me you never fed the bleedin' thing? Strike me pink, lady, it only needed a sprinkle o' birdseed." ' The customers were laughing, and Cheap-Jack went on, 'Ole Silas was raving. 'E reckoned the lady should 'ave known 'ow to look after pets, she 'ad enough of 'em on 'er bleedin' coat . . . Oh now don't laugh, girls, the story's true. Sure as Gawd made little apples.'

The woman with the card of collar studs finally left satisfied, and the market settled down to normality. The hustle and bustle of the place contrasted with the peace and quiet of the little backstreets. Conner Street though had its fair share of activity. The Eagle and a small hatter's shop occupied the corners at the market end, and then the row of houses continued on each side until they were halted by the two factories: the leather works and a small custard powder factory.

At the Kent Road end were two small corner shops. The one on the left was owned by a little old lady who sold sweets and tobacco, whilst the shop opposite boasted a multitude of things, from vinegar and hearthstone, paint and putty, to tin-tacks and shoe leather. Behind the counter, hanging high from a large hook in the ceiling was a bundle of canes. They had crooked handles and were looked upon with awe by the visiting children.

On this Sunday, the shops were closed and shuttered and the stalls and barrows stored away in a backstreet shed. The only one to be seen was the shrimp and winkle stall that stood outside the hatter's shop. On the stall was a white cover, nailed in place over the wooden boards. An aproned lady with a ruddy face scooped up a pile of winkles into a pewter pot and dropped the pint-worth into a brown paper bag. A customer waited while the lady scooped up a pint of shrimps. The ice-cream man had just arrived and was tightening the red and white canopy above the four brass poles that stuck out of his barrow. He then opened up a box and stacked up columns of wafer cones ready for the children, two of whom were already waiting, copper coins held tightly in their sticky palms.

There was a strange tension in the air on that warm Sunday morning. Everyone felt it, as women snapped at their children and men stood in small groups talking quietly. It would soon be eleven o'clock and the waiting would be over. The suspense had grown during the past few months when signs and posters began to appear on hoardings, walls and lampposts. The signs pointed out first-aid posts, gas mask fitting stations and gas cleansing stations; the air-raid shelters and the wardens' posts, which were set up inside sand-bagged and strengthened buildings. The posters issued terrifying instructions, 'What to do in the event of an air raid or an invasion'.

The past few months had also heralded in a new sound; the air-raid siren. There had been demonstrations of this new, frightening device that screamed out a warning from the roofs of police stations and public buildings. The tone of the siren rose from a low pitched moan to an ear-splitting scream and, although broadcasts and leaflets had warned them what to expect, the sound still struck fear into the hearts of everyone who heard it. Bridie Flannagan called the siren a 'scream from hell'. Her husband Patrick used somewhat earthier adjectives to describe the noise.

The periodical 'try-out' of the air-raid warning was sure to awaken the Flannagans' baby, and as soon as Bridie had settled James again the long high-pitched sound of the all-clear would reverberate through the streets. James immediately woke up and made his own contribution to the cacophony.

The Spencer Street Primary School was a gas mask fitting station. Every day the people came with their children, the young leading the old. They came for their gas masks and they stood patiently in line as the uniformed workers fussed and instructed. The conversations were repeated daily: 'No, Mrs Smith, you musn't worry over your hair . . . That's right, pull the straps over your head . . . I'll try you with a medium one . . . It's only condensation, Mrs Smith . . . Yes, put your chin right into it . . .' So it went on. They brought out the children's masks, the red and blue ones with the two eye-pieces and the flat nose that rasped when the wearer breathed out. So it went on: 'No, Johnnie, don't frighten your sister . . . Don't pull the nose off, sonny . . .' The 'Mickey Mouse' masks were not at all frightening and the children rushed to try them on. 'That's all right, Mother. If he won't take it off, let the little dear walk home in it.' And mother walked from the centre with little Johnnie still wearing his mask and terrified two old ladies on their way in. The frailer of the two clung to her sister as a rasping noise came from the 'Mickey Mouse' mask. Johnnie's mother cuffed his ear and a wailing sound came from inside the mask as she led her son away.

The Fletcher sisters entered the centre to be confronted with a strange scene. One of the workers was demonstrating how to place a baby in a large container that was then zipped up. A hand pump supplied oxygen to the infant, who could be seen gurgling happily through a large cellophane visor. 'C'mon, Mother, let's see you use the pump . . . No, not so fast! It isn't a bicycle pump . . . That's better, a nice steady action.' There was a tearful outburst, and a reassurance, 'Look here, I don't suppose you'll ever need to use this, but it is as well to be prepared, isn't it?'

Maud Fletcher whispered to her sister, 'I wonder if they have anything here for the parrot?' and was rewarded with a despairing look.

One morning, Mrs Jenkins walked into the centre and stood patiently in line until it was her turn. Someone put on a mask and adjusted the strap over her head. When they had picked her off the floor they tore the mask off and applied the smelling salts. Later they tried again. Mrs Jenkins was picked up once more and eased into a chair. She sat ashen-faced for a while; then, when the colour had returned to her cheeks, they made towards her with a mask. Mrs Jenkins was adamant, 'If you think I'm goin' ter put that bleedin' contraption on again, yer got another think comin'. Take it away, an' if there is a gas attack I'll piss on my 'ankey an' 'old it round me face. They say it's just as good!'

Mrs Brown nudged Mrs Jones, 'That won't worry 'er much, she's always pissed anyway.'

Nan Roberts sauntered into the centre and fluttered her eyelids at one of the male workers. She was soon attended to and left the centre with a gas mask case slung casually over her shoulder. Mrs Jones nudged Mrs Brown 'Did yer see that?'

'See what?'

'Didn't yer notice? 'Er gas mask box. It was marked "large". I always said she 'ad a big 'ead.'

Having decided that there was little more to interest them, Mrs Lizzie Brown and Mrs Emmie Jones left the centre. Both were carrying a gas mask in a box, and on the side of each box the word 'medium' was stamped with indelible ink.

Soon after, the Fletcher sisters left the centre and slowly made their way home to Conner Street; Minnie stern-faced, Maud tearful. Like everyone who collected their gas masks, the sisters were worried, and they knew better than most about the effects of a gas attack. Their younger brother had been gassed during the Battle of the Somme and had never fully recovered. They would never forget the silence when, a few years ago, the laboured breathing from his blistered lungs had finally ceased.

Each day people came and went. The mothers left the centre with large cartons resting on their prams, and the youngsters with small cases slung over their shoulders. Everywhere the preparations went on . . .

As the sun rose higher in the sky, the tension mounted. In Conner Street, as with other streets in dockland, the inhabitants gathered around their wireless sets. The tension was mounting too in the Flannagans' home, but for a different reason. 'I'm goin' to be late, woman, where's my boots?' the big Irishman said as he glanced at the clock.

Bridie puffed and handed him a pair of elastic-sided black boots from under the table. Patrick Flannagan took a brush and started to apply some polish to the dull toecaps. Two-year-old Terry grabbed one of the brushes and threw it at the cat who darted under the table. Patrick retrieved the brush and Terry kicked his foot under the table in an effort to get at the cat. 'Terry, you leave that cat alone,' screamed Bridie, her shrill voice waking up little James. The baby started to cry and Bridie cooed to him as she rocked the pram. 'You naughty boy, now see what you've done.'

The seven-year-old twins, Sheena and Sally, played in one corner, watched closely by Patrick junior, who waited his chance to poke at the doll's glass eye. At five years old Patrick junior was beginning to feel the urge to take everything to pieces, and he wondered what his father would say when the dismantled alarm clock was found.

Maureen came into the room, placing her hands on her hips. She puffed at Terry who immediately scuttled away to the scullery. Maureen was the eldest of the brood and at ten she felt sufficiently grown up to scold the children. Maureen was Patrick's favourite, although he would not admit to it. The child had her mother's colouring, with raven hair and very deep blue eyes. She had her mother's mannerisms too and the children knew when Maureen was angry with them. Bridie spoke to her daughter, 'Will you see what Terry's up to, darlin'?'

The two-year-old was standing on a chair in the scullery, watching the goldfish as they swum lazily around inside their glass bowl. He imitated their mouth-gaping movement for a while before his eyes lightened on the iron wringer. In his wisdom he knew why the fish were so sad. Anyone would be sad if they had to stay wet all day he reasoned. He'd seen his mother put the dripping wet clothes from the boiling copper into those wooden rollers and had seen how dry the clothes had become at the other side. If only . . .

'Terry, you naughty, wicked boy,' Maureen shouted. Terry removed his hand quickly from the bowl and the fish settled back to their lazy swim. The girl tucked Terry under her arm and carried him along to the parlour. Terry was crying. 'Terry dry fish,' he sobbed.

Patrick was nearly ready. He scooped up a pat of brilliantine and rubbed it between his palms to soften it, then plastered the grease over his dark wavy hair.

Bridie was watching the operation, 'Don't be late, Pat, promise me you won't be late.'

The man looked puzzled. 'I'll not be late, woman,' he answered.

Patrick Flannagan let himself out of the house and walked quickly along the street. The Eagle did not open until noon on Sundays but the conniving Irishman would taste his first beer well before then. He had struck a deal with Florrie Braden, the 'Missus' of that pub, and he smiled to himself as he recalled the incident.

It had been a quiet night in the Eagle as he stood against the bar counter listening to Florrie's protestations. 'Do you know, I have to do everything here,' she was saying. 'I've got to stack the shelves, empty the drip trays, polish the counter, and everything else before I open. He's become absolutely useless. The drink's killing him, so the doctor told him.'

The subject of Florrie's tirade stood at the far end of the bar. He was trying to roll a cigarette, watched by the only other customer, who was leaning on the bar counter. Florrie glanced at him, her eyes showing her disgust. 'Look at him, doesn't it make you sick. He's like that first thing in the mornings, can't keep still. It wouldn't take me long to get out.'

Patrick nodded in sympathy. 'Why don't you get some help in, Florrie?' he asked.

The woman shook her head. 'I wish I could afford it, but I already pay the two girls for the evenings, and the cleaner. This is only a small pub remember.'

Patrick was thinking hard. 'What you need is a little unpaid help.'

Florrie looked puzzled, 'Now where on earth am I going to get . . .'

Patrick cut her short, 'You need look no further,' he said quickly. 'Why, I could help out on Sundays at least. If I got here at around eleven o'clock I could stock the shelves, polish the bar and have everything ready by the time you open up. What d'ya say?'

Florrie Braden thought hard. On the surface it sounded a good idea, but there had to be a catch somewhere. 'I couldn't let you work for nothing, Pat,' she remarked.

The Irishman was ready to deliver the 'coup de grace'. He leant forward, 'I wouldn't consider payment, but I'll tell you what. If I should get a little thirsty, then I could open a bottle of beer, now couldn't I?'

Florrie became wary. She was well aware of the man's liquid appetite, and the bottle he mentioned could become a crate full. She cupped her chin in the palm of her hand, the little finger toying with her bottom lip, as she glanced again at her husband. John Braden was in trouble with his cigarette. He was trying to twirl the paper around the strands of tobacco but his hands wouldn't stop shaking. The other customer got tired of watching the performance, ''Ere, give it to me, John,' he said, and the landlord gave him a cross-eyed stare, 'S'alright, I can manage, it's my fingers, they're a bit stiff,' he slurred.

Florrie's mind was suddenly made up: 'Okay, Pat, it's a deal,' she said quickly. She poured the Irishman a tot of her best whisky, and a double gin for herself. 'This one's on the house.'

Patrick's mouth was already dry as he rang the bell of the pub. It was a few seconds away from eleven o'clock on that Sunday morning, and the impending war was not in the Irishman's thoughts. Flannagan's war would start the night they bombed the Eagle.

*

At number 22, they were getting ready for the broadcast. Joe Harper switched on the wireless set and it started to crackle. He checked the terminal leads on the square glass accumulator, cursing to himself as he tightened the caps. The oscillations became louder as Joe twiddled with the tuning dial. The sound of Big Ben boomed out the hour and a voice came over the air, saying that the Prime Minister would speak at eleven fifteen. Joe turned off the wireless to conserve the accumulator and sat in silence, hands clasped, his thumbs revolving round and round each other. No one spoke as the minutes ticked away. Joe stared at the floor and occasionally glanced up at the clock on the high mantelshelf. Slowly, very slowly the minute hand crept towards the quarter hour. Finally, Joe got up and turned on the wireless again. The oscillations sounded louder than ever in the quiet room. Joe cursed under his breath and gently adjusted the tuning dial. There was a crackle, then the announcer's voice introducing the Prime Minister.

The Prime Minister's voice sounded tired and deflated as he began: 'I am speaking to you from the Cabinet Room at 10 Downing Street. This morning the British Ambassador in Berlin handed the German Government a final note, stating that unless we heard from them by eleven o'clock that they were prepared at once to withdraw their troops from Poland, a state of war would exist between us. I have to tell you that no such undertaking has been received and that consequently this country is at war with Germany . . .'

His voice was interrupted by Bridie who burst into tears. Rosie Harper went pale and put her hand up to her face. Skipper stared down at the floor, his pipe held unlit in his hand. Joe shook his head sadly as the voice on the wireless continued.

'You can imagine what a bitter blow it is to me that all my long struggle to win peace has failed. Yet I cannot believe that there is anything more or anything different that I could have done and that would have been more successful . . .'

Joe turned the volume down and said, 'Well, we expected it, didn't we?'

'Holy Mary Mother of God, Holy . . .' started Bridie, only to be cut short by Rosie. 'Now stop that, luv, you've got the children to think of. It's no good lettin' 'em see you upset. War or not, I've got a shoulder of lamb to cook, an' the spuds ter peel.'

'Holy Mother . . .' sobbed the little woman as Rosie put her arm around her shoulders and led her out of the room.

Joe Harper turned up the volume in time to hear the Prime Minister's concluding words, 'Now may God bless you all. May He defend the right. It is an evil thing that we shall be fighting against. Brute force, bad faith, injustice and oppression, and persecution and against them I am certain that the right shall prevail.'

Joe turned off the wireless set and turned away. 'Where the 'ell 'as she put it,' he puffed as he bent down to look in the cupboard. He brought out a flask of brandy from the back and placed it in the middle of the table, the contents pale-looking in the light of the sun's intruding rays. He found two glasses and, pouring a measure into each, handed one to Skipper.

The old man downed his in one gulp, and immediately started to choke. Joe slapped the seaman's back, making him gasp. With his eyes streaming and his voice coming out in a cracked whisper, Skipper said, 'Gawd a'mighty, Joe, that stuff's bloody strong.'

'It's good brandy, Skip. I got it when Rosie 'ad that bad turn last year. Anyway, 'ere's to us all,' Joe said as he put the glass to his lips. Skipper looked dolefully at his empty glass and then at the brandy flask. Joe smiled and filled the old man's glass.

'Gawd bless us all, son,' said Skipper as he sipped the drink.

Joe Harper looked through the parted curtains and caught sight of a tall, stooping individual who carried a service gas mask pack and steel helmet slung over his shoulder, and wearing an armband on his right arm. Joe recognised the long-striding individual and watched him stop by the shelter. It was just like Bob Bowman to have volunteered as the Street warden.

At the shelter the warden opened the gates and secured them. Best to be ready, Bob thought, we don't want any panic. Like Tom Carter, his pal who lived at number 34, and many of the men in the Street, Bob Bowman worked in the docks, which meant that he was exempt from call-up. He had been a docker for most of his working life in the Pool of London. His father, who was a stevedore, had first taken him along to the Pool when Bob was a tall, thin youth of eighteen. He was accepted for work with some reluctance due to his frail appearance, but he soon showed he could work with the best of them. On his twenty-first birthday Bob was made a 'ganger' in charge of a team of dockers. He had developed physically, growing to well over six feet in height. His hawkish features were dark and accentuated by large pale blue eyes. His shoulders were rounded, and his black hair was brushed back and parted in the middle. His strong, white teeth were gapped at the front and his bottom lip was inclined to droop over a dimpled chin.

On Bob Bowman's twenty-second birthday his father was killed in a dock accident. Bob was heartbroken, and when the chance came to him to train as a crane driver he took it. It was to be in a different wharf in the Pool and away from the place where his father had met his death. Now, at thirty-five, with lines forming around his mouth and eyes, he looked even older. Bob had one hobby; an abiding passion for growing flowers, and in particular, geraniums, which he grew in his backyard. As he secured the shelter gates in the open position, though, geraniums were farthest from his mind. There was a war to fight and Bob Bowman was determined to do his share.

The taste of brandy was still hot on their tongues when the wail of the air-raid siren filled the Street and reverberated through the houses. Joe Harper and Skipper looked at each other for a second or two then Joe grabbed for the old man's coat. 'Quick, Skip, get it on! I'll get the women.'

Rosie came running into the room accompanied by the terrified Bridie. 'O my Gawd, Joe!' she gasped.

Joe shouted at her. 'Bridie get yer kids over the shelter!'

Bridie ran out and Joe went to take Rosie's arm. 'Wait, the gas! I've got ter cut the gas!' she yelled.

Conner Street became alive, as everyone rushed from their homes. Joe held on tightly to the old man and Rosie as they joined the crowd. Down the street they came, like a scene from the *Pied Piper*, urged on, not by the sound of melodious pipes, but by the horrendous wail of the siren. The Davis boys were holding on to their aged father, Bridie was clutching her baby close to her, and the twins held on to her coat. Maureen held the two youngsters' hands as they hurried to the shelter entrance. At the gate Bob Bowman and a policeman waved them in, and Bob called out, 'Now don't panic. That's right, nice an' easy'.

As Bridie came down the shelter slope the warden gave her a wink. 'C'mon, Bridie, where's Pat?'

The little woman gave him a wicked stare and the warden winced.

The Conner Street folk filed down the two tunnels, into the dark, musty smelling place that they had prayed they would never have to visit. They screwed up their eyes in an effort to get accustomed to the dim light that was supplied by two bare electric light-bulbs hanging from the damp ceiling. They staggered over the duckboards that covered the stagnant pools of oily water and sat down on the rows of wooden benches that were placed along the walls and down the centre. The room was cramped and airless and the reek of carbolic from the toilet compartment filled the shelter.

Outside, the Street was deserted, except for one couple hurrying along; a big elderly woman and a shuffling idiot who held on to her arm. They reached the shelter and the policeman ushered them inside quickly. He then walked back to the gate and looked up and down the now quite empty street. Overhead, a flight of pigeons in ragged formation swooped low over the roof tops and a lone dog appeared from an empty house. It chased its tail for a while, then stopped to look along the Street, before trotting back inside. The faint sound of a tug's whistle echoed briefly from the direction of the river, and then it was quiet.

Bob Bowman ambled up casually to the policeman and gave him an enquiring look before placing his hands behind his back and walking back down the shelter slope and into the dark cave.

Conner Street was at war . . .

Chapter Three

Bobbie Wilkins was an idiot. He had become a victim of children's ridicule, and an object of comparison by adults. If a child from Conner Street was caught pulling faces in the mirror, then the child would be scolded with, 'D'you want to grow up to be like silly Bobbie?' If the recalcitrant youngster skipped his lessons, then the same comparison was applied. None of the Street's children wanted to grow up to be like Bobbie, so they went back to their lessons, and they tried hard to stop pulling faces in the mirror. But the children just had to pull faces at someone, and that someone was usually Bobbie Wilkins.

Bobbie wasn't born an idiot, and it didn't just happen overnight. The idiocy simply grew on him. It would be more correct to say that the sickness had been beaten into him, because Bobbie had a father who went to sea and a mother who tired of the long separations. There were nights when his mother found solace in the company of available men, and on such nights the little lad pressed his face deep into the pillow as the woman writhed and moaned in adulterous adventures. There were times when the seaman came to his home port and sought out his wife.

As the boy grew older he began to fear his father, and often threw his puny weight against the enraged man to protect his mother. In a drunken frenzy, the father would attack the woman, and cuff the boy out of his way. The screaming and fighting became more frequent, and so did the beatings. One heavy cuff around Bobbie's head made his nose bleed, and put him into a daze. The boy was just nine years old. From that moment on, the boy was changed. He became absent-minded and dull at his lessons. He would wander off for no apparent reason. His speech became slurred and he developed a tic. They sent him to a special school where the boy became worse, and where the headmaster believed in the cane as the finest therapy. The treatment failed, so they sent him to the kind nuns at St Mary's School.

When Bobbie was fourteen his mother had become very ill and had been taken from her home screaming and raving. She had met a seaman who not only gave her a share of his shore time, but also left her with a memento of his one-time visit to a Far Eastern whore-house. Bobbie's father was repulsed by the boy, who now dribbled incessantly because of his partially paralysed tongue. He decided to get rid of the idiot, and spoke to the parish priest about finding a home. Word got around the Street and reached the ears of Lizzie Brown, who became outraged by the news.

Lizzie Brown was treated with caution, and a good deal of respect, by the Conner Street folk. Although she was well into her sixties, and stood barely five feet in height, Lizzie was a veritable giant. She held her ground against any and everyone. Her frail appearance belied her strength, and it was said that she could fight like a man, and often had when her husband was around. Lizzie now lived alone at number 17 and was often seen in the company of Emmie Jones, a younger and much larger woman, and Ada Dawkins, a large red-faced widow who lived at number 4. Lizzie Brown had a sharp tongue and many a shopkeeper and market trader had taken a verbal lashing from the diminutive lady. Everyone knew Lizzie, and everyone was aware that she had a heart as big as the Street.

On the day that Lizzie heard the news about Bobbie Wilkins her faded grey eyes watered. She had walked back from the market and stopped in a doorway to re-tie her garter string which had slipped from above her knee to around the ankle. As Ada Dawkins greeted the bent figure, Lizzie straightened up with a sigh.

'What's all this about that poor little Wilkins boy, Liz?'

'I tell yer, Ada. That dirty tyke's goin' ter put the poor little bleeder in an 'ome. Breaks me 'eart it does. Never known a day's lovin' 'e ain't, not from the day 'e was born.'

Ada shook her head. 'Poor little sod, where's 'e at now?'

Lizzie Brown knew. She had made it her business to find out. 'St Mary's are lookin' after 'im, at least fer the time bein'. They'll get 'im into one o' them places, you see,' she said, with a knowing nod of her head.

Ada knew of those places. 'It's a cryin' shame. If my Charlie were alive, Gawd rest 'is soul, 'e'd'ave sorted that bastard out,' she said, her fist clenched to emphasise the point.

Lizzie Brown looked up and down the street, to make sure that they were quite alone. 'You 'eard about 'is mother?'

'Whose, Bobbie's?'

'Yes, Bobbie's,' said Lizzie Brown impatiently. 'Took 'er away they did. Last night it was. Screamin' an' callin' out. Gone to 'er kidneys it 'as.'

'What 'as?' asked Ada.

'Why the syphilletics of course,' answered Lizzie Brown.

Ada went home and stood for a long while in front of a picture of her Charlie. She had never yet made a decision without first consulting him. The tall guardsman stared out of a sepia photograph that was framed in carved ebony, and below the picture was a display of medals mounted on green beige and framed in the same type of wood. Ada spoke softly to the photograph, and felt the uncertainty flowing from her. 'Gawd bless you,' she said, then left her home to see the priest. The next day, two nuns walked into Conner Street and knocked at number 4. The children watched with curiosity as the two long-robed figures walked back along the street, their hands tucked demurely in their sleeves, rosaries swinging from their waists and supporting the large crucifixes.

A week later, a big black car drove slowly up Conner Street and stopped at number 4. It was driven by an old nun who had hairs sprouting from her chin. Two younger nuns climbed out from the back, one holding the hand of a scared boy, and the other, a large suitcase. The children gathered around the car and one young lad, bolder than the rest, moved forward to touch the gleaming headlight. The nun with the bristling chin sounded the horn making the boy jump back. The two younger nuns went into the house and later emerged without the boy.

'Did you see who it was?' asked one of the little girls.

'Course I did, it's silly Bobbie,' another answered.

''E's been in a silly school,' the first girl said.

'I don't care if 'e 'as, 'e can still play wiv us, can't 'e?' replied the other girl.

The young lad who tried to touch the car stepped forward once more. 'I don't s'pose 'e knows 'ow to play marbles anyway,' he said with a grin.

'Don't you be so wicked, Albert Conlin,' the second girl said. 'If your dad kept 'ittin' you on the bonce, you wouldn't be able to play like normal children, so there.'

Albert grinned. 'Did you see 'is tongue? Kept pokin' out, it did. I s'pose it's cos 'e's firsty.'

The second girl folded her arms and swung her head away

from Albert, who stuck out his tongue and shuffled along the street. 'I 'ate you Albert Conlin,' shouted the girl, and Albert laughed. The big black car finally drove off down the narrow Conner Street and turned into the Tower Road, leaving the idiot boy behind in the care of Ada Dawkins.

Bobbie Watkins settled in with the kindly Ada, and he found some much-needed love for the first time in his young life. Ada Dawkins fed him, clothed him and protected him as best she could from the taunts and jibes. Bobbie was happy growing up in the close, friendly atmosphere of a small dockland street. The children eventually accepted and tolerated him as he tried to join in their fun. He grew to manhood physically, but remained a child in his mind, his mental development having been clubbed to a permanent standstill. He walked the street as a man because he was told to do so, but loved to watch the pretty marbles as the boys rolled them in the gutters. He tried to talk like a man because he was expected to, but he was only happy with the children. He wanted to sit with the boys as they played cards, and threw the ball at a tin can with sticks crossed on top, but he did not do so. He knew he was supposed to feel like a man and act like a man, and he tried. He watched the men as they smoked cigarettes and wore their caps on the side of their heads. When he tried to wear his cap at an angle it fell off, and the one time he had tried a cigarette, it made him sick. He tried hard to become like the men, but his head hurt and his body was clumsy. He found peace in his little room at Ada's with his comics, and with the pretty marbles that he found in the gutters of the street. When his head hurt bad, he went to bed and watched the patterns that danced on the ceiling, formed by the moving shadows that the coal fire created. Sometimes, the pictures formed by the glowing coals would frighten him and he pulled the bedclothes over his head, as a child would do.

Sometimes, the pictures formed reminded him of things half-remembered, half-forgotten, and his head ached.

The events of that Sunday morning didn't mean anything to Bobbie, until that terrible noise made his head buzz. He had seen Ada crying earlier, but that was not so very unusual. Ada often cried when she looked at the man in the photo, and when her wireless played hymns on Sunday evenings. The mounting tension over the last few weeks was beyond his comprehension and he went about his simple tasks in the market in his own innocent way.

As the wail of the siren sounded and Ada grabbed his arm and hurried him out of the house, Bobbie became scared. His idea of war was from the pictures in his comics, with the enemy shaded green and the guns that fired beams of light. He could shut bad things from his mind by closing the comic, but the sight of everyone hurrying along the street and that awful noise frightened him. The box that was slung over his shoulder frightened him too, but Ada grabbed the gas mask and told him to take it with him when the siren started up. Bobbie felt he could not breathe when he tried it on and hid it under his bed. Ada had found it and told the idiot to keep it in a safe place and as they both hurried along Conner Street the box bounced about on Bobbie's back.

When the two reached the shelter the policeman ushered them inside, where most of the seats were occupied. They made room for Ada on a bench near the door, but Bobbie had to stand. Outside on the concrete patio the men stood talking, and Bobbie signalled to Ada that he wanted to join them. The woman was worried. 'Stay under cover, Bobbie, for Gawd's sake, keep with the others.'

The idiot nodded and shuffled out from the stuffy tunnel.

''Ello, Bobbie, what you doin' 'ere? Come out for air?'

38

remarked Ginger Davis as he nudged his brother. Bobbie grinned and stood against the wall, his gas mask box hanging down in front of him. Ginger's brother Fred leered at the idiot. 'See you've got your mask all ready, does it fit?'

Bobbie nodded and pointed to the box, 'Small one, Bobbie got small gas mask, lady said it fits.'

'I don't know about that, Bobbie boy,' Ginger said. 'I reckon you should 'ave a medium, what d'ya say, Fred?'

Ginger's brother rubbed his fingers along his chin. 'Yeah, I reckon so, that small size ain't no good.'

Bobbie started to shuffle about in his agitation, and Ginger grinned at the group of young men standing around the entrance.

'Why don't you try it on, Bobbie? Let's see 'ow it looks,' he said.

The idiot shook his head vigorously. 'Bobbie don't like gas mask, makes me sick,' he whined.

Joe Harper was sitting on a wooden bench by the wall watching the performance. Skipper, who was sitting next to Joe, spat out a stream of tobacco juice and said, 'Tricky little snapper, that Ginger Davis. One of these days someone's goin' to take 'im down a peg, mark my words.'

Ginger made a grab for Bobbie's box and succeeded in removing the mask. The idiot snatched it away from his tormentor and backed away. Joe Harper had seen enough. 'All right, Ginger, you've 'ad your fun, leave 'im be,' he said quietly.

Bobbie's tongue hung out as he backed towards the shelter door.

Big Albert Conlin sidled up to Joe. 'What's 'a matter, Joe? The boys are only 'avin' a laugh.'

'Yeah, well the laugh's over,' replied the signalman.

Ginger Davis came up towards the idiot and Skipper

shouted to him, 'Why don't you leave 'im alone, you flash little monkey.'

'Shut up, Grandad,' Ginger sneered.

'If I get up off this seat . . .' began Skipper, but Joe interrupted him by grabbing Ginger's coat lapels. 'Talk to 'im like that an' I'll tear your 'ead off your shoulders,' he spat out.

'Now what's goin' on,' the warden called out, 'you two tryin' to start your own war?'

Bobbie seized the opportunity to dart back inside the shelter. He still had the gas mask in his hand and as he entered, Lizzie Brown screamed out, 'O my Gawd, it's a gas attack!'

People began to panic, and some of the children started to cry. Bob Bowman heard the noise and he rushed in. 'Calm down, it's okay, it's all quiet outside, take it easy.'

Ada grabbed Bobbie and pulled him down beside her. 'Sit 'ere an' don't move, you've frightened everybody.'

Bobbie tucked the mask back into the box and held it tightly on his lap. The shelter returned to the quiet mumble of anxious conversation and some of the children started to congregate around Ernest Jacobs, a fat boy clutching a tin box.

'Come on, Ern', show us your pitchers,' said one little lad.

'No fear,' replied Ernest. 'Them's me stakes.'

'Wot, fer pontoon?' said the little lad.

'Pontoon or brag,' replied Ernest in an authoritative tone.

'Can't play brag, but I can play pontoon,' said the little lad hopefully. 'An' I've got some cigarette cards too,' he chirped.

Ernest Jacobs looked at the group, a gleam crystallising in his eye. Here was a chance to build up his supply of cards. He addressed the group of children, 'Anyone want to play pontoon? Cigarette cards is stakes.'

Four of the lads fished out some tattered cards, and one little boy took a bag of marbles from his pocket. 'I've got these,' he said as he rattled them in front of Ernest.

'Them's no good, only cigarette cards,' replied the 'card-sharp' of Conner Street.

The game began in a deadly serious mood as the boys placed their stakes in front of them. Granny Flint was trying to take a nap and she clicked her tongue, aggrieved at the noise.

'I'm banker, cos' them's my playin' cards,' announced Ernest.

Bobbie Watkins was sitting quietly beside Ada when he heard the rattle of the marbles. He saw the boys gathering and decided to investigate. He edged his way down the row of benches and stood in front of Granny Flint to get a view. The old lady gave him an icy stare and closed her eyes once more.

'Busted!' shouted one of the lads, and Granny Flint half-opened her eyes and clicked her tongue at the children.

'Can Bobbie play?' asked one lad.

''E's got no cards,' said Ernest in a tone of disgust.

Bobbie slowly put his hand into his top pocket and pulled out a few tattered cards. A grin spread over his round face.

'Okay, but no dribblin' over the cards,' said Ernest.

Bobbie put the little pile of cigarette cards down in front of him and folded his coat-ends under his legs. Ernest licked his thumb and dealt one card to each of the lads. The card that he placed in front of himself was deftly manipulated from the bottom of the deck. The stakes went down and the idiot rubbed his hands together. 'You got to bet more than one card,' shouted Ernest, and the lads laughed. Bobbie took the pile in front of him and placed them all, with the exception of one card, in the centre of the game. The fat boy dealt the next card to each of them, and one to himself, again from the bottom of the pile.

'Stick,' said the first boy, and then the second boy.

'Twist,' said the third lad, then quickly picked up the card dealt to him. 'Busted,' he said sadly.

'Buy one,' said the remaining lad as he laid down his stakes.

Ernest eyed the boy with caution as he dealt him a card.

'I'll stick,' said the lad with satisfaction.

'Buy one,' mumbled the idiot.

'Do what?' shouted Ernest.

'Bobbie buy one.'

''Ow can you buy a card wiv' no stakes?' sneered the cardsharp.

The little lad next to Bobbie nudged him. 'Go on, Bobbie, put your card down,' he said loudly.

'Buy one,' repeated the idiot as he laid down his last dog-eared cigarette card, grinning as he did so. He held two pretty pictures in his hand and he wanted to buy another.

The little lad next to Bobbie had caught a glimpse of the two queens in his dirty grasp. His face took on a look of horror. 'No, Bobbie, you mean stick,' he said urgently.

'Bobbie buy one,' the idiot repeated.

'No no, you can't buy one with them cards,' said the little lad.

'If 'e wants to, let 'im buy one,' Ernest butted in. He put a card face down in front of the idiot, who laid his two pictures down for all to see. A gasp went up and Ernest leered. 'Turn your card over,' he said with scorn.

Bobbie slowly turned the card to reveal an ace. The boys stared for a second then erupted in laughter. Granny Flint nearly hit the roof as the noise woke her up, and fat Ernest snapped his tin box shut. 'I'm not playin' anymore,' he said in disgust.

'Twenty-one! Bobbie's got twenty-one!' they cried.

The little lad nudged Bobbie, 'Pick yer winnin's up,' he said with a grin that spread from ear to ear.

The idiot made his way back to Ada and sat down next to her. His tongue hung out of his mouth as he felt for the winnings in his pocket. The little lad was sitting near him and he grinned at Bobbie as the victor felt his pocket. Bobbie grinned back, and the lad beamed. A stream of saliva ran down the idiot's chin and dripped onto the floor. His tongue hung out as he felt once more for the cigarette cards. Bobbie looked again at the lad and they grinned at their secret joke. The look that passed between them was for the world of children; the doors had long been closed on the adults for all their sage understanding. The exchanged smiles were innocence, a pure feeling that reflected their thoughts, an acknowledgement so open that for an adult it would be betrayal. The smile, that turned into a chuckle from the lad as Bobbie hunched up his shoulders in delight, was not understood by the adult mind of the boy's mother. She was talking to her neighbour when she heard him and promptly slapped the boy around the head. 'I've told you before, an' I won't tell you again. Stop laughin' at silly Bobbie, you know 'e can't 'elp it.'

The little lad stared at the floor, his eyes misting. The idiot's doleful eyes seemed to mist too and he searched for the cards in his pocket.

The long, even wail of the all-clear sounded and the people broke into spontaneous cheering. Feet clattered over the duck-boards as they hurried for the door. Bobbie found himself standing next to the boy as they waited their turn to move out into the sunlight. Bobbie tugged at the lad's sleeve and saw the tear that had traced a line down his cheek. As they walked up the sloping path to the street, the idiot pressed a handful of cigarette cards into the boy's palm. The lad looked fearfully in the direction of his mother before giving Bobbie a huge grin.

The Conner Street folk went home to cook their Sunday meal and talk of the day. They feared for the future and their fate, and they waited. Bridie waited too and, long after the all-clear, Patrick Flannagan staggered home for his meal.

Chapter Four

The cold, wet, mid-November evening settled over a blacked-out Conner Street, with a gusting wind that lashed the rain against the little houses and along the near-deserted turning. It had rained non-stop throughout the day and the gutters were running with water that poured down into the dark drains.

The homeward-bound folk held their heads down and their coat collars up against the weather. One or two late workers trudged into the back street, holding their torches low, the beams of which were diffused by tissuepaper discs affixed to the glass. The late folk looked forward to a hot meal and roaring coal fire, and later they would listen to the nightly broadcasts, as did the rest of the Street. They would hear of the occasional skirmishes, and the sporadic shelling on the Western Front. The news was very limited from that area, as was the information about fighting at sea. The war was two months old, and there was a lull on the continent as the armies faced each other. It was different on the oceans, where battles raged. A regular toll of merchant ships and their cargoes went to the bottom, together with a large part of the crews.

The nightly broadcasts did not name the doomed vessels, although sometimes a whole street already had news of the disaster. They knew of the men, and the ships they sailed in and they kept count. Conner Street knew Alf Morgan, for he was born in the Street and lived there until he decided to see the world. Alf Morgan thought that the merchant service was the answer, so he joined as a stoker. He saw a good many ports and harbours, one of which was Halifax, Nova Scotia. It was from there one dark night he boarded an old coal-burner, and set sail for London.

The ship joined a convoy, but started to lag behind with engine trouble. Four nights out, a U-boat attached itself to the convoy, and singled out the old coal-burner; the torpedo was straight and the aim was true, and the ship was caught foursquare in its boiler room. Halifax, Nova Scotia, was the last port Alf Morgan ever saw.

On that cold November night, a telegram boy pedalled into Conner Street on his red bicycle and stopped at number 5. The buff-coloured envelope had an official heading and the boy sighed as he rat-tatted on the door, the telegram held tight beneath his coat against the rain. The Morgans were startled as only the collectors and policeman rat-tatted in dockland, and it was too late in the day for the collectors. The dread on Mrs Morgan's face turned to horror as she saw the boy. The *Southern Star* had gone down, and the whole Street knew it. Mrs Morgan understood only too well the news the telegram boy brought.

The lull was having effects, since the dreaded bombs had not fallen, and apart from the first day of war, the shelter had not been used. Some of the evacuated children were brought home, and there was even talk of a swift end to hostilities. The market traded as usual and there was plenty of food in the shops. Of course, some things had changed, such as the now closed cinemas, and certain new laws that were strictly enforced;

petrol was rationed, and exotic fruits became non-existent. People who broke the 'blackout' regulations found that heavy fines were imposed, and sometimes even imprisonment.

The blackout regulations brought with them a few problems for the odd trader. The man who sold black material from his stall in Tower Road market could not satisfy his customers' demands, and one day he upset Lizzie Brown. 'I'm sorry, luv, but I've 'ad a run on the stuff. There's only wot you see.'

Lizzie looked at him in disbelief. 'This all you got?' she snorted, holding up a small piece of cloth. 'This wouldn't even cover me carsey.'

Another who was on the receiving end of Lizzie's acid tongue was the man in the hardware store. 'Tin tacks? Sorry, lady, sold out.'

'Sold out of bloody tin tacks?' Lizzie choked. ''Ow the bleedin' 'ell can you run out of tin tacks?'

'I'll 'ave some in next week,' said the man helpfully.

'Next week's no bleedin' good. I wanna get me blackout up this week.'

'I've got some nails,' he suggested.

'Nails is no bleedin' good,' ranted Lizzie Brown. 'I'll never get me bloody winders open.'

'Sorry, luv, it's the shortages,' he said apologetically.

Lizzie Brown hammered the counter. 'I tell you what,' she shouted. 'If you ain't got 'em in by next week, I'll get me vinegar an' me 'earthstone somewhere else, so there!'

'I wish you would,' mumbled the man under his breath.

'What did you say?' said Lizzie, her eyes popping.

'I said it's understood.'

'Well, that's all right then,' said Lizzie as she stormed out of his shop.

*

On the same cold November night that the telegram boy knocked at number 5, something happened to Albert Conlin that made him wince every time he thought about Florrie Braden.

Albert was a big man who sold salads from a stall in the market, and at the end of that particular day Albert Conlin was soaked through. He had the beetroots to cook for the next day and he had to get up early the next morning to go to the Borough Market for fresh supplies. So he was feeling a little sorry for himself as he carried the beetroots into his lodgings at number 15. Nell Jones, his landlady, had the copper boiling ready and, as soon as Albert had finished, she started to serve up his supper.

'Keep me meal in the oven, will you, Nell? I fancy a pint,' he said.

Nell Jones puffed. 'Don't be long then, Albert, it'll get all baked up.'

Albert hoped it would, as he hated mutton stew with the same passion that he loved a pint of ale. He put on his still damp coat watching as Nell placed the covered dish into the iron oven, next to the open coal fire.

The Eagle was busy on that night as Albert slid through the heavy blackout curtains and entered the smoky bar. He recognised a few of the traders who were playing darts and the old man who stood talking to Florrie, a clay pipe hanging from the corner of his mouth. ''Ello, Skip, 'ow yer doin'?' he asked.

'Okay, son, just bin askin' Florrie if she fancies a night out wiv me.'

Florrie laughed and slapped the old man's hand playfully.

''Ow's the 'arpers?' Albert asked.

'They're all right. Joe's on nights this week,' Skipper replied.

Florrie looked at Albert. 'What'll it be?'

'Give us a pint of ale, luv,' answered the big man.

'I 'eard the Davis boys got called up,' remarked Skipper.

'Last week, gone in the infantry,' Albert said.

Skipper remembered the episode at the shelter. He tapped the clay pipe on the bar counter and started to refill it. 'Do 'em good if you ask me,' he remarked.

Albert grinned and took a gulp from his glass. 'God I needed that.'

Florrie was watching him. She had a soft spot for the big man who sometimes helped her with the barrels. Florrie had a good understanding with the traders. She would often ask them to help her move a barrel onto the stillion or carry up a crate or two from the cellar. She especially liked it when Albert was available. She liked to watch as his muscular arms strained against the weight and his neck muscles tightened as he lifted the barrel. There was always a pint at the end of the chores and the traders were happy.

Florrie waited until the man drained his glass. 'Another?' she asked, and the man nodded.

'Bad day, Florrie,' he said.

The woman filled his glass and placed it down in front of him. 'Looks like you've got a thirst on.'

'Well, I've been wet outside all day, might as well get soaked inside,' quipped Albert.

'What you need is a nice warm bed, luv,' smiled Florrie.

The remark was lost on the man as he took a large draught from his beer. He put the glass down satisfied, and lit a cigarette. The man standing next to him vacated his stool and Albert gratefully sat down.

Skipper waved goodnight as he left and Albert stared down at his half-smoked cigarette.

Wheezy Morris called over, 'Fancy a game, Al?'

'No thanks, I'm dead beat,' Albert answered.

Florrie Braden was serving a customer, her eyes glancing in the direction of the big man. Wheezy Morris noticed this and he nudged his partner, 'See Florrie lookin' at our Albert? Fancies 'im, she does!'

Wheezy's darts partner was having trouble sighting the board, and his eyes crossed as he tried to follow the speaker's gaze.

'Sad I calls it, wot wiv 'er ole man in 'orspital,' went on Wheezy.

The customers were leaving, and Florrie came over to where Albert was standing. 'Al, be a dear, can you move a barrel up on the stand ready for tomorrow?' she asked sweetly.

'Okay,' the man replied, and drained his glass.

Wheezy Morris had left his partner, who was having trouble finding the exit, and propped himself at the bar counter near Albert. He watched as the big man walked behind the bar and down the narrow stairs into the cellar. Wheezy looked at Florrie. 'Good 'earted our Albert, Florrie.'

The 'missus' ignored the remark, but Wheezy was not to be beaten. 'Shame about Albert,' he said, looking into his empty glass.

Florrie Braden looked puzzled. 'What about him?' she asked.

'Well, 'e gets these funny turns.'

'What do you mean, funny turns?' Florrie queried. 'He seems okay to me. Never noticed anything when he's been in here.'

Wheezy rubbed his hands together below the counter. He had Florrie on a hook and he wasn't about to let her go. ''Aven't you wondered why 'e never got married?' he asked in a low whisper.

'I've never really thought about it,' lied the 'missus'.

Wheezy glanced behind Florrie to make sure that Albert

was still in the cellar. 'Women make 'im violent. 'E gets sort of over passionate. Gets a bit rough wiv 'em, 'e does.'

'You don't say?' Florrie said in mock disgust. 'I'd never have thought it. Not our Albert.' The woman was secretly intrigued, the thought of Albert Conlin taking her in those massive arms of his and crushing her to him gave Florrie shivers of pleasure. She looked at Wheezy, who was savouring the conversation.

'O, 'e's 'ad a few girls in the past but when they find out wot 'e's really like they soon ditch 'im,' he said, trying hard not to betray himself. 'All the dollies round 'ere won't 'ave nuffin to do wiv 'im.'

Florrie wanted to lick her lips, but shook her head instead.

The sound of Albert climbing the cellar stairs stopped Wheezy in his tracks. 'Well, I must be orf,' he said quickly.

The last of the customers had left and Florrie ran a wet cloth over the bar counter. Albert was just about to leave when the woman spoke to him, 'Al, slip them bolts over and we'll have a nightcap.'

Albert wasn't sure whether he needed a nightcap but he did as she bid.

Florrie placed two glasses on the counter and filled them both to the brim. 'Taste a drop of the best, Al,' she said with a wink.

The man took his glass and took a swig. The feeling of heat went from his throat down to his stomach and his eyes watered.

Florrie drained her glass in one gulp. 'That's my best Scotch, I keep that for my friends,' she said pointedly. 'Look, Al, I've got some cheese and pickles upstairs, why don't you come up for a while?'

The pints of ale were having an effect on the big man and the last drink seemed to set his insides alight. Albert realised that it was hours since he had eaten, and the thought of that mutton stew in the oven at his lodgings did not seem too objectionable now. He looked at the clock. By now, that stew would no doubt be in Nell's dustbin. His stomach was sending him messages. 'Okay, Florrie, that sounds good,' he said.

Florrie waved him round the counter. 'Turn the lights off then, Al, and mind your head,' she warned him.

The stairs spiralled up to the small flat above the Eagle and Albert had to duck low as he went through the archway at the foot of the flight. At the top of the stairs three doors led off and Albert entered the room facing him. The small sitting room was lit by a table lamp and the glow of the brightly burning coal fire. There was a large armchair in front of the fire and Albert slumped down into it with a contented sigh. He stretched out his legs and yawned. He could hear Florrie moving about in the next room and closed his eyes. The heavy veil of sleep was beginning to descend over him when the door opened. He opened his eyes quickly and saw Florrie standing before him. She held two drinks in her hands, 'Get this down you and I'll bring in the supper,' she said.

Albert took the drink and looked at it, then nodded his thanks. As Florrie tripped out of the room Albert suddenly realised she had changed into a dressing gown. He drained his glass in one gulp, his thoughts racing. It was almost identical to the one that the Embankment woman wore, and he shivered as the thoughts came back of that night on the foggy Thames Embankment.

It had been loneliness that took him up West. The desire to be with a woman sometimes caused him to ache inside, and he would walk the busy, well-lit streets until he saw the women. They stood in doorways, and smiled at passers-by. Albert Conlin wanted to seek their company and made towards the shadowed figures, only to walk quickly by as they smiled at him. He would make for the nearest pub and reflect over his beer, and then stroll down to the Embankment to catch the last tram home to dockland.

Women had not figured in Albert's life since his early days, when his widowed mother frightened girlfriends away. Her hold on Albert tightened during her last years, and when she died he found it impossible to carry on living in the dreary old house. He moved into lodgings, and very soon realised that he had hardly any friends of the fair sex. His easy ability to talk to the young available maidens faded quickly over the last dominating years of his mother's life, and now Albert had completely accepted his position. The occasional need was sometimes drowned at the Eagle, and sometimes repressed by his fear of those shadowy figures who smiled from the doorways.

He recalled that night with the bitter cold and fog. Yellow, sulphuric fumes had settled down over the town and he decided to hurry down to the Embankment before the last tram left. It was hopeless, with the swirling fog much more dense by the river, and he missed the tram.

He started to walk the long journey home when suddenly the woman appeared out of the fog. She was dressed in a fur coat with a scarf tied around her piled-up hair. Her face was heavily made-up, with spots of rouge beneath her eyes that made her look doll-like. Her lips were scarlet-painted and thin and her eyes watery and sunken. She smiled at him; a grin that made him start. 'Ello, dearie, nasty night ain't it?'

Albert stared, his mouth hanging open.

The woman winked at him. 'I'll give yer a nice time an' you can stay the night, wha'dya say?'

The big man nodded dumbly and the woman took his arm. 'It's only a couple of minutes from 'ere, luv.'

They crossed the tramway and took a narrow, rising street

that led away from the river. Halfway along the street the woman stopped and took her key from the large handbag hanging from her shoulder. 'Listen, dearie, I don't usually bring me fellas 'ome 'ere, but it's a terrible night, an' it's quiet.'

Albert wondered where the woman usually took her men. He had visions of her selling her body against the cold statues that lined the Embankment.

'First floor, luv, an' keep quiet.' She opened the front door which led into a dingy hall. The stairs creaked as they climbed to the room above. The open fire had died down and the woman threw a large knob of coal onto it. Without wiping her hands she poured a colourless liquid from a bottle into two glasses that stood on the table by the covered window. 'Cheers, dearie,' she said and swallowed the contents.

The smell of gin made Albert heave but he gulped his drink down and shuddered.

'Give me a minute,' said the woman with a wink as she disappeared behind a Japanese screen. Albert took off his coat and started to unbuckle his belt.

'Put the money on the table, luv, it's custom,' came a voice from behind the screen.

Albert felt foolish sitting in that cold room clad only in his underpants. The fire was beginning to pick up and the lump of coal started to spit out its gases.

The woman came around from behind the screen. She wore a dressing gown that gaped open at the front. It had a fluffy collar and cuffs and was adorned with large red roses.

The recollection of that night in the cold room off the Embankment made Albert wince as he felt again those clammy hands on his back. He remembered the giggles from the woman that turned to disbelief, as she realised that her ample charms were being lost upon the hulking man at her side. He remembered the effect of the gin and the sickly smell of her cheap perfume. 'God Almighty,' she said incredulously as he retched into the bowl. 'Don't I just pick 'em!'

Albert remembered the early morning tram ride home to dockland, the clackety-clack that said over and over again, 'Don't worry, luv, you'll do better next time.'

His train of thought was interrupted by the door opening and Florrie entering again, carrying a tray which she set down on a small table.

'There we are,' she said as she pulled up another chair to the fire. The tray contained buttered rolls, a large square of cheese with a knife pressed into it, a dish of pickled onions and two mugs of tea.

Albert gratefully started into the food and Florrie smiled at him.

'You didn't mind coming up with me, did you, Albert?' she asked. 'I simply can't abide being here alone.'

The man was staring at her dressing gown, with its fluffy collar and cuffs and the large red roses. 'Course not,' he replied.

'John will be away for a couple of days, they're giving him some treatment,' Florrie went on. 'The days are not too bad, it's the nights I can't stand. It's the being alone, although we've not slept together for over a year,' she hastened to add.

The meal was eaten and the fire burned low. Florrie stood up, her large breasts standing out beneath the flimsy night-gown. She reached out and took his hand, steering him out onto the landing and into the darkened bedroom. Heavy drapes over the window were pulled back and the weak light from the moon shone down on the bed. Florrie pulled the covers over the window and lit a candle.

Albert sat on the bed and took off his shoes with deliber-ation as the woman watched him. She smiled and stretched and in the same movement let her dressing gown fall from her shoulders. Her thighs were heavy and her hips rounded, contrasting with her narrow waist and slender shoulders. Her breath came in gasps as she bent over him and tore at his shirt. Albert moved back but the woman smothered him with her open mouth, her fingers searching and probing. She finally managed to get him derobed and into the bed, her fingernails biting into his back as she fought against his immobility. She gasped 'O my God, Albert, take me, do it, for God's sake do it!'

The man was drowning, immersed beneath the raving woman, whose breath was coming in screams. He fought for supremacy, as her nails bit deep into his perspiring body and drove red lines from his shoulders down to his waist. He was terrified. She was an animal, savage-like in her desires. Albert felt he was losing consciousness and he heaved upwards with his arms and threw the woman from him. She rolled from the bed and fell backwards onto the floor. Albert sat up and grabbed at his side where a trickle of blood had started to flow, dripping onto the sheet. He looked down at Florrie and saw that she remained still.

She lay on her side, her head by the washstand. Albert gasped and went from the bed to where she lay. He felt her head, gently turning her over as he did so. There was no blood but he could feel a large bump forming behind her ear. He wet a towel and pressed it to her forehead and the back of her neck. She moaned and her eyes flickered.

'Thank God,' he said aloud as he picked Florrie up and placed her on the bed. She groaned and turned onto her side. Albert quickly dressed, glancing at her as he did so. The candle flickered and burned bright again as he opened the door. With a last look at Florrie, the man hurried down the winding stairs and into the bar. The night air hit him through his open shirt as he made his way quickly to his lodgings in the street.

In the small bedroom above the Eagle, Florrie turned onto

her back and gazed up at the shadowy ceiling. Her head hurt and her body ached, but she felt a warm feeling inside. She called his name, then closed her eyes, her hand searching the empty space beside her.

Chapter Five

Christmas was only a few days away when certain things happened to brighten up the lives of the dockland folk. Cinemas started to open up again, and some of the theatres too. The big West End stores advertised that they would stay open late for the Christmas week and they promised to put on their usual treat for the kids, a Santa Claus complete with reindeer. People started to breathe a little easier, for they reasoned that it would be unlikely for any bombs to fall on London, at least until after Christmas. Children who had been evacuated were to be allowed a visit from their parents, and special trains were laid on for this purpose.

The Carters had two youngsters who had been evacuated to the country and their letters were giving Tom Carter and his wife Mary a few worries. It seemed that Reg, who was ten years old, and his sister Marjorie who was seven, were having to do certain chores for the local squire and his wife with whom they were billeted. One letter said that Marjorie had to make beds and do housework and Reg was helping on the farm with the animals.

Tom Carter was a docker who had little in common with country squires, and knew nothing of country life, but it seemed to him that his children were a little young to be put to work, especially by 'them dung-caked landowners', as he put it.

'We'll write to 'em an' arrange a visit,' Tom said to his wife Mary, ''an' if there's anythin' untoward goin' on then they'll 'ave Tom Carter to deal with.'

Mary looked at her broad-shouldered husband and winced as his massive clenched fist pounded the table. She dearly hoped that all would be well, else the dung-caked landowner would probably become even more dung-encrusted. She tried to put her fears to one side as she hunted for presents to take to the children. After all, they may be with kind people, she thought. The children were probably very happy at the farm. But her doubts still nagged as she tied up the presents in their coloured wrappings. Mary had also managed to find a bottle of real Scotch whisky, which they would take as a present for the squire and his wife. Tom had his reservations, but as he said 'Oh we'll give 'em the whisky, even if I break it over 'is 'ead.'

Mary hushed him quiet. 'Now don't go jumpin' to conclusions, let's wait till we get there, Tom.'

They took the early morning train from Paddington during the Christmas week. Mary wore her best coat and hat and her smart shoes. Tom Carter refused to wear a tie. Instead he chose his white silk scarf which he knotted over his blue and white striped shirt. He wore his best blue serge suit and his brown button-up boots, and his check cap set at a jaunty angle.

Paddington station was crowded with waiting servicemen, who sat around with huge piles of equipment. More uniformed men and women milled around the RTO hut seeking instructions. A few others sat back on the seats, trying to snatch a few minutes' sleep. Red-capped military policemen patrolled in pairs, watching the servicemen and answering questions. The atmosphere in the station breathed confusion and uncertainty, currently aggravated by families trying to find the trains which would take them to their children. Tom and Mary were also confused as they approached the ticket barrier, for their experience of trains was confined to the very rare day trip to Southend. Mary carried two paper bags of presents, and Tom held the tickets.

They spoke to the ticket collector. 'Does the train stop at Gloucester?'

The man merely raised his arm towards the train.

'Miserable git,' remarked Tom, and Mary squeezed his arm.

Eventually the train pulled out of Paddington and the couple settled down in the smart compartment with its fold-away armrests, its carpeted floor and white linen head-squares. Mary snuggled back into the deep cushioned seat and smiled contentedly at Tom. An army captain occupied the window seat opposite the couple, and in the far corner an elderly cleric sat twiddling his thumbs. Facing him sat his wife, in her tweeds and gold-rimmed spectacles.

Presently Tom pulled out his pocket-watch and looked at it. They had been travelling for one hour. Mary also glanced at his watch and decided it was time to have something to eat. She pulled out a pack of sandwiches from a zip-up bag, which she held on her lap.

She leaned over and tapped the captain on his knee. 'Care for a fish-paste sandwich?' she asked softly. The officer declined and buried his face in a copy of *John Bull*. Mary looked at the vicar and his wife, who was twitching her nose like a rabbit. 'Would you care for one?' she asked. The tweed-dressed lady looked over her spectacles at Tom's wife and shook her head. 'No thank you,' she said coldly. The vicar declined with a slight smile that must have caused him some pain because he quickly reverted to his serious observation of the carriage roof. In fact, Mary had disturbed his contemplation upon the coming Sunday's sermon. He had considered the 'feeding of the five thousand', but the dreadful smell of those fish-paste sandwiches had changed his mind.

Tom Carter took a sandwich and munched it, occasionally wiping the crumbs from his lap onto the carpeted floor. The vicar's wife looked at the crumbs, at Tom, then returned her gaze to the rolling countryside. Tom finished his last mouthful, and was wiping his hands on a red spotted handkerchief, when the door slid open. A tall, stooping ticket inspector entered the compartment and held out his hand. The captain showed the man his pass and went back to his copy of *John Bull*. The vicar held out his tickets and the inspector clipped a chunk out of them.

Tom Carter was searching his waistcoat pockets for the tickets when Mary nudged him. 'Your back pocket,' she whispered.

Tom jumped up and accidentally knocked the inspector's hat from his head. The man stooped to retrieve the hat, noticing as he did so the crumbs on the carpet. He sighed as he remembered that feeling he had experienced when he woke up. It was going to be one of those trying days when it may be an advantage to turn over and switch off the alarm. The man had decided against it, and was beginning to think that all would be well, until he entered this compartment with its odour of fish.

Tom had now found the tickets and smiled at the stooping, mournful representative of the Great Western Railway. ''Ere we are, mate, knew I 'ad 'em somewhere,' he said cheerfully. Mary's eyes went up in anguish as the train lurched and Tom stepped on the inspector's toes. The man winced noticeably and almost snatched the tickets. His face took on a look of pained authority as he said 'These are third class tickets, sir, and you are in a first class compartment,' the word 'sir' delivered with sarcastic intonation.

'Oh, is it?' replied the docker with an air of innocence.

'This way if you please, sir,' said the inspector, standing back for safety. Mary gathered up her parcels, her face flushed in embarrassment. Tom grinned sheepishly and the vicar's lady looked at the pair over her gold-rimmed spectacles. The captain muttered, 'Good God,' and buried his face in his magazine.

The inspector led the way to a part of the train that had no carpet on the floor, and no white linen head-squares. He was determined to see to it that the cockney sandwich-eaters would cause him no more tribulation between Paddington and Gloucester. As he returned to punch more tickets, he tried to recall the last time there had been fish-paste sandwiches consumed in the upper section. Meanwhile, the occupants of the upper compartment were taking their own measures to combat the lingering odour. The captain lit a 'Gold Flake', and the cleric's venerable lady took out a lace handkerchief impregnated with toilet water and dabbed at her nose. The cleric gave her one of his holy smiles, and continued to twiddle his thumbs as he contemplated the ceiling of the carriage.

The train finally puffed into Gloucester station. The Carters bade farewell to their cramped, third-class fellow travellers, and hurried from the train out onto the forecourt. Mary gave her husband a look of disgust. 'I felt a proper fool. Didn't you know it was a first-class carriage?'

'Course I did,' Tom replied. 'I always wanted to travel in one o' them posh carriages!'

The day was fairly mild with a slight wind. Tom took a deep breath. 'Beats Conner Street, luv, you can smell the country.'

Mary just wanted to get to the children. 'Let's ask that man the way,' she said, pointing to an aged driver who leant against his battered taxi.

Tom took out a letter and looked again at the address, then sidled up to the ancient man. 'I say, me ole mate, d'you know this 'ere place?'

The man gave Tom an icy look. He did not particularly want to be a mate of this man in his blue suit and brown boots. He'd seen the pictures in the papers of those London louts, as they stood on street corners during the strikes. He looked at Tom's cap and knotted scarf and knew that the man before him was definitely a troublemaker. He looked at the address at the top of the letter in Tom's hand. 'That's the squire's house, be up Church Lane, off 'n village,' he said slowly, wondering what the townie wanted with the squire. Then the ancient driver remembered the scruffy children he'd seen that day in Comstead Village. 'Your children be stayin' with the squire then?' he asked.

Mary nodded. ''Ave you seen 'em, are they all right?' she asked urgently.

'O, they be fine, you want me to drive you there?' asked the man.

Tom grinned at the driver, 'That's right, me ole mate.'

The Conner Street couple, sitting with their bags of presents, held on tightly as the driver pulled away from the station forecourt, and very nearly knocked the postmistress off her rusty old bicycle. The village of Comstead was three miles from the station, although to Mary it seemed much more. The driver turned left just past the village pump and took a narrow lane hedged by tall bushes. The lane continued for a quarter of a mile then opened out into a wider road that was laid with cobblestones. A hundred yards along the road, the driver stopped by a short drive that led to a stone-built house. 'Taxis are not allowed on squire's drive,' said their chauffeur curtly.

'Right you are, me ole mate,' said Tom cheerfully, unaware of the ancient man's look of disgust.

The two hurried up the drive, Mary holding on tightly to the parcels. The stone house was three-storied, with flint stones placed here and there on the façade. Two stone columns supported a balcony over the large oak front door. Tom looked at his wife, 'There's no bleedin' knocker,' he exclaimed.

'They've got no bleedin' curtains up either,' remarked Mary.

Tom hammered on the door with his fist, but the sound was evidently not heard within. Then Mary noticed a knob poking out on the door lintel. She pulled on it and the sound of a distant bell reached their ears.

'Don't like this place, Tom, it gives me the creeps,' Mary whispered.

'Them kids better be all right, luv, or I'm goin' to 'ave a few words wiv mister squire.'

The door suddenly opened to reveal a tall, gaunt man in tweeds. His coat was belted and he wore a brown cravat over a green shirt.

'Mr and Mrs Carter I take it?' he asked in a cultured voice.

''S'right, guv, we've come to see the kids,' answered Tom.

'Won't you come in,' said the squire as he stood aside.

The couple entered the hall and looked around. There was a wide staircase leading from their right, up and round to the landing above. The floor was marbled, and at the bottom of the stairs stood a grandfather clock in dark wood. Facing the clock was an ugly suit of armour, the metal arm crooked around a wicked-looking axe. Doors led off the hall on all sides, and one that was opened by their host led into a warm study. Books covered the walls, and brass statuettes were placed about the room. There was a large settee in the middle of the floor space, with a small table in iron and marble placed nearby. The large bay window was without curtains, and a huge table filled the alcove. On the centre of the highly polished oak table an aspidistra sprouted from an unglazed pot. The leaves were limp and brown. A log fire burned in the massive grate, and by the side of the fireplace stood a set of brass fire-tongs and pokers.

'Nice place you've got,' Mary said.

'Yeah, very nice,' agreed her husband.

'Won't you sit down. I'll tell my wife that you've arrived.'

'Are the kids okay?' Mary asked him impatiently.

'Yes, they're fine,' replied their host. 'Can I take your coats with me?' He added, as he made for the door.

Mary handed him her coat and scarf but Tom preferred to keep his coat on. ''S'okay, guv, I'll just undo it,' Tom answered.

The man left the room and Mary nudged her husband. 'For goodness' sake take your 'at off, Tom,' she implored him.

The docker removed the cap and ran his fingers over his hair.

The squire re-entered and announced that the children would be down in a few minutes. Tom studied the man and noticed that he had a habit of frowning, a pronounced movement magnified by his bushy eyebrows, which seemed to sprout outwards. The squire looked ill at ease, his hands continually going in and coming out of his coat pockets. 'Would you care for some tea?' he asked.

Mary nodded her thanks and the tall man went over to the door and pulled on a tassel. After a few seconds the door opened and a tired-looking woman appeared. She had dark hair that was pulled to the back of her head in a tight bun. Her eyes were deep-set and her face was thin, with a nose that bent round from the bridge to the tip. She wore a dark dress with a white apron tied around her waist.

'Will you serve tea for two, Anna?' The man asked loudly.

The woman watched the man's lips, then left.

'Deaf as a post,' remarked Tom to his wife in a whisper, and Mary gave him a meaningful look.

The host walked to a cabinet in one corner of the room and took down a cherry-wood pipe which he started to fill. 'You had a good journey down, I take it?' he asked, and Mary nodded affirmatively and glanced wickedly at her husband.

66

'Yeah, we 'ad a comfortable ride, at least most of the way,' Tom said, a ghost of a smile playing around his mouth.

The man looked at the door impatiently. 'Where's the wife got to?' he muttered and Mary looked at Tom.

Footsteps sounded outside and the door opened. A large woman stood framed in the opening. She held the hand of a girl and rested her other hand on the shoulder of a boy. 'Say hello to your parents now, children,' she prompted.

The couple looked at their youngsters in astonishment. Reg was dressed in a pair of trousers that were sizes too big. His hair was unkempt and his pullover had holes in places. Marjorie hugged a small doll and stared at her parents, hardly able to believe that it was really them. She wore a dress that was meant for summer, and her grey-looking socks barely covered her ankles. Her shoes were dirty, and one of the straps flapped undone.

Mary sobbed as she tried to greet them and Tom felt a lump rising up in his throat. A cold feeling gripped at his insides and he gritted his teeth in rage.

The children stood for a few seconds, then the girl ran sobbing to her mother. 'Mummy, Mummy, are we goin' 'ome?' she sobbed.

The boy walked bravely towards his father, holding back his tears, and the broad-shouldered docker swept him up in his arms.

The woman who stood in the doorway gave her husband a look of disdain and she closed the door behind her.

Mary was holding the sobbing Marjorie to her breast. 'It's all right, luv, it's all right,' she whispered.

The large woman walked over to her husband and stood by his side. The door opened again and the maid came in bearing a tray which she put down on the marble table. She sniffed and left the room silently. There were two cups of insipid looking tea and two plates, each of which had a tiny scone sitting in the centre.

Reg looked up at his father, 'Are we goin' 'ome, Dad?' he asked, tears welling up in his eyes.

'You bet you're goin' 'ome, son, you're not stoppin' 'ere, that's for certain,' Tom said with venom.

Mary looked at the woman, who stood impassive. 'Where are their winter clothes? They brought plenty wiv 'em,' Mary asked, a look of dark anger showing in her eyes.

'These are only the children's working clothes. They have their work to do you know. Daily tasks, in fact,' answered the large woman.

Tom Carter nearly choked with temper, 'Work? Tasks?' he spat out. 'You mean to tell us you work these kids?'

'They have to earn their keep. Marjorie makes the beds and keeps the house clean – I mean she helps the maid with sweeping up and suchlike,' replied the woman.

The gaunt man butted in, 'Reg is learning how to care for the animals, isn't that so, Reg?'

'Animals? What animals?' screamed the infuriated Tom.

'The animals out at the back,' ventured the man.

Tom reached out and gripped the man's arm in a vice-like hold. ''Ere, show me them animals, mister squire,' he said through gritted teeth. He made the squire lead the way out of the study and out through a door at the back of the hall.

Mary meanwhile was looking hard at the large woman. 'You 'eard what my Tom said, missus, you'd better get their cases packed, an' leave out their warm coats.'

As Tom reached the courtyard the smell hit him like a blow. 'Gawd Almighty, what's that stink?' he uttered.

The man felt his fingers going numb and tried to wrestle himself free of Tom's grip.

'Don't try, me ole son, you're likely to break your arm,' Tom said, looking at the man with hate smouldering in his eyes. They walked over to the corner of the courtyard and there Tom saw the pigsty. Mud covered pigs fought to get at the swill. They pushed and shoved and slithered in the filth to get to the trough. Tom felt sick. 'You mean to tell me you got my little lad to clean out this?' he shouted at the man.

'They're only pigs, they wouldn't hurt him,' the man protested.

Tom's self-control snapped completely. He grabbed the squire by the seat and collar of his tweeds, and heaved him bodily into the filth of the sty. The man's face went deep into the swill and, in trying to get up, he only slipped deeper into the mess. Tom turned and walked back to the house.

Mary was waiting for the woman to bring down the cases. 'What you done wiv 'im, Tom, you ain't killed 'im 'ave you?' she asked fearfully.

'No, luv, just sorted 'im out, nuffin' ter worry over,' he winked.

Presently the woman came down the stairs and put two cases by the front door. She held the children's coats over her arm. 'Where's my husband?' she demanded.

'Wiv the pigs,' answered Tom, and the woman gave him a funny look. 'Come on kids we're goin' 'ome,' Tom announced.

The youngsters grinned from ear to ear and Mary picked up her bag of presents. Tom grabbed the cases and walked out of the house. Behind them, they could hear the woman shouting, 'Cyril, come here at once!' As the little party marched down the drive, the woman appeared at the front door. 'If you've harmed my husband I'll call the police.'

'Don't worry, luv,' Tom replied. ''E's all right. Better run a bath, though!'

The London-bound train stood ready to leave as the tired but happy family reached the platform. The guard was ready with his green flag and whistle. Tom opened a carriage door and threw the cases in. 'C'mon, this'll do,' he shouted as he bundled them all into the compartment. The whistle sounded and the train puffed out of Gloucester station. Tom nestled back into the deep cushioned seats with their white linen head-squares and pull-down arm rests. He looked at Mary, and she gave him a huge smile. The two youngsters sat by the windows. They looked tired out but happy, and Tom, watching them, felt a lump in his throat.

Mary put her arm on his. 'What's the matter, luv?'

'Dunno, got a bit o' grit in me eye I reckon,' Tom said quickly.

An hour later the compartment door half-opened, then shut quickly. The representative of the GWR hurried down the corridor, mumbling to himself as he tried desperately to put as many coaches as possible between him and his tormentor. As he went on his way he bumped into a ruddy-faced old colonel from Much Deeping in the Fold. The mumbling ticket inspector caught the colonel's shoulder and knocked the monocle out of his eye. The old officer's face went even redder. 'Good Lord,' he gasped as he polished his eyepiece. 'Fish-paste and brown boots?' he repeated incredulously. 'The man's a raving bloody lunatic. Whatever's the GWR coming to?'

Chapter Six

The Christmas holiday passed peacefully, with no air raids and very little news from the land front. Broadcasts did, however, tell of the continuing battles that raged at sea. The telegram boy pedalled around dockland on his red bicycle, slipping into the back streets to knock on doors with a rat-tat, then handing over the buff-coloured envelope with its official heading. But the boy on the red bicycle had already completed his business with Conner Street, at least for the time being. The only seafarer from that backwater had gone and would never return.

The Eagle had been very busy during Christmas, with John Braden returning to contribute his dubious talents. The Bradens were particularly busy during the New Year's Eve celebrations, as Conner Street toasted in 1940 very loudly, but with some trepidation. In the new year, as in every year past, hangovers and headaches assailed the jollificators.

Early on New Year's Eve, Patrick took his tiny wife to the Eagle and sat with their neighbours the Harpers, Joe and Rosie, and their lodger, Skipper. Joe's friend and workmate Fred Harris and his wife were also in the merry group. They joined in with the rest of the customers to sing their favourite songs, accompanied by the rusting tones of a battered old piano which in its long life had more pints of beer tipped into its innards than had Patrick Flannagan!

Early in the evening a young woman entered the Eagle public house and hesitated at the door before walking up to the counter. She put down the small attaché case she was carrying and fumbled in her handbag for her purse. Florrie Braden was busy pulling a pint of ale and did not immediately notice the newcomer, but a few pairs of lecherous eyes coveted the slim figure of the woman, whose blonde hair barely reached her coat collar, and whose shapely calves were accentuated by her fashionable high-heeled shoes.

When Florrie Braden looked along the bar counter and saw the young woman standing there, her eyes suddenly widened and her face broke into a huge grin. 'Well I'll go to the foot of our stairs! Is it really Julie?' she exclaimed, spilling beer over the top of the pint mug.

The young woman's white, even teeth flashed a smile and her pale blue eyes lit up. 'That's who I was when I woke up this morning, Florrie. How are you and John?'

Florrie reached across the counter and clasped Julie's hand in hers. 'You're the last person I expected to see in here. Where are you staying?'

Julie blinked back happy tears. 'I'm staying at the Women's Hostel in New Kent Road. Just for a couple of nights. I'm looking for regular lodgings,' she replied, putting a half-crown down on the wet counter.

Florrie straightened up and shook her head. 'It's really you. I can't believe it.'

John Braden shuffled past at that moment, holding two pints of beer in his unsteady hands. His wife blocked his path. 'Look who's just walked in, John.'

It took the man a second or two before he reacted. 'My God! It's young Julie?' he gasped.

'Oi! John. What about our beer then?' an irate customer called out.

John Braden pulled a face and shuffled away with the beer to placate the solemn-looking individual, who leaned on his elbows at the end of the counter.

'He's not altered,' said Florrie, jerking her head in her husband's direction. 'Still upsetting the customers.' Her eyes looked down at the half-crown. 'Put your money away, girl. What you having?'

Julie felt embarrassed. People were looking at her and customers were waiting to be served. Florrie ignored their entreaties and grinned happily at the young woman before her.

Julie's cheeks flushed red. 'Let me come round the counter and give you a hand. I haven't forgotten how to pull a pint you know.'

Florrie waved her plump, ring-bedecked hand in the air. 'You don't need to do that. You stay where you are and enjoy yourself.'

'No really, Florrie. I'd sooner help. I'd feel more at home. Honestly.'

'O all right then, luv. Don't stand no old nonsense from this crowd though,' Florrie laughed. 'We'll have a nice chat later. I might just know someone who's looking for a lodger, fingers crossed though.'

Julie felt uneasy at first, but a pub atmosphere was not alien to her and soon she was laughing and joking as she helped the Bradens to deal with the ever increasing flow of customers. The piano melodies stirred the past for the young woman but the trade was too brisk for her to dwell on it.

''Ere, darlin'. G'is a pint o' Best fer Dinky. 'E's gotta be kept oiled,' said Skipper, jerking his thumb over his shoulder in the direction of the pounding keys, and at the same time rewarding Julie with a huge wink.

Julie placed the beer on the counter and watched as the little old man weaved an unsteady path towards the piano. She sighed and swallowed hard. It seemed like she was home at last.

'Dinky' Richards the pianist was blind. His sightless eyes rolled around as his skilful hands found the introductory keys, then closed as the melody rang out. It was as though the blind man wallowed in a love affair, raptured by every note, as his head tilted to catch the passing chords. His face often took on a pained expression, when his highly sensitive hearing caught a flaw in the already part-oxidised piano string. And his face took on yet another expression when his hearing picked up the vibrations caused by the placing of a full pint of ale upon the piano top. A wide grin would flash over his countenance for an instant. Then, like a snake delivering the fatal bite, Dinky reached out a long, thin arm and his hand closed perfectly around the glass. The operation was covered with his other vamping hand and the tune struggled on without the Eagle choir being any the wiser. Even when the ensemble were in top key and the melody vibrant, Dinky could hear the soft tap if one of the customers bought him a pint and placed it to hand.

That night Dinky Richards was playing a selection from a popular musical show that was appearing up West. One of the customers was thrilled by the blind man's performance, and stood near to Dinky to watch his fingers as they caressed the keys. As the chorus rang out the man put down his glass, which was still three parts full, to join in the singing. The top of the piano, being the most convenient place to stand his glass, was also convenient for the pianist. After an hour or so, the customer came to the conclusion that the quality of the ale in the Eagle left a lot to be desired. He'd calculated that he had drunk seven pints of beer, at twice his normal speed, and ended up being as sober as when he walked in the place. Not only was the ale losing its potency but the pianist too seemed to be flagging. Five minutes after the customer walked out of the bar, Dinky Richards did an unusual thing. He fell forward and played the last few notes of the song with his forehead.

'Get 'im a drink,' someone shouted, 'it must be the 'eat.'

The last thing that Dinky wanted right then was a drink.

It happened on that merry occasion on New Year's Eve, 1940, that Patrick Flannagan also got a little more inebriated than the rest. The next morning, the Irishman found it impossible to raise his head from the pillow. 'Jaysus,' he croaked, 'the room's spinning round.' Bridie provided him with black coffee and a headache powder, then warned the children of his condition. Maureen put her hands on her hips, because she was the eldest, and she also raised her eyes in disgust, as her mother would do.

A short while after the medication had been administered, Patrick entered the parlour to state that he felt somewhat better, but not so that he could go to work. 'If I should fall down, woman, then I may end up in hot water.' The statement was probably true, for Patrick's job was to stoke the boilers of the local bagwash factory.

Bridie gave the man his breakfast and, as he sat, eating implements held in shaking hands, eyes glued to his plate, his two young sons climbed onto a chair at the other end of the table to watch. Two-year-old Terry knew that if he licked his lips and stared hard enough at the egg on his father's plate, he would get a 'dip' on a piece of bread.

Terry tried licking his lips. In fact he tried two or three times, but the 'dip' was not forthcoming. It was not that the Irishman's behaviour was unreasonable, it was just that he could only barely focus his eyes on the plate. Anything further away was a blur. But the results of his father's over-indulgence the night before could not be understood by the two-year-old

Terry and he went off in disgust to get the toy pistol that made a loud clacking noise, so he could shoot his father.

The sound of the toy pressed to the back of his head as the trigger was pulled, gave Patrick the agonising feeling of nuts and bolts being shaken beneath his skull. He groaned, his head in his hands and Bridie, coming into the room, got Maureen to carry the protesting Terry from the parlour, and Patrick junior settled down again on his chair to watch his father's discomfort. The man was still trying to find a way to eat his breakfast, but without much success, for he felt very sick. Young Patrick watched fascinated as his father, after checking that Bridie wasn't looking, slowly cut the rind from his bacon, then slid the rasher over the edge of the plate and into his lap. Patrick roared and thumped the table, and Patrick senior groaned once more. Bridie grabbed the boy, and spoke to Maureen, 'I need to go to the market, I'll take this one with me,' she said, giving the boy a stern look.

The weather was cold but bright on that first day of the year, and the market was in full swing, although some of the traders looked the worse for wear. Bridie finished her shopping at Albert Conlin's stall. She had taken her time so that the house would be left reasonably quiet. She knew that it would be around ten minutes to eleven before Patrick returned to the state of partial mobility. He would then announce that he would wash, shave and get a 'breath of fresh air . . .'

As Albert Conlin weighed up the tomatoes, Patrick junior's eye was caught by a shuffling figure that worked away behind the stall. The man's tongue hung out as he levered at a box of fruit. A stream of dribble ran down his chin as his face contorted with the effort. The boy watched closely as the idiot fought to get a case-opener under the lid of the box. The tongue slid around towards his cheek, then dropped to lick his chin as the operation became more and more difficult.

76

The young Patrick grinned at the idiot and poked his own tongue out. Bobbie realised that he was being watched and decided that he must show the little lad the best way to open a case of apples. He put the case-opener down while he turned the box round, then he picked up the implement and decided to turn the box round again. Patrick junior could see, even allowing for his tender years, that all was not right.

Albert too saw the mess the idiot was creating for himself. 'Bobbie, for Gawd sake leave it alone. 'Ere, take this an' get me a mug o' tea,' he said, handing the unfortunate a tin mug and two pennies. 'Bridie, that poor bleeder'll be the deaf of me, you see if 'e don't.'

As he spoke, Albert tipped the tomatoes into a brown paper bag and flipped it over so as to twirl the ends. The bag split and some of the tomatoes spilled onto the pavement. Bobbie saw the mishap, and quick as a flash he dropped the mug and picked up the fruit, some of which had squashed. When he had a handful he threw them into Bridie's shopping bag. Unfortunately, it happened to be the wrong bag, and the tomatoes landed on top of a half-dozen new laid eggs!

'Not that bag, you heathen,' Bridie screamed. 'Will you look at my eggs? They're all smashed,' she wailed.

Bobbie was not to be beaten. He dived his hand down into the mess and pulled out a handful of egg shells, broken yolks and squashed tomatoes.

'Holy Mary, Mother o' God, take him away!' Bridie cried, and Albert Conlin burst out laughing, his eyes watering, and his shoulders shaking violently. Bridie screamed at him, 'You big pudden, what you find so funny?'

'I'm sorry, luv, I couldn't 'elp it. I tell you, 'e'll be the deaf o' me for sure.'

Bobbie ran to the safety of a pile of boxes and peered over the top of them, his deep-set, dark eyes staring in anguish, his tongue licking the box as he watched Albert replace the tomatoes.

At ten minutes to the hour of eleven, Patrick spoke to Bridie, 'You know, I feel a bit better, I'll get a wash and a shave, and then I'll take meself off for a breath of air.'

Bridie puffed and got on with her washing, and the twins put their dolls' clothes onto the pile of dirty linen which was awaiting the copper.

At ten minutes past the hour, Patrick called out to say he was taking his stroll and Bridie grumbled to Maureen, 'As far as the pub is all the stroll your father will take, darlin', and that's for sure.'

Patrick reached the Eagle and realised that he felt a little weak. This walking is tiring, he thought, I'd better sit down somewhere for a spell. The fact that the pub was at hand, he put down to sheer coincidence. After all, thought the Irishman, it could just as easy have been the undertakers.

By the time Patrick had consumed a few pints of ale he felt much better. His headache had left him and his thirst had returned.

The pub was fairly packed, with most of the traders who were regulars coming in for their 'liveners'. One or two people waved at the big Irishman, and one old character came over to ask about the rebel song. 'You know, 'bout the bloke wot's goin' ter git shot at dawn or somefing?'

Patrick scratched his head. He knew the song well enough, but he had no recollection of ever trying to sing it. He bought the old fellow a drink and the two got into conversation. The man had spent a lifetime in the docks, and Patrick enjoyed his company. They drank a few more beers and then the old man asked him again about the rebel song. 'Yer gotta sing it, Pat. Yer good lady stopped yer last night. Kept on treatin' the pianer player, so's 'e wouldn't play yer song. I's always got me eyes open, spot fings I do.'

'Well, if you want to hear all about *Kevin Barry* I'll sing it, Pop,' announced the swaying Irishman, as he banged his empty glass down on the bar counter.

The piano player was recovering from the night before, and the instrument stayed silent. Nevertheless, Patrick went over to stand with his arm resting on the top of that battered, scarred old upright and he started to sing. His hands waved and gestured and tears came into his eyes as the song rolled from his lips. The crowd in the bar were listening to the rendering when a little man pushed his way through. He carried a bar stool by its leg, and when he got within range of Patrick he promptly laid the Irishman out with one swift blow across the head.

They quickly bundled the assailant out of the pub, and then carried the unconscious man into the street. They propped him against the wall of the Eagle, to the chagrin of Florrie Braden. 'I'm not having him lying there giving my pub a bad name. You'll have to take him home.'

An emergency meeting took place and it was decided to commandeer Sammy Israel's fish barrow, which had been parked outside the Eagle for the past two hours. Sammy brushed a few fish-heads off the barrow with the back of his hand and said, 'Now him I don't mind on my barrow, but to push it down the street is too much. What if the Rabbi saw me, an' me a good Yiddisher boy? With a Catholic on the barrow would be too much.'

Wheezy Morris had an idea. 'Let's get Bobbie Wilkins, 'e'll push 'im 'ome fer a few coppers, I bet.'

Sammy Israel looked much happier. 'That's okay, but just don't ask me . . .'

Wheezy cut him short, 'Don't worry, Sammy boy, we won't tell the Rabbi, will we, lads?'

Sammy threw his hands in the air. 'You please yourself, but just don't ask me . . .'

'Sammy, fer Gawd's sake stop whinin' an' do somefing useful, go an' get Bobbie!'

They made Patrick comfortable on the barrow, with his head propped up on a kipper-box and they fetched the idiot. Wheezy borrowed a cloth money-bag from Florrie and slyly placed two metal washers inside. 'C'mon everyone, 'ow about a whip round fer good ole Bobbie?' He shook the bag and Bobbie grinned in surprise.

Sammy put a couple of pennies in and Albert Conlin, who'd followed the idiot over to the pub, dropped a silver threepenny bit into the bag.

'C'mon, let's get Bobbie a nice collection, folks,' sneered Wheezy.

Someone found a fish-head and an apple core, a few more washers, and a nut and bolt, all of which found their way into the bag.

Patrick was coming round as Bobbie pushed the barrow away from the Eagle. The customers cheered and the shuffling figure grinned back, his tongue rolling around his face and his dark eyes shining.

It was tea break in the leather factory, and the girls sat in the window to drink their tea and watch the people as they walked by. As they chatted and giggled together, Sally Jones's eyes became like organ stops. She suddenly screamed out and pointed to the street. The girls fought to get a better view and, as the idiot passed by, straining against the weight of the barrow, the girls burst into a frenzy of cheering. Patrick heard the row through his befuddled senses. He sat up and saw the girls waving through the open window. He waved back and nearly fell off the cart. Then Bobbie decided to join in and he put the barrow down on its legs so his hands were free to wave. The girls cheered back and waved their arms in the air and Bobbie grinned, his face contorting with pleasure.

As suddenly as it had started, the cheering stopped and the girls' faces disappeared from the window. In their place was a stern old martinet, who looked at the scene with disgust. Bobbie did not want to wave to that face; he liked the girls' faces better, so he picked up the barrow and turned the corner, then marched the few yards to number 30, where gently he set down the legs once more and wiped his face on the back of his sleeve. Patrick meanwhile had regained his senses to a degree and tried to get off the barrow. But he chose the wrong end and, before Bobbie could help him, Patrick tumbled on to the pavement.

Bridie had been doing her wash and heard the cheering. She peered through the lace curtains of her parlour to see her husband struggling to get up from the floor, with Bobbie standing over him grinning like the devil. Bridie clenched her fists in anguish and asked the saints for guidance. As if they obliged, the pail of soapy water caught the woman's eye. She grabbed it and opened the door. Patrick was trying to sing to her, and Bobbie moved away, the broken eggs still registering in his mind. He saw the woman draw the bucket back and smartly dodged out of range.

'You drunken heathen, and to come home on a fish barrow!' cried the tiny woman as she threw the contents of the bucket over the unfortunate Irishman, who stood shaking before her. 'And you,' she screamed, pointing to the idiot, 'you're haunting me today, begone with you!'

Patrick meanwhile had decided to give up the drink. He would go in his house and keep well away from the Eagle, for it was getting dangerous to even sing a song in there, he thought.

As the shuffling figure of Bobbie came into sight, his landlady and guardian Ada Dawkins was cleaning her doorstep. She looked puzzled as Bobbie approached her grinning widely, his hand holding a bag.

'What you doin' 'ome this time, Bobbie? Ain't they got no work fer you to do?'

'Bobbie pushed drunk man in cart, Sammy's fish cart.'

'Who the bleedin' 'ell you talkin' about, Bobbie?' urged Ada.

'You know, man who speaks funny. Firty, number firty,' said Bobbie.

'Oh my Gawd,' moaned Ada. 'You didn't push Patrick Flannagan 'ome in a barrow, did you?'

'Bobbie don't mind. Men gave Bobbie money,' he grinned.

'Money, what money?' asked Ada.

Bobbie held up the bag for Ada to see. 'Bobbie got money, look.'

Ada snatched the bag and peered inside. 'Gawd Almighty, they 'ave 'ad a whip round, ain't they?' she said, with cold malice in her voice. 'Who gave it to you, Bobbie?'

'Wheezy gave it Bobbie,' the idiot said grinning. 'Can Bobbie 'ave it?'

Ada tipped the money out and handed it to the grinning Bobbie.

'I'm goin' to take the bag back, you wait 'ere,' she said, her eyes flashing furiously.

The Eagle was getting ready to shut as Ada Dawkins walked in. Albert Conlin saw her and spoke, ''Ello, girl, want a quick 'alf a pint?'

'Thanks, Al, I'm lookin' fer someone,' she said.

Albert got her a drink and handed it to the woman, whose gaze was resting on the foxy figure of Wheezy Morris. The man was laughing and joking with a couple of traders and he held a fresh pint of ale in his hand. Ada beckoned to Florrie and the woman came over.

'Hello, Ada, what's wrong, luv?'

'Florrie, do us a favour, girl. There's a woman outside, won't come in 'cos she's scared o' pubs, said she wants to speak to Wheezy. Looks a bit funny to me,' Ada said, making a circular motion over her stomach with her hand.

'Okay, Ada, I'll tell him on the quiet.'

Ada Dawkins watched as the landlady of the Eagle called Wheezy to the counter and spoke in his ear. The foxy little man put his beer down and left the bar. As soon as he shut the door behind him, Ada sidled up and dropped something in Wheezy's glass of ale.

'C'mon now, time, gentlemen, please. Drink up now,' shouted John Braden.

Wheezy dived back into the bar. He looked relieved. 'Couldn't see anyone, Florrie, must 'ave gone.'

'C'mon now, drink up,' John urged again, and Wheezy picked up his glass. The ale disappeared into the man's stomach, and as the glass drained, a fish-head floated up, staring balefully at the man.

'Oh my Gawd,' screamed Wheezy, as he threw the glass away from himself. 'I feel ill, a stinkin' fish-'ead! I bet that Sammy Israel 'ad somefing to do wiv it.'

Albert Conlin glanced at Ada, who was just leaving. She gave him a huge wink, and strolled back along Conner Street as though nothing had happened.

Chapter Seven

The early weeks of 1940 were very cold, with east winds that rattled doors and windows and whistled through draughty houses. The wind blew down trees, lifted slates from roof-tops, and performed other ominous tricks. It blew under front doors and lifted the passage mats so that they seemed to float like magical carpets. It took the chimneypot from the roof of 24 Conner Street and nearly caused the demise of old Granny Flint.

The chimneypot landed in the almost empty street, just missing the few passers-by, but pieces from the crumbling stack fell into the hole and down into Granny Flint's fireplace. The room became filled with soot and smoke which enveloped the old lady, who was snoozing at the time. As she remarked later, 'I thought I'd died an' gone down to "old Nick"!'

The reason Granny Flint didn't go downstairs, or even upstairs to escape, was Maureen Flannagan, who happened to be passing the old lady's window. She saw the smoke and heard Granny Flint screaming. And, with Bridie and Rosie Harper, carried the old lady out, still sitting in her armchair. They covered her in mounds of blankets while they tidied up and aired her parlour.

Skipper managed to find the brandy flask and gave the old

lady a tot. The old seaman grinned at her. 'I gotta say it, girl, but you look like one o' them there music 'all minstrels, what wiv that soot all over yer face.'

With a look that spelt out 'be careful', Granny Flint held out her glass towards Skipper, who drained the brandy dregs into it. 'Pity this is the lot, Gran, one more o' these an' you'd be able to sing us all a song,' said the man.

'I'm sure,' puffed the old lady. 'Would yer like me to do *Swanee River* an' tap-dance down the street?'

Skipper laughed and old Granny Flint waved her stick at him. 'Be off wiv yer or I'll put this across yer shoulders yer young bleeder.'

The early months of 1940 remained quiet except for the continuing battles at sea. The German U-boats were picking off the convoys, and the cost of getting food and supplies into Britain was very high both in lives and ships. Food supplies were low, and rationing laws were tightened up. The ration book became a way of life for everyone, and it caused quite a few headaches for the shopkeepers. The paper work was a gigantic task, with forms that had to be sent to the Ministry, and registration of all customers. Coupons, cut from the ration books, were counted and used to get further supplies. The one-man business became a round-the-clock operation and many of the solo shopkeepers had to find assistants to help them.

Stanley Nathan ran a little one-man business. He had mixed feelings about food rationing, for although it caused him many headaches, it also brought a new woman into his life.

The Nathan Provision Store stood at the Kent Road end of the market, and had been there as long as anyone cared to remember. Stanley's father had founded the shop, and when he died Stanley took over the business. He was now forty years old, fat, short and balding. He had a rosy face that beamed at the customers, and a manner that was charming. Stanley had tact, guile and personality, and he needed every bit of it with some of his customers. They marvelled at his cheerfulness and his memory. He never forgot to ask after his clients' ailing family members, and how little Johnnie's cold was. He was admired especially for the way he coped when his wife upped and left him, preferring the more ambitious man, as she put it, to the staid, contented Stanley Nathan.

When he had brought his new wife with him to help in the shop, the customers seemed to change. It was as though they resented her coming between them and their favourite shopkeeper. The woman did not have Stanley's personality, nor his tact, and many times she fell out with the more difficult customers. She finally stopped helping in the shop and everyone, including Stanley, breathed a sigh of relief.

Things were starting to go wrong, and the letter awaiting him one night as he got home confirmed his suspicions. He sat in his little house in leafy suburbia and read the contents over and over again. His wife had left him for a businessman who was someone in the fish trade. He puzzled, as he read and re-read the letter. Should he have taken that next-door property when it was available? Should he have expanded, and taken on assistants, and enlarged his store? He already knew the answer. He was happy, as his father was before him. Stanley did not see himself as an employer, paying out the wages and sitting behind a desk, instead of sweet-talking the acid-tongued Mrs Brown. He knew he was happy and he intended that it should stay that way.

The months that followed were very lonely, and he tried not to let the customers see pain in his face. He did not take into account the fact that they were dockland folk, people who were born into a tightly knit community. They were masters at reading faces. The chances of anyone fooling them with lies and deceit were very small indeed. Those rough diamonds stared at the eyes, the open gaze, daring the person to lie, and they knew. They did not sympathise with empty words, but shared the pain; the eyes said it, and the open faces absorbed the ache. It had always been that way; from the raw times when tall-masted schooners tied up at the docks, and the women waited on the wet, foggy jetties for their men to come home. They sometimes stood outside the brightly lit pubs with their children hugging their skirts and the baby wrapped around in the end of the woman's shawl. They pleaded with their drunken men for money for food and were slapped into the gutter, or abused with a drunken tongue that flayed them with barbed nautical obscenities. Their life was hard and the area was bleak, with cold, foggy streets that led to the wharves and docks, and damp verminous tenements that festered and ate away at the very soul.

The reformers worked hard in dockland. They got the worst of the tenements pulled down. They founded the Seamen's Homes and the welfare organisations, and they planted trees along some of the soulless byways. They cleaned the filthy streets and altered the course of the open sewers. The reformers changed the lives of the dockland folk, but the image that was etched on their souls had descended from generation to generation. The look of suffering still lingered in their eyes. They recognised the symptoms, and saw them in their fat, balding shopkeeper.

Stanley Nathan often wondered about his wife, how her fortune fared with the ambitious businessman in the fish trade. He was to find out one sunny day during the summer of '39, when the Eagle held their annual outing to Southend. Stanley often used the pub during his lunch hour, and he joined the party which strolled along the sea front for a bowl of jellied eels and a smell of real sea air. The friends joked and jostled each other, and they pointed out the pretty girls. They stopped at a stall that sold bowls of fresh jellied eels, together with hunks of bread. A tired little man served the portions, his face a picture of misery. The woman who washed the bowls behind the counter looked even more miserable. The dirty apron tied around her skinny waist, and the head-square tied over her hair, seemed to define her face, and it became imprinted on the mind of Stanley Nathan. His wife had sought her fortune with the businessman who was someone in the fish trade. Stanley turned away quickly when he recognised her, but he need not have bothered. The woman worked away as an automaton, neither seeing nor hearing. She would, no doubt, finally leave the man for someone with more ambition. Or would she? Stanley wondered.

The rationing had become a nightmare for the shopkeeper. So one morning in January he took a piece of cardboard and a black crayon and drew up a notice which he pasted in his shop window. He realised that he must get some help, and hoped the assistant would get on well with the Lizzie Browns and the rest of his customers. He looked at the notice and pondered on what she would be like. Now the young woman who had just passed his window would be ideal, thought Stanley. She looked fine, with her honey-blonde hair tied back with a thin black ribbon. He was suddenly jerked back into reality as the girl turned and came into the shop. She walked up to the counter and gave him a sweet smile. 'Please, I've come about the job in the window.'

Stanley stared open-mouthed for a second. 'I'm ... I'm sorry,' he said hesitantly. 'Didn't you just walk past?'

'Yes I did,' replied the girl. 'Is the job taken then?'

'No, no,' replied Stanley, staring into her pale blue eyes.

'I have references, and I did work for the Bradens – from the Eagle, when they had their last pub in Kent!' the girl exclaimed, holding out some letters. 'I worked as a barmaid, but I've done shop work,' she added.

Stanley looked at her open, rounded face that flushed slightly as she spoke, and her dimpled cheeks, and he liked what he saw.

'Okay, when can you start?' he asked with a smile.

'Don't you want to see the references?' enquired the girl.

'Oh that's all right, I can see you'll do fine,' said Stanley, shocked by his own outspokenness.

'I can start tomorrow, if that's okay?'

Food rationing was not the only thing that upset the dockland folk. Their beer was being tampered with. Apart from the fact that it became dearer, it also got weaker. The locals noted it and when they spoke to Florrie about it she lied to them by saying that it was the hops, which seemed to satisfy them, for they still came in for their pint and a chat.

A few of the regular customers were missing. The Davis brothers were already drafted and others were getting their papers. Wheezy Morris was one, but he walked into the medical centre holding his back. 'Your back, you say?' asked the doctor. 'What's wrong with your back?'

'Twisted it years ago, I did,' answered Wheezy. 'It ain't bin right since.'

'Okay then, we'll just have a look, old man,' said the doctor.

Wheezy gave him a funny look, and the medic pointed to a chalk mark on the floor, 'I want you to stand here and drop your trousers.'

The little man did as he was bid.

'Now raise your hands over your head,' said the doctor, pressing a bell as he spoke.

Wheezy had been making it seem a major operation to drop his trousers, and as he stood there with his hands held high he winced convincingly at the doctor. The door opened suddenly and a nurse walked in. Quick as a flash, Wheezy dived down to hoist up his trousers, and the medic raised his eyes. 'Seems fine now, Mr Morris, doesn't it?' he said, pointing to the offending part.

Wheezy bit his lip. He'd been caught out by one of the oldest dodges in the medical profession. As far as the army was concerned, Wheezy needn't have worried, for the doctor looked at him and said 'I'm sorry to tell you that you have a perforated eardrum, old man.'

'You mean I can't go in the army an' do me bit?' asked the little man, trying hard to muster up a look of disappointment.

'Sorry, old man,' said the medic as he stamped a card.

Wheezy hurried back to the Eagle and got into conversation with Sammy Israel, who was going for his medical the next day.

'I tell yer, Sammy, I was disgusted. Pleaded wiv the doc' I did. "Let me go, I want to do me bit, Doc'," I says. "Can't yer ferget me wonky ear 'ole?"'

'What did 'e say, Wheezy?'

'Wouldn't 'ave it. Said a sharp noise in me ear could kill me.'

Sammy Israel was beginning to get an idea. ''Ow did the doctor find out about yer perforation, Wheezy?'

'Put great big lights in me ear'ole. Though I don't fink they know what they're lookin' for. They didn't find out what was wrong wiv me bruvver.'

'What was wrong wiv 'im?' Sammy asked.

'Stone deaf 'e was, but the doctors couldn't find a fing wrong wiv 'im. I could 'ave told 'em. It was 'is bleedin' wife wot caused 'im ter go "mutton".'

'Yer bruvver's wife, 'ow come?' asked Sammy.

'Well, 'e liked a drink, did Alf. Trouble was 'e couldn't get up in the mornin' an' Mona, 'is wife, kept screamin' in 'is ear 'ole. Not only did it send 'im deaf, it sent 'im round the bend. 'E tried to cut 'er froat one mornin' an' they carted 'im orf to the looney bin.'

Sammy had it all worked out when he presented himself to the army medical board.

'Shut the door behind you, Mr Israel,' said the doctor, and Sammy walked right in.

'The door,' barked the medic, and Sammy grinned.

'You have a problem with your hearing then?' queried the doctor.

'Do what?' said Sammy.

'You can't hear too well?'

'I'm sorry I can't . . .'

'Never mind,' cut in the doctor, 'we'll examine the rest of your anatomy anyway.'

Later, when the doctor had finished, he said to the yiddisher boy, 'I'm glad to say that apart from your hearing, you're a perfect specimen.'

'What yer say?' asked Sammy.

'It's okay,' said the medical man as he stuck a probe into the unfortunate one's ear. 'Looks perfectly okay to me,' mumbled the doctor.

'Do what?' asked Sammy.

'I said okay.'

'Pay?' queried Sammy.

'Good God,' moaned the nerve-wracked doctor, as he beckoned the nurse over. 'I've filled the form in, nurse. I want you to give Mr Israel his expenses, and a half-crown for his dinner. Sign this form please, Mr Israel.'

Sammy picked up the pen, then threw it down in disgust.

'Strange,' remarked the doctor. 'Shall we take one more look in your ears, Mr Israel?'

The yiddisher boy went home to await his call-up, and to tell Wheezy Morris of his impatience to get into uniform. The subject was discussed at length in the ale bar of the Eagle.

'You can't fool them panel doctors. Sharp as me ole mum's carvin' knife they are.'

Sammy Israel nodded, ''S'right. You can't pull the wool over their eyes.'

Skipper sat at the table, listening. He took out his tobacco pouch and proceeded to fill his clay pipe. 'It depends 'ow much yer wanna swing the lead,' he remarked.

'Wha'd'ja mean?' asked Wheezy.

Skipper took out a Vesta and struck it on the table top. Clouds of smoke enveloped him and Sammy coughed. 'Are you still there?' he asked through the fog, and Wheezy laughed.

'Well, it's a question of 'ow far yer prepared ter go, ain't it?'

'I don't get yer,' Sammy said.

'I knew of a chap once,' began Skipper, 'who got out o' the last lot. The '14 war I mean. This chap was fit as a fiddle, but 'e was determined 'e wasn't goin' ter get put into a uniform. When 'e got 'is papers fer the medical, 'e tore 'em up. Course they sent the police down. Found 'im wiv 'is 'ead in the gas oven.'

'Was 'e dead?' asked Wheezy.

'Course 'e wasn't. There was a smell of gas, an' the police broke in an' saw 'im layin' there wiv 'is 'ead on a cushion. Couldn't a bin there more'n five minutes. Must a seen 'em comin' down the turnin'. Took 'im to 'orspital an' checked 'im over, then they sent 'im 'ome. Couple a days later, down comes 'is medical papers. Anyway, this chap, I'm tryin' ter fink of 'is name, Woods, that's it, Billy Woods. Well Billy ain't goin' an' that's fer sure, so 'e outs an' dives under a tram.'

'Was 'e dead?' asked Wheezy again.

'Course 'e wasn't. They got grids at the front o' trams, ain't you ever seen 'em?'

'What 'appened?' asked Sammy.

'Tram was stoppin' anyway,' went on Skipper. ''E got cuts an' bruises, an' a bit of a shakin'. The tram pushed 'im fer a few yards that's all. Anyway, back 'e goes in the 'orspital again, an' they look 'im over. Out 'e was, in under a week. Missed 'is medical, so they decided to send 'im some more papers.'

The seaman paused in his narration to re-light his pipe. Sammy Israel and Wheezy Morris were eager for Skipper to go on.

'Well, what then?' asked Sammy.

Skipper wasn't satisfied with the performance of his pipe. He tapped the bowl on the edge of his chair and started to re-pack it, pressing the strands of tobacco carefully into a tight wad before putting a match to it.

'Go on, Skipper, what 'appened next?' asked Wheezy impatiently.

'Well, Billy Woods gets these papers,' went on Skipper, 'an' 'e gets a bright idea. 'E's got some sleepin' tablets, an' 'e decides ter wait till the police come fer 'im again. When 'e sees 'em comin' 'e swallers two tablets. The rest is already down the closet. Well, the police see the empty bottle, an' Billy Woods out like a light. Anyway orf they go to 'orspital again. Give 'im a stomach pump, an' a good talkin' to an' send 'im 'ome.'

'What about the papers?' asked Sammy.

'I told yer, Billy tore 'em up like all the rest.'

'No yer never.'

'Well 'e did anyway,' Skipper said with a shake of his head.

'What next,' said Wheezy, who was desperate to get to the end of the story because his glass was nearly empty.

Skipper cleared his throat. 'By this time, the 'orspital's gettin' fed up wiv our Billy Woods, so the doctor writes a letter to the army panel, sayin' that Billy's a lunatic, an' the panel send Billy a grade four card, which means that 'e's not needed.

Anyway, when poor Billy sees the envelope, 'e don't open it. 'E already knows who it's from by the look of it. Well, 'e runs out of 'e's house, down the street, like the devil's after 'im, an' straight across the road. Didn't even look. Straight under a dray 'e went. Trampled by the 'orses an' crushed by the barrels.'

'Was 'e dead?' asked Wheezy.

'Well, they never sent 'im any more medical papers,' grinned Skipper.

Chapter Eight

The early spring of 1940 was very mild, with the winds coming from the south. The season's flowers opened their petals atop air-raid shelters and between sandbags. They sprouted from sand-filled fire buckets and from every window box in Tanners Alley. The profusion of colour helped to tone down the ugliness that was war-time dockland.

Bob Bowman was pleased with his geraniums. They were budding well and he was looking forward to a good show this summer. The little backyard of the street warden's house was full of small earthenware pots. They stood crowded together on the scullery windowsill and on the cracked concrete floor of the yard. More pots stood in a row on a rickety wooden shelf that Bob had nailed up on the wall beside the lavatory door and each of the potted plants reached out for the restricted sunlight that shone grudgingly down into the yard.

Unlike Bob, his wife Grace was not very pleased with the way things were out back. It wasn't so much that she had to tread warily when she hung up the washing or when she used the wringer. It wasn't the fact that she had to be careful not to open the lavatory door too far in case the pots went flying. What Grace could not abide was 'The awful pong of that bleedin' 'orseshit.'

Bob just laughed it off. 'Let me tell yer, woman, that's the finest fertiliser yer can get, 'specially if it's fresh.'

Grace became resigned and just shook her head every time her husband disappeared from the house with a bucket and shovel and then returned carrying a bucketful of steaming geranium food.

In the early spring Bob Bowman was sure he would get a nice show. 'I'll stick a couple in the front winder soon as they flower, pet.'

'Not wiv that bleedin' 'orseshit on 'em yer won't,' vowed Grace.

May began with warm spells, which helped to add to the complacency that abounded. The news was the same from Europe, with the large armies facing each other along hundreds of miles of fortifications. There was renewed talk of a swift end to hostilities, and people prayed that it would be so. They offered up prayers from Spencer Street Methodist chapel in Thursday evening's bible class, and it was as if the prayers were heard as an urge to get the war moving. Which was precisely what happened.

On the next day, as the dawn broke, thousands of German soldiers and machines by-passed the defended front and swept through the Ardennes. Parachutists landed in Holland, Belgium and Luxembourg. The real war had begun.

In dockland, little groups gathered around to talk about the developments. They read the evening papers and heard on the wireless how the Prime Minister had resigned, and they were informed of the new leader, Winston Churchill. They discussed the events. 'I tell yer, it'll be a long, drawn-out affair,' remarked Skipper to Joe Harper.

'I tell yer, Skipper, we've got ter be grateful for that little strip o' water. If it wasn't fer that, we'd be fightin' 'em in the streets right now,' said Joe.

'Yeah, they might be good soldiers,' said Skipper, 'but they can't walk on water yet awhile.'

Joe Harper shook his head. 'They seem to be goin' through the Low Countries like a dose o' salts. It's frightenin'.'

'Them bastards wiv them parachutes, that's what's causin' the panic,' Skipper said, with a shake of his head.

'Yeah, it must be frightenin' seein' 'em floatin' down,' Joe agreed.

'I don't trust Germans. We 'ad one aboard ship. Officer 'e was.' Skipper stated.

Joe sensed a story, and he made excuses, 'Sorry I can't stop, mate, I've promised to slip over to see Fred Harris. Bin orf sick 'e 'as.'

Skipper reached for his tobacco pouch as Joe stepped out of the house.

The sun had set, and the long spring evening was turning to dusk. Joe walked slowly along the turning towards the Kent Road. As he neared Fred's house at number 8, he saw his daughter Mary walking in his direction. She saw him and smiled. 'Hello, Dad, I'm just on my way round to see you and Mum.'

Joe kissed her. 'You go on down, I'll be along in a minute, just poppin' in to 'ave a word wiv Fred, 'e's bin under the wevver.'

Mary's eyes were red and puffed. 'I'm on nights this week, Dad.'

'Yeah, I can see, or 'ave you bin cryin?'

'Well, I'm worried over Bob now that it's all blown up out there.'

'Don't worry too much, luv. Bob knows 'ow to take care of 'imself. 'E'll be okay, you'll see.'

The tall, slim woman walked on down the street, and Joe went into Fred's house, where he stayed awhile talking.

Lizzie Brown had a few comments to make on the day's

events. She stood by her front door in Conner Street, hands tucked into her apron. Emmie Jones stood with her in the gathering gloom. 'I tell yer straight, if them parachuters land in this street they'll get wot for.'

Emmie shuddered. 'O I'd die if I saw 'em floatin' down, I'm sure I would,' she said, looking over her shoulder as if one of the parachutists were standing there.

'Die nuffink,' thundered Lizzie Brown. 'I tell yer wot I'd do. I'd tie me carvin' knife on the end of me broom 'andle, an' I'd rip the bastards up afore they touched the ground, that's wot I'd do, mark my words.'

Emmie Jones shuddered again, and tucked her hands into her apron like Lizzie. The conversation was beginning to scare her.

'I saw Joe 'arper's eldest girl a while ago. Looked worried she did. 'Er feller's out there at the front.'

Lizzie nodded. 'Nice girl. Works in an army 'orspital, so Rosie 'arper told me.'

Emmie Jones caught sight of Mrs Smith, who was hurrying along in the dusk. The two watchers screwed up their eyes in an attempt to see what the woman was carrying.

'Is that one of those tram sheets?' Emmie asked.

'Looks like it,' agreed Lizzie.

Betty Smith reached the two women and set the bundle down on the pavement. 'Gawd, that's bleedin' 'eavy,' she gasped.

Lizzie and Emmie stared at the bundle.

'I carted that all the way from me sister's over on Spencer Street. Me arms feel like they're droppin' orf.'

Despite the fact that Betty Smith was concerned about pieces of her aching anatomy, she looked pleased with herself. Tram sheets were now prized possessions in dockland, and increasingly difficult to come by. There was a time when the ageing destination sheets got thrown out for the dustmen, until some enterprising soul found that a good day or two's soaking in soda-water loosened the black paint. The linen sheets could be picked clean, then split, seamed and ironed, to produce a pair of high quality bed-sheets.

For a while the tram depot became sieged with applications for the sheets, until they realised why. From then on signs went up advertising old sheets at seven-and-sixpence a time.

Betty Smith picked up her bundle. 'I'm goin' 'ome an' put this in to soak wiv a nice knob o' soda. I'll leave it in the bathtub. My 'arry'll 'ave to wash in the sink.'

'Your 'arry's goin' ter give yer a black eye if yer not careful,' remarked Lizzie, with good reason. Harry Smith was a heavyweight coalman with a well-known short temper. Mrs Smith's plan looked in jeopardy.

The knowledgeable Mrs Brown was usually consulted regarding the happenings around the dockland community, and Emmie Jones was aching to find out about Stanley Nathan and his new assistant. ''Ere, Lizzie, I know what I was goin' to ask yer. Is our Stan courtin' 'is shop girl?'

Betty Smith's bundle was getting heavy, but she decided to wait around for Lizzie's pronouncement on the matter.

'Well, it's funny you should mention Stanley an' that girl of 'is. Seems that she used to work as a barmaid for the Bradens, when they 'ad their pub down in the 'op fields. Tom Carter's wife was tellin' me. Got it from 'er 'usband's mates. Turns out there was a bit of a scandal. Can't get the rights of it, but this 'ere barmaid runs orf. Now she turns up workin' for ole Stanley Nathan of all people.'

Betty Smith decided to get her heavy bundle home to the bathtub, and Lizzie Brown thought it time she went in out of the blackout.

'I 'ope our Stan's a little bit more careful this time,' she said to Emmie as a passing shot.

*

The subject of the ladies of Conner Street's concern was at that moment sitting in the ale bar of the 'Eagle'. His assistant Julie Brett was with him. She had a serious look about her face, and Stanley was talking. 'I don't understand, Julie. You've settled in nicely, and the customers have taken to you. Why, even old Lizzie Brown gives you a smile now and again.'

Julie smiled at the joke. 'Stan, it's difficult, and you've made it worse.'

'I still don't understand,' repeated Stanley. 'You say you're thinking of leaving, because I asked you to walk out with me?'

'Let me try to explain,' said Julie. 'You hired me without even knowing my name. You didn't even look at my references, and now you want us to get serious?'

'Yes, yes I do,' said Stanley. 'We work well together, don't we?'

The girl nodded. 'You don't know anything about me, it wouldn't be fair to you, and besides, I . . .' She stopped suddenly, and began instead to move her finger around the rim of the tumbler.

'Look,' said Stanley, taking her empty glass. 'I'll get us a refill and then we're going to have a serious chat, okay?'

It was early evening and the pub was quiet. John Braden served Stanley with the drinks.

'How's Florrie, John?'

'Okay, Stan. She's got some work upstairs,' he answered.

Stanley Nathan took the drinks back to the table and put the gin and orange in front of the girl. He sipped at his whisky and soda, watching the girl as she put the glass to her lips. 'Enough orange?' he queried.

'It's fine,' replied Julie, as she took out a silver cigarette case from her bag.

Stanley glanced at the case. 'That's nice. Unusual in fact. I bet it was expensive.'

Julie wished she had left the case at home. 'Yes, it was a present,' she said quickly.

Stanley did not proceed with the conversation. He sipped at his drink thoughtfully.

Julie studied the man. He had a kind face, and his eyes were soft. He had proved nice to work for, but the thought of becoming his girl awakened her pain and suffering, and she found it very hard to come to terms with it. If he persisted, he would have to know, and the telling would mean the end for her as his assistant. She looked into his eyes and saw the concern there. She knew that she must tell him everything, and if that proved to be the end for them, well it would just have to be. There could be no other answer. The woman knew it deep inside her.

'Stan, I'm going to tell you something, and I want you to listen,' she said as she picked up the glass, looking at it for a second or two before downing the contents in one gulp. She then lit the cigarette she had been toying with and exhaled a cloud of smoke.

'You remember when I first walked in the shop, I told you about me working for Florrie and John as a barmaid? Well, it was a few years ago. I was just eighteen and very innocent. There was a chap who used to come in very often. He was smart, and had all the right answers for a girl like me. Well, I thought I was in love with him. I couldn't wait for him to show up. If he didn't make an appearance one night I'd be really upset, that's how bad it was. Anyway, one night he asked me out, and it soon became the usual thing for me to be with him on my nights off, and even after work. He told me about himself. It seemed that he was waiting for a divorce to come through. He said his wife had got herself another man. I felt sorry for him, and it wasn't long before I'd become his mistress.'

Stanley put his hand on hers, 'Look, I don't want to hear, Julie,' he said, his large eyes soft and pleading.

'You've got to hear it all, Stan,' she said sadly. 'If there's going to be any future as far as you and I are concerned, then you must listen. You can guess what happened next; I became pregnant. I was happy at first. I saw it as the thing that would bind us together. I didn't realise how wrong I could be. The man changed completely the moment he found out. It was then he really told me about himself. He had a devoted wife and three lovely children. He said that I should get an abortion. Money was no problem, and he knew of someone who could perform the operation. God, I felt as though I wanted to die.'

Stanley squeezed her hand until she winced. 'I'm sorry, Julie, but I don't need to know about it. What happened was in the past. It doesn't matter.'

'But it does. That's why it does matter. Don't you see? There's always ghosts that come up to haunt you. Someone from the past who comes on the scene and spoils everything. No, Stanley, it's important that you know everything there is to know.'

'Okay, Julie, but you know it won't make a scrap of difference to me,' Stanley said softly.

'I couldn't stay where I was,' said Julie. 'I went to stay with my sister in North London. It was a bad decision, because my sister was on the streets. I hadn't seen her for some time and I didn't know. She looked years older than she really was, and every penny went to her keeper. He was a monster, a sadist who liked to beat women. I know, because I saw him attack my sister more than once while I was there.'

Julie sighed, and fingered the silver cigarette case. 'It was a couple of months later when I lost the baby. My sister was shopping and I was cooking a meal for the three of us. Her man tried to get familiar and we started to fight. I remembered scratching his face, then he knocked me down the stairs. I can just about remember falling, then waking up in hospital. I'd lost the baby. The terrible thing was that her pimp was there in the ward, waiting for me to come round as though nothing were wrong. He had a bunch of flowers, and an evil grin that dared me to say what really happened.

'I was terrified for my sister as well as myself, so I kept quiet about what happened. That man was capable of anything. I was determined to get away as soon as I could, but when I got out of the hospital nothing seemed to matter. The rush to leave wasn't important. I suppose if you live with evil and degradation, then some of it is bound to rub off. Anyway, I started drinking. Then I frequented the places my sister used. It wasn't long before I was taking men back home. Yes, Stanley, I became a prostitute.'

The man dropped his gaze. He did not want her to see the tears that welled in his eyes.

'You wanted to walk out with me, Stanley. I had to tell you, surely you must understand?'

'Yes, I understand,' replied Stanley. 'But as I said, the past is the past. God Almighty, woman, we may never live to see the end of this war. Do you really think that because you've had a rough time it gives you the right to take it out on anyone who walks into your life?'

Julie gripped the cigarette case. 'Do you know how I got this,' she said, holding it out towards him. 'It was for services rendered, do you understand?'

'I understand,' replied Stanley. 'Tell me, why do you carry that case around with you. Is it to punish yourself? A penance, so that every time you reach for a cigarette, you remember the life you led and the men you slept with?'

Julie's eyes filled with tears, and she made to leave.

Stanley gripped her arm and spoke. 'Now listen, girl. Listen good. I'm not a priest in a confessional box. I can't issue you with so many Hail Marys. I'm a fat, balding man who's gone through a shambles of a marriage, with a woman who thought it was more exciting to sell jellied eels on Southend pier than spend her married life in Stanley Nathan's shop. Yes, Julie, my wife ran off with another man. I've had pain and suffering. I wanted to cut my throat, but somehow things get put into a different light when you least expect it.'

The woman looked at him, and saw the soft eyes that stared back at her. She saw the pain reflected there, and she gave a deep sigh.

'I opened my shop as usual the next day,' went on Stanley. 'I was missing her, and it must have shown on my face. Do you know who my first customer was that morning? It was Lizzie Brown. She came in and looked at me. It was the only time I can remember her actually smiling. What's more she even said "good morning", would you believe?'

Julie smiled, and Stanley was encouraged.

He winked at her, and went on. 'When I weighed up her bacon, she even said, "Thank you, Stanley". I tell you, girl, the whole community helped me through that period. They ached for me, if you can understand what I'm trying to say. They're lovely people, and I'll never forget them. They didn't try to judge me, they helped me. They taught me something, Julie. You don't judge people, you accept them, with all their faults. Yes, like the Lizzie Browns and the Emma Jones of this world. Christ, Julie, can't you understand what I'm trying to say? I want to walk out with you! I want to stroll along the riverside, and watch the sun dipping over the wharves. I want to see the ugliness of the place, and think that it's the most beautiful sight I've ever seen. I can only do that with you, girl. Now do you see?'

Julie reached out for his hands and clasped them tightly. She laughed through her tears, 'I see, Stanley, I see,' she sobbed.

'You're staying on then?' he asked.

'What do you think?' she replied.

Chapter Nine

Throughout May 1940 the news got steadily worse. The British army was being squeezed back onto the French coast, into a pocket around a place called Dunkirk. The news bulletins were all very grave, describing the struggle to keep the Dunkirk area open for the eventual evacuation of the army.

By the end of the month, an armada of small boats had been assembled ready to leave for France. In fact the evacuation was under way during the last days of May. Thousands of wounded, soaked, exhausted troops were lifted off the beaches, under constant enemy fire, and taken out to where the large ships lay at anchor. Many of the small craft struggled all the way back across the Channel, laden to the gunwales with human cargo.

Two people in the local community were immediately concerned with the progression of events. Joe Harper's daughter Mary was one. Her husband Bob was somewhere in France. Mary listened to all the bulletins with a dread that became almost unbearable. Alberto Vitelli was the other. He also listened to the news with a deepening sense of futility and fear. He knew that very soon his country of birth would be at war with his country of adoption. The signs were all there and the inevitability was burning into his mind as the days wore on.

On the evening of June 11th 1940, Alberto Vitelli locked up

his greengrocery shop in the Tower Road market and climbed the stairs to his small flat above. Maria, his wife, was visiting her cousin and would not be home for quite a while. Alberto sat in the quietness, his head buried in his large hands. He was unaware of the changing shades as the warm evening's sun dipped down in the reddened sky. The lengthening shadows darkened the room until it was night. Still the man did not move. A train whistle drifted across from the freight yard, with the sounds of shunting wagons as they were assembled for the night journey. The vague note of the steam whistle roused old memories, unlocking the door to the past. The man reviewed the fleeting thoughts from his supine position. He allowed himself to drift along with those memories beneath a feeling of despair that was an agony.

It was hot. Stifling hot, with the smells of the drains and the swill-bins at the rear of Leonardo's restaurant vying for supremacy. The stench rose unnoticed around the young boy as he crouched down behind the swill, waiting for the danger to pass. His hand gripped a fat wallet of pig skin, and his fingers traced the pattern as he waited. He crouched very still, allowing his breath to become normal and his heartbeats to slow to a boyish rate. He listened to the sounds of screaming and shouting as they became more distant. Still he did not move. They might return and he had to be sure.

It had been easy, except for that old witch Caterina. He had sidled up to the large foreigner with the cane and the white covers that draped over his shoes. He saw the bulge and reached it without the slightest slip. He removed the wallet and had started to back away when that crone called out. The foreigner spun around and shouted to the boy, who darted into the maze of alleys. Old Caterina pointed the way, her hand held out for a reward, only to be brushed aside.

It was hopeless, as the trail led nowhere in the dark byways. The boy had taken them in a wide arc, away from his abode, so that he would not be recognised by someone who would betray him for a silver coin. He had shaken off his pursuers and now he waited. He had learned to be patient, to trust his intuition, and that way he did not starve, and he remained free.

At last he moved. The wallet was in the swill-bin but the contents, lira and foreign notes, were hidden about the boy as he carefully picked his way home. Home, where his mother lay ill, and where his sister Carla brought the men who would pay for her services. He entered the street and climbed the dark stairs, two at a time. He sensed something was wrong before he pushed open the door. His mother had gone, and a priest stood comforting his sister. Carla sobbed, as the man of the cloth held his arm about her thin shoulders.

'Mamma, where's Mamma?' cried the boy.

The priest spoke, his deep voice ringing around the stone-walled apartment, 'The suffering soul who is your mother is very ill. She has consumption, Alberto. She must have care, so we have taken her to a hospice of the Daughters of Christ. There she will be properly cared for. We must pray for her often, my children.'

Alberto cried bitter tears. The money that Carla had earned in her room across the hall, and the lira he filched from the pockets of the rich, had now become enough to pay the price of a bed in the green-painted wards of the Daughters of Christ.

Carla was troubled about the boy, and she sought her answers at the church after mass that evening.

'I know of someone, Father, who will help me to get the boy away from here. There is a family in England related to our dear mother. The one who will help me has agreed to pay Alberto's fare on the ship to England. I want you to see the boy.

Talk to him, Father. He must go from here before he ends up in the prison.'

'Do not trouble yourself, my child. I will talk to the boy, and we will see to it that he starts a new life. Come now, let us pray.'

It all worked for Alberto, and he found himself standing on the quayside, looking up at the great ship that would take him to the country where everyone became rich and famous. He was nearly sixteen, almost a man; so he could not cry. His eyes blinked back the tears as Carla brushed her cheek along his. 'You must write often, and you must learn to speak the English tongue, Alberto. You must come home to see us when you are rich and famous.'

Alberto kissed his sister and she fled, too heartbroken to watch her little brother depart, maybe for ever.

The arrival at Liverpool was a relief for the boy. He did not like the dipping ship and the food that his stomach would not hold. He felt better as he walked down the gangplank and into the customs and immigration shed.

'You are from Naples, young man?' asked the tall man in Italian.

'Yes, and I have a letter of introduction, and my documents here.' He held out the bundle of papers to the smiling man, who spoke to his companions.

'I see that you are sixteen today,' said the man, and Alberto smiled proudly.

'There is your passport, you must guard it very well. Come, I will show you where to get the train for London.'

The young man walked hesitantly along the platform and glanced once more at his ticket. He was tall for his age and already the grey suit that he wore was beginning to come apart at the seams around his shoulders. A soft cap was pulled down tightly on his head but did not hide all the black curly hair. Dark eyebrows stood out on the lad's pallid face and large brown eyes stared out in awe at the bustling scene. His black pointed boots squeaked as he walked beside the stationary train searching for an empty compartment. The young man carried a brown paper bundle under his arm and occasionally felt his breast pocket to reassure himself that he still had his documents.

Soon Alberto was seated alone in a compartment that reeked of cigar smoke and stale perfume. He glanced idly through the window as the train slowly moved out from the station and quickly gathered speed. He sighed, looked down at the parcel on his lap, then up at the luggage-rack. He was loath to part with the bundle. Although it contained little of value, the contents were his only possessions and he was determined to guard them with his life. Carla had warned him about the dangers of being alone in a big city, but for Alberto London held no fears. He'd run the back alleys of Naples and learned to take care of himself at an early age. Besides, there would be someone to meet him who would show him the ways of London.

The lad's thoughts were interrupted by the compartment door being slid open and two men entering. They laughed loudly as they threw their small suitcases onto the luggage-rack and flopped down facing him. For a time they talked together but the lad could not understand what they were saying. Once or twice they talked to him but he could only smile and raise his hands in a friendly gesture. The men were looking at his bundle and obviously talking about him, he could sense it. He became uneasy and averted his eyes to the autumn landscape that flashed past the window. Later the two men became silent and presently drifted off to sleep. Alberto studied the sleeping men. They were both heavily built. The taller of the two had massive hands that rested in his lap. The man's hair was ginger in colour and close-cropped. His suit looked expensive and his button-up boots were of the sort Alberto had seen in the smart shops back home. The sleeping man's face was flushed, with a small, livid scar just below his left cheekbone. His thick lips hung open and occasionally his face twitched. His companion was a foot shorter, with wide shoulders that slumped down as he slept. His face was pale, with tiny blotches of blue veins on both cheeks. His hair was fair and thinning and was combed back. He wore metal-rimmed glasses that looked too small for his face. Alberto noticed that both men wore the same colour ties; a red and black design of vertical stripes. He wondered about the ties.

The train thundered on towards London and soon Alberto's eyes started to droop. The changing landscape had levelled out and could not hold his attention. Sleep overtook him and he dreamed of Carla. He saw her standing on the quayside, her small lace handkerchief held to her face. She was waving but he could not raise his arm in answer. He awoke with a start to find that his arm had become numb. Alberto rubbed the circulation back into it and put the parcel onto the seat beside him while he stretched. He could hear someone calling out along the corridor and the sound got louder. A white-coated figure passed by and the two men awoke. They stretched and the taller man nudged his companion, 'Shall we eat?' For an answer the bespectacled one stood up and straightened his tie. The two glanced at Alberto as they left the compartment.

The lad put the bundle back onto his lap. Now that he was alone he would eat. He carefully unwrapped the paper and removed a small, crinkled parcel. Making sure that his possessions were secured once more, he took out the food. It consisted of a hunk of black bread, a thick slice of salami, an apple and a screw-top bottle containing cold tea. The food tasted good and he washed it down with the tea. His stomach stopped complaining and he stood up for a while to stretch his legs. Away across the fleeting fields he could see the spire of a church and his thoughts drifted back to his home. He wondered about his sick mother and Carla. Soon he would earn money and then, when his mother was well again, he would send for them both.

In the dining car, the two subalterns of the King's Own Light Horse sat sipping coffee. Second Lieutenant Rodney Fallon addressed his companion, 'I'm willing to wager a few pounds, Cyril, the regiment will be ordered overseas before Christmas.'

Second Lieutenant Cyril Nunn looked up over his metal-rimmed glasses. 'I hope you're correct. Egypt wouldn't be a bad proposition this time of year. It'll beat the blasted climate in Scotland.'

Rodney Fallon nodded. 'These past months have been hell, haven't they? What with the rain during all the training, and the Old Man kicking up about the standard of discipline.'

Nunn winced. He'd been on the receiving end of the Colonel's acid tongue on a couple of occasions. 'Let's try to forget old "Cannon Balls". We've got the ladies to concentrate on.'

That suited Rodney Fallon. He was beginning to enjoy his leave. It had started the previous day when they both stopped off in Liverpool to spend a day and night in living it up before pressing on to London. Rodney licked his lips eagerly at the thought of the big city.

With their coffee cups refilled once more the two sat idly watching the changing view. Tall chimneys replaced open fields, and large factories emitted sulphuric smoke clouds that hung over the industrial heart of England. Presently, Cyril Nunn turned to his companion. 'You know, Rodney, I'll be glad to get in a spot of overseas. This country of ours is slowly going to the wall. It's becoming a dustbin for all of Europe. We've had the Irish, the European Jews, and now we've got the rubbish from Italy flooding in,' he said.

Rodney nodded in agreement. 'It's this Mussolini. Seems he's organising everyone, and the peasants don't like it. They're mutinous, Cyril. Can't wait to leave the country.'

'Quite. Take that blighter in our compartment. I'd wager a month's pay he's from Italy. Shifty-eyed. Can't trust the blighters. Give him a few months and he'll be selling hot chestnuts on a street corner.'

Rodney laughed. 'I'll tell you something more. Give him a year and I wager he'll put some young woman up the duff.'

Cyril roared with laughter and a few heads turned in their direction. 'I'd like to know just what he's got in that parcel he's holding on so tightly to, Rodney. He hasn't let it out of his sight.'

'Probably a supply of chestnuts,' joked Rodney.

The two subalterns laughed loudly and there was a tut, tut, from two elderly ladies sitting nearby.

'I think we'd better return to our compartment, Rodney. I do believe the ladies are offended.'

The autumn sky was leaden and let no sun through. Alberto could only guess that it was past midday. London would be reached in about an hour or so according to his reckoning and there he would begin his new life. He leaned back in the seat, allowing the rhythm of the train to lull him into a semi-slumber. His eyes were heavy from the continuous lack of sleep during the journey from Italy, and he was only vaguely aware of the two men coming back. The mention of the name Mussolini immediately jerked Alberto back into alertness. He tightened his grip on the bundle and feigned sleep. Something warned him that he must be careful. His early training in the slums of Naples had made the lad's senses razor-keen and he was ready.

Cyril Nunn leered at Alberto. 'Our dago friend appears to

116

be sleeping peacefully, Rodney. What say we take a peepums at that parcel?' he suggested.

'I shouldn't, Cyril. You've got to be careful with that sort. Probably got a stiletto tucked down his breeches.'

Cyril eased himself onto the edge of his seat and adjusted his glasses. He leaned over and gently prodded the parcel. Alberto remained perfectly still. Cyril looked at his companion and put a finger to his lips in a sign. Rodney mouthed the word 'careful' as the bespectacled one stood over the young Neapolitan. Just at that moment the train gave a lurch and Cyril tipped forward. He put out his hands to save himself and fell against the seated figure.

'Awfully sorry, old chap. Just about to go to the closet,' he mumbled.

Alberto's hands had reached out suddenly to contain Cyril and as the two became untangled the lad uttered the only English he knew, ''S'okay.'

Cyril kept up the pretence by leaving the compartment, while Rodney stared out of the carriage window, his interest in the bundle now dissipated.

For the rest of the journey, Alberto kept a tight grip on the parcel. When the train reached the London terminal, he waited until the two men left the compartment before he made any move himself. He felt safe now that he was alone. At last he was in London. Presently he stepped out onto the platform and joined the milling crowds. Alberto felt strangely elated and his thoughts raced. First he would become rich. He would learn good English and maybe one day marry a beautiful woman from England. He would then . . . His thoughts were interrupted by a voice talking to him in his own tongue, 'You are the little one, then? The boy they call Alberto Vitelli?'

Alberto spun around to see the large man facing him. There was a white flower in the buttonhole of his coat.

'You are Gino Campanari?' the boy asked.

'Yes, I am Gino Campanari.'

The young Neapolitan reached into his coat pocket. 'I have a letter for you. It is from my sister, Carla. I have a letter from the priest as well.'

Gino smiled, his thick moustache twitching. 'I can look at the letters later. First we will go to my home. You must be hungry, and you must be in need of a bath.' He slipped his arm around the lad's shoulders. 'Come on, we'll get the bus. The journey's not long.'

Outside the station entrance two men, who both wore ties of the same pattern, hailed a taxi, 'New Bond Street, old man, and step on it, we've got a rather important engagement.'

The London cabbie was not in the least impressed, but he weaved his way quickly through the traffic and turned into Shaftesbury Avenue. The fog was thickening and a dampness settled on the cobbled streets.

'Soon as we get to the club we'll grab a bath, then a bite to eat, what say? I'm feeling positively famished.' Rodney suggested.

Cyril nodded and tapped on the driver's window, 'I say, old chap, step on it. We're rather late.'

The cabbie spat a stream of tobacco juice from the corner of his mouth and gave the horn a squeeze, although his path was clear.

'This'll do, driver,' shouted Cyril presently, reaching for his wallet. Suddenly his face changed dramatically. 'Good Lord, it's gone!' he said incredulously.

'Gone?' repeated Rodney. 'Gone?'

'I say, Rodney old chap. I suppose you couldn't loan me the price of the fare?'

'Sorry, old bean. Haven't a brass farthing till I get to the bank.'

The cabbie looked around and then spat another stream of tobacco juice into the gutter. 'Where will it be now, gents? The bank, or the police station?'

Chapter Ten

When young Alberto Vitelli left the empty wallet under the carriage seat, he made a vow never to steal again, though he felt the two men had brought the punishment upon themselves, or at least upon one of them, by their actions. Alberto was going to become rich and famous. But he would have to change from the swift-footed little thief he had been back in Naples.

As he rode the top deck of the bus to Clerkenwell, Alberto looked down on the foggy London scene. He was aware that his long journey was almost over. Here in this big city he would find work. He would then be able to take care of Carla and his sick Mamma.

Gino Campanari sat beside Alberto, pointing out a few items of interest as they bounced over the cobbles. Alberto thought that the area was exciting. The streets were wider and cleaner than in his home city. He would surely become very rich here in London.

'We get off the bus here, Alberto,' Gino said, pressing the red button on the ceiling.

'There are so many of our people's names here above the shops,' said Alberto in wonderment.

'That is so,' replied Gino. 'Our countrymen call this place "Little Italy", and you can see why.'

The lad looked up at the shop signs. There were names from all over Italy. Famous Roman, Neapolitan, and even Sicilian names on greengrocer, hardware and butchers' shops. The names were everywhere, and Alberto grinned happily.

The boy was given a room at the Campanaris'. Gino's wife, Rosanna, took to him and treated Alberto as her own son.

The Campanaris' daughter Maria was a year younger than Alberto, and her natural curiosity slowly turned into an adoration of the young, good-looking boy from Naples. She was very careful to hide her feelings from her parents. Gino and Rosanna were very strict in such matters. Maria felt that her God-fearing Mamma and Papa would treat her feelings as sin in one as young as sixteen. But to harbour such thoughts, sinful as they were, was very exciting, and one day her parents would know.

Maria could speak English with hardly any accent, and she taught Alberto so well that very soon he could hold a limited conversation in his adopted tongue. He wrote home to tell Carla of his progress, and of his plans to become a rich man. He told Carla of how he worked in the business of Gino Campanari, and of the daughter who taught him the English. He wrote of the girl who one day would be beautiful, but was now a nuisance to him because she was always getting under his feet in the shop.

When Alberto was seventeen, he went to the market with Gino in the man's battered old Ford van. Gino showed the boy how to select the produce and how to barter with the traders. The two men returned, Alberto sitting proud as a peacock beside the older man. He learned very fast, and soon took on the responsibility of ordering the goods. Alberto also learned how to drive the Ford van, and from then on went alone to the market.

Gino was getting on in years and the young Neapolitan took

more and more of the responsibilities upon himself. He buried himself in the running of the shop and the days flashed by. Slowly he began to become more aware of the young Maria. She had blossomed into a beautiful woman. Her rounded breasts and slender thighs, her flowing hair and dark, smouldering eyes stirred the young man. He began to watch her as she walked in and out of the shop. He missed her when she stayed away and tried to ignore her when she hung around him. His eyes gave away his thoughts, and as their glances met she saw the need and it warmed her.

A few days before Alberto's eighteenth birthday, a cable came from Italy. It told of the death of his mother. Alberto was distraught and shut himself away from the family. He had planned it very differently. He was to go home and buy the very best house for his mother and Carla. Now his plans were shattered. It took a very long time to become rich. The ache stayed with him, and he took to walking alone. The ageing Gino was troubled by the boy's attitude and he noticed the effect it was having on his Maria. He talked to Rosanna of this and the woman smiled. 'You mean that you have only today noticed that our Maria is a woman? You have only today seen the glances, the looks they share, Papa? You must be blind,' she said, her hands held up to the sky.

Gino smiled and kissed his wife. 'I too have seen the looks they share, Rosanna. I too have seen the way they are happy together. One day I think they will get married, or one day Gino Campanari will become very angry.'

Maria was determined to talk to Alberto. She knew that he took an evening stroll, and tonight she would meet him. She would tell him of her feelings towards him and ask of his. She would try to make him feel less sad, and tonight she would pledge herself to him.

The thoughts running through her head made her feel

breathless as she followed the young man. He walked slowly, hands in pockets, with his head held low. He stopped by the old churchyard and gazed at the flaking headstones that leant against the wall. Maria reached him and, as he turned, she slipped her hand into his and looked up into his eyes. She saw the pain there, and she nestled her head against his arm.

He squeezed her hand and smiled at her. 'I know that I have cut myself off from you, Maria. It is the pain, the knowledge that I could do nothing to help my mother. That I could not pay the doctors who would make her well.'

The girl looked into his eyes. 'The pain is one you can share. The guilt is not yours, Alberto. Your mother had consumption. She could not have lived, even if you gave a million pounds. She was a victim of the poverty, the misery that is turning Italy into a country the people run from. Your sister Carla knew that when she made the arrangements for you to come to England. She knew, Alberto.'

Alberto put his arm around the girl's shoulders and kissed her clumsily on the side of her mouth. She responded by lifting her mouth to his and throwing her arms around his neck.

As the months went by, Alberto put more and more time into the shop. Gino had become ill with heart trouble. His wife Rosanna nursed him constantly. She was younger than her husband by twenty years, but the strain imposed on her turned her into a prematurely old woman. There was also the worry of the business. The local landowner had been putting pressure on the shopkeepers. Land prices were rising as industry moved into the area. Shop rents were pushed up until it became a struggle to run the business profitably. Pressure was applied to frighten the shopkeepers. Flashily-dressed characters appeared. They spoke of the terror of the gangs and the protection only they could offer.

Johnnie Arpino was sent to talk to Gino Campanari. He

warned of the dangers of not paying for protection. When Gino tried to throw him out, his poor body succumbed to a terrible heart attack. Alberto was at the market when the racketeer called; he returned to find Rosanna bending over the prone figure of Gino. The man was very ill and Alberto knew that he had to act quickly. He picked up the old man and placed him in the cab of the Ford. Rosanna squeezed in to hold her husband's head against her as Alberto raced to the hospital.

The young Neapolitan returned to the Campanaris' alone. Maria was waiting for the news.

'Your father is in a coma, Maria. Your mother is beside him. There is nothing we can do now, except pray.'

Alberto climbed back into the Ford, his face set hard. Maria ran to him but Alberto pushed her aside. 'You must wait,' he said quietly. 'Your mother will need you. I have something that I must take care of.'

The boy drove westwards. He knew of Johnnie Arpino and of his gambling club in Soho. The cold feeling in his stomach persisted as he drove through the theatre traffic and over into the seedy area off the Charing Cross Road.

Johnnie Arpino sat behind his desk. One of his henchmen stood by the door. 'Come in, Alberto, I hear you want to speak with me,' he said.

The boy walked to the desk and put both hands down, fingers spread on the linoleum top. 'Your visit today, Arpino, put Gino Campanari into a hospital. It is doubtful that he will ever come out again. You have gone too far this time. If I see you in my part of the city then you will have to answer to me.'

'You are a brave boy,' grinned the gambler. 'But you are only a boy. You do not threaten Johnnie Arpino.' He nodded to the heavy man who stood by the door.

The man walked over to Alberto and grabbed him by the collar. The boy's hand closed over a large glass ashtray that stood on the desk, and as he was pulled round, he brought the heavy object down on the man's head. Blood spurted from the man's skull as he folded up in a heap on the carpeted floor. Alberto backed away as Arpino stood up, a wicked-looking knife in his hand. There were sounds of footsteps and voices in the hall. Alberto grabbed a chair and wedged the backrest under the doorknob. Arpino crept towards him, the knife flashing under the light.

'I'm going to cut your heart out, little man,' sneered the gambler.

Alberto crouched down, his hands wide apart. He feinted a jump at the gambler, then stepped to one side. Johnnie Arpino lunged at him, the knife held waist high. Alberto's toe flashed up and into the man's groin. As Arpino went into a heap, screaming in agony, Alberto grabbed the knife and a searing pain shot up his arm and blood ran down his fingers. He realised that he held the knife by the blade and it had laid his palm open to the bone. Arpino tried to rise but the boy kicked out at the man's head and felt the thud as his toecap caught Arpino's temple.

The men in the passageway hammered at the door and Alberto looked around him desperately. It would have to be the window he thought, grabbing up the heavy chair by the desk. The chair took the window frame with it as it went through, and Alberto followed, landing on all fours in the alley. He heard the men coming after him. They were shouting and calling for assistance. He ran up the alley, out into the glare of Soho's lights. He found his van and quickly drove away from the area, his badly cut hand clenched to stem the flow of blood.

Gino was still unconscious. Maria told Alberto how the traders had gathered together when they learned what had happened. There was to be a meeting at Morrelli's the next evening, and everyone would be there. The boy was relieved.

Now that he'd tangled with the racketeers there were bound to be repercussions.

Alberto's wound was stitched, and the next night the traders met. The meeting started by the boy telling of the fight with Johnnie Arpino and the possible reprisals. He spoke of Gino and the debt he owed the man for taking him in as a son.

One by one the men spoke. They vowed to form a group to fight the gambler and his mob. The meeting drew up a declaration that was to be delivered to Johnnie Arpino. In short, it said 'keep out'. Just as the meeting was about to break up, a messenger hurried to the front of the gathering and spoke to Alberto. The news was that Gino had died.

The days and the months that followed were sad for the Campanaris and their adopted Alberto. The business had to be conducted and a watchfulness had to be maintained. There was a depression settling over the country, and the traders suffered with the rest of the community. Money was in short supply. Unemployment reached terrible levels, and existence for most was little short of starvation.

Rosanna could not get over the loss of her beloved Gino. She became a recluse. Maria and Alberto tried to take her out for walks, and sometimes for rides in the Ford, but it was no use. The woman had given up her will to live. Maria talked to her mother about Alberto and of her desire to marry him, but the woman only stared at the girl, not hearing what was said, and not caring. Maria was heartbroken. Something would have to be done.

'I will have to write to Mamma's cousins. They have business far from London. She will be better away from this place. There are too many bad memories to bury the good ones, Alberto.'

'You are right,' the boy said. 'I will speak to your Mamma.

It is time that we thought about the marriage, too. We must talk to the priest.'

On Alberto's twentieth birthday, the couple were wed. Mamma Campanari sat impassive as the service took place in the little Italian church in Clerkenwell. The ceremony that followed was subdued, but the couple were greeted by all Gino's friends, who were now also friends of Alberto. They were grateful for the way he had taken on the racketeers and worked to strengthen their group. They bade the couple good weather and Godspeed as they left for their honeymoon at a little seaside resort.

The early days of marriage was a happy time for Alberto and Maria, marred only by their concern for Mamma Campanari, who was staying with her cousins. The woman was clearly brokenhearted and, even when the two young people visited her, her eyes never lost their glazed look. It was as though Rosanna were waiting to join her beloved Gino. She sat listening to the news from her daughter, but would suddenly tilt her head as though she heard something. He face would then relax, become more serene, and it frightened Maria.

The business progressed. Neither Maria nor Alberto could forget the early days, when he first met her and brushed her aside as a nuisance. They both smiled at memories as they looked around and saw the changes. It was not the happy place it had once been, and they spoke about it: 'I would like to leave here, Maria. Sell this shop and move south of the river. There are shops to buy, I've seen advertisements in the papers.'

'I feel the same, Alberto. The memories sometimes tear my heart out. I want to start somewhere new, away from the past.'

The young man grabbed his Maria and kissed her. 'I will go to see about it tomorrow. We will start afresh and become very rich, no?'

Maria laughed as she recalled the plans they had made, on

those long summer evenings that seemed ages gone.

Six months went by. Maria and Alberto were beginning to get restless when the offer came, via an old friend of Gino. He knew of a business that was going up for sale in the Tower Road market. It was south of the river, a good, homely place to begin again. The people were friendly dockland folk who would make a newcomer welcome, the man said.

The room above the greengrocer's in the Tower Road market was warm and dark on the evening of June 11th, 1940. The curtains were opened, and no breeze came in through the raised window, only the muted sound of the whistle from the freightyards. Alberto Vitelli sat very still, his head resting in his hands as he pondered. There was much to do and time was short. Maria would soon be home. He must write the letter, it was very important to explain.

Alberto reached for a writing pad and pen. There was ink in the drawer of the sideboard, he remembered. A late tram rattled past as he drew the curtains and lit the gas mantle. He sat down at the table and removed the stopper from the ink bottle. A small blob of ink dripped onto the white linen tablecloth and spread out from the centre of the stain like a searching octopus. Alberto stared hard at the mark and shivered violently, the pen shaking in his grasp. There were many words he must put down on paper. He owed it to himself and to Maria, and to all those who had left a troubled and violent Italy, to begin a new life in England. The words must tell of the love he felt in his heart for his country of adoption, even though he, and many of his people, had encountered much ill feeling since the outbreak of war. He must write of his despair, his heartache, now that all his dreams, his visions of the future, had been destroyed. There was much to say, much to put down on paper, about the plight of those of his people who had escaped a tyranny, and who had come among friends, to become as brothers and sisters, now to be seen only as the enemy. He rose and lowered the open window and drew the lace curtains. Seated once more at the table he studied the nib of the pen and the drying inkstain. There was much to say, but he found he could not begin. The events of the day came crowding in, blotting out everything else. It was as though a black curtain had descended. Some minutes later the clock on the mantelshelf struck the hour and Alberto Vitelli began to write.

Chapter Eleven

At number 14 Conner Street five young men sat around an improvised card-table. They drank beer which they poured from quart bottles, and they played cards with a dog-eared pack. They passed copper coins to and fro over the blanketed surface, and they grumbled over the snores and grunts of old man Davis who sat slumped in his armchair.

The night of June 11th, 1940 was warm and still. Blackout curtains kept out what little air there was, and caused the tobacco smoke to hang in dense layers about the room. The gaslight splayed down on the table and on the white faces of the men. It illuminated the scorch marks in the grey blanket, impressed there by the flat iron, and it shone down on the crates of ale by Jack Davis's armchair.

Wheezy Morris had 'cleared the board' and as he swept up the stakes of copper coins he gave a little chuckle, 'Me luck's in ternight, boys!'

'Yeah, we can see that,' agreed Ginger Davis. 'Keep it up an' I'll 'ave ter ask me old sarge fer a sub.'

''E'll give yer a sub all right. The only fing 'e'll give away is about nine inches o' baynit,' remarked his brother Freddie.

The men laughed and old man Davis grunted.

'You awake, Pop?' asked Ginger. 'Wanna drink?'

The old man shook his head and settled down in his chair.

'Who's fer a top-up?' asked Albert Conlin, leaning across the table to reach the bottles.

'Turn the wireless on, Freddie,' said his brother. 'Let's get the news.'

The cards were forgotten as the men listened to the reports of violence against the Italian population around London. Windows had been smashed, people attacked and fires started in some places. Feeling was running high against the Italians at the news of Italy's declaration of war on the side of the Germans. It had been a topic of conversation all day at the market.

'Bloody treacherous lot,' growled Wheezy. 'Yer can't blame people fer givin' 'em a pastin', can yer?'

'Serves 'em right,' mumbled old man Davis.

''Ello, Pop, you awake, fancy a drink?' asked Ginger.

The old man licked his lips, and sat up straight.

''Ere we are, Dad,' said Freddie, handing over a glass of brown ale.

The man gulped the beer down and wiped his mouth on the back of his hand. 'I ain't bin asleep. Bin listenin' ter the wireless. Serves 'em right I say. Fink they're clever, linin' theirselves up alongside them bleedin' Germans. Wait till our boys git at 'em wiv the old cold steel. Don't like the old cold steel, they don't.'

'I wouldn't fancy a baynit up me arse either,' grinned Wheezy.

Jack Davis wagged his finger at Wheezy. 'We used ter put the fear up them Germans in the last war, mark my words. When them bleeders 'eard our orficer call out "fixed baynits" they shook in their boots, I tell yer.'

'All right, Dad, take it easy. You'll start your ticker orf again,' said Ginger.

'Ticker nuffink. I seen the whites o' their eyes, I 'ave. Stuck a few as well, let me tell yer.'

'Yeah, I bet yer did, Pop,' laughed Ginger.

The old man stood up and took his tobacco-pouch down from the mantelshelf. He slowly filled his clay pipe, then lit it from a rasping Vesta, sending clouds of smoke ceilingwards.

The fourth man in the room sat thoughtfully tracing his finger along the pattern made by the flat iron in the blanket. Then he spoke for the first time. 'Well, I reckon they was right ter 'ave a go at the wops. It's all right them politicians sayin' about keepin' calm. They ain't got ter live wiv 'em, 'ave they?'

'Yeah, but it's bad when they turn on people they've known all their lives. People like Vitelli, and ole Giuseppe the ice-cream man,' remarked Albert Conlin.

'Accordin' ter the news, they're gonna intern 'em all,' said Freddie.

'Don't you believe it,' interrupted the fourth man. 'They won't intern 'em all, not English natrilised wops.'

'Wot worries me is that these wops can carry on tradin', an' all the time keep their ear 'oles open fer scraps of info', an' Bob's yer uncle. Straight ter the uvver side,' remarked Freddie.

''E's dead right,' shouted the fourth man, banging the table. 'I reckon a little bit o' rough stuff wouldn't 'urt none. It might warn 'em against tryin' anyfing funny.'

'You're not suggestin' we go an' duff ole Vitelli up are yer?' exclaimed Albert Conlin. 'Old Alberto is as much of a cockney as me or you.'

'Yeah, well I wouldn't trust 'im wiv a bit of info', like a convoy sailin' time, that's fer sure,' said Ginger Davis.

'I'm fer goin' round an' put the fright'ners in, what say you?' the fourth man asked.

Big Albert Conlin stood up and looked hard at the man. 'Listen, 'Oppy. I don't go a lot on wot you're suggestin'. I reckon you're gonna cause a lot o'trouble. In fact duffin' the man up is more likely ter send 'im over ter the Germans, so yer can count me out.'

Hoppy Dyke stared down at the little pile of coins in front of him as Albert put on his coat and bade goodnight to the old man.

Jack Davis had been listening to the conversation. He thought that it was time he gave the boys the benefit of his experience. He stood up, placed his pipe carefully upon the grate, and rolled up his shirt-sleeves over bony arms. ''And it over,' he said suddenly, pointing to the corner.

''And wot over?' asked Wheezy, perplexed.

'The bleedin' broom in the corner,' shouted the old man.

Wheezy complied, standing back quickly, and the old man pushed the chair back to make room. 'Now I'm a Tommy, an' you're a bastard German,' he said.

'Am I?' asked Wheezy.

'C'mon, let's be 'avin' yer,' the old man said, pointing the broom bristle foremost at Wheezy.

'Now c'mon, Pop, sit down, you'll 'ave an accident if you're not careful,' said Ginger, waving to the armchair.

'It's all right, son, c'mon yer bastard, come an' get me.'

Wheezy Morris wasn't too keen to get within range of the old man's weapon, even if it was only a broom. In the old chap's hand, even the bristles looked menacing.

'C'mon then, yer cowardly git!'

Wheezy sighed. He would have to humour the old man. 'Okay, yer English pig-dog,' he screamed as he jumped forward.

'Got yer, yer bleedin' cabbige 'ead,' shouted old man Davis, as he prodded the broom into the face of the advancing Wheezy.

'Gawd Almighty, wot yer got on that broom,' Wheezy

screamed, his face blackened by the bristles and contorted in disgust.

'Sorry, son, I fergot. I 'ad ter sweep the yard down yesterday. That bloody cat shit everywhere.'

'Why, you silly ole bleeder,' ranted Wheezy as he rushed out to the scullery, his hand held over his mouth, and the echoes of the men's laughter ringing in his ears.

A few minutes later Wheezy made an appearance, his face scrubbed clean with the aid of the old man's carbolic soap. He sat down sheepishly as Hoppy Dyke gathered up the playing cards and spread them out before him. 'I take it we're all in this, ain't we boys?' Hoppy said.

'Yeah, we're in,' they all said in unison.

'Right then. 'Ere's the shops,' Hoppy said as he pointed to the line of cards. 'We'll go down the alley by the pet shop, okay?'

The three men nodded. They were quite content to let Hoppy take charge. He usually did, from the time he first made an appearance in the Street.

It was a long gone summer when the days were warm and balmy, and the only people who knew about blackout were Patrick Flannagan and Mrs Jenkins. It was during the hot spell that the boys of the Street became restless. They were looking around for something now to amuse themselves with, when young Bernard Dyke moved into the precinct. He hobbled into the circle of boys and announced himself. They looked at his club foot and listened as he told them of a new game. The circle of hunched shoulders and bent heads opened up like a sunflower, the faces were beaming.

They found an old cap, then they sat like sentries, waiting for the first horse to fertilise the cobbles. When the deed was done, they surrounded the lad with the club foot, who proudly carried the cap full of steaming horse manure along Conner

Street. The cripple had volunteered to climb the lamppost with the cap and the boys were curious. They had never seen a boy with a club foot climb a lamppost, and they had never seen the feat accomplished with a cap full of horse-shit.

The sun beat down on the pavement as the little boy stood alone at the base of a Victorian gas lamppost. He looked distressed and held his head in his hands, occasionally peeping to see if any person tall enough were walking in his direction. He waited alone, patiently, until an ideal candidate appeared. He walked tall and proud. He carried a wooden cane that was silver-tipped, and the man looked kind.

'Well, well, now what seems to be the matter, little boy?' asked the good Samaritan.

'Th-the big b-boys put m-me cap up-up there, mister,' sobbed the boy, moving his shoulders up and down, the way he'd seen Jackie Cooper do it at the Tower Road Kinema.

'Now stop that crying, d'you hear,' said the man, owner of the local leather factory. 'I'll get your cap down for you, you shall see.' And he raised his cane to the cap which was perched on the ladder-arm poking out from beneath the lantern.

'Good Lord,' gasped the man as he staggered back, covered in fresh horse droppings. 'I'll tan your hide, you little guttersnipe!' he raved, shaking the manure from himself.

They appeared from everywhere, from behind dustbins, out of doorways, from corners, and out of houses. They appeared like a ravening hoard, screaming out 'Shit-finger Dick, old shit-finger Dick!' They danced around him, just out of reach, waiting for him to react.

The man was enraged. He looked for a victim, and thought he'd found one in the shape of Bernard Dyke. By the gods, he thought, here was a laddie that would feel the cane across his shoulders. 'Stop, you little swine,' the man shouted as he took off in pursuit of the cripple.

The boys of Conner Street were shrewd in their selection of a lamppost for the plot. The one that stood outside the Flannagans' house was ideal because it was near the Tanners Alley, and Tanners Alley afforded an extra escape route. It was this route that Bernard Dyke chose, and as he hopped along his pursuer realised that he was not making any headway. The cripple had perfected a movement which led from a hop onto the club foot to a skip with the other leg, then onto the club foot again, a movement that carried him over the ground at a remarkable rate. The factory owner was soon outstripped, and he returned to his office to recover.

The grinning, leering doorknockers might have looked down on the scene, seeing one of their own, a misshapen thing that grimaced as it hobbledegooked through their domain, with the figure of outraged virtue hard on its heels. It was a singular spectacle which would no doubt be discussed at the next coming-together of the night-people, when the church bell peals the midnight hour, and the rusty chimes drift down the narrow path, when the lion on the door would shake his flowing mane, and roar his approval, when the grinning devil would turn to watch the mailed fist give the Roman salutation. The ashen figures would rattle their delight on their plates without disturbing the sleepers in the cottage bedrooms, summoning the creatures of the night who would marvel at the events, and slink away before the going down of the moon, and the coming of the human dawn.

The fomenter of the nocturnal whisperings had swaggered from the alley, and had taken a roundabout route home. He was met with backslappings and words of praise, 'Cor, 'e never got near yer,' said one.

'I bet 'e stinks like a drain,' said another.

'Serves 'im right. 'Is factory's bin stinkin' our street out long enough.'

A little boy with a wheezy cough spoke up, 'I fink we oughta call 'im 'Oppy. 'E 'opped down Tanners Alley like a grass'opper.'

'Wot's a grass'opper?' said a boy with a running nose and large ears that stuck out like sails.

'It's wot's down 'oppin'. There's fousinds of 'em down 'oppin'.'

Hoppy Dyke ran his finger along the line of playing cards. 'We walk up 'ere, stop to see if it's all clear, then slip into the alley, an' creep along to the Vitellis' backyard. Okay?'

The trio nodded.

'We chuck a dustbin over 'is wall, then when 'e opens 'is winder, we pelt 'im wiv the rotten fruit an' cabbiges,' Hoppy expounded.

Ginger Davis slapped Hoppy on the back, 'We're wiv yer, ain't we, Freddie?'

'We sure are, 'Oppy,' said Ginger's younger brother.

'I 'ope we can get 'old of some rotten fruit,' remarked Wheezy.

'Don't be stupid,' said Freddie quickly. 'There's always piles of it in the alley every night.'

'Right then. We'll 'ave another drink, then orf we'll go,' said Ginger.

'I'm comin' too,' said Ginger's father, squaring up like a prize-fighter. 'I can still 'ave a go,' he said, thumping Wheezy in the back of the neck with his clenched fist.

'Gertcha, silly old bleeder,' moaned the victim of Jack Davis's right hand.

The four men walked purposefully up Conner Street and over the deserted Tower Road. They walked along past the shuttered shops until they came to Silas Cornbloom's pet shop. There was an alley beside the shop which the four entered, their torches shining a dim path before them.

It was a black night, with the thick cloud blanketing off the moon and stars. A slight breeze had got up and it threatened rain. A dog barked in the distance as the men crept along the dark alley. The path ended in a T-junction and the four turned left.

'It's the last but one,' whispered Ginger Davis.

'This is it,' said Hoppy. 'You get a dustbin, Ginge. You 'elp 'im, Wheezy, me an' Freddie are gonna get some spunky apples.'

Ginger Davis and Wheezy returned carrying a dustbin between them. They placed it up on the wall and gave it a shove. It toppled into the Vitellis' backyard with a loud clatter.

'Who's there?' shouted a voice as a window was thrown up.

A woman's voice answered the man's, 'Yer silly bleeder. D'yer fink anyone's gonna answer yer?'

'Might be a cat,' the man said meekly.

'Oh that's different, 'course a cat'll answer,' mocked the woman.

'Put that light out,' screamed someone else, and the window slammed down to the sound of 'cobblers'.

It was quiet once again in the alley. The sound of the dustbin did not seem to have disturbed the Vitellis.

'Tell yer wot,' said Hoppy. 'Let's aim a cabbige frew 'is winder.'

—Wheezy grinned and let fly. The sound of breaking glass carried up the alley.

'What the 'ell's goin' on out there?' shouted a man's voice.

A dog barked somewhere, and the woman's voice exploded, 'What is it, them cats again? Started jumpin' frew winders now 'ave they?'

'Put that bleedin' light out,' shouted another.

'Yer muvver wasn't married,' screamed the woman as she slammed down the window.

'There's nobody in,' said Wheezy.

'I'm goin' over the wall,' announced Hoppy. 'Watch out fer me.'

'I'm wiv yer,' said Ginger as he clambered up and into the Vitellis' backyard. Freddie followed them and Wheezy sat up on the wall, watching out.

'Try the door, it mightn't be locked,' whispered Hoppy.

Ginger lifted the latch and pulled on the door. It creaked open, letting light from the landing gas mantle flood into the yard. It lit up the passage and the patent-leather shoes that were suspended about a foot above the floor.

Hoppy Dyke joined Ginger and the pair stood, eyes popping as their gaze travelled up the figure, from the shiny black shoes to the bulging, grey waxen face. They held each other's hand, like young children, as they looked on death for the first time. They shook as they slowly backed out into the yard.

'Is it 'im?' asked Freddie in a whisper.

'Wot's wrong?' muttered Wheezy as he jumped down from the wall.

'It's the wop,' said Hoppy. 'Strung up wiv red cord 'e is. 'Ung 'imself from the bannisters.'

'Gawd a'mighty, wot we gonna do? We've gotta tell someone. We can't go ter the cops, can we?' wailed Wheezy.

'Right, over the wall quick. We'll tell the priest,' said Hoppy.

'I bet 'e's asleep,' mumbled Wheezy.

'Well we'll 'ave ter wake 'im up, won't we?' answered Hoppy.

The double funeral stopped the market. The shops shut for two hours in respect, and the stalls did not appear at all. The dockland folk from the little backstreets lined the Tower Road as the horse-drawn carriages trotted up to the Vitelli Green-grocery. Sad-faced women watched as the two coffins were slowly carried out and placed on the highly polished chromium dais. They put their handkerchiefs up to red eyes as the cortège slipped slowly along past the shuttered shops. The sleek black horses wore their tall plumes and dipped their noble heads as if in respect.

The trio, Hoppy, Ginger and Wheezy, stood silently together. They were among the first to arrive and they hardly took their eyes from the goings-on across from where they waited. They talked in whispers, as though the dead souls might hear, and they crossed themselves with feeling.

Further along the road three women stood paying their last respects. When the procession had passed, they turned to face each other.

'I bin finkin', Lizzie. Where they goin' ter put 'em?'

Lizzie Brown gave Emmie Jones a quick look. 'What d'ya mean?'

'Well, 'e done away wiv 'imself, didn't 'e? I didn't fink they buried 'em in 'oly ground.'

'Well I don't know about 'im,' interrupted Betty Smith, 'but they gotta do the right fing by that poor little bleeder, ain't they?'

'That's right,' agreed Lizzie Brown. ''E might 'ave done 'imself in, but that poor little cow never. She 'ad 'er froat cut.'

Chapter Twelve

July 1940 was very hot and during those long, dry midsummer days the news of war got steadily worse. France had capitulated and the German armies were massing along much of the continental coastline facing England. The narrow strip of water was the only factor that prevented an immediate invasion. More British ships had been sunk, and the German airforce had started to bomb English coastal towns. Papers were making gloomy reading. There were items on what to do in the event of an invasion, an announcement that there was to be no more ringing of church bells and, most depressing of all, the horrendous news that the English habit of tea drinking was to be interfered with. Papers carried the news that tea was to be rationed at two ounces per week, per person.

As usual, the folk of Conner Street had something to say about the latest round of news. 'Why 'ave they stopped them church bells, Lizzie? I love to 'ear 'em on a Sunday mornin'. It makes me feel all sort of peaceful, it does really.'

'Well you better 'ope you don't 'ear them bells any more on a Sunday, or any other day for that matter, 'cos if yer do it means we're being invaded, Emmie.'

Betty Smith looked up the street and saw the two women talking. She put on her clean apron and trotted out to join the discussion. 'I saw that bit about the tea bein' rationed an' I was really shocked. Why, my ole man drinks a potful before 'e goes ter work of a mornin'. Gawd knows what I'm gonna do now,' Betty complained.

Lizzie looked up and down the street to make sure there was no one listening. 'Save the grouts, put 'em in a bag an' add 'em to the pot, next time yer brew up,' she urged conspiratorially.

'Gawd, Lizzie, if my ole man caught me doin' that he'd give me a back-'ander, I'm sure 'e would,' said Betty with a horrified look.

'Well, if my ole man tried that on me I'd open the tyke!' exclaimed Emmie.

The concern of the dockland folk for the safety of their children was reflected in the sudden increase of those sending their youngsters out of London. Many children left their homes for the first time, though there were others who had already been evacuated once and were going for the second time. Other families were worried by the stories from parents who had visited their youngsters and found them not being properly cared for. The Carters' account was instrumental in Bridie's decision to keep her brood under her wing. 'I'm not letting them chicks out of my sight. If the Holy Lord wants to take us, then He can take us all together,' she said in a hushed voice.

On the domestic scene, there were a couple of events that helped to brighten up the depressing atmosphere which seemed to be slowly absorbing everyone. The engagement between Stanley Nathan and Julie Brett was announced, and Albert Conlin started to visit the 'Eagle' once more. The two items were of course discussed by the 'Ladies of the Street', a description formulated by Skipper, who had the good sense to utter the words in a confidential manner, and only to his trusted confidants. Even the old seaman realised that the wrath of the ladies would be too terrible to contemplate, should they hear that their immaculate behaviour was being questioned by such a scurrilous sobriquet.

These paragons of virtue gathered outside Emmie Jones's house to hold council. She had cleaned her windows, changed her curtains, hearthstoned the front doorstep, and served her Arthur with his tea, 'a nice piece of 'addock, fresh out the water,' she'd told him. Emmie had earned her rest, and she stood with her hands tucked into her apron, listening to Lizzie Brown.

'Well all I 'ope is 'e's doin' the right fing. 'Specially after the last turn-out. Made 'im ill fer weeks when she run orf,' Lizzie was saying.

'She wasn't much good to 'im, Lizzie,' Emmie pointed out.

'That's wot I'm sayin'. Mind you, this one seems all right. Yer can't take much notice o' wot people are sayin', after all, she works 'ard in that shop of 'is, an' she gets on wiv people,' Lizzie said to her nodding friends.

'By the way,' Emmie said. 'I saw Albert Conlin come out o' the Eagle last night. Drunk as "old 'arry" 'e was, could 'ardly keep 'is feet.'

Lizzie cupped her hand around her chin and pursed her lips. 'I thought 'e stopped usin' the place. Didn't 'e 'ave a set to wiv Florrie Braden?' she asked.

'Well, that's what my bruvver-in-law's wife told me, an' she ought ter know, Albert lodges there,' answered Emmie.

'Well, I 'eard 'e was usin' the Crown in Spencer Street. Rough 'ole that is,' remarked Lizzie.

'You're tellin' me, I . . .' A shout from inside the Jones' house interrupted Emmie's conversation. 'I'd better get in, Lizzie, it's Arfur. 'E's 'urt 'is back. Twisted it down the ship's 'old. I gotta rub it fer 'im.'

'Wot yer usin'?' asked Lizzie. 'I always use that

Wintergreen. Luvvly stuff that is,' she remarked, as the voice rang out again from inside number 7.

There was another little affair which punctuated that hot July. It became known as the 'spy business', and the leading character might easily have jumped out of a boys' magazine. He was long, thin and wore a dark beard. He was dressed in a black suit, with a black cape that hung from his narrow shoulders like a dust sheet. He wore black shoes with patent toe-caps and a black trilby hat that rested upon his large ears. He seemed to drift along rather than walk. His feet danced over the cobbles like a ballet dancer, fleeting across the stage during some grand performance.

''E's like some bleedin' fairy,' pronounced Hoppy Dyke.

'Well, we'll 'ave ter watch points. See if 'e shows up again. 'E might be a bleedin' spy,' said Wheezy.

The man did show up the next afternoon. He stopped outside the leather factory and took out a dog-eared notebook from inside his coat. He started to write, flipping over the pages, wetting the tip of the pencil with his tongue. He growled at young Maureen Flannagan and made little Terry cry. Then as speedily as he entered the turning he departed, observed by a worried Bridie.

'I'd like ter know wot 'e's puttin' in that bleedin' notebook,' grumbled Wheezy Morris.

'Well, we'll 'ave ter catch 'im. 'E must be up ter somefing,' said Hoppy.

'I tell yer wot we can do,' said Wheezy. 'It's 'arf day termorrer. When I put me stall away, we'll 'ave a couple o' pints in the Eagle, then we'll 'ang about the Street. See if 'e shows up.'

'Okay, I'll meet yer in the ale bar, 'bout one o'clock,' arranged Hoppy.

The next day was warm and sunny, with the Conner Street

146

folk bathing in the lazy atmosphere. Flies buzzed in the heat.

Good as their word, the two friends kept watch in the street. They strolled back and forth, eyeing the folk who used the turning as a short-cut. They were beginning to think the 'spy' would not show when Hoppy spotted him. 'Look, there 'e is! Comin' past the alley.'

Wheezy chuckled. 'Looks a right eighteen-carat character, don't 'e?'

The two men watched as the 'spy' walked up to the custard powder factory and stopped. He got out his notebook and proceeded to take particulars, dabbing the stub of a pencil on the tip of his tongue. He then crossed the street and started to address the lamppost that stood outside the Flannagans' house.

'What yer doin', mate?' asked Hoppy, trying to keep a straight face.

The man tapped his notebook. 'It's all down in here,' he said in a cultured voice. 'I have to write it all down and then assess it.'

'I don't get yer,' Hoppy said, scratching his head.

'Sizes. Doors and windows, They all have to be put down you know.'

'Oh, I see,' lied Hoppy. 'Gotta put 'em all down, 'ave yer?'

'Of course. Building regulations. Heavy penalties involved if the regulations are not complied with.'

'What about the lamppost then?' asked Wheezy. 'I see yer talkin' to it. Is the lamppost okay?'

'Oh, it's fine. We don't need to move that.'

Wheezy nudged his friend. ''Ere, I've bin finkin', what's 'e dressed up like that for? It's a bakin' 'ot day, an' 'im dressed up like it's the middle o' winter.'

'I dunno, p'raps it's cold in Germany in July,' grinned Hoppy.

The caped figure circled the lamppost and returned to

147

where the two friends stood. 'Carpenter's the name, Benjamin Carpenter. How do you do?'

The two men grinned at the 'spy'.

'Me an' me mate was wonderin', d'yer feel the cold then?' asked Hoppy.

'Cold, of course it's cold,' said the caped intruder, rubbing his hands together and walking off.

'Take no notice, the man's a loony, nutty as a fruit cake,' observed Hoppy Dyke, struggling to keep a straight face.

The cripple's diagnosis proved correct, for the next day Benjamin Carpenter was apprehended as he read the riot act out to a pair of dray-horses. The law, represented by PC Smith, arrived in the nick of time, for Benjamin Carpenter was about to receive a severe cuff around the head from the outraged drayman, who took umbrage over his steeds being lectured to by this 'bloody lunatic'.

'Take 'im away, mate, or I'll smash 'is bleedin' 'ead in,' said the foaming drayman.

Benjamin Carpenter was taken away, back to the hospital from which he had absconded. All in all though, he was not too sorry to be back home. He hadn't cared much for the places he had seen while he was out, and it felt nice to be back in the peace and comfort of the familiar surroundings.

The Street settled down once again to gloom and despondency. The days were long and became longer because the government decided to play tricks with the clock. They introduced 'Double British Summertime', which meant that the nights got shorter and the days began with folk going to work in the dark mornings. It was as though a piece of the early night had been lopped off the front and stuck on at the end. It was a good idea as far as throwing the enemy into fits of hair-pulling at the antics of the mad English, but it had a tiring effect on the worker, who now had to try to get to sleep while it was only just getting dark, and who had to go to work holding a torch to light the way.

Tempers were getting short-fused and there were incidents.

'Wha'd'ya mean 'e kept yer ball? 'E's got no right ter keep it.'

'Well 'e did, Dad. Said we shouldn't kick a ball in the street.'

'Oh 'e did, did 'e?'

The man's wife joined in. 'Now don't go getting all upset, Tom.'

Tom Carter did get upset, and he stormed along the street to number 7. He knocked on the door and when Emmie Jones answered he demanded to see the man of the house.

''Fraid 'e's at the Eagle,' said Emmie.

'Well, I'm gonna 'ave a word wiv your ole man,' said Tom Carter.

The fuming docker pushed his way into the smokey ale bar, and found Arthur Jones holding a pint glass in his massive fist.

'I want a word wiv yer, Arfur,' said Tom.

'Wot yer drinkin', Tom?' asked the man.

'I'll 'ave arf o'mild,' said Tom.

''Arf's no good, 'ave a pint.'

'Okay, Arfur, give us a pint.'

'News is bad, ain't it, mate?'

'Yeah you're right, 'nuff ter drive yer round the twist.'

'Wanna fag, Tom? Got 'em orf the ship, they're Senior Service.'

Back in the Street Mary Carter sat worrying and watching the clock.

Young Reg looked at his mother. 'Is Dad gonna fight Mr Jones?'

'Course 'e's not. Dad's only goin' ter get yer ball back. Now drink yer cocoa an' get in ter bed.'

'But Mum, Mr Jones is bigger than Dad.'

'I don't fink that'll worry yer farver, Reg. Now are you gonna drink that drink an' get ter bed?'

'Mum, why ain't Dad bin called up like Jimmy Bennett's dad?'

''Cos yer farver's too old ter fight, that's why.'

'Well what's Dad doin' sortin' Mr Jones out then, Mum?'

'You ask too many questions. Now look, you've got skin on yer cocoa.'

Two hours later, Mary Carter put her coat on and walked along to number 7. Emmie answered her knock. 'Emmie, 'as my ole man bin 'ere?'

'Yeah, I sent 'im up the Eagle, luv. 'E wanted Arfer, an' that's where 'e is.'

'Did 'e say what 'e wanted 'im for?'

'No, Mary, 'e just wanted ter talk wiv Arfer.'

Mary nodded and turned away.

'By the way, Mary, I got your Reg's ball 'ere, 'e wouldn't knock fer it.'

'Fanks, luv, g'night.'

'Night, Mary.'

Two men sat in the Eagle sharing a joke. One of them had a nagging feeling that he had omitted to do something. The warm glow inside and the convivial company put Tom Carter at his ease. There would be time tomorrow. He would surely remember then what it was he had to do, he thought.

The Eagle was doing a fast trade during those hot summer days and nights. The regulars from the Street and the market came in and discussed the latest news bulletins over their ale, and they became more and more fearful for the future. Little groups sat around the tables to debate on what exactly went wrong in France. They planned the future battles, and the more knowledgeable of the group terrified the rest with their pronouncements. If the speaker was an optimist then everyone went home happy, but if his tone was pessimistic, then the sense of fear prevailed and the customers went home feeling miserable.

As there seemed to be more pessimists than optimists among the pub's customers, the listeners of the group soon sought to insulate themselves from doom. They were fed up with pronouncements upon the future bombing of London, the use of poison gas and the date of the invasion. They turned to the storytellers. They sought the pedlars of the adult fairy tale, the orator who could relate strange happenings and amuse them. The listeners desired to be transported to some eastern market-place, to hear the soothsayer at work. They longed for the spinning of old tales, of kings and princes, yarns that could be bought for a coin or two. The listeners would hear of hot nights filled with the wild scent of jasmine and dotted with silver points of light shining down from a sky of deep blue velvet, and where the yellow orb-like moon hung low, casting its powdery glow upon the stage.

There was no soothsayer in the Eagle, but there was an able storyteller. There were no eastern carpets that could whisk the listeners off to a Persian harem; the carpets in the Eagle were holed and dirty, although their origin may have been further east, perhaps even as far as the end of the Mile End Road. As to the perfume, the modest Eagle could not boast jasmine, but it had a fine scent of 'Nosegay' and 'Goldflake'. There was also a full moon on the night the Eagle storyteller wove his tale, although it was hidden from view by the blackout curtains. There was no dish for the listener to drop his coin into, but a glass of dark liquid to quench the speaker's thirst throughout the saga of the *Damselfly*.

'Well it must 'ave bin '94 or '95, if me memory serves me right,' said Skipper as he packed his old clay pipe. 'I was up in Liverpool lookin' around fer a ship when I saw it. It loomed up out of the fog like a great sea monster. Docked an' still it was, although it appeared ter be breathin', strike me if it didn't. Anyway, I saw the name, the *Damselfly* it was called. Funny name, I remember finkin' ter meself. The lines was all slimy an' wet, an' the plankin' looked sort o' greasy, like the ship 'ad travelled in a sea of oil. Very strange it was.'

The audience watched the old seaman as he deliberately lit his pipe, blowing the smoke upwards. When he was satisfied that the bowl was drawing well he continued. 'I was young an' ready fer anyfing, an' I signed on fer a trip. The *Damselfly* was bound fer the Orient an' it suited me. You could reckon on bein' away fer a year or more when you signed on fer such a trip. I'd 'ad enough of Liverpool an' I fancied the noise of the wind in the canvas. I liked the windjammers an' the *Damselfly* looked a challenge. Ter be honest, I was a'feared of that ship but, as I say, when yer young the fear is a prod in the back.'

The listeners, sitting around the table in the little ale bar nodded their agreement and motioned for Skipper to go on, but the old mariner had spotted Joe Harper coming his way with a frothing pint of ale held in his hand.

'There we are, Skip,' said Joe as he put the glass down in front of the storyteller.

'Gawd bless yer,' grinned the seaman as he sipped at the froth. When he had taken a large gulp, and wiped his mouth on a red handkerchief, he continued with his tale.

'Well, as I was sayin', I signed on an' went ter me lodgin's ter make preparations. The ship was leavin' on the evenin' tide next day so I decided ter get well an' truly drunk so's I'd get a good night's sleep. I went in a pub I know near the docks 'cos some of me ole chums was there most nights. Anyway, I was beginin' ter enjoy meself, an' the rums was comin' up fast, when I spotted this ole seaman. 'E 'ad a patch over 'is eye an' a gold earin' in one of 'is lug-'oles. I don't know what it was but 'e seemed ter look strange. Couldn't put me finger on it, but I just 'ad a funny feelin' about 'im. I must 'ave bin starin' at 'im, 'cos 'e nodded an' asked me if I was sailin' on the *Damselfly*. Gawd above knows why 'e should ask that question, there must 'ave bin nearly a 'undred people in that pub, an' 'e asks me that. Anyway, I says yer, an' we get inter conversation. We must 'ave bin talkin' fer a decent while when I suddenly felt funny, like I was gettin' 'ot. I started ter sweat, an' I felt really ill. The ole seaman with the patch reckoned I'd caught a dose of the Mersey fever. I felt really rough, so I decided ter get back ter me lodgin's. I remembered gettin' under the blankets an' goin' from 'ot ter cold. Well, I must o' dropped orf ter sleep. I was 'avin' this dream. It was a terrible dream, not a nightmare. Nightmares are mumbo-jumbo ter me, but this dream was real.

'I was aboard the *Damselfly*, an' we was in the tropics. The sun was beatin' down an' I was ill. They 'ad me laid out on a plank up on deck. I was sweatin' an' me mouth was parched. I couldn't speak 'cos me tongue was too swollen, an' I jus' laid there. Two o' the crew were talkin'. "Dyin' 'e be," one of 'em said. Then the captain comes up. "Fetch me the sailmaker," 'e says in a deep voice. The sailmaker turns out ter be ole "one-eye" from the pub. 'E looks at me wiv a wicked grin spreadin' all over 'is face, an' 'e rubs 'is 'ands tergevver like 'e was enjoyin' me sufferin'. Then the captain opens a bible an' starts sayin' the burial service. Gawd I was scared. I looks at the sailmaker an' I nearly 'as a fit. There 'e is, large as life an' twice as ugly, stitchin' the canvas inter a shroud fer me. 'E was leerin', an' d'yer know what? I saw 'orrible 'orns startin' ter sprout from the top of 'is 'ead. 'E was the devil 'imself. Then I see the tail growin' from behind 'im. It 'ad a tip like a snake's tongue, terrible it was. Anyway, I'm layin' there 'elpless, when I spots the large darnin' needle e's usin'. It seems ter be doin' the stitchin' all by itself. The needle was shining like it was made of silver an' it really glistened in the sun. The captain finished the service an' then they came over ter put me in this canvas shroud. As they picked me up I woke up.

'I found that I was soaked in sweat. The blankets felt like someone 'ad poured a bucket o' water over 'em. I 'ardly 'ad the strength ter lift meself up in the bed. I looked out an' I could see it was daylight. I got up an' washed an' shaved, then I went down fer me breakfast. The landlady was surprised ter see me up. She told me I'd bin in a fever fer more'n two days. The doctor 'ad bin in an' 'e was due ter call back. Course, I'd missed me ship, an' I 'ad ter kick me 'eels up in Liverpool 'til anuvver chance come along.

'A couple o' days later I felt better, an' I went fer a drink in the pub I used the night I got took bad. I asked the landlord if 'e remembered me, an' 'e said 'e did. 'E also remembered me gettin' took bad. Funny fing was, 'e 'ad no recollection of the seaman wiv the patch who was talkin' ter me. It seemed strange ter me. I kept on finkin' about that ole one-eyed seaman, an' that silver darnin' needle that sewed by itself. Sent shivers down me back it did. Still I 'ad ter pull meself round, so I got anuvver berth an' I was away fer over a year.

'It was next year, '95 I believe, when I was in Liverpool. I 'appened ter go in that pub I bin tellin' yer about. There was a couple o' seamen talkin' an' I got ter "ear-wiggin". "Yeah, went down wiv all 'ands," this seaman said. "In the China Sea last year," 'e went on. "Must o' copped a typhoon, there was some nasty storms out that way last year." Well I pricked me ears up an' I 'eard the seaman mention the ship: it was the *Damselfly*! Gawd, if I 'adn't bin taken bad, I'd 'ave bin feedin' the fishes by now!'

Wheezy Morris broke the silence. 'Funny ole world ain't it?'

Skipper nodded. 'Yer can say that again. 'Cos the strangest part of all 'appened years later. I was shippin' out wiv a seaman whose 'obby was paintin' small pitchers of butterflies an' insects, an' the like. Well, I saw this paintin' 'e done of a damselfly, an' underneath 'e'd printed a name in Latin. I asked 'im what the inscription meant. Know what 'e said? It means "devil's darnin' needle". 'E told me that they sometimes called damselflies by that name. Well, I don't 'ave ter tell yer 'ow I felt. I stayed cold fer a bleedin' week. Funny fings dreams is, funny fings . . .'

Chapter Thirteen

On Saturday morning, August 7th, 1940, Maureen Flannagan put on her mother's apron and busied herself about the house. Her father was at work and her mother was shopping in the market. James the baby slept peacefully in his pram outside the front door, and beside the pram the twins Sheena and Sally played 'five-stones'. The two boys Terry and Patrick junior were constructing a deadly trap for their feline pet, who watched their endeavours from a safe distance, its green eyes unblinking.

The morning was warm, and along the Street the usual rituals were being performed. Women hearthstoned their front door steps and cleaned their windows. The menfolk stood with thumbs tucked under their braces, and with clay pipes burning orange as they conversed. They blew clouds of tobacco smoke into the air and sent the aroma of 'Nosegay' and 'Old Returns' drifting down the Street. The men wore worried frowns that morning as they spoke of the impending invasion. They tried to appear unruffled in the presence of their wives, but the women knew how they really felt, and gained no comfort from their conclusions.

Only the children remained unaffected, and they went about their usual Saturday pleasures. They got under the feet of adults, and upset the peace of Conner Street with their requests: 'No you can't 'ave me 'ammer, you'll smash yer fingers wiv it.'

'No, yer can't borrer me chopper, yer farver'll box yer ears.'

'Don't chop up that box outside me front door, I've just done that step.'

The youngsters of dockland were adept at making a few coppers from their labours, and the sale of good dry firewood provided them with the means to see the latest films on show at the local 'bug-hutch', as they named it, or the opportunity to consume a plate of pie and mash at Cuthbert's pie shop. The problem was obtaining a weapon to decimate the large orange or apple boxes, and then packing the fragments in such a way that their customer would believe he or she was getting a bargain in domestic fuel. The children of Conner Street were expert at foraging for boxes and selling the produce. They worked in small groups, and enlisted the aid of a tiny helper who would be responsible for the sale.

''Ello, son, wot yer want?'

'Wanna buy some firewood, mister?' puffing heavily.

'Wot yer puffin' for, son?'

'It's the bag, mister, ain't 'arf 'eavy,' said the tiny tot.

''Ow much?'

'Only sixpence, mister, an' yer git tons o' wood.'

The angelic features swayed the customer, and another sixpence found its way into the pocket, along with the usual assortment of string, bubblegum, and a fold-up knife with its instrument for removing stones from horses' hooves.

On Saturday August 7th, the Solomon brothers, Ron and Ernie, went into the firewood business. They obtained an egg box and an apple box and they looked around for a tool to break up the wood. They sneaked into their house and removed the chopper from its resting place under the stairs, and broke up the boxes, selling the sticks to Mrs Jenkins. They also sold the bits of wood to other people in the Street, for they made sure there was plenty of wood to go round.

'Look, don't go puttin' in that much, Ern, watch me.'

Ron Solomon placed three sticks upright in his canvas bag and then laid a sprinkling of sticks on the top. He then demonstrated how to walk along as though carrying a heavy burden.

'Yer gotta puff, Ern, an' let 'em see yer can't 'ardly carry it.'

The young one grinned and tried the technique on Mrs Jenkins. 'Cor blimey, lady, this bag ain't 'arf 'eavy.'

'I s'pose it is,' agreed the bleary-eyed lady, and rewarded the budding actor with a South African sixpence.

Maureen Flannagan enjoyed Saturdays too. She usually took the twins to Cuthbert's on most Saturdays and she tried to dodge meeting silly Bobbie there. Bobbie slurped when he ate his pie and mash, and liquid ran down his chin and onto his coat. He pulled faces too and made the twins giggle, which prompted the forthright Maureen to ask Bobbie to 'stop being so silly'.

'Gawd 'elp us, luv,' laughed the owner of the pie shop. 'You might just as well ask the Thames to stop flowin'!'

Bobbie liked Saturdays too. He got paid on Saturday morning, and he liked to wander along to the pie shop. He stood and watched the slithering eels in the galvanised tanks outside the shop. He enjoyed watching the shop-owner grab an eel and quickly cut off its head. A deft flick of the knife and the eel was gutted. A chop, chop, and the inch-long pieces were ready for the boiling pot. The man cleaned the chopping-board with his knife and then repeated the process, but the idiot had seen enough and he went inside.

Patrick Flannagan had finished his shift at the furnace and he had reached the Eagle in time to consume a few pints of ale. He now sat in the backyard with his feet up on the window-ledge. The chair in which he sat spewed out its contents of horsehair stuffing, and one leg was missing. It remained usable though with the placing of two house-bricks under the seat. The big man sat comfortably with his cap pulled down over his face. His steady breathing moved the cap up and down as he slept in the warm afternoon.

In the scullery, Patrick junior stalked a buzzing bluebottle that had got itself trapped behind the curtain. The boy carried a pint glass that he sought to drop over the 'buzzer'. He looked through the window at his father and grinned at the moving cap, then went on with his hunt. As the bluebottle flew away a roar filled the air. It came from the police station roof and screamed out its stark message of fear.

Joe Harper sat in his signal-box at Bermondsey Crossing and waited. He had received a call to hold the signal at red. He thought about this and wondered. There might be a raid on down in Kent, or maybe only a mishap down the line. He lit a cigarette and waited. The war was getting to be bad for everyone, he thought. Bad for his daughter Mary, who had seen her husband wheeled into her hospital ward exhausted and with shell fragments in his arm and leg. The war was bad for his daughter Josie, whose husband Brian had been called up, leaving her to manage the two young children. Joe ran his fingers through his hair and stared down at the floor.

The noise seemed to start from way down the track. It rushed along the rails and enveloped the signal cabin, and at the same time the phone rang.

Silly Bobbie sat in his quiet bedroom while Ada Dawkins sat downstairs listening to the wireless. Strains of *Old Monterey* drifted on the warm air and Ada's head dipped down onto her chest. It was late afternoon as Bobbie reached under his bed and took out a square wooden box. He opened it and leaned down to smell the varnish. The box was about nine inches long and wide and just a fist deep. It was well made, with strong brass hinges and a bone catch that looped over a brass stud to secure the lid. The top of the lid was inlaid with a paler wood than the mahogany from which the box was made. The whole casket was highly polished, with a shellac that lifted the grain and colour to a reddish brown. The box was made to hold something valuable, as indeed it did.

Bobbie smiled as he took out the contents of the box. There was a small bag tied up with a bootlace. The bag contained Bobbie's complete collection of marbles. In one corner of the casket there was a pile of money. The idiot took out the coins and started to count the smooth, worn pennies. He never reached more than eleven or twelve before he tired of concentrating, and today it was too warm to count all the coins. In the box there was a knife that had many gadgets. Bobbie cleaned the knife with his shirt sleeve and then inspected the blades. There was a large blade that was very sharp and a smaller one which Bobbie used to cut string with. The rest of the gadgets were a mystery to the idiot, although some of the children had told him of their uses. Bobbie opened up the long curved prong which he had been told took stones from horses' hooves. There was a corkscrew that one of the children said was used to pick up twisty worms in the garden. Bobbie shut the corkscrew quickly when he remembered what the child had told him. There were a couple of old army badges and a few broken pencils, a dice with a few counters and a folded up piece of paper. Bobbie carefully unfolded the square and looked at the coloured picture with interest. It showed an Indian elephant. The beast was adorned with the glorious silk and satin trappings of a maharajah, and its tusks were encased in silver tubes with jewels encrusted along their length. Atop the beast there was a seat made of padded velvet and covered with a sunshade. On the seat sat an evil-looking prince, who held a stick aloft. Bobbie stared at the half-naked figure of the mahout, who sat at the elephant's ears. He seemed to be beating the animal with a bamboo cane and Bobbie frowned. He hoped that one day that man who beat the elephant would fall off and be crushed beneath those massive feet.

The idiot carefully replaced all his treasures and slid the box back beneath the bed. He handled the casket very carefully. He had owned it for as long as he could remember. In fact the box had been given to the boy by the kind nuns when they left him with Ada Dawkins. The box was very old and had been made to hold a ship's sextant. For years the box had kept the instrument safe and dry beneath the tight-fitting lid. It had lain on the railed shelves in the cabins of tall-masted schooners and ships of the line. Later, when the owner of the box left service, it rested forgotten in dark cupboards. Hard times caused the box to see the light of day once again as it passed through the doors of an establishment that advertised its benevolence with three brass orbs hanging from chains above the portals.

The box with its sextant was never reclaimed, for the owner now travelled in fluffy cloud schooners across the heavens in the company of his nautical ancestors and had no need for such a piffling instrument of mortals. So the box remained on the dusty shelf. The romance and mystery were lost on the scrawny pawnbroker; he made his living on a thousand such treasures left and sometimes never claimed back. He looked at the sextant and decided it would sell if properly exhibited, and on the glass shelf it went, in pride of place in his large window. The box remained, as the buyer of the instrument did not need the case. It stayed until the unromantic pawnbroker was touched by the pleas of the visiting salvationists who asked for gifts for their charitable ventures. The box passed through the hands of godly people and into the grimy hands of an idiot, who lavished as much love on that box as it had ever known in its long existence. It was now placed back in its cache, and as the idiot slid out from beneath the springs he heard the roar start up. It filled the room and Bobbie quaked.

The wail of the siren sounded unreal on the soft warm afternoon. It seemed so improbable and impossible on that lovely day with the few wisps of cloud hanging high in the azure sky. It grated on the relaxed folk of Conner Street and they rushed out into the sun to stare skywards with disbelief. The wail diminished into a dying moan, but before it stilled the sound of a heavy drone reached their ears. Machines flying high and following the ribbon of twisting water approached in tight formation. Among them tiny pieces of cotton opened and expanded as shells burst but the aircraft still flew on.

'Gawd Almighty, there's fousands of the bastards, they're everywhere,' screamed Emmie Jones.

'Get yerselves in the shelter quick,' shouted Bob Bowman the warden, his face red from running.

'The bleeders are after the docks, they're after the Surrey,' Skipper said as he hurried across the street on the arm of Rosie Harper.

The sky became streaked with vapour trails and the black smoke of exhausts as the aircraft went into their bombing run. The streaks widened and drifted over the virgin blue canvas as the picture dissolved in nightmarish apparitions.

'Look, they've got one, 'e's goin' down!' screamed Wheezy Morris.

A bomber left the formation and turned. It dipped earthwards and dived down towards the Kent hills, one of its engines billowing smoke.

Most of the inhabitants of Conner Street did not enter the

shelter but stood instead on the pavement totally transfixed. They saw the formation turn and make their return run. Flashes could be seen over the chimneypots and explosions rocked the homes. Here and there a window shattered from the blast, and a couple of slates rattled off the roofs. Pigeons flew round the houses and settled for an instant, before flying off again in stark terror.

'Gawd 'elp them poor bleeders downtown, they won't 'ave a chance,' moaned Lizzie Brown, her hands tucked in her apron and carpet slippers on the wrong feet.

As the flying armada bore down on its target once more, the bombers could see that down below the whole of dockland was burning. Their excitement showed in their voices as they spat out instructions to their pilots. They pressed the buttons with their gloved thumbs and sent more bombs screaming down into the inferno. From high above, the docks were like a grate that was ready laid and waiting for the spark from the devil's tinderbox.

On that first run the spark was dropped among the docked piles of Russian fir and Finnish pine. The blazing mass spread to Norwegian spruce and Canadian cedar. The whole of the timber burned, and sap and resin flowed in sticky, red-hot streams. It dipped into the water and set the Thames alight. The timber sheds crumbled. The galvanised panels blew outwards and the girder skeleton melted and took on frightening shapes. Sparks crackled and leapt skywards, and water turned to steam as white-hot iron sank down into the mud. All of the docks were ablaze; a mammoth smoke cloud rose up in the sky and was visible for miles, the indiscreet pall of a funeral pyre.

The engines of destruction had flown away and now the all-clear sounded. Fire engines roared to the Surrey Docks from all over London. There were whole streets by the Surrey that were burning. Hoses melted but the exhausted firemen battled on, their faces grey with shock and emotion. The wall of the dock threatened to collapse on the fire tenders but the firemen would not move. Oxygen-starved, they had to be pulled away bodily as they fell over the hoses and were too tired to pick themselves up again. Their desperate battle against the roaring flames was witnessed by the families who were trapped in the streets adjoining the docks. They waited quietly, the women sometimes crying silently until a path out of the inferno was made safe. The red-eyed inhabitants marched away carrying pitiful bundles containing few of the smaller, and most treasured possessions.

A fire tender rushed along the traffic emptied road and turned into a side street. Chief Fire Officer Smart sat beside the driver, a lad of twenty, who drove like a demon. He shouted encouragement as the driver steered the tender over fallen debris. The heat was intense as they skidded to a halt and started to set up their hoses. The flames had spread into the houses in the street, and a fire engine that had arrived earlier had its paint scorched black.

'Are they all out?' shouted Officer Smart above the din.

'They're all clear,' answered a blackened fireman.

'Let it burn, that wall's goin' any minute,' the fire chief shouted. 'We'll get into the next turnin' see if we can contain it.'

There was a roar as the dock wall collapsed, sending a sheet of flame outwards and completely enveloping the tender. Officer Smart saw his driver sitting upright in the cab, his hands gripping the steering wheel, his body taking up a posture of death on his funeral pyre. There was nothing that could be done for the man and Officer Smart turned back round to the fireman he had just shouted to, shaking. The man lay prone across the fire hose, with his uniform smouldering. There was no time to lose, the whole street was about to be swallowed up in the engulfing flames. The fire officer grabbed the man and struggled painfully to get him up onto his shoulder. A burning pain ran down the length of his back as he staggered along to the end of the street. His breath came in gasps and his legs started to give out. Gawd don't let me drop him, he prayed to himself.

'C'mon, mate, let's 'ave 'im,' a voice said, and Officer Smart fainted.

Earlier that fateful Saturday, a scruffy individual was strolling along by the dock wall holding a paper bag. He looked through the locked gates and saw the duty dock policeman leaning against his office door and talking to a colleague. The man's befuddled brain managed to deduce that it must be afternoon if the gate was locked. He knew the dockers all rushed out at twelve noon on Saturdays and then the gates were locked. Then a thought struck him. It might be Sunday, in which case it could still be morning. The man's brain reacted against the pressure put on to it and it refused to respond. It decided it must be Saturday because there were too many people about in working clothes for it to be Sunday and, after that great piece of detective work, it went back to working at its usual pace.

The man was used to sleeping rough, and recently he had found a very nice place way inside the Surrey Docks. It was easy to get in, all that was needed was the knowledge of the exact spot. The tramp found the place by watching a young boy squeeze through some loose planking near the jetty and retrieve his ball. Later the tramp gave the spot a hefty kick and sure enough the bottom of the board gave way from its nailed joint. Carefully replacing the board, the tramp waited until it was dark, then made his way into the docks to find a safe, warm place to lay his head. The only danger was the dock police. As long as he was quiet and kept out of sight he was sure he'd be all right. That night the tramp found the perfect bed on a stack of veneer. The wood smelt pleasant, and it held his warmth. The tramp had found some sacks which enhanced his comfort and there he stayed. The place was tucked away down by the most quiet part of the docks where even the dock police hardly deemed it necessary to venture.

The tramp walked past the gate and down towards his secret spot. He stopped and taking out a quart bottle of ale from the paper bag took a large swig. He had scrounged the price of the beer by helping to push the laden fruit barrows from market, and having drunk most of his wages the tramp felt unusually tired. The day was very warm, and the sun beat down relentlessly on his tattered old overcoat making him long for his veneered bed in the shade. He staggered in the right direction and upon finding his private place he lay down at full stretch, his heavy eyelids dropping down to shut out the light. It was peaceful, he thought listening to the gurgling water and the far away sound of a steam engine as it pulled out of the station. He heard the chatter of the starlings that rested high up in the shed girders and the creaking sound as the barges strained against the mooring ropes. This was perfect, thought the tramp as he took another swig from his quart bottle.

'How do you plead?' asked the magistrate.

'Not guilty, your worshipful.'

'But you took the shoes from the shop without paying for them,' said the tired-looking beak.

'Well, your 'ighness . . .'

'Sir will do,' said the stern man in the lofty chair.

'Well, your 'ighness, I mean sir, I meant to pay, but I was tired an' I just forgot.'

'Is the man ill, or without all his faculties?' asked the beak of the solicitor.

'Arnold Thomas has been a model of good behaviour recently, sir, and I think it was just an oversight on this occasion.'

'An oversight, an oversight,' repeated the magistrate.

'Yes, sir,' said the tall skinny-looking solicitor. 'You see, the defendant was trying the shoes out by walking around the shop when someone called him from outside. My client states that as the shoes were so comfortable, he didn't realise he was wearing new ones and he just kept walking.'

'What about his old shoes?' asked the beak.

'He left them in the shoe box,' said the solicitor meekly.

The magistrate sat bowed in his high-backed chair, his head resting upon his two closed fists. It was time to speak his words of wisdom to the unfortunate soul before him, and he took a deep breath. 'It appears to me that you, Mr Arnold Thomas, sought to deprive the owners of the shoes, the company of Messrs Comfywear, of those said shoes, without due and proper payment. I am loath to consider what may have happened should you have succeeded in your evil scheme, when at a later date some person asked for a pair of shoes and was shown a pair of singularly shabby boots, minus the soles and parts of the uppers, minus the laces, and smelling of Billingsgate fish market, the place where I understand you earn money by pulling laden fish barrows. No, Mr Thomas, I cannot permit this situation to arise in the future by allowing you to walk out of this court unpunished. You will go to prison for fourteen centuries . . .'

The tramp woke with a start. He had dreamed he was back in Wandsworth and he felt his heart pounding. He sat up and observed his tattered footwear. He knew that he would have to think of another, less dangerous way of replacing them. The thought of exchanging his newfound bed for the hard prison cot was abhorrent to him and he shook his head. It was peaceful here, and the distant drone made him feel sleepy again. He closed his eyes but the drone became louder. It now sounded directly overhead and the tramp opened his eyes.

The first explosion knocked him off his resting place. The pile of timber some distance away had turned into a burning mass. He saw the timber shed opposite his position billowing smoke and flame. The tramp started to run, wishing he was back in Wandsworth right that minute. He heard the clatter as more bombs landed, his eardrums perforated by the first explosion. He had to get out of here fast, he thought as he made for his secret entry spot. The way was barred by a sea of flame that made him gasp for breath.

He retraced his steps to his hideout and took another path. In front of him he saw the dock gate that he had passed earlier that day. It was burning. He heard a shuddering noise that hurt his ears, then a flash that swept away the gates. He ran for the opening and saw a policeman fighting to free himself from a pile of logs that had been blown down from their stack. The policeman saw the tramp and screamed at him to help.

Arnold Thomas ran past. He knew he was trespassing and he wanted to put distance between him and the law. He reached the opening by the street and stopped for breath. The policeman's cries rang in his ears and he hopped about in agitation. I can't leave him to roast, he thought, and he went back. The pile of logs was burning and the flames would soon envelope the trapped man. The tramp grabbed a short log and used it as a lever, prising at the rest, straining until he trembled with the exertion. The pile moved and the policeman dragged himself from underneath. He moaned and then fainted, and the tramp saw that his leg was crushed. He would have to carry him out, but he knew he would never make it. Already the fire was filling the dock and sweeping towards him. He left the policeman and ran for the opening once more. Halfway there he stopped and looked back. The policeman lay perfectly still. It was no use, the tramp knew he couldn't leave him there. He hopped around again in panic as he tried to think. His gaze caught sight of a wheelbarrow propped against the burning logs nearby. The tramp grabbed hold of it and hurried to the fallen man. He managed to roll the policeman onto the barrow and lashed him tight with his belt. The flames were licking at his heels as the tramp trotted out of the dock, the moaning policeman gritting his teeth from the pain of his shattered leg.

Late in the evening, the sky was coloured red from the still burning docks. Two exhausted firemen stood by a canteen van and sipped tea from large enamel mugs.

'I've never seen anyfing like it,' said one. 'I turns round an' there 'e is, pushin' this wheelbarrer out wiv a copper tied on it.'

'Go on,' said his mate.

'Yeah, I tell yer, I couldn't believe me eyes. This feller looks like a tramp, proper scruffy 'e is. 'E wheels the barrer up ter me an' says, "Don't say anyfing about me, I've already bin in trouble over me shoes." I ask yer, fancy worryin' over 'is bleedin' shoes. 'E 'ad the clothes scorched orf 'is back an' the flames lickin' round 'is arse an' 'e's worried over a fing like that.'

The fireman set down his mug and put his arm around the shoulder of his friend. 'I reckon the 'ole world's gorn bleedin' crazy, Bert.'

Chapter Fourteen

As the blood-red sun dipped down behind the chimneys of dockland, the sky took on a dark, smoky tinge. In the east, flames still spurted up from the savaged Surrey Docks. A smoke cloud rose high into the heavens. It seemed unreal to the Conner Street folk as they watched the spectacle. Fire bells rang out almost continuously as reinforcements hurried to the blazing inferno. People stood in their doorways staring up at the flashing, reflecting sky. They looked on in disbelief and in horror. It was as though the war had only just started. And for most of them it had.

Fire tenders were arriving from many areas around London. They came to relieve exhausted, grey-faced men who were dropping with fatigue and the lack of breathable air, their lungs almost bursting with the pressure created in the cauldron that had once been the peaceful last resting place for the produce of the vast North European forests. Fir and spruce, pine and cedar had lain in huge piles about the docks, seasoning and drying to become tinder for the bombers.

Inside the Surrey Docks the floor space had become a molten lake of treacle as sap boiled and ran from the logs. It was like volcanic lava, and certain death to any living thing in its path. It ran down into the river, turning the water into liquid fire. It ran up against sheds, setting them alight. The whole scene was one of weird, twisted shapes that shifted and changed as the girders buckled in the heat. The planks of wood piled up inside the sheds generated terrific heat and blew out the corrugated walls with tremendous force. Firemen were pulled back, for it was impossible to combat the blaze at its source. It was becoming hard to save the surrounding streets from destruction.

The loop of land that pushed out into the Thames contained not only the docks, but many wharves and small factories. It also housed the local workforce, in tenements and small terraced houses. That Saturday night saw the end of many of these homes, and the exodus of refugees continued all evening. Pitiful groups of tired, sad-faced folk trudged from their destroyed homes downtown to rest centres and church halls which had been hurriedly made ready for them. They used horse-drawn carts, barrows and manpower to transport the salvaged pieces of their possessions, their prized flotsam that no amount of money would induce them to part with. There was Granny's photo, and the old jug, now chipped, which had once stood on a wash-stand, the wedding present from a departed. Bales of soaked bedding balanced on a kitchen table, alongside a chiming clock that only 'donged' the half-hour. Tired children sat on carts and barrows, a girl cuddling her doll, and a boy stroking a terrified pet tom-cat. They came away from the hell to kindly solace from helpers and allowed themselves to be herded into rest centres. They muttered their thanks as hot soup and mugs of tea were handed out. As they trudged along to safety they passed fire tenders on their way to the scenes of destruction. They sometimes waved, and the firemen waved back shocked at what they saw. The firemen shouted encouragement to the homeless stream of folk, then held on tightly as they were rushed to the mouth of the inferno.

That night, as darkness drifted in slowly, the fires were still out of control, lighting up the sky. Sparks shot up from the crumbling sheds and wood-piles, night being turned into day by the magnitude of the blaze. It caused the pigeons to fly at midnight, and the children to believe it was still too early to go to sleep. The size of the inferno increased until the whole of the docklands were burning.

In Conner Street the folk were out on their doorsteps. They looked up at the sky, some in silence, some in earnest conversation.

Lizzie Brown stood with hands tucked under her apron. 'The bastards 'ave done the Surrey in,' she said bitterly.

'Gawd a'mighty, Gawd,' Emmie cried out. 'Whatever's ter become of us?'

'We'll be all right, yer silly mare,' Lizzie said reassuringly.

'My Arfur's gone ter see if 'is mates are okay. Some of 'em live downtown.'

'It's no good us 'avin' blackout up, no bleedin' good whatsoever,' remarked Mrs Jenkins, a glass of ale held in her shaking hand.

'All I 'ope is the bastards don't come back ternight,' said Lizzie. 'All London must be lit up.'

'Gawd 'elp us if they do,' Emmie Jones said, shaking her head.

The initial shock had passed, but now the dread of what might come filled the Conner Street folk as they sought the company of their neighbours. Each individual handled the fear in a certain way.

Ada Dawkins found that it helped to talk to her dead husband Charlie. She told him of the day's events and the eyes that stared down at her seemed to fill her soul with calm.

Bobbie sat up in his room. He could not understand the reason for the sky to be so red, light enough for him to read his comics without the gaslight being turned on. He did not want to see the pictures of war. Instead he looked at the animal pictures. He grinned at the matchstick men and the talking duck. He liked the pictures of the farmyard, where a huge sun smiled down on cows, and sunflowers with shy, drooping faces that looked down on frolicking lambs. He wished he and Ada could be there, where Ada would not cry any more and he would sit in the sun, watching the animals.

Patrick Flannagan had his own way of coping with his fears; he got drunk. Bridie cuddled her baby close to her and kept her brood near by. Joe Harper and Rosie sat with Skipper in their parlour. The wireless set emitted soft music, and the old seaman puffed away at his brown stained clay pipe. He was lost in his thoughts of a better time, long gone, where men battled the storms at sea and not each other. He thought of his days before the mast, listening to the rising wind in the rigging. He reminisced of the days in far off ports and in rusty old tramp steamers, and occasionally he sighed deeply.

Lizzie Brown had her two friends in for a chat. She shared a few bottles of stout with them as they sat in her parlour, among the glass ornaments and ebony-framed pictures hanging on the walls. Lizzie talked of her departed husband, who had one day walked out and never came back.

'Real right bastard 'e was,' she said. 'Never any good from the day I married the tyke.'

''Ow long's 'e bin gone, Liz?' asked Emmie.

'Winter it was, Guy Fawkes night, 1936,' answered Lizzie Brown.

'Still, yer better orf wivout 'im, gal,' said Betty Smith.

'I should say so,' Lizzie laughed. 'I reckoned someone claimed 'im fer a guy.'

The two women laughed, and Lizzie filled their empty glasses. 'You know, I never could remember 'im doin' a full week's work all the time I was married ter the bleeder. Wasn't as if 'e didn't 'ave a trade. Tanner 'e was, worked in the leavver market, when 'e was sober. I've seen 'im lose many a good job over the booze, an' uvver poor sods scratchin' aroun' fer work.'

'Bleedin' shame,' said Betty Smith.

'Well at least my ole man don't piss all 'is wages up the wall,' said Emmie. 'Good ter me is my Arfur, never sees me short 'e don't.'

Betty Smith glanced at Lizzie, a trace of a smile showing on her face. 'Well it's all right if yer got an ole man in steady work,' she said with envy.

'My Arfur's 'ad it bad in the docks,' Emmie answered quickly. ''E 'ad ter fight fer a decent day's pay. Bin frew a lot o' trouble 'as my ole man, wot wiv the strikes, an' the 'black-leggin'. Many a time I 'ad ter take 'is suit over uncle's ter get the price of a loaf o' bread.'

Betty Smith snorted. 'You was lucky, Emm. My ole man didn't 'ave a best suit till lately. Tell a lie. 'E did 'ave one, till 'e 'ad ter take it ter work when the arse fell out of 'is working trousers.'

Lizzie Brown took a draught from her glass. 'I fink we've all 'ad our share of the pawnbroker. Trouble wiv my ole man, 'e used ter sleep in 'is Sunday best when 'e came 'ome pissed. I 'ad ter press the bleedin' fing afore I could take it over uncle's.'

'I tell yer one fing,' said Emmie Jones, looking at Betty Smith. 'I bet your ole man wuz the smartest coalman round these parts. Fancy deliverin' an 'undred-weight 'o nutty slack in yer Sunday best.'

*

At the Eagle conversation was flowing. Everyone discussed the bombing. Wheezy Morris and one of his darts partners leaned on the bar counter talking to John Braden the landlord. Big Albert Conlin sat on a bar stool smoking a cigarette and staring woodenly at the empty bottles lined up on the bar. Florrie Braden had been too busy to remove them; she was fussing between customers, giving her husband wicked glances. Occasionally, she looked over in Albert's direction. Florrie still had a warm feeling for the man and often thought about renewing the liaison. John would never be any the wiser, she thought. Most nights he went to bed in an intoxicated condition and it would be so easy. She sighed as she cleared the glasses and the line of bottles in front of Albert. Recently Florrie had dropped the odd hint or two, but it seemed to be in vain. Her words were falling upon deaf ears. Albert was determined to stay clear of any emotional entanglements with the hot-blooded Florrie. There was an element of pity in her attraction towards Albert. Florrie knew that he lived alone and that he was a lonely man. He had told her that, when he was not sitting in the Eagle, he spent his time reading. She felt that warm glow deep down inside as she looked at him on that Saturday night, and she sighed again.

At the warden's post a few streets away, Bob Bowman sat with two other wardens. The men wore armbands and carried tin helmets that were strapped to canvas gas-mask cases. They spoke of the bombing of the docks and the destruction that was surely to continue.

'They've bin puttin' anti-aircraft guns in Southwark Park all week,' said one.

'And on the factory roofs,' said another.

'Well I tell yer wot,' informed Bob Bowman, 'they better not try an' put anyfink on the factories in our Street. The bleedin' lot'll cave in.'

The conversation was interrupted by the entry of a messenger, bearing a sealed envelope.

'Wot yer got there, son?' asked one of the men.

'It's from headquarters,' announced the pink-faced youth.

'Give it 'ere then,' beckoned the man.

The youth stepped forward and handed the message over, then stood back.

The warden read the sheet of paper and signed the receipt.

'Okay, son, on yer way,' he said.

'Anyfing wrong?' asked Bob Bowman.

'It's a "red alert" warnin',' replied the controller. 'The bastards are due back.'

Conner Street's warden ran his hand over the back of his head. He stood up and stretched, his long angular frame arching as he did so. Bob was tired. The river traffic had been very heavy recently, with the cargoes being unloaded late into the evening. He had also noticed that the strain showed on the ships' crews who moored their vessels and went about their business in the Pool. The oceans of the world were getting progressively more hazardous for shipping, and more and more seamen's lives were lost to the lurking U-Boats.

Bob Bowman looked around the warden's post as he slipped his arm through the strap of his service pack. He felt he was at last going to be able to do something useful. He had not had much to do so far, apart from keeping an eye on the shelter and checking that the Street was fully blacked out during the hours of darkness. He was beginning to wonder if he had been right in volunteering for the job of warden. His wife Grace had shed a few tears when he first walked into his home and put the steel helmet on the table. Funny thing about that, he thought. It was the first time he had seen her cry. She hadn't cried when the doctor told her she could not have any more children after young Brenda was born over five years ago. She hadn't cried that time they sent for her when he fell down the ship's hold and they thought he'd broken his back. Grace wasn't one to create a fuss.

A telephone bell startled Bob and jarred his thought back to the business in hand. 'I'd better get back, they've bin pumpin' water out o' the shelter. It's seepin' in from somewhere.'

The controller was speaking into the phone. As Bob was leaving the man put his hand over the mouthpiece and shouted, 'I nearly forgot. There's a bike there. Take it, it might come in 'andy.'

Bob looked at the rusted frame and worn saddle. 'You sure you can spare it? It looks like it came out of a Salvation Army sale.'

The controller ignored Bob's comments. 'There's some bicycle clips on the 'andlebars.'

Bob Bowman put on the clips and pedalled back to Conner Street.

Fred Harris walked down Conner Street and knocked on Joe Harper's door. 'Can't stop, Joe, just ter tell yer, ole Jerry the rag-an'-bone man copped it. 'E lived by the docks apparently. Dragged 'im out awhile ago, so one of the lads told me. Burnt to a cinder 'e was, poor bleeder.'

'Gawd a'mighty,' gasped Joe. 'We're gonna miss 'im comin' round on Sundays. I loved to 'ear 'im call out.'

'Take my tip, Joe,' warned Fred Harris. 'Keep yerself 'andy ter get in that shelter. It's odds on the bastards'll be back ternight. The bloody 'ole o' London's lit up fer 'em.'

Further along the Street, Mary Carter sat in her parlour looking at her husband Tom as he read the evening paper. 'Tom, do you think there'll be another raid ternight?' she asked.

Tom Carter didn't answer right away. 'If yer like,' he said.

Mary puffed and spoke sharply, 'Tom Carter, did you 'ear what I said?'

Tom put the paper down and smiled at her. 'Sorry, luv. I was readin' a funny bit in the paper. What did yer ask me?'

Mary ignored the question and looked down at her knitting. 'I can't seem ter get started on that pullover of Reggie's. Fair put the fear inter me, that bombin'.'

'Now it's not worth upsettin' yerself, Mary. Yer don't want the kids ter see yer upset, now do yer?'

Mary picked up her knitting. 'I was talkin' ter Lizzie Brown a little while ago an' your mate Bob came past. Went ter look at the shelter. Ridin' a bike 'e was.'

'Ridin' a bike? Bob Bowman ridin' a bike?' Tom laughed.

'Rusty ole thing it was. Wobblin' all over the place 'e was.'

Tom laughed even louder. 'If ole Bob was on a bike it 'ad ter be rusty, 'cos 'e'd never buy one. Someone must 'ave give it to 'im.'

Mary was infected by her husband's laughter. Her face relaxed as she remembered something. 'Bike clips. 'E 'ad bike clips on.'

'Well that's not unusual. People usually wear bike clips when they ride a bike,' Tom remarked, looking at Mary as she burst into loud laughter.

Mary took some time before she could answer him. She dabbed at her eyes and swallowed hard. 'It made me notice 'is socks. They were odd ones.'

Tom Carter shook his head. 'It's that warden's job. Drivin' 'im round the twist it is.'

Mary regained her composure and started on her knitting. Tom picked up his paper as the children came into the room. 'Now don't get all them games out, you've got ter get washed soon.'

'Just five minutes, Mum.'

'All right. Just five minutes.'

For a while Mary knitted. Then she stopped and looked at the back of Tom's newspaper. Her face had taken on a stern look again, her eyes reflecting her worry, and her young son, who was playing snakes and ladders with his sister, clearly noticed. The boy's eyes kept glancing in his mother's direction and his sister became impatient.

'For goodness' sake, will you frow them dice,' she pleaded, her hands propping up her tiny pink face.

'Okay, fusspot,' laughed her brother, and he threw two sixes.

'I'm not playin' wiv you, you're cheatin',' she complained.

'Now come on, kids, put that game away, it's time you got washed for bed,' Mary ordered.

Marjorie yawned and left the table, while young Reg gathered up the counters. 'Will there be any more bombin', Mum?' he asked quietly.

'We don't know, son,' answered his mother. 'If the siren goes in the night, I want you ter get yer sister up, but don't frighten 'er. We'll 'ave ter go over the shelter, okay?'

'Wot, over that stinkin' place?'

'Yes, over that stinkin' place, Reg,' Reg's father butted in. 'It may not smell very nice, but at least we'll be safe there.'

'Okay, Dad,' said little Reg, and he walked out of the room.

Presently the children came in to say goodnight, and when they were at last alone Mary confided to her husband. 'I'm scared for their safety, Tom. I wonder if we did right in bringin' 'em back inter this.'

Her husband put down the paper and stretched his legs out. 'Now look, luv, it's no good you gettin' yerself all worked up about it. We couldn't leave 'em wiv that pair o' carrot crunchers, now could we? Besides, if we'd 'ave found 'em new people, 'ow could we be sure they were bein' looked after properly?'

Mary nodded agreement. 'I only 'ope it don't get too bad,' she sobbed.

Tom reached out and took her in his arms, cuddling her head to his chest. He could feel the softness of her body and her sweet response as she nestled in to him. The trace of cologne from her hair was pleasant in his nostrils, and his hands gently stroked her back.

'Wait, Tom,' she whispered, as she pulled the curtains tighter.

'Close the door, case the kids come in.'

The evening wore on, and in that little parlour in Conner Street two bodies joined together to forget the carnage and destruction for a few precious moments.

The news of the bombing reached the Davis brothers as they sat in their billet in an army camp in Cambridge. They cursed the Germans and feared for their old father who was now living alone. The ginger-haired Davis boy put down his army boot and cleaning brush, and spoke to his younger brother, 'I'm worried over the ole man, Fred. They didn't say 'ow bad the damage was, only mentioned the bleedin' docks.'

''E'll be okay,' his brother said reassuringly. 'Our street's a couple 'o miles from the Surrey.'

'S'pose you're right,' Ginger said. 'Trouble is, yer feel so 'elpless stuck in this bleedin' God-forsaken 'ole.'

'D'yer fink ole four-eyes'll give us a pass ter get 'ome?' Freddie said.

'No chance,' replied his brother. 'Mister Second-left-bleedin'-tenant wot's 'is name ain't got no 'eart. We've got about as much chance of gettin' a leave pass orf of 'im as gettin' a pork chop out of a synagogue.'

'Well I'm goin' over the canteen, want any fags?' asked Freddie.

'Yeah, can yer get me five Woodbine?' Ginger replied.

Ginger lay full stretch on his camp bed and stared up at the ceiling. Above, on the dusty beams, a small spider hung from a delicate strand of web. The sound of snoring came from the corner of the hut, farthest away from the door. The only other occupant of the room was in the land of dreams and, from the happy expression on his face, Ginger guessed rightly that the soldier was back home doing something much more suitable for a Saturday night. Ginger cursed and aimed his boot brush at the spider, who ran up the strand and disappeared into the dust on the beam. The brush travelled in an arc and landed on the sleeping soldier. He turned over, grunted and started to snore once more, his face now wearing a miserable expression. By an unhappy coincidence, the brush hit his back at the exact moment that the girl in his slumbers rejected him.

The billet was quiet except for the snoring. Most of the men were either in the canteen or in town. Ginger was due for guard duty the next morning, and there were brasses to polish and boots to shine. He felt depressed without any knowledge of his father's welfare, and helpless at being so far from Conner Street. Ginger paced the room; if he could slip out of camp without being challenged, he could maybe hitch a lift to London, and scrounge the fare back in time for the guard mounting at 8 am. It may work, he thought. He would have to be quick. If he couldn't make it back in time and Freddie was with him, then they would both be in trouble. It would also be easier to hitch a lift if he were alone. His mind was made up. There was no way he would be able to dissuade his younger brother from accompanying him. So he had to leave before Freddie got back from the canteen. Grabbing his small pack and gas mask, Ginger slipped out of the billet and sauntered down to the main gate. He held his breath as he reached the guard post. If he was asked for his pass he would have to make some excuse and hope for the best. As it happened there was a truck waiting to enter and the duty sergeant was deep in conversation with the driver. Ginger walked past casually and got a nod from the soldier on guard. It was easy, he reflected as he walked swiftly up to the main London road. Twenty minutes later, he was sitting in a meat lorry that rattled on towards London.

The driver was a man in his fifties, a Londoner whose firm was based at Kings Cross. He whistled tunelessly as he crashed through the gears and wrestled with the large steering wheel. Ginger sat back and stared at the ribbon of dark road. The beam from the screened headlights gave only a limited view ahead, and Ginger marvelled at the driver's ability to travel at such a speed.

'Slippin' 'ome fer a weekend then, son?' asked the man.

'Yeah, mate,' replied Ginger. 'I'm gonna see me ole man, 'e lives near the Surrey Docks.'

'Whereabouts?' asked the driver.

'Conner Street, orf the Tower Road,' answered Ginger, taking a drag on a cigarette that the man had given him.

''E should be okay,' said the man reassuringly. 'The bombin' was round the dock area, 'cording ter the news. 'Eard it when I stopped fer a cuppa. So I wouldn't reckon that Conner Street got touched.'

'Gawd I 'ope not,' said Ginger. 'Me ole man's bin on 'is own since me an' me bruvver got called up.'

'Ain't yer got no muvver then?' asked the friendly driver.

'Died when I was a kid,' replied Ginger. 'Me young bruvver don't even remember 'er.'

'Christ, that's 'ard luck,' sympathised the driver. 'Ne'mind, son, the ole man'll be all right, mark my words.'

The two men lapsed into silence, and Ginger started to doze off. He was awakened by a jolt and found that the lorry had stopped.

'Time ter get orf, son,' said the driver.

'Fanks, mate, all the best.'

'That's all right, 'ope yer find the ole man 'ale an' 'arty.'

The driver turned his lorry into the depot gates and Ginger felt in his pockets. He just about had the bus fare from Kings Cross to Bermondsey. It wouldn't be long now, he'd be home soon. Better get across the road to the bus stop. Hope I don't have to wait long, he mused.

He started to move away from his position near the railway station entrance when he spotted two military policemen walking out of the forecourt. They strolled along in his direction, their boots sounding loudly on the cobbles. Ginger held his breath and started to walk across the wide road.

'Just a minute, soldier,' one of the men called out to him.

Ginger didn't wait to find out what they wanted. He took to his heels and darted over the road and into a dim side street. The two policemen followed hard on his heels.

Ginger felt his breath coming in gasps as he tried to put space between them. It was no good, they were gaining on him. He turned into a dark alleyway and realised his mistake. It was a dead end! He turned and crashed into one of his pursuers. The military policeman hit the ground with a thud and Ginger ran off, the other man following closely behind him. Ginger gained a few yards and darted into another side street. He spotted a dark doorway and jumped into the recess. It was now or never, he thought as the policeman turned into the street. Ginger stepped out into the man's path and aimed a blow at him. His lashing arm caught the pursuer between the eyes, and the man's headlong running magnified the force of the blow. He went down hard, completely stunned.

Ginger took off along the darkened street, not daring to look back. The street led out into the Kings Cross Road, and Ginger noticed a bus some distance away, moving in his direction. He ran the few yards to the bus-stop and leaped on board before it had even stopped.

'Bit of an 'urry, son, ain't we?' the conductor asked him.

Ginger grinned sheepishly at the man and glanced out of the rear window of the bus. There was no sign of the two military policemen. Ginger ran up the stairs and sat down gratefully on the nearest seat, his heart still pumping furiously.

As the bus crossed the Blackfriars Bridge, Ginger Davis looked along the river eastwards. The night sky was red with the fires that were still raging at the Surrey Docks. The bend of the Thames made the glow seem as though it were emanating from way inland. Ginger knew the river well. The twisting, turning lifeline of the metropolis ran very near to his part of town. He loved the smell of it, the mud, the fresh fruit, as cranes hoisted the boxes on to the quayside. He loved the tang of the air and the empty coconut-carrying barges that he used to climb into so that he could gather the broken husks that lay on the deck. He remembered his boyhood; slipping past the dockers and stevedores as they toiled on the incoming cargoes. He would sit on the quayside watching the big ships spewing forth their wares, from the Orient, from Cape Town and northern ports, as slings of yellow timber emerged from the depths of the holds. Ginger gritted his teeth as he realised that much of the area he loved was now disappearing in the inferno. He looked away from the east, tears welling up, and he heard the wail. It rose above the sound of the bus engine. The scream increased until the slumbering pigeons awoke and flew away from the rooftops. It sent a shiver of fear through the young soldier.

The bastards had come back.

Chapter Fifteen

The air-raid siren had hardly stopped before a salvo of gunfire from the factory and park emplacements vibrated through the twin caverns of the Conner Street shelter. People were still spilling into its evil-smelling interior, cursing and crying out against the alien air fleet above. They glanced up fearfully as searchlights pencilled the sky in white, converging to criss-cross and hold the odd invader in the glare. Guns were trained on the mechanical moth and shells flew upwards. The local guns in the Southwark Park and on the jam factory roof opened up and the sound rattled the shelter doors and hurt the eardrums. The exploding shells puffed around the aircraft, like little balls of cotton wool. Jagged shrapnel fell to earth, still glowing red as it fell in pieces to lie on the pavements.

As the air armada reached their overhead position above dockland, they unleashed their deadly cargoes. Bombs fell to earth, whistling down as the air rushed the tailfins. Heavier high-explosive bombs fell with a juddering sound, like the ire of some unimaginable fiend who shuffled sheets of corrugated iron. The bombs fell downriver at first, then more locally. Explosions rocked the shelter and seemed to lift it off its foundations. Bombs fell through roofs and tore buildings apart in one almighty flash; the blasts lifted chimneypots and threw them streets away; explosions tore up huge chunks of roadway, then spat out mangled metal into the craters. One bomb blew up a small home and snatched up a policeman sheltering in a doorway, dropping him on a rooftop many yards away. The man was dead, and still completely unmarked.

In the shelter, the terrified Conner Street folk prayed to their particular gods with some token sign; the clasping of hands, the twiddling of rosary beads, shaking gestures resembling the sign of the cross. The people sat huddled together for comfort, and one old woman dozed off to sleep.

'Gawd a'mighty! 'Ow the bleedin' 'ell can she sleep?' someone cried out.

'She's stone bleedin' deaf, that's why,' cried another.

'Gawd in 'eaven, I wish I was deaf right now,' cried Lizzie Brown.

The raiders flew on, choosing new targets. They aimed for the railways, the wharves upriver, and large buildings, all choicely illuminated by the still burning Surrey Docks. Guns fired at the aircraft, and bombs continued to fall. Stockpiles of shells became low at the gunsites as the gun barrels got white hot. Crews swivelled their weapons round in an arc to face a new flight of bombers that appeared downriver. In the park a bomb fell through the bandstand roof, hit the floor and rolled down the few steps on to the dry, yellow grass. It lay there grey and daunting, and was seen by the gunnery sergeant some distance away. He calmly walked towards it and then dragged it by the tailfin away from his men. As he started back, a bomb landed on his gun emplacement, enveloping the site in flame. When the sergeant picked himself up he was aware of hot blood trickling on to his chin. Of his crew, there was no sign.

The gunfire flashes lit up the deserted Conner Street and illuminated the way for a crouching figure who ran, head held down in a futile gesture of self-preservation. He stopped at number 14 and banged on the door. There was no answer. The figure cursed, then saw that the door-string had been left out. He pulled on it and entered.

'Well I'll be striped!' gasped the old man inside. 'It's me boy, Ginger, ain't it?'

'Well it ain't the bloody tallyman, Dad,' the soldier laughed.

'Wot yer doin' 'ome?' Jack Davis asked.

Ignoring the question, Ginger looked closely at the hunched figure of his father who sat in a chair by the empty grate. 'Why ain't yer in the shelter?' he asked.

'If yer fink I'm gonna sit down that bleedin' deaf trap wiv all them women, listenin' ter Lizzie Brown an' 'er cronies, well yer got anuvver fink comin'.'

'But, Dad, the bleedin' bombs a' fallin' like rain. Yer can't sit 'ere.'

'Oh can't I? You jus' watch me. Listen, son. Yer muvver died in that room upstairs, an' if I'm ter go 'ere, wot's okay fer yer muvver is okay by me.'

'But, Dad,' implored Ginger.

'There's no buts, so don't stan' there lookin' all mean an' 'orrible, go 'n put the kettle on.'

Ginger did as his father bid and noticed that the gas jet was very low. 'Kettle'll take a while, Dad, the bastards must 'ave caught a main,' he shouted.

'Can't 'ear a word yer sayin', wot wiv the noise. 'Ow long's the kettle gonna take?' asked the old man.

Suddenly there was a rumbling explosion and the house shook.

'Gawd above they must 'ave 'it the gas works,' the old man croaked.

Ginger came running into the parlour, and stood by his father.

'T'ain't the gas works, the gas jet's still alight,' Ginger said.

'I 'eard a sound o' glass, I bet the upstairs winders 'ave all broke. There'll be glass all over me bleedin' bed now,' his father moaned. 'I told you an' that bruvver of yours ter tape 'em up.'

Ginger ran upstairs to the tiny front bedroom. The whole of the window frame lay across the old man's bed. There was glass everywhere.

Ginger ran down to his father, who was pouring the boiling water into a teapot. 'It's a right old mess up there, but don't worry, I'll clear it all up in a minute,' he said reassuringly.

'It's a good job we've got those shutters on the downstairs winders,' Jack said. 'I'd 'ave 'ad the 'ole bleedin' Street lookin' in.'

Father and son sat sipping the steaming tea. The sounds of the bombing now seemed farther away. The local guns still kept up the bombardment, and every now and then the house rattled.

''Ere, I never asked yer, wot yer doin' 'ome, anyway?'

'Got a weekend pass, Dad,' lied the soldier.

'I 'ope yer ain't deserted. They shot deserters in my time,' croaked the old man.

'Course I ain't deserted. I told yer, I got leave.'

'By the way, 'ow's young Freddie doin'? 'Ope yer takin' care of 'im? Always a little mite wild was our Freddie.'

'Fred's okay, Dad,' replied Ginger.

'Why couldn't 'e get a weekend pass?' asked Jack suspiciously.

'Cos 'e's on guard,' said Ginger, looking away.

'I remember when I was courtin' yer muvver. Went over the wall ter see 'er. There was this colour-sergeant. Tricky bit o' goods 'e was. Anyway, I ups an' belts 'im, I did. Put one on 'is chin. I see yer mum fer a few 'ours, but they got me. Twenty-eight days in the glasshouse I got. If it 'ad bin wartime, I'd a bin shot.'

The guns kept up their pounding as the raiders tired of their game and turned for home. Behind them they left a wake of destruction. Homes were destroyed. Wharves and factories were burning. The Thames was alight from the spilling oil. Firemen battled desperately as water mains burst, and their hoses ran dry. The carnage was widespread throughout London. Fire tenders rushed along debris-strewn streets and quickly turned away as their path was blocked. Gas mains flared, and water shot upwards in fierce jets from fractured pipes. Buildings burned and homes lay in ruins, with rescuers delving into the piles of rubble. They often stopped their digging and were silent, listening for the sound of a voice that would tell them there was someone alive beneath the ruins.

A merciful dawn broke, and light lifted over the chimneys. With the dawn came the even wail of the all-clear, and the folk of Conner Street emerged from their place of refuge. Ada Dawkins wore the beginnings of a black eye. It had happened some time during the height of the bombing, and as the idiot's landlady and protector walked up the slope of the shelter to the street she felt stiff. Her hair was hanging down, and there were scratches on one side of her face. Beside her, the shuffling figure of Bobbie looked diminutive as they made their way to number 4. It was not all due to the cramped night inside the shelter. Ada had become involved in a fracas.

Earlier that night Bobbie had been sitting beside Ada, and facing them were the Flannagans. Bridie held the baby tightly and little Terry slept, his head resting on her lap. Maureen had her arms around the twins and Patrick junior sat beside them. Bobbie was getting fidgety. He wanted to be back in his cosy room away from the noise that frightened him. When the guns sounded and the bombs exploded, the idiot felt sick. His ears were paining him and his back was aching from sitting so long in one position. He wanted the noise to end. When the bombs stopped he would be able to get his box out and look at his treasures. He shifted his position and felt the one treasure he had carried with him to the shelter. It was a marble, green in colour, with a milky streak running through the centre. Bobbie took the marble from his pocket and held it in the palm of his hand. Across the space between the benches, Patrick junior watched the idiot's actions. When Bobbie looked up, Patrick poked his tongue out and Bobbie replied, his own tongue rolling round his chin. A stream of saliva ran down onto the idiot's coat-front and Patrick abruptly burst out laughing.

Ada looked round and nudged the idiot. 'Keep still, Bobbie,' she said irritably, kocking the marble from the idiot's palm as she prodded him.

Bobbie watched horrified as the glass marble rolled down the aisle and disappeared under the bench where Granny Flint slept. Bobbie gasped. He couldn't bear to lose his best marble, and he decided to fetch it before forgetting where it had gone to. He shuffled down the aisle, ignoring Ada's plea for him to come back. Bobbie went down on all fours and felt under the bench. His fingers touched the marble, but he only sent it farther along under the bench. Impatiently he grasped the old lady's ankle to move it out of the way. Granny Flint awoke with a start and saw the dribbling idiot kneeling at her feet. She let out a piercing scream and Bobbie jumped back.

'Get 'im away,' Granny Flint shouted.

'Bobbie Wilkins grabbed Granny Flint,' someone said.

'What's goin' on?' asked another.

'Bobbie Wilkins attacked the old lady,' someone else shouted.

'The idiot tried ter rape old Granny Flint,' the first one said to the woman sitting next to her.

The fat figure of Dolly Mason stormed up and slapped the idiot hard around the face. Bobbie reeled back, his eyes watering.

Ada jumped up and tore into the fat woman, grabbing her hair as she lunged. The two staggered back and fell in a heap between the benches, tearing and scratching at each other. They were finally pulled apart, with Ada sobbing in her anger.

Bobbie, meanwhile, had retreated to his place on the bench, his face scarlet from the slap.

Patrick Flannagan began to cry, upset at the idiot's sad expression, and Bridie held the boy against her. 'It's all right, darlin', it's all right,' she said quietly.

'Poor Bobbie,' sobbed the boy. 'That 'orrible lady 'it poor Bobbie.'

The noise of the incident carried outside, and brought Bob Bowman in. 'What the bloody 'ell's goin' on in 'ere? I could 'ear you lot above that bleedin' mob,' he shouted, pointing with his thumb to the roof.

'She 'ad no right ter bash my Bobbie, 'e was only tryin' ter get 'is marble,' Ada sobbed. 'If she comes near him again I'll do fer 'er, so 'elp me I will.'

Bob Bowman turned to the idiot. 'Where's yer marble, son?'

'Dere, over where lady sleepin'. Bobbie only get 'is marble.'

'Okay, son, I'll 'ave a look.'

The warden felt under the bench and fished out the cause of the trouble. He handed it to Bobbie, who quickly put it back into his pocket.

Later, as the Conner Street folk emerged, they smelt cordite fumes, and smoke from the nearby fires. A smell of gas also hung in the chill morning air, and the folk shivered. They were relieved to see that their Street had remained intact. Most of the little homes had wooden window shutters that had been closed tightly. The upstairs windows were, in most cases, taped against blast, and they were still intact. A few untaped windows had been smashed, and here and there a roof tile lay in the street. Half of a red chimneypot lay outside Bridie's house. Beside it was a jagged piece of shrapnel. Almost stately above the minor debris, the Street had survived.

The Sabbath morning was like no other as the early morning sun climbed up over the chimneypots. The rays shone blood red through the filter of smoke that hung in the sky, and lingered heatless and troubled. The sun climbed higher and became hotter as it lifted over the wall of smoke. The Street remained almost empty. For the most part, the inhabitants were catching up on their sleep. They tried to get the cramped, stiff feeling out of their bones and sighed with pleasure to realise they were still alive. It was a miracle that no bomb had fallen in the Street. From the flames and smoke, they knew how lucky they had been.

In the Davis's house Ginger was sipping a cup of tea. 'I'll 'ave ter get back soon, Dad. They 'ave a roll call early mornin's an' I'm gonna be missed.'

'I knew it,' the old man said. 'I knew yer bunked 'ome. Gawd, son, wot yer go an' do a fing like that fer, don't you fink yer ole dad can look after 'imself?'

'I was jus' worried, Dad. We 'eard all about the first bombin' on the wireless in the canteen.'

'Yer better 'ave a bite o' breakfast an' get on yer way back. If the bleedin' red-caps come round 'ere snoopin' they'll get me boot up their backsides, you mark me words.'

Ginger grinned and placed his arm around his father's bony shoulders. 'I'll fry a rasher an' put it between a couple o' slices then I'll be orf.'

''Ow yer gettin' back?' asked Jack.

'Don't yer fret,' replied Ginger. 'I'll get a 63 bus ter Kings Cross an' see the RTO. Tell 'em I've lost me travel warrant. I'll get back all right.'

The soldier slipped a couple of slices of streaky bacon into a frying pan and while it was sizzling he cut two thick slices of bread. He spread a dollop of butter across the bread and, when the bacon was starting to blacken, he made the sandwich.

'I knew yer bunked 'ome when I see yer bruvver wasn't wiv yer. You look after 'im, Ginge. Freddie's not as steady as you.'

'Yeah I know, Dad, that's why I didn't let 'im know I was comin' ter see yer.'

'Is there any news of where yer bein' posted to?' the old man asked.

'Gawd knows,' replied Ginger. 'Could be anywhere. I wouldn't mind Buckin'am Palace,' he joked. 'I could get 'ome every night then.'

The sun had risen overhead as Ginger stood at his front door. 'Now don't ferget, Dad, if it gets bad, get down the shelter, d'yer 'ear me?'

'Okay, boy, I will. Might even sit next ter old Lizzie. I used ter fancy 'er a few years back, though it was 'er tongue put me orf. Proper ole gas-bag. Mind yer though, a few o' these would soon tame 'er,' he joked, raising his hand in a threatening manner.

Ginger grinned and walked a few yards before his father beckoned him back. ''Ere, I almost fergot, put this in yer bin, I got a bit put by.'

Ginger started to protest at the proffered ten-shilling note.

'Don't argue, put it away in yer pocket,' his father insisted.

'Fanks, Dad, I'll pay yer back.'

The slight, hunched figure of Jack Davis watched his son reach the elbow of Conner Street and turn back to wave before he disappeared from sight. The old man closed his door and walked into his parlour. 'Sod the rent, they'll 'ave ter whistle fer it,' he said with conviction.

As midday approached, the smell of cooking drifted out

onto the Street. A few children appeared and played close to their own front doors. They were under strict orders not to stray far. They played five-stones, and drew hopscotch lines on the pavement. They stopped at the sight of the police car that drove into Conner Street. They gathered around as the man next to the driver got out and hammered on the door of number 14. Two red-capped army men sat impassively in the back seat of the car. The policeman hammered again and Jack Davis's voice barked out from within, 'All right, all right I'm comin', can't yer wait a minute?'

The door opened and Jack Davis confronted the policeman. 'Wot yer want?' he asked in an aggressive tone.

'We want to have a word with Private Ronald Davis. He was reported "absent without leave".'

As he spoke to the old man, his two companions got out of the car and walked up to the door.

'Yer can't come in 'ere. I don't allow any ole Tom, Dick or 'Arry in my 'ouse,' protested Ginger's father.

'I've got a warrant, Dad. You can't stop us, and I warn you, if you try, I'll take you down the station. Now c'mon, stand aside.'

The old man muttered as the three men went into his home. 'Bleedin' comin' in ter people's 'omes. Kick up the jacksey, that's what they need.'

The men ignored Jack Davis's muttered threats and searched the house.

Finally they emerged and drove away.

As the Conner Street folk prepared their Sunday midday meal they listened to the wireless broadcasts. The news was bad. There had been widespread damage with many lives lost. Fires were still burning, although the Surrey fires were now under control. A lot of the backstreets near to the docks were destroyed and thousands of people had been made homeless. The broadcasters issued repeated warnings, urging families to allow their children to be evacuated and to take precautions against bomb blasts. Instructions were issued advising that windows should be taped, pails of water made ready to fight fires, and gas masks placed in a handy position. People were also requested to board up windows and make some of their rooms blast-proof. All the news was depressing that bright Sunday noon.

Conner Street's warden had been very busy during the past week. There were food supply ships sitting in the Pool, and their vital cargoes had to be discharged as quickly as possible. The docks and wharves were a prime target for the German Air Force, and the river men were working at a tremendous pace to get the berths vacant for incoming vessels. Bob Bowman had his own special responsibilities as warden for Conner Street. There was the shelter to take care of. Sand and water buckets had to be kept filled. Kerosene lamps had to be primed and made ready for emergency use, and then there was the Street blackout. Twice every night Bob Bowman patrolled Conner Street to make sure that no light shone out from the houses. More and more the inhabitants came to rely on their good-natured warden. Bob was asked about how to get sandbags, how to board up windows, and once he was asked how ''er tom cat could be dissuaded from pissing in my back yard.' Nan Roberts also required Bob's services. She called him in one night to have a look at her leaking tap. Miraculously, the tap had stopped of its own accord by the time Bob arrived. Nan Roberts offered the warden a drink and Bob was tempted. But after rubbing his hand over his stubbled chin he politely declined her offer. Bob didn't want to get too comfortable, and he didn't want Grace to hear about his nocturnal visit to the Street's own siren.

As the sun climbed up over the chimneys and its rays pierced the parlour window they shone on the resting warden. Bob's eyes were closed, his mouth hung open, and his long legs stretched across the small room. Grace came in quietly and was obliged to step over his legs to get the box of Swan Vestas from the mantelshelf. She was worried about her husband. Already he was beginning to show signs of exhaustion. His thin features were white and drawn. Grace realised also that last night was only the start of a terrifying time, and she went quietly out of the parlour.

Although the Conner Street folk were still suffering from the experience of the previous night, their cockney humour won through.

'I told me ole woman ter get down those stairs fast. Know what she said? "I'm lookin' fer me clean drawers." I told 'er, the bastards 'ave come ter bomb yer, not rape yer. Sod yer drawers I told 'er.'

'My ole dutch went ter church,' someone else piped up. 'Jus' got back she 'as. When the vicar said "Let us all pray", she shouted out, "Wot yer fink we've bin doin' all night?".'

'I 'eard one o' the German planes got shot down,' related yet another. 'Anyway, the pilot baled out. Sailin' down all peaceful like, when 'e sees ole Lizzie Brown beneath 'im. 'Oldin' a carvin' knife she was. Couldn't face 'er. Turned round an' went back 'e did.'

'Did yer 'ear about that fight in the shelter last night?' asked another man as he strolled up to the 'Eagle'.

'No,' replied his drinking partner. 'Wot was it all about?'

'Well, I 'eard silly Bobbie Wilkins took a shine ter that ole biddy Flint. Gits up, an' away 'e goes over ter see 'er, so I 'eard. The ole gal's out like a light. Snorin' 'er bleedin' 'ead orf. Well, young Bobbie strokes 'er leg. Up she sits an' screams out,

"Don't stop!" Everyone gits the wrong impression. They all fink she's sayin' "Don't! Stop!" Gawd, she should be so lucky. Must be ages since anyone's stroked 'er leg.'

The storyteller's companion laughed. 'I reckon she didn't mind 'im strokin' 'er leg, it was 'im dribblin' all over 'er feet she didn't go a bundle on.'

Chapter Sixteen

Early on that Sunday morning, John and Florrie Braden came up from their place of refuge in the cramped cellar of their pub. They looked around and saw the bar was a complete shambles, with glass and debris everywhere. All the windows facing the Tower Road were smashed and the frames hanging out. A strong smell of alcohol came from behind the bar, and the large, flower-etched mirror on the wall behind the counter had a crack running the length of it.

'Gawd,' moaned John, 'seven years' bad luck.'

Florrie gave him a disdainful look. 'Sure it's only seven years?'

From their shattered bar, the Bradens could see the origin of the blast damage. Along the Tower Road, on the other side of that debris-strewn thoroughfare, they could see the bombed shop of the late Alberto Vitelli. Where not so long ago the Vitellis had served their customers with cheerful smiles, there was now a pile of smoking rubble. The shops on either side had miraculously escaped destruction, though their shutters had been blown right off.

Florrie dabbed at her eyes as she stared at the ruins. 'It's terrible. Just terrible,' she cried. 'Look at that wood sticking out on top of that heap.'

John Braden's eyes were bleary and he squinted in an effort to follow the direction of Florrie's pointing finger.

'There's a lump of wood sticking out in the shape of a cross. It makes me go cold looking at it. It's like a memorial,' she said.

'Makes you wonder,' John Braden said. 'First bomb in the street and it lands on one of their own.'

'Alberto wasn't one of them, nor was Maria. They were as much English as you or I. Alberto was beginning to talk like a cockney,' Florrie sobbed.

John Braden went to a small space behind the bar and emerged holding an unbroken bottle of brandy. His face was glowing. 'Here's one they never got,' he grinned.

'Don't stand there grinning like an idiot, pour us a drink,' Florrie demanded.

The two sat among the dust and broken glass sipping their drinks. The sun was beginning to rise up in the sky and early morning rays shone on the bar, faintly lighting up the dust that lay on its beams.

'Heaven knows how we're going to get this lot cleared up by opening time,' wailed John as he put his glass of brandy to his lips with a shaking hand.

'Well, we're going to have a good try, that's for sure,' asserted Florrie.

John Braden blinked his bleary eyes and sighed. The previous night he had taken his last spare bottle of whisky into the cellar, and during the terrible bombardment had drunk the entire contents. Florrie had taken her small brandy flask with her, and she too had taken a tot or two, her mind concentrating on her warm, intimate bedroom, and a certain big man who had once shared that room with her.

'Come on then, John. Let's make a start,' said the woman, getting up and fetching the broom.

As the couple set about the task of removing the broken

glass from the bar, a voice called out, 'Are you two all right in there?' The figure of Patrick Flannagan stood framed in the place where there had once been a window.

'Come on in, Pat, and mind yourself, there's glass everywhere,' warned Florrie.

'Holy Mary! What a mess,' Patrick remarked.

'Sit yourself down and have a drink,' invited John, waving his hand at the bottle on a dusty table.

'Look at it all,' moaned Florrie. 'We'll never get cleared up in time for twelve.'

Patrick poured himself a large tot of brandy and surveyed the damage. He looked up at the windowless gaps which let in the insipid light, then gulped up his drink. 'I'll not be long,' he announced, and was gone.

Florrie glanced at her husband and shrugged her shoulders.

As the two toiled away they heard the sound of wheels on the cobblestones outside, and the voice of Hoppy Dyke, 'Push the bloody fing then, Wheezy, lost yer strength?'

'Wot yer fink I am, a bleedin' 'orse?' moaned Wheezy.

The Bradens looked out and saw a barrow parked in the kerb. It was laden with planks of wood, and they saw the puffing figure of Wheezy Morris leaning on the load, mopping his brow. Hoppy was already sizing up the frames. 'Don't worry, folks, me an' my mate'll 'ave yer winders boarded up in no time.'

The Bradens dared not ask where the makeshift workmen got their timber, but John whispered to his wife, 'I bet the bleeders pulled a fence down somewhere.'

'I'm not worried where the wood came from, so long as we can open come twelve,' said Florrie quickly.

Albert Conlin left his lodgings and walked up Conner Street. He saw the work going on and he offered his help. Hoppy Dyke grabbed a saw and handed it to Albert. ''Ere, Al, you do the sawin'.' He pointed to Wheezy. ''E can't do anyfing straight, not even a saw-cut.'

'If you was ter take yer bleedin' coat orf an' do a bit o' work 'stead o' jus' measurin' we'd get a bit more done,' Wheezy moaned.

'It's no good you goin' on,' Hoppy said with a grin. 'Some of us was born ter work, an' some ter supervise. It's the way of the world, me son.'

Wheezy carted a plank of wood to the window frame and started to nail it in place. Patrick Flannagan came along and spoke to Hoppy. 'It's okay. The watchman said we can have more, as long as he gets his drink later.'

'Right y'are, Pat. I'll tell the Bradens it'll cost 'em drinks all round, 'ow's that sound?'

'Good lad,' said Patrick. 'Now I'm away to get meself ready. I've still got the stacking to do, to be sure.'

Hoppy waved as the Irishman sauntered down Conner Street, then he found a piece of board and wrote the words, 'Business as usual'. When he had hammered the board to the door of the Eagle, he called his workmen together.

'Now listen, men,' he said in a whisper. 'Ole Percy only wants a drink fer this lot o' wood. We'll tell the Bradens it came ter firty bob, okay?'

Wheezy rubbed his hands together and Albert Conlin just grinned. 'Okay then, chaps, let's get a drink.'

The announcement of 'Business as usual' was not strictly true, for there was one character conspicuous by his absence. Dinky Richards did not make an appearance at the lunchtime session. The battered old piano stayed silent and was used in its secondary capacity as a stand for pints of ale. It also served as a place to lean against when the beer started to take effect. The blind piano player was not forgotten however, and he was toasted in his absence. The Eagle clientele hoped that Dinky would show up for the usual sing-song that evening.

Dinky Richards had every intention of getting to the Eagle as usual that Sunday lunchtime. He left at his regular time and made good progress from his home in Spencer Street. Dinky used his stick as usual to feel his way along, but today he suddenly felt an obstruction in front of him. He could tell that the pavement was blocked. There was no option but to go round it. He stepped out into the road and immediately fell headlong into a crater. Luckily his fall was broken by the soft earth and a pool of filthy, muddy water. Dinky spluttered as he found his feet and the water stung cold as he wiped the mud from his face. Although soaked through, he was unhurt, apart from a few sore places. Standing up to his waist in the pool, he cursed. He cursed the German airforce, the cold water, and the whole filthy war. Dinky did not curse his blindness. For him it was a condition he'd lived with since birth. He knew the area and found it easy to get around. At certain times, when he waited at the kerbside for assistance to cross the road, there was always a hand that touched his arm, and a few kind words as someone helped him across to the other side. On this particular morning, however, there was no one about, and Dinky realised that he could quite well remain in his present position all day if he didn't do something about it.

Police Constable Smith strolled along the debris-strewn backstreets until he came upon a hoarding that had been blown down by the blast. It lay across the whole of the pavement, and PC Smith put his hands on his hips and considered the situation. As he stood there he heard a voice call out. It cried for help, and the custodian of the law bent down and tried to lift the hoarding. He managed to move it up slightly, but it was too heavy for him. As he let it go that faint cry for help was repeated. 'Christ, there's someone underneath,' he said aloud to himself. 'Don't move, I'll 'ave yer out in no time,' PC Smith called out.

''Urry up, I'm gettin' cold,' the voice shouted out.

PC Smith knelt down and tried to see beneath the hoarding. 'Are you 'urt?' he shouted.

'Don't fink so, jus' soakin' bleedin' wet an' bleedin' cold,' replied the faint voice.

PC Smith scratched his head. The morning was warm and there was no sign of water beneath the hoarding.

''Ow comes you're wet?' he asked.

'Gawd a'mighty, wouldn't you be wet, up ter yer waist in water?' said the now frantic voice.

PC Smith turned round and looked at the crater.

'Of all the people round 'ere, the first one on the scene's a bloody idiot,' wailed Dinky. 'Over 'ere, sod yer! Over 'ere!'

The long arm of the law finally reached into the crater and hauled Dinky out, setting him down on top of the hoarding. He was then taken to the hospital, where he was given a bath, a change of clothes and, to the delight of Dinky, a promise to get him to the Eagle in time for the evening session.

One of the shops that adjoined the destroyed greengrocery was the provision store belonging to Stanley Nathan. He had been informed that his shop had been damaged and was already at the scene, working to replace the broken shutters. Julie Brett joined him later, and the two began to replace the tins and packages that were strewn over the floor. They worked hard right through the morning and by lunchtime the task had been finished. The shutters were secured and the shelves tidied and restacked. Stanley fitted a new padlock and winked at Julie. It would be 'Business as usual' for the Nathan store as well.

In the Eagle trade was brisk. Tired, shocked men stood quietly talking of the night's bombing, and their normal quick humour was tempered with anguish. The usual faces were there: market people, folk from Conner Street and the few regulars from neighbouring streets. There were always one or two strange faces that popped in, and normally they merely got an inquiring glance, but the stranger who walked into the Eagle that Sabbath mid-morning received slightly more than a casual look.

He was tall, with thick, greying hair that was brushed back carefully. His face was wide, with a few lines around the corners of his pale blue eyes. The man carried himself with confidence, his walk was almost a swagger. The suit he wore was expensive, and the shirt was obviously silk. He walked up to the bar and ordered a beer.

'I can see you've received some damage,' he remarked in a cultured voice.

John Braden handed the man a pint of ale and nodded. 'Wasn't too bad, mainly glass. The windows,' he said, pointing to the planks at the window frames.

The man glanced around the bar as he sipped his drink.

Hoppy Dyke studied the man and whispered to Wheezy Morris, 'Mind wot yer say, that feller there's a tec.'

'Is that wot 'e is? Looks more like a pox-doctor's clerk if yer ask me. Look at the gear 'e's wearin'.'

Sammy Israel was enjoying his leave from the Rifle Brigade and was determined to get drunk before he returned to his camp the next day. He had seen the stranger walk in and he sidled up to Hoppy and Wheezy.

'That's a nice bit o' "schmatter" 'e's wearin',' Sammy said, nodding in the man's direction.

'I tell yer 'e's a dick. Look 'ow 'e keeps clockin' everybody. Lookin' fer you, Wheezy, I bet,' grinned Hoppy.

'I ain't touched a bit o' stolen since Gawd knows when. Strickly straight I am,' Wheezy said, hooking his thumbs through his waistcoat.

Florrie Braden was busy at the other end of the bar and did

not immediately spot the stranger. When her husband had finished serving him, she turned and started sharply. For a second she stared as though not sure. The man had aged somewhat, but it was definitely him.

She called John over. 'Didn't you recognise him?' she asked.

'Recognise who?'

'The stranger you just served.'

John looked over at the man, trying to focus his red-rimmed eyes.

'It's Alan Denman. What's he doing round here? As if I didn't know,' said Florrie with concern.

At that moment, the door opened and Stanley Nathan walked in with Julie Brett. He ushered her into a corner where there was a vacant seat and then went up to the bar to order his drinks.

While he waited to get served, Julie fumbled in her handbag and took out a mirror which she studied, touching her hair with the palm of her hand. Julie did not relish the thought of going into what she considered a man's domain on Sunday at lunch-time. But Stanley had persuaded her, saying that they had both earned a drink. She felt uneasy and looked around to see how many other women were there. She could only see two. One old lady sat near her, who had a drink in front of her and was staring down at her clasped hands. Julie saw the troubled look in the old lady's eyes as she twiddled her thumbs endlessly. The other woman sat near the door. She was heavily made up, with blobs of rouge on her cheeks. She was joking with the market men, prodding at one of them as she spoke. Julie cast her eyes in the direction of Stanley who was just getting served.

Two men on Stanley's far side took their drinks and walked away from the bar, affording Julie a sight of the tall stranger. The first sight of him hit her like a hammer. Her body started to tremble, and her breath came fast. It was him! He looked much older, and his hair was now streaked with grey, but he was still very much the same as when he had first walked into her life. What was he doing here after all this time? Julie wondered. The dread of meeting someone from her days on the streets was one thing that was often in her thoughts, but this was totally unexpected. She never dreamed she would meet Alan again.

The shock hit her hard, and when Stanley returned to her table with the drinks he noticed that something was wrong.

'Julie, you're as white as a sheet, is there anything wrong?' he asked with concern.

'I'm okay, Stan,' Julie replied, trying to gain control of herself.

Stanley took her hand and said, 'I'm sorry, love, I must have worked you too hard.'

'Of course you didn't. I'm just feeling a bit shaken after last night.'

Stanley patted her hand. 'Now I want you to listen to what I've got to say. There's plenty of room at my house. It's far enough away to be a lot safer than living round here. When we've finished our drinks I want you to go to your digs and pack. We can get to my place before it's dark.'

Julie shook her head. 'I can't move just like that, Stan. It was very good of the Morgans to let me have their son's room. I can't just leave them, not after getting on with them so well.'

Stanley's face looked a picture of disappointment, and Julie squeezed his hand. 'It's not that I don't thank you for offering, and I know you'd be the gentleman, but I just can't leave them, not just now. When I first went there, the Morgans were still trying to cope with their boy's death. I felt like an intruder. There were times when I bundled in on Mrs Morgan and saw her sobbing over her son's photo. Slowly I managed to ease her grief by talking to her. She still sits in her little room with that photo nearby, and we talk about her son. She says it helps to ease the pain. They treat me like a daughter, Stan. I just can't leave her, not yet anyway.'

Stanley sighed and gave her a grin. 'Okay, Julie, I understand. It's just that I worry over you.'

He picked up his drink and took a swig. Over his shoulder Julie saw the tall figure from her past put down his empty glass and turn to leave. As he did so their eyes met for an instant. The spark of recognition showed in his eyes before he looked away and walked to the door.

An hour later, Stanley and Julie left the bar and walked the short distance to the girl's lodgings. She held on to Stanley's arm, her troubled thoughts hid from him. He must never know. It was going well for both of them and Julie felt happy with the kind Stanley. He had taken her to his heart, and the knowledge of her past did not make any difference to him. Julie often wondered if he was pained by it. He never spoke, nor hinted. It seemed that he had denied the very existence of her dark past and never discussed it, and Julie was grateful.

The sun was high in the heavens as the two people stood by the Morgans' front door. Stanley kissed her gently on the lips and looked hard into her eyes. 'Don't forget what I said. There's plenty of room, and there's a lock on the bedroom door.'

Julie smiled. 'Stanley, the way I feel right now you'd need one to keep me out.'

The shopkeeper raised his eyebrows in mock reproof, and his assistant looked down at her shoes. 'Stan, you don't mind if I stay in tonight, do you? I don't feel very well, I think I've got a chill coming.'

Stanley Nathan squeezed her arm. 'You get an early night. I'll see you tomorrow.'

Julie kissed the man gently on the cheek and watched as he

walked out of the Street. As she turned to enter her lodgings she saw Alan Denman. He sauntered along across the Street, walking away from her. He must have spotted her, and now he knew where she lived. Julie went inside quickly and ran up to her room. Her heart was pounding and she felt faint.

'Julie, is that you?' called out Mrs Morgan. 'Dinner'll be in five minutes.'

'I'll be down right away,' the girl answered in a voice she hardly recognised.

Later that afternoon, Julie found herself sitting on her bed. The Sunday meal was over and she had helped Mrs Morgan with the washing-up. The elderly couple were sitting in their parlour listening to the radio. Julie could hear the strains of *La Cumparsita* drifting up from below. The violins, stringing at the tango, evoked a feeling of melancholy within her heart and she threw herself down onto the bed. She laid her head on the cool pillow and thought about Alan Denman. Why did he suddenly appear out of her past? What was the significance? He would be aware that in presenting himself at the Eagle, Florrie would recognise him. He expected the news of his visit to be passed on.

Julie twisted fretfully on to her back and stared up at the flaking ceiling. He saw me at the door, she thought. Even if the visit was just a twist of fate, he now knew of her presence in the dockland area. If he intended to get in touch, he would only have to drop a letter through the door. Her breath was quick and shallow as she contemplated his move. She felt strangely frightened, a feeling that was mingled with excitement. The girl also experienced a feeling of guilt at the prospect of a letter. It was as though she were betraying the kindness of Stanley, but she could not shake off the feeling of expectancy. She closed her eyes and allowed her thoughts to drift back in time, then she turned and buried her face in the pillow as she sobbed softly.

*

When the Eagle shut on that Sunday lunchtime, three characters remained loitering outside. Hoppy Dyke leaned on the pub wall, as he found it easier to keep his feet that way. Wheezy Morris stood beside him, listening to the cripple's oration. Sammy Israel sat on the kerb, his army uniform unbuttoned and his beret and belt pushing through the lapel of his tunic. Sammy was on leave from the Rifle Brigade, and he was determined to get drunk at least once more before he turned his attention to bayonet practice. He held his head in his hands as he listened to Hoppy's scheme. It sounded all right, and what did it matter? In two days he would be back at Winchester, well away from any repercussions, and with a few shekels in his pocket.

'I tell yer, it's easy as taking a tanner from a blind man,' Hoppy was saying. 'I went up the alley last night to 'ave a look. The fencin' looks like it's ready ter fall down on its own. We can get in an' lever up the winder. There's a nice few quid's werf of 'ats in there. Top 'ats, bowlers, an' even wimmin's straw 'ats. Ole Solly Goldberg said 'e'll take the lot. Said 'e'll pay us right away. Come on, wha'd'ya fink?'

Sammy Israel looked up at Hoppy, disbelief showing on his face. 'I've never known Solly Goldberg ter pay anybody right away. Good businessman is Mr Goldberg. Even keeps me waitin' for the 'errin's I sell 'im, an' me one of 'is own.'

'I tell yer 'e's promised ter pay up sharp,' Hoppy insisted.

'Well I'm not so sure,' went on Sammy. 'I've known Solly fer years. 'E was at my Schmickling, an' that's ages ago.'

'Gawd blimey, Sammy boy, can't yer speak the King's English,' Wheezy complained. 'Wot's "Schmickling"?'

Hoppy Dyke laughed. 'It's when the yiddishers get circumcised.'

'Gawd 'elp us,' moaned Wheezy. 'You lot 'ave ter get an

audience, even when yer gettin' the top o' yer dingle sliced orf.'

'It's custom,' said Sammy proudly. 'We 'ave a party fer the child.'

'Don't they frow all nuts an' raisins over yer as well?' asked Wheezy.

'Silly git, that's a Barmitzvah,' corrected Hoppy.

'A wot?'

'It's when we come of age,' said Sammy.

'Well I still fink it's stupid,' insisted Wheezy. 'Wot did they do when yer got called up, all get pissed did they?'

Hoppy got impatient with the trend of the conversation. There was more pressing business to decide. 'Well, wot about it? Are yer in?'

'Yep,' said Wheezy.

'Sammy?'

'Okay. Long's Solly coughs up sharp.'

'Right then, now listen. We'll wait till it's dark. 'Ave a couple o' pints, then Bob's yer uncle, in we go.'

The three strolled off in an unsteady manner; Sammy to his flat in Spencer Street, Hoppy to his house at number 21 Conner Street, and Wheezy to the buildings in the Kent Road.

Chapter Seventeen

Orange streaks showed across the evening sky, fading to violet with the setting sun and the folk of Conner Street became anxious. Night was approaching, and with it the dread of another air raid. The children were shepherded from the Street and given an early supper. It might be another night in the shelter, and with that in mind the youngsters were hurried off to bed for a few hours' sleep. The long summer evenings were not conducive to sleep however, and the cry of the toffee-apple man, peddling through the Street late in the evening, caused a few problems.

'Mum, I can't sleep.'

'Well try.'

'But, Mum, it's still light out.'

'Listen, Johnnie, they've altered the clocks ter trick the Germans. It's really late.'

'Mum, I can 'ear the toffee-apple man. Can I 'ave a toffee-apple?'

'No yer can't. I'm not gettin' toffee all over me bedclothes, now get ter sleep.'

'But, Mum, Reggie Carter's dad lets 'im 'ave a toffee-apple in bed.'

'Now listen 'ere, yer little tyke, if yer don't get ter sleep this

215

minute, I'll go up the Eagle an' fetch yer farver 'ome. 'E'll give yer wot for.'

'Oh all right then,' puffed Johnnie.

As if to justify her actions, the boy's mother added, 'Anyway, those apples are all rotten. They've got worms in 'em.'

'Cor.'

'An' they'll rot yer teef.'

'Wot, the worms?'

'No, the toffee. Now will yer get ter sleep?'

The lad lay twisting in his bed, thinking of a nice, juicy, sweet-tasting toffee-apple on a stick. It wasn't fair. Reggie Carter ate toffee-apples in bed. Reggie Carter even had a scooter with real ball-bearings. Perhaps if he ran away they would realise a little old toffee-apple wasn't much to ask for. It would be different if he asked for a scooter with ball-bearings. He would run away in the morning. Then he could have lots of toffee-apples, and eat them all in bed. He could stay up till it was black as ink, and stand outside pubs like Reggie Carter, and eat arrowroot biscuits, and drink gallons of lemonade. Just wait. He would show them. A drummer boy in the army, that's what he'd be, or a cabin boy on a large ship.

The sandman called, and the little lad's eyes shut. He saw the toffee-apple man in front of him, holding out huge treacle-covered apples on sticks. The man wore a candy-striped suit and a top hat dotted with jelly beans. The lad took a bite from the sweet toffee-apple, and saw the man grinning evilly at him. The lad saw that the bite had exposed a worm-eaten core and he awoke. He tried to look down at his tongue. It was dark in the room, and he heard a voice that seemed to come from a long way off. 'You, Johnnie, get yer clothes on quick, it's the bloody siren.'

*

At the corner of Conner Street, a shaft of light hit the pavement and a voice shouted, 'Watch that light.'

The Eagle was full. Three young men, one in a uniform, sat in a corner.

'It's no good goin' yet. The bleedin' Street's full o' people.' Wheezy moaned.

'We'll wait fer an hour, it'll be quiet by then,' said Hoppy.

'Wot we gonna put 'em in?' asked Wheezy.

'Don't worry, I've already seen ter that. Yesterday I lobbed a couple o' sacks over the wall,' answered Hoppy, tapping his head meaningfully.

'All I 'ope is Solly pays up sharp,' said Wheezy, sipping his beer.

'So do I,' added Sammy Israel.

Joe Harper walked into the bar accompanied by Rosie and Skipper. The old seaman winked at Florrie, his faded eyes drifting down to the woman's ample bust.

'A few years ago I'd a bin over that counter,' Skipper muttered out of the corner of his mouth to Joe.

'A few years ago I'd a bin wiv yer, Skip,' grinned Joe.

'You two goin' ter stan' whisperin' all night,' piped in Rosie.

Skipper licked his lips in anticipation and he fished in his coat pocket for his pipe. 'I likes 'em wiv a bit o' meat on 'em,' he went on. 'Can't stand a skinny lookin' woman.'

'Wot yer mumblin' about, Skip?' Rosie asked.

Joe got the drinks and the three sat at a table next to the conspirators.

'When yer goin' back, son?' Skipper asked Sammy.

'Termorrer,' answered Sammy, wishing the old man hadn't asked.

Joe Harper looked at the uniformed Jew. 'Got many yiddisher boys in your lot, Sammy?'

'Cor not 'arf, Joe. Most of 'em come out o' the Mile End Road.'

Joe picked up his pint of ale. 'Well 'ere's to yer, son.'

'Cheers, Joe,' Sammy said with a wink.

Skipper was looking at his pint with a frown.

'What's wrong Skipper?' Rosie asked. 'Don't yer fancy it?'

'It's either me mouth, or that bleedin' landlord's bin waterin' it down,' Skipper said with a glance in John Braden's direction.

'I wouldn't fink so,' Wheezy piped in. ''E never touches the stuff.'

Florrie Braden was busy serving. She could not help thinking about the visit from Alan Denman. She had noticed the look of horror on Julie's face when she had spotted him. After all the trouble he had caused her, why should he appear again? Florrie had liked Julie and was upset when she decided to leave Kent. For a while the two women had kept in touch, until Julie went onto the streets. What was the reason for Alan Denman to come to the Eagle? She hoped it was just a coincidence. Even so, what was he doing in London? Perhaps he had heard from someone about Julie, and had decided to try his luck again. In any case, she was determined to have a quiet word with the stranger if he showed up again. Julie seemed happy with Stanley Nathan, and Florrie aimed to keep it that way.

Dusk was slipping down like a cloak. For the past hour the half-daylight had stayed unchanged. Blackout curtains had been drawn and lights lit, although it was still possible to see the length of the Street. Now suddenly it was black. Stars winked down from the velvet sky, and a full moon appeared over the chimneypots.

'C'mon lads, we can't wait no longer,' said Hoppy.

The three conspirators waved goodnight to the Harpers, then slipped quickly out of the pub.

'Funny,' observed Joe Harper. 'Either they don't like our company, or they've gorn orf beer.'

Rosie grunted. 'I can't abide that 'Oppy feller. I bet they're up ter no good.'

'Wouldn't be surprised,' remarked Skipper. 'First time I've seen Wheezy leave without Florrie 'avin' ter shoo 'im out.'

The three young men walked quickly up the alley that led off from Tower Road. They moved silently, until Sammy's foot made contact with an empty tin can. The rattling noise over the cobbles clattered loudly through the quiet Street, and the three stopped.

'It's no time ter play bleedin' football,' hissed Hoppy.

'Got no consideration, some people. Fancy frowin' their rubbish up bleedin' alleys,' moaned Wheezy.

Sammy was silent. The escapade did not seem such a good idea now. Sammy was a born costermonger who, like most of his faith, had a shrewd business brain. He had recognised that anything was saleable, but the thought of Solly fencing top hats and straw bonnets in wartime made him shake his head.

The alley ran along the side of an empty, boarded up shop. Hoppy pulled on a part of some corrugated fencing and it bent outwards. 'Quick, lads, in yer go,' he whispered.

The three were soon inside and standing in the yard. There was a six foot wall that separated them from the hatter's. Hoppy spotted the outline of an oil drum, which he moved to the foot of the wall. 'It's empty, lads. This'll make it easy,' he said.

The three men clambered one by one on to the drum and slipped over into the hatter's yard. Hoppy worked on the window catch using a kitchen knife. Soon he grunted with satisfaction and gently slid the window frame up. The men climbed over the sill and stepped into a dark room. The moon had risen, but its pale beam barely reached into the room. What light there was enabled the three to pick out a few wooden crates, and a door in one corner of the room.

'C'mon, lads, upstairs we go,' hissed Hoppy, his heart pumping fast with excitement.

'Where's yer torch, 'Oppy?' whispered Wheezy. 'I can't see a bleedin' fing in front o' me!'

'Can't shine it 'ere. Too risky. Wait till we get upstairs,' answered Hoppy.

The three men started to climb the stairs when Hoppy, who was leading, suddenly stopped.

'Christ! The sacks! We fergot the sacks!'

Sammy was last in line. 'I'll get 'em,' he volunteered. He climbed back into the yard and scrambled over the wall into the next yard. He went to the fencing and felt around in the dark. The sacks were lying near to where they had entered. The corrugated sheeting was gaping outwards and, as Sammy retrieved the sacks, he saw a light shining up the alley. The sound of slow, deliberate footsteps reached him and he quickly threw himself face down among the rubble. A beam from a torch shone over his body and Sammy held his breath.

PC Smith had been on duty along the Tower Road and found the urgent need to relieve himself. When he had finished, PC Smith buttoned up his trousers and sighed with contentment, then he walked back out of the alley.

Sammy stood up and looked down at his uniform trousers. The bottom half was soaked in urine.

'My God!' he mumbled aloud. 'To be pissed over, and by a gentile!' The insult made the yiddisher boy grit his teeth. He quickly clambered over the wall and rejoined the two men.

'Wot kept yer, Sammy?' asked Wheezy.

'Will yer just look at me uniform?' moaned Sammy. ''E pissed all over me. 'Ow 'e didn't spot me, I'll never know.'

'Who the bloody 'ell yer talkin' about?' asked Hoppy.

'PC bloody Smith, that's who. What a place ter 'ave a riddle. I couldn't move, 'e'd 'ave seen me,' wailed Sammy.

'Well I'll be blowed. Yer mean ter say yer just lay there an' let a cozzer piss all over yer?' Wheezy said in mock horror.

Hoppy interrupted them. 'Never mind about that now. Fill these sacks quick as yer can, an' let's get goin'.'

The room at the top of the stairs was both workroom and showroom. Hats of all descriptions were lined along shelves. The light of Hoppy's torch picked out top hats, brown Derbys, straw bonnets, bowlers, and fine, flower-bedecked creations.

'Cor, look at those,' whispered Wheezy, pointing to a row of lace bonnets. 'Wonder wot me ole mum would say if she could wear one o' those.'

Hoppy was busy stuffing the loot into the sacks. 'Them ain't fer the likes o' me an' you. Up West. That's where this lot was goin'. Look at the label.'

The three peered at the stitched label inside the brim of a top hat. The light of Hoppy's torch shone on the words, 'La Parisienne'.

'Yer lords an' ladies an' the rest o' the toffee-noses buys this stuff. Bloody idiots. Buy a brick o' shit if yer stuck a fancy label on it,' Hoppy said with feeling.

Wheezy was filling a sack with ladies' bonnets. 'I fink me ole mum would look good in one o' these,' he said.

'We told yer, they ain't for the likes o' the people round 'ere,' remarked Sammy.

'Oh, an' why not?' asked Wheezy. 'Nuffink wrong with cockney people. Least they got manners. I seen some of them there dooks an' earls. Seen 'em at Epsom once. Bleedin' carry on it was. The gippos on the Downs 'ad more decorum. I saw . . .'

Hoppy stopped him. 'We gonna 'ave a lecture on manners, or are we gonna piss orf while we can?'

The three men made their stealthy exit from the hatter's shop without being seen; each carrying a sack of loot slung across his shoulders, they turned into Conner Street. Their plan was to stow the sacks behind the shelter, in a small recess that afforded an emergency exit. They reasoned it would be safe there until Solly called around next morning. Down the Street they went, in single file and bent forward with the bulkiness of the sacks, like extras from *Snow White*, unseen, until PC Smith turned the corner by the Eagle.

Sammy was trailing, and he turned to make sure they were not being followed. He saw the beam of light from the policeman's torch. 'It's the cozzer!' he cried.

'Quick, run!' shouted Hoppy.

The beam of light flashed along the Street. 'What's occurrin' then?' shouted PC Smith.

In the light of the torch, PC Smith saw what looked like three hunchbacks disappearing around the corner. He stood and scratched his head.

'Must be goin' crackers,' he said aloud. Voices coming out of holes was one thing, but hunchbacks running abroad in the neighbourhood was too much. PC Smith longed for the end of his spell of night duty.

The three ran towards the shelter. 'Quick, get inside!' shouted Hoppy, thinking the policeman was following them.

'Blimey!' gasped Wheezy. ''E would 'ave ter show up.'

Into the stuffy-smelling shelter went the three. They sat in the darkness, the sacks stowed by the door.

Wheezy lit a cigarette and puffed out a cloud of smoke. 'That was close,' he muttered.

'Shush!' barked Hoppy. ''E may be outside.'

The men were silent, listening for the sound of the

policeman's tread outside. It remained quiet, and Wheezy stamped out his cigarette.

'C'mon, boys, let's get them sacks stowed,' said Hoppy.

As they stood up, the moaning wail of the siren started. It picked up in sound until it turned to a scream.

'Cor blimey,' moaned Wheezy, shuffling around in agitation.

'Quick!' shouted Hoppy. 'There's no time now. Put 'em right in the corner.'

The three sacks were hidden just in time. Into the shelter came the folk from the Street. White-faced and hurrying they came; wide-eyed and scared, but some still managing to crack a joke.

Granny Flint tottered in, puffing and panting with the effort. 'Gawd a'mighty Gawd, this'll be the deaf o' me.'

'Shut up, Gran, that bastard 'Itler can't kill you,' said Lizzie Brown, sitting down heavily beside her.

The three conspirators sat wooden-faced, watching the Conner Street folk pile in.

'Wot you free doin' 'ere?' asked Lizzie Brown. 'Ain't you s'pose ter be outside watchin' out?'

'I'd sooner be inside watchin' out, Liz,' joked Wheezy.

'Not so much o' yer cheek,' said Lizzie sharply. 'Piss orf out there an' leave room fer the wimmin an' kids.'

The three left the safety of the shelter and joined the rest of the men in the covered area at the front of the refuge. Inside, the women were talking quietly. Children sat yawning, miserable at being dragged from their warm beds. One lad, ignored by his mother who was talking to her neighbour, started to pick at the string on one of the sacks.

Suddenly the guns opened up, and a loud explosion rocked the shelter. It was followed by another loud salvo of gunfire and another explosion. Dust fell from the concrete roof and the lights flickered.

'Holy Mary,' muttered Bridie Flannagan, cuddling her baby close to her.

Maureen had her arms round the two boys and the twins sat on each side of Bridie, their heads leaning on her. 'It's all right, children, it's only the guns,' she said reassuringly.

Granny Flint gave Bridie a cold stare. 'She said that last night.'

Lizzie Brown patted the old lady's hand. 'She's only sayin' it fer the kids' sake, they're all scared.'

Granny Flint sniffed. 'Shouldn't be 'ere. Should all be 'vacuated,' she said quickly.

Yet another explosion and another roar of gunfire rocked the shelter. With the drone of planes came a whistling sound as a bomb fell earthwards. There was a dull thud, but no explosion.

'Did you 'ear that? Must o' bin a dud,' said Lizzie.

'Bastards!' Emmie Jones cried. 'If this keeps up we'll 'ave ter start sleepin' 'ere.'

'Gawd ferbid,' said Granny Flint. 'I couldn't sleep a wink in this stinkin' place.'

Lizzie Brown grinned. Granny Flint soon nodded off to sleep and her head tilted to one side and her mouth hanging open.

It had suddenly gone quiet. The droning of the planes diminished and the gunfire ceased. The lad in the corner had untied the knot on one of the sacks and was delving inside.

'Cor, look wot I got!' he said loudly, holding up a top hat.

'Where did yer get that?' asked his mother.

'Look, Mum, there's lots of 'em in the sack.'

The boy's mother fished in the open bag and removed a lady's bonnet.

'Turn the sack up, let's 'ave a look wot's inside,' someone said.

''Ere, gi's one,' said someone, and 'Pass us one,' said another.

Within minutes, the loot from the hatter's shop was on display. Even Granny Flint wore a bonnet. Joe Harper heard the laughter and popped his head inside.

'Wot's goin' on in there?' asked Bob Bowman, the Street warden.

'Well I'll be!' said Joe. 'They've all got party 'ats on. Gawd knows where they got 'em from.'

Someone from the adjoining shelter heard the laughter, and came in to see what was going on.

''Ere, take a few next door,' said the boy's mother, passing a sack to the woman.

Outside, the three men responsible for the hilarity sat with downcast faces as the woman ran past them and into the next shelter.

'Wonder who put them 'ats in there?' grinned Joe, looking directly at the three.

'Gawd knows,' said Hoppy.

'Solly Goldberg's goin' ter be pleased,' groaned Sammy.

'I'm not too 'appy meself,' moaned Wheezy.

'I wouldn't 'ave minded if we'd 'ave earned a few shekels,' said Sammy, his face registering disgust. 'I've bin pissed on an' not earned a penny. I knew it wasn't a good idea from the start.'

'Well yer didn't 'ave ter come wiv us, did yer?' snapped Hoppy.

''Ere, Sammy, d'yer know wot yer smell like? That piss-'ole in the pitchers,' Wheezy cracked.

Sammy ignored the remark and sat glumly, his head resting against the wall behind him.

Overhead the droning started again as the night raiders turned for home. The guns started up and explosions sounded in the distance. The drone became louder and the explosions got nearer. Above the din came the rising sound of singing from within the shelter. Lizzie Brown's voice could be heard. 'There's an old mill by the stream,' she shrieked, and the chorus answered her, crying out, 'Nellie Dean!'

'Where I used to sit and dream,' she sang. 'Nellie Dean,' they cried.

The adjoining shelter, not to be outdone, started up with their own chorus.

The gunfire was deafening, and pieces of shrapnel clattered down the cobbles. The full moon was high, and the pale, cold light was changed to a pink glow from the nearby raging fires. Flashes of light followed by loud bangs went on for the next hour, as the anti-aircraft guns in the park aimed at the new flight of bombers overhead. The raiders spewed from their bellies of death and turned over the edge of London to make their return run. Buildings collapsed. Fires started and roared out of control. Hospitals were hit, and everywhere craters gaped, smoking and filling with sewage. Firemen found their hoses ran dry as water mains were hit. Factory walls fell outwards, down onto the firemen below. Ambulances ran a gauntlet to and from the hospitals. Doctors and nurses worked on, almost out on their feet, and police and rescue squads delved into the rubble for sobbing, terrified survivors.

It continued through the night. Shrapnel and shell cones fell, still glowing hot. Tower Road was cratered; in Spencer Street, an oil bomb fell slap in the middle of the tannery. The place burned fiercely, threatening the adjoining houses. Little Dixon Street was hit by a landmine and wiped out. A high-explosive bomb landed in Conner Street and made a hole in a backyard. Conner Street was lucky that night; it suffered a few cracked windows.

At the height of the bombing, a strange and unreal incident was taking place. Inside a cavern of concrete, an old lady and an idiot were facing each other. The lady wore a bonnet, tied under her chin, and the idiot wore a top hat. The old lady held her skirts high, and the idiot stuck out his chin. They were dancing a jig to the accompaniment of a mouth organ. The audience clapped and laughed as the two performed. Lizzie Brown was light on her feet and danced in tune to the music. The idiot dribbled onto his chin and shuffled on the spot. The woman locked arms with the man and spun him around to the delight of the bedecked audience. It might have been a scene from a Victorian music hall, with the top hats and flowered bonnets, and a dancer showing a glimpse of her pink, knee-length drawers. Instead, the light came from an electric light bulb, and the thunderous applause came from the guns in the park and the bombs from the sky.

The old docker shook the mouth organ and wiped it on his coat-sleeve. Lizzie Brown kissed the idiot on the cheek and sat down heavily on a bench. Bobbie shuffled along to where Ada sat, a top hat resting uneasily on his ears. He sat beside her, a happy light showing in his eyes. Ada squeezed his arm and gave him a warm smile.

Later, as the bombers flew out over the sea and the all-clear shrilled out, they emerged. Tired, thankful, and still wearing their fancy headgear. They went in their houses to brew tea, to get some sleep, and for one young lad, to make a discovery.

Reg Carter slipped into the backyard of his home to see if his rabbits were all right. Two dust-covered pets were out of their cage. They were sniffing around a hole that hadn't been there a few hours ago. Reggie peered down and saw the fins of a bomb sticking out of the rubble in the crater.

Chapter Eighteen

Not all the inhabitants of Conner Street used the shelter. Old man Davis refused to budge from his home. The Morgans stayed together in their parlour and Julie Brett sat with them. Mrs Morgan had a philosophy about the bombing. 'If yer number's on it, love, it won't matter a scrap where yer at, it'll find yer.' As for old man Davis, he fully expected to be found, but he was adamant: 'My ole dutch died upstairs, an' when I go I wan' it ter be in this 'ouse. Wot was good enough fer 'er is good enough fer me.'

Patrick Flannagan hardly ever used the shelter. When the siren wailed out its eerie warning, he gathered up his tribe and despatched them all across the Street to the refuge. For himself, the house was shelter enough. When he wasn't on night shift at the bagwash factory, he would be snoring the moment his head hit the pillow. With help from the Eagle, Patrick slept well, and even the German night raiders could not rouse him. There was only one person who could waken the big Irishman, and that was Bridie. She'd gently touch his shoulder, and say a few words such as, 'Pat, the Eagle's open', and he'd be wide awake.

Early on Monday morning, when young Reggie Carter discovered the unexploded bomb, the police and air-raid wardens moved in to arouse the Conner Street folk. Everyone

229

in the Street was moved to a nearby rest centre, hastily prepared by volunteer workers. The Street was roped off, and a notice was placed at each end of the turning. It said simply, 'Danger, Unexploded Bomb'. A policeman patrolled by the rope, and only lifted it when an army lorry drove up. The vehicle had a sign over the cab with a red flag flying both sides of the notice. Royal Engineers of the Bomb Disposal Squad hurried into the Street and set about shoring up the bomb. They worked through the morning, and by mid-afternoon the officer and a sergeant climbed down into the enlarged hole. At five o'clock that evening the safely defused bomb was loaded on to the back of the lorry. As the policeman lifted the rope for the vehicle to leave, Florrie Braden ran from her pub bringing the last bottle of whisky with her. Each man was given a huge tot, and Florrie spoke loudly enough for the policeman to hear, 'If I get summonsed for serving outside of hours then it'll be worth it.'

The policeman turned away to look down the Tower Road.

When Julie Brett returned to her lodgings that evening, she found an unstamped envelope propped against the china soap dish that stood on the washstand. The envelope was addressed, 'To Julie'. With trepidation the girl opened the letter and read the contents.

Dear Julie,

I'm sorry if I upset you by my presence at the Eagle on Sunday. I refrained from talking to you as I noticed that you were with someone. I expect you are wondering why I should suddenly appear after all the time that has elapsed. Well, it was no accident. After all that happened between us, I just had to see you again.

When you left, I tried to pick up the pieces and repair

my marriage, but it was no good. From the day you left I have not shared the same bedroom as Elaine. We still live together, but there is nothing there anymore. She has taken the two children to her mother in the West Country to get away from the bombing and I have a flat in the East End which I use during the week. The reason for this is that I have opened another factory in London, and we are doing war work.

It was Percy my manager who saw you at the Eagle. You don't know him, but he knows you by sight, and in fact often covered for me while we were together. Percy has been with me a long time and he was on some business for me when he went into the Eagle by chance. I feel that it was fate that our paths should cross once more.

I don't expect that you want to see me anymore, Julie, but for old times' sake I would dearly like to talk to you to discover what you have been doing since we parted.

Say that you will meet me. I will be in the Boatman at Greenwich on Wednesday of this week. I will be there at 8 o'clock and I will wait till 9. Please try to come.

Yours,
Alan Denman.

Julie Brett sat on her bed. Her hands were shaking, and her eyes misted. Boldly scrawled words on the sheets of paper flowed together as she tried to re-read the sentences. A large tear slipped down her cheek, and she threw herself face downwards into the pillow. It was impossible. She could not meet him. In any case, Stanley always took her out on Wednesdays. She could not deceive him after all he had done to help her rebuild her life. She dare not consider the meeting. Slowly she turned over onto her side and looked at the letter once more. A strange feeling of excitement made Julie shake. The old flame of passion had not quite burned out, after all.

Julie clenched up the letter and threw it to the floor. She knew that once she spoke to Alan Denman again there would be a danger of a new involvement. She simply could not trust herself. She bent down and retrieved the crumpled letter and straightened it out on her lap. Putting it behind the clock, she went down to talk to the Morgans.

Florrie had made up her mind to talk to Stanley Nathan. Ever since the first time her young barmaid had walked out with Alan Denman, Florrie had predicted trouble. There was only one way for it to end for the girl, and that was for her to get hurt. When Julie had lost the baby and ended up on the streets, Florrie's dislike for the man responsible turned to hatred. When he walked into the Eagle on Sunday, Florrie knew that unless she did something shrewd, Julie was going to get hurt again. And this time, more than one person was involved. Stanley Nathan was a good man. She could not stand back and see the new object of Julie's affections upset by what might happen. She would go to see him. Now would be the right time, she knew that every Monday evening Stanley worked late in the shop. It was his practice to work on his rationing forms and to update his ledgers. Julie would not be there in the shop, so it would give her the opportunity to warn him.

Stanley Nathan was just finishing off filling in a large form when Florrie knocked on the shutters. Stanley pushed aside a huge pile of papers and went to the door. Florrie repeated her banging before he reached the front of the shop.

'Sorry to trouble you, Stan, but I knew you'd be here late,' said Florrie.

'That's all right, Florrie, come on in.'

He led the way to the back of the shop and beckoned Florrie to a chair by the table. 'I was just about to make a cup of tea, care for one?'

'Well it would make a nice change to the stuff I've been drinking lately,' joked the landlady.

Stanley lit the gas and placed a small tin kettle over the flame. 'What can I do for you?' he said as he tipped out the contents of a brown china teapot into the sink.

'Well, it's about Julie that I've come, Stan,' Florrie began.

'She's okay, isn't she?' the man said quickly, concern showing on his face.

'She's fine, Stan, it's just that I'm worried.'

'Worried?'

'Alan Denman has shown up,' she said, watching for the reaction on his face.

Stanley showed no surprise. His mouth creased into a serious smile. 'I know.'

'You know?' queried Florrie. 'You saw him?'

Stanley did not answer right away. Instead he walked over to the table and spooned some tea leaves into the teapot. Florrie watched his broad back, surprise showing on her face.

'He was in the pub yesterday, wasn't he,' remarked the man.

Florrie nodded. 'I didn't think you knew him.'

'I didn't, until then. Somehow I knew, the moment I saw Julie's reactions. Oh, I made out I hadn't noticed anything, but Julie went white. I just knew that it had to be him,' said the shopkeeper.

'Have you spoken to Julie about it?' asked Florrie.

'No. If she wants to talk, then I'll listen. It may be too painful for her, so I'm not going to ask her,' Stanley said.

The kettle started to boil, and the man filled the teapot with the water.

'Do you think he'll try to contact Julie?' Florrie asked.

'I think he will,' replied the shopkeeper, 'but for his sake, he'd better stay clear.'

Florrie looked at the man, a surprised frown causing her eyebrows to arch. She had known the shopkeeper for some time, and it was the first instance she could recall when he had spoken so grimly. She noticed the way he emphasised the sentence, his jaw muscle knotting as he spoke.

'I've been turning it over in my mind, Stan. I know that Julie has told you all about her past, but I expected her to try not to let on that the stranger was him. She was too scared of your reaction. You might have done anything. Julie loves you, Stanley. She's really happy now, and I know the girl. I think she's terrified of the past. What it might do to both of you. She's trying hard to bury her memories, but when he walked in my place yesterday it was like a bad dream come true. Don't let the past destroy your lives, love. I think a lot of both of you, and I wouldn't want something like what happened yesterday to spoil it all for you.'

Stanley gave her a friendly wink. 'You take sugar?'

'Two, please.'

He poured out the tea into two large mugs, and added the milk and sugar.

The two sat facing each other across the desk. Florrie sipped her tea, and Stanley studied her. The woman was aware of his gaze and she put down the cup. 'Does it worry you, Stan?' she said quickly.

'You mean about Julie's past?'

'Yes.'

Stanley looped his finger through the handle of the cup and moved it around on the desk top. His forehead creased into deep lines as he answered. 'There are nights when I lay in the dark and can't get to sleep. I try not to dwell on it but I can't help it. I see those men, buying her body, and I break out in a cold sweat. I find it hard to take sometimes. The problem is, I think so much of her, I can't bear to think of her with anyone else.'

'Listen, Stanley Nathan,' Florrie began, 'I've been around myself. When I first met John I was not exactly altar-pure. He knew it, and he wouldn't let me forget it. There would always be remarks and jibes. He never, ever talked about it openly. I think he tried to bury the memory of it, and his way was with the bottle. There was this fellow that he knew about, and the only time my John would mention him was when the drink was saying it for him. We never tried to sort out the problem, and I suppose I was as much to blame as he was. Anyway, the drinking got worse, and now there's only the pub that keeps us together. We've only got a business relationship now. What I'm trying to say is, don't make the same mistakes. Forget the past, it doesn't matter. She's yours now, and when you get married make sure you're happy. I'm going on a bit, but I hate to think what might happen if you don't accept the past, then cast it out. Think of the two of you. The way things are now, we've all got to grab at happiness. Just you make sure that you don't miss the opportunity.'

As Florrie left the shop, Stanley kissed her lightly on the cheek. 'I thank you for being concerned, and don't worry. I'll sort my problem out, and we'll be okay, Florrie.'

'Course you will, Stan. See you soon.'

'See you soon,' he repeated as he watched the landlady cross the road.

As she reached the other side, she turned and gave him a wave before walking along to the Eagle. She felt better for the chat with Stanley, although the feeling of something bad still persisted inside her. She was aware of her serious face, and she paused at the door of the pub to compose herself. It would not do for the landlady of a pub to be miserable. She looked up at the evening sky. The setting sun stained the clouds red. Streaks of a 'shepherd's delight' would soon pale, and the full moon would rise high into the heavens. A bomber's moon they called it.

The pub was filling up, and Florrie went behind the bar. John Braden gave her a quizzical stare and got on with serving a customer. Wheezy was leaning on the counter. Hoppy stood beside him.

'Where's Sammy?' Florrie asked.

'Gorn back early,' replied Wheezy.

'I fink 'e prefers the sergeant major to us,' said Hoppy, grinning at his friend.

'I hear the hatter's shop got broken into last night,' Florrie said.

'Yeah. Whoever done it dumped the stuff down the shelter,' answered Hoppy, a look of angelic innocence sweeping over his countenance.

'The police were asking questions today, although it was awkward, what with that bomb in the Carters' backyard. They'll be back tomorrow though,' Florrie predicted.

'Well I don't know who nicked them 'ats, but it livened up the shelter. Silly Bobbie 'ad a top 'at on. Dancin' wiv ole Lizzie Brown 'e was. Looked a proper card,' said Hoppy.

'Looked like a pox-doctor's clerk, if yer ask me,' added Wheezy.

An old man who was leaning against the bar straightened up and faced Wheezy. 'I tell yer wot. 'E may not 'ave all 'is marbles, but 'e 'ad that shelter in stitches. While they was all laughin' at 'im they was fergettin' the bloody bombs, son.'

Hoppy nodded. 'Bobbie Wilkins is okay by us, Dad. You gotta agree though, 'e did look eighteen-carat.'

The old man returned to his pipe and ale, and Wheezy went over to the dartboard. Hoppy leaned dejectedly against the counter. His crippled foot was aching, and he placed it on the foot rail. Hoppy watched Florrie's rear as she walked along to talk to John. He picked up his glass and drained the contents. There were better things to do than just standing here drinking, he thought. Florrie figured in those things. He ogled the woman as she came back along the bar. Her large bosom bounced as she walked and Hoppy sighed to himself. He missed Sammy, and now Wheezy was playing darts. He looked around the bar. He saw Albert Conlin walk in, and noticed Florrie's eyes light up. The woman leaned on the counter, her bust spread on the oaken wood. The big man grinned sheepishly as Florrie jested with him.

'Hello, Al. Come in just to see me, have you?'

'I 'ad ter get out o' the 'ouse. Nell's sittin' there snorin' an' there's nuffink werf while on the wireless,' Albert complained.

'So you've decided to take me dancing or something, have you?' Florrie joked.

Albert Conlin fumbled for some coins. 'Give us a pint o' usual, Florrie.'

The landlady pulled on the pump handle and filled a pint glass to overflowing. 'A pint o' best for the best,' she said, a gleam in her eye.

Wheezy Morris was waiting for his turn to throw the darts. He ambled over to Hoppy. 'See Florrie? She really goes a bundle on 'im, don't she?'

Hoppy nodded, and Wheezy went on, 'The man's too dopey ter see it. Wish it was me. I'd give 'er wot for.'

Hoppy looked at his friend in disgust. 'She'd smuvver yer wiv 'em,' he cracked, nodding at the woman.

'Wot a way ter go,' answered Wheezy, lighting a Woodbine.

Time was weighing heavily on Hoppy and he felt restless. He looked around the little bar and saw the Harpers' old lodger sitting alone by the door. The man was puffing away at his pipe, a near-empty glass in front of him. Wheezy had gone over to take his turn at the dartboard and Hoppy felt the need to talk to someone. He ordered two pints of ale and carried them over to the table. Skipper looked up and stared at the beer.

'There we are, Pop, 'ave a drink on me,' Hoppy said.

'Cheers, lad. I was just about ter get meself one.'

'All right if I sit 'ere?' asked the cripple.

'Sit yerself down, son. I expect yer miss Sammy, don't yer?'

'I tell yer, Skip, if they'd 'ave me I'd be orf termorrer.'

'Fink yerself lucky, lad,' said the old seaman, tapping his pipe on the table leg. 'There's gonna be a lot o' fightin' ter be done afore this war's over. A lot o' young blood's gonna be spilt. Don't be too anxious ter put yerself in the way of a bullet.'

'Yeah, I s'pose yer right, but d'yer know I really envied Sammy when 'e left. At least 'e ain't sittin' around 'ere waitin' fer a bomb ter fall on the Street.'

'Well I'll tell yer wot,' Skipper began. 'Sammy's okay fer the present, but mark my words, there's gonna come a time soon when young Sammy's gonna be wishin' 'e was in your shoes. A PBI is the worstest job in the army.'

'PBI?'

'Poor bloody infantryman, that's wot,' Skipper went on. 'Up the sharp end every time, cor blimey.'

Hoppy took a sip from his glass. 'It ain't much fun sittin' in that bloody shelter every night, waitin' ter see if one o' them bombs is gonna find yer. Fair gives me the creeps it does.'

Skipper looked at his pipe and decided that it needed re-lighting. He struck a match and puffed hard on his brown-stained clay briar.

Hoppy watched him drawing on the pipe, and noticed how gnarled the seaman's hands were.

'Yer don't fink you're the only one who's scared o' the

bombin', do yer? I've lived a few years, an' I want ter go on fer a mite longer yet.' Skipper said, through a cloud of tobacco smoke. 'I tell yer, I used ter 'ave a sayin' when I was a young stripplin'. I used ter say that I'd like ter live till I was ninety, an' die in a brothel, on the job. Long as I didn't kick the bucket in the waitin' room I'd be 'appy. I'd still like ter reach ninety, though I don't worry too much about the brothel. Wot I do fink about is goin' under a pile o' rubble.'

Hoppy laughed. 'I reckon you could still make them dollies know wot's wot.'

Skipper burst into a fit of coughing. When he had regained his breath, he looked at his pipe. 'Bloody fing wants a good pipe-cleaner, it tastes like the inside of a tram driver's glove,' he moaned.

Hoppy finished his drink. 'D'yer fink the bastards'll be back ternight?' he asked.

'Gawd knows. I 'ope not. I ain't 'ad a good night's sleep fer a week,' the seaman complained.

'It's the waitin',' said Hoppy. 'Just sittin' without bein' able ter do anyfing. That's wot I can't stand.'

'We're all in the same boat, son. All we can do is just sit there, bein' scared. I remember bein' scared at sea, but it wasn't as bad as now. I was scared when the wind got up, an' the waves almost swamped the ship. I was scared when I 'ad me first woman, but nuffink beats this.'

Hoppy grinned. 'I bet that was a long time ago, Skip?'

'Wot's that?'

'Yer first woman.'

'Blimey, it must be donkey's years ago,' agreed the seaman. 'Big ole Bertha up in the Pool.'

'Wot's the "Pool"?' asked Hoppy.

'Liverpool. That's wot us seafarers call it. Got some big uns up there. Never ferget it. Me first trip it was. Down ter Aussie

239

we went. Anyway, back I comes, wiv money in me pockets an' feeling like a dog wiv two dicks an' the waves almost swamped the ship. I was scared lookin' around. Didn't 'ave ter look far, I can tell yer. I spots 'er in the pub. Built like a brick carsey she was, an' enough paint on 'er face ter cover all the rust on our ship. It didn't stop me buyin' 'er a drink. Never ferget it. Stout she wanted, an' a pint at that. I've never see'd a tart drink like it. Gulped the stout down like soap suds down a drain-'ole. Well anyway, she takes a shine ter me, an' orf we goes to 'er 'ouse. She jumps inter bed, an' she's shoutin' fer me ter 'urry up. I was wearin' those 'igh buttoned boots at the time. I 'ad a bleedin' knot in one of 'em, an' there's 'er screamin' fer me ter get a move on. In the finish, I gets on the bed wiv one boot left on.'

'Cor, I bet that was uncomf'table?' remarked Hoppy. 'Fancy sleepin' all night wiv one boot on.'

Skipper gave the cripple a disdainful look. 'All night! Blimey, son. Under ten minutes an' I was back out on the cobbles. 'Arf a crown it cost me. Wouldn't even let me give 'er a kiss. Said it'd spoil 'er make-up. Bloody make-up! Anyfing yer done ter that face would 'ave been an improvement. She 'ad a dial like Big Ben.'

Hoppy laughed and for a few minutes forgot the war, his aching foot, and the fact that very soon the air-raid siren would most certainly scream out again.

Distressed by the nightly blitz, the Conner Street folk were coming together. Lizzie Brown spoke to Nan Roberts in the market one day, the first time the two women had done so for years. 'Cheap-Jack' sold Mrs Jenkins an article even though she was a penny short in her purse. Someone had even seen the old hawker in Tower Road attempt a smile. It was a time to come together in the fact of adversity, and the folk of Conner Street did it in their own special way.

Chapter Nineteen

Nightly, and without pause, the bombing blitz went on. During the hours of darkness the folk of Conner Street became shelter-dwellers. They sat cramped and miserable, young ones asleep in their parents' arms and older children leaning exhausted against their mothers' bodies. They spent the terrible nights fitfully sleeping, or crying silently. The menfolk stood outside under the concrete canopy, taking turns to sit on the two benches that spread end to end between the two caverns. It was exhausting for everyone, and to add to the misery children in particular began to suffer from skin eruptions. Boils and sores started to appear. Scabies spread from child to child, and head lice were discovered on the cleanest of children.

It was into the second week of the blitz and, miraculously, not another bomb had fallen on to the Street. Spencer Street was not so lucky. They had a second bomb that knocked down a row of houses and made the whole Street homeless. The folk of Conner Street heard about the two families that were killed and felt helpless with rage. Spencer Street was only two turnings away, and it was reasoned that the bombs were getting nearer. Conner Street was getting desperate and, although the danger was being driven home to them, some families decided they could take no more. They spurned the safety of the shelter and stayed in their frail homes. For those who continued to go to the shelter nightly, something had to be done. Some of the men brought back doors from the bombed houses and placed them down in the gangways. They propped them on bricks to keep the wood away from the smelly, dark water, and the children slept more peacefully. For the parents the continuing agony of trying to catch a few hours' sleep sitting up on the hard benches remained. Legs and feet started to swell and backs developed cricks that were hard to get rid of. As the bombing got heavier and the nights longer, so the torture became worse. Mrs Jenkins got sick, and Granny Flint developed pneumonia. They put her to bed in her little home, and Lizzie Brown and Emmie Jones took turns to sit with her. The men boarded up the old lady's windows, and piled sandbags outside to catch any blast.

Not far away from the Street was the jam factory. Its owner, a benevolent soul, opened the gates of his factory to give refuge at night. The woeful manager tried to warn him of the consequences, but the paragon insisted. In they came, carrying their bundles of bedclothes, people who were desperate for a night's sleep in safety. They climbed up on the huge piles of sugar that were stacked in the ground floor warehouse. In the warm, stuffy atmosphere, they slept well. The thick walls deadened the sounds from without, and soon the morning came. They told their friends and more came. They climbed even higher on the stack to find a spare space, and trampled over the already established refugees of the night. Arguments broke out as children were trodden on. A fight broke out between two large women, who rolled over and over to the bottom of the pile. It was getting impossible to control the situation, and more people came.

The authorities learned of the jam factory and its teeming sleep-seekers and they spoke to the owner. The following night the people were turned away as they arrived. A hastily printed letter told of the dangers in case of fire. Sugar would run like treacle. Panic would mean loss of life. The letter told of the new incendiary bomb that was being used in the blitz. It was a small, silver-coloured tube that ignited on impact and burned with a white hot ferocity. One incendiary device on the factory would be an unmitigated disaster.

The people read the letter and trudged away. The manager rubbed his hands together.

'They've been pissing over the sacks, sir. Actually urinating over the sugar, sir.'

The owner of the jam factory sighed deeply and walked away. That night the warehouse was quiet, scoured of ragged foundlings and left to the rodents, and other creatures of the night.

There was a strange fatalism developing amongst the dockland folk. The news of someone's death by bombing did not raise their emotions so greatly now. Death in some violent form was expected and accepted. The living shook their heads and went about their day. The night was spent clinging to the thin strand of life, waiting and hoping. The grace between walking out of the shelter or a fragile home next morning and being blown into eternity during the night lingered like a candle flame, flickering and spluttering in a draught, burning brightly, then suddenly extinguished. Such was acceptance of the terrible times; exhaustion and physical weakness produced the only respite, the overriding need to sleep. Folk began to sleep through the most violent of nights. They began to lose their comprehension of events. The thought of a warm bed, and being enveloped in soft, clean white sheets, was paramount. Brutal death, even when witnessed, was no more such an awesome thing.

'Johnnie, run up the top an' get yer Granny a pinch o' snuff.' Johnnie grasped the sixpence. 'Up Catchpoles?'

'Yes,' replied his mother, 'and hurry up, Granny don't feel very well.'

The little lad skipped up the street, dodging the broken glass on the pavement and the pieces of window frame that littered the place. He danced around a pile of sandbags and turned the corner. 'Catchpoles' was not open. Johnnie, being rather young, did not know anywhere else he could buy snuff. He did not recall having seen the brass scales hanging from brass chains, and the little weights that were put into one of the scale pans. He could not recall having seen those large, brown earthenware jars where snuff was kept. Only 'Catchpoles' had those things. It must be the only shop in the whole of London that sold snuff, he concluded.

'No good you standin' there, son. 'E's not open,' a voice said.

Johnnie stepped from the doorway, and stopped twisting the sixpence around in his palm. He looked up at the tall man, a question written across his jam-streaked face.

'Why, mister?' he asked with all the innocence of youth.

''E's gorn. Killed 'e was, last night,' replied the tall man.

'Cor,' was all the boy could say.

The man nodded at a pile of red-dotted sand on the pavement nearby, and walked off. The boy twisted the sixpence around in his palm again, and walked away from the doorway. As he passed the sand, Johnnie kicked it curiously. A cold, dead eye, attached to red strands, stared up at him, and the boy ran all the way home.

During the early days of the blitz, Julie Brett found herself faced with a heartrending decision; whether or not to meet Alan Denman. She had not confided in Stanley about the man's reappearance. She did not wish to hurt him by reminding the man of her past. Stanley had accepted her without question and she wanted it to stay that way. Julie knew in her heart that if she did not keep the appointment, she would never know for sure if she would have been able to go through with their marriage had she met Alan again. This way, by keeping the appointment, she would know what her feelings were once she had spoken to him. She wanted to be sure in her mind, to know that it was possible to turn away, and to finally bury the past once and for all.

It was Wednesday evening, and a fresh wind was rising. A few leaves dropped from the grimy plane tree near the tram stop as Julie waited. She pulled the collar of her coat up against the wind and sorted some copper coins from the depths of her handbag. The tram rattled up and stopped. As Julie climbed aboard, two young people ran up and jumped on just as the tram accelerated away from the stop. The young couple sat on the seat in front of her. The man, dressed in a naval uniform, sat staring ahead. The girl held his arm tightly, her head resting on his shoulder. They did not speak, simply sharing the intimacy of the moment. Julie sighed and held out the fare. The grey-haired conductor flipped out a ticket and punched it on his tin ticket machine. The couple were wrapped up in each other, not noticing the collector. As the man passed back along the aisle he winked at Julie, and glanced back at the lovers.

Presently the church spire came into view and Julie got off the tram. She walked along by the little shops and turned into a narrow street. At the end of the turning Julie saw the sign 'The Boatman' swinging in the wind. She entered and looked around in the smoke-laden air. The ceiling beams were low and the bar smelled of stale beer. The girl felt uneasy at entering the pub alone. A few faces stared at her, then resumed their wooden expressions. She could now see Alan Denman. He stood some way down the bar, his fist clenched and resting on the counter. His hair looked even greyer than she'd remembered. He did not look her way until she had almost reached him. When he turned, Julie saw the pale blue eyes, and the thin, clipped moustache. He looked older; less ruddy, but more lined.

'I knew you would come,' he said, a ghost of a grin on his face.

Julie gave him a cold smile. The man was so sure of himself. In that department he hadn't changed one bit, she thought. He still stood in the same relaxed manner, still conducted himself with an air of confidence. Somehow though, he was different. Julie could not fully understand it, but there was something that puzzled her. Perhaps it was the passing years. The picture of him, his manner, never completely shut out from her mind, was a picture of the past.

'What can I get you?' he asked.

'I'll have a port and lemon,' the girl replied.

He placed the order, and while the barman poured the drinks, Alan Denman looked hard at Julie. 'You've hardly changed. In fact, you look even better than I remember you,' he said.

The drinks were paid for and Alan motioned Julie to a vacant table. 'It's better here,' he remarked.

'How are you?' Julie asked, fishing for words.

'Fine, fine. You know I just knew you would come,' Alan Denman repeated.

'Well I almost didn't,' Julie said, annoyed at his manner. She was thinking of when she had lied to Stanley not more than two hours ago. Her excuse of a severe headache, and the man's cheery wave as he walked down the Street made her cringe inside. God, she thought, he is so trusting, so innocent. Instead of being in her man's company, she was here, rekindling the past. Alan had spoken to her but the words passed unheard. She was aware that he had asked her a question.

'I'm sorry,' she said quickly, noticing Alan's eyes staring at her, waiting for an answer.

'I said, is the man. I saw you with on Sunday your steady?'

'We're going to be married. We've set a date for November,' Julie answered.

Alan toyed with the half-empty glass in front of him. His lips parted slightly in a faint grin. 'Shopkeeper, isn't he?'

'That's right,' said Julie quickly, her eyes on his face.

'Do you love him?' Alan Denman asked, taking the empty glasses to the bar before Julie could answer.

Julie watched his self-assured saunter to the counter, and she gritted her teeth. She was aware of her face getting hot and she opened her handbag and took out a small mirror. She could see the two red blotches on her cheeks. By the time Alan Denman returned to the table, Julie had composed herself somewhat.

The man sat down and looked at her, his eyebrows raised as if begging the answer to his earlier question.

'I'm very fond of him,' Julie said.

'I asked you if you loved him.'

'Yes,' answered Julie.

'You don't sound too convincing,' replied Alan.

The red blotches were appearing again. Julie looked down at the drink in the middle of the table.

Alan Denman passed it towards her. He could see that the girl was uneasy.

'Are you sure you love him?'

Their eyes met. 'I love him,' repeated Julie. 'Though not in the way I was with you. It's a quieter, more settled thing. With you I felt on edge half of the time. Up in the air one minute, then down in the depths the next. With Stanley it's even, no upsets. We just feel good together.'

Alan Denman smirked. 'I bet you sometimes wish it was a little more exciting, Julie, eh?'

The girl looked at him and noticed his smirk. She caught her breath. It was wrong for her to have come. He was acting like a hunter, with all his traps set, and his prey coming head on. Well it wouldn't work. She would spring the trap, from the outside.

'Did you know about the baby?' she asked suddenly.

The man winced noticeably, his eyes dropping down away from her gaze.

'Yes, I heard,' he said.

'Did you hear about me after that?' Julie asked quietly.

'No. I tried to contact you, but I heard that you went to live with your sister. In fact I pestered Florrie Braden, but she insisted she didn't know your address.'

Julie caught his eye and held his gaze. She wanted to see his reaction when he heard the next bit.

'I was a prostitute.'

'What!?'

'I went on the game. The streets.'

'You mean you . . .'

'That's right. I went to bed with men. For money.'

'God Almighty, Julie. D'you mean you was like a common tart?'

'No like about it, Alan. I was a common tart. Paint and powder, high heels, black stockings. Believe me, I was as much a tart as you'll ever see. Are you shocked?'

'I don't believe it. You! No, you're just saying that.'

Julie watched Alan closely. Gone was the suave, cocky manner. In its place was a look of disbelief. The man's eyes were popping and his mouth hung open. Julie almost felt sorry for him.

'No, it's not true. It can't be true! You wouldn't do it. You couldn't,' he spluttered.

'I could, and I did,' replied the girl, revelling in his

discomfort. The roles were now reversed. The man was on the defensive.

'I took their money and they took me. It was simple. At least they all paid for the pleasure. You used me, and when I needed you most you cut me off, running back to your wife with your tail dragging the floor. You know, I feel sorry for your wife right now, 'cos if I'd have agreed, you'd be making plans right now, wouldn't you?'

'Julie,' he protested, but Julie wasn't finished.

'You told me about your wife in the letter. Was it true? Are you sleeping apart?'

'I already told you, Julie. My wife is away with the children.'

'I mean did you sleep apart before she went?'

'Yes, I swear.'

'Then knowing you, there must have been other women.'

'I've not been celibate. But they don't mean anything, none of them. You're different. I need you, Julie. I make no secret of the fact. Come and stay with me. The flat is nice, you'll be happy there, I promise.'

Julie shook her head, then reached for her handbag from the chair beside her. 'I must be off. I knew it was foolish to come, but now I can be happy. No wondering, no troubled thoughts about whether or not I could turn my back on you and walk away.'

'Julie, you must give it time. Think about it for a while. You'll come to realise. You couldn't be happy for the rest of your life being the partner of a shopkeeper, you'd go insane with boredom.'

Julie smiled and got up. She looked down at him, her eyes glinting. 'You know you're so different, Alan. You're poles apart, the two of you. There was a time when I'd have gone to the ends of the earth with you. But I've changed. We've all changed, and there's a war on. None of us know how much more time we've got. I'm going to leave now, and I'm going to get back to Stanley as quick as I can. I'm going to tell him of this meeting, and if he still wants me, I'll gladly marry him tomorrow. As for you, I wish you well, Alan, and I hope you will get back with your wife.'

Julie walked quickly to the door of the Boatman, her heels, clicking on the wooden floor. Alan Denman watched her go and sighed.

She did not turn, but walked out into the dusk. Her heart beat fast as she made her way to the tram stop. Birds were singing in the trees which lined the pavement. Dark clouds gathered and blotted out the early stars. Few people were about, and those who were on the thoroughfare did not linger. They all seemed to be making for somewhere, using the limited amount of time for their calls, then hurrying to their own places which offered them safety. For some it was the deep shelter of the Underground: the train-free stations that had become a nocturnal home. For others, it was the surface shelter, or the 'Anderson' shelter, a corrugated affair sunk in the little town gardens. For many, their own home provided them with frail safety, and they refused to leave for a more substantial haven.

Stanley Nathan shut up his shop that evening and walked across to the 'Eagle'. It was usually his night out with Julie, but tonight he was at a loose end. He didn't feel like going straight home. Instead, he walked into the bar, and bumped into Lizzie Brown who was coming out.

The old woman carried a jug of beer. ''Ello, Stan. No Julie ternight?'

'She's not feeling too good, Liz. I'm having a quick 'un then I'm off home.'

Lizzie Brown nodded and walked off along Conner Street,

her stockingless feet encased in huge, fluffy slippers. She went a short way, then turned to make sure that Stanley really did go into the Eagle. It was Lizzie Brown's way. She took salt with everything, including anything she was told.

Stanley really did go into the pub. He ordered a pint of ale, then sat with his back to the partition that divided the bar from the off-sales. The night was cool, with a hint of a storm. Dark clouds were gathering over dockland, and the darkness was deepening. The fears of another blitz still lurked. Although the pub folk laughed and joked as usual, their laughter was becoming more forced lately, and the jokes were old hat. Conversation was strained and staccato; now and then men's eyes darted up to the bar clock. Perhaps the threatening storm would come, perhaps it would pour all night, they thought, and the bombers would stay grounded; better still, it might even get foggy. Now that would really be something; clean sheets, and a good night's sleep. Even during a storm the bombs could fall, but a pea-souper would be really nice.

Stanley was deliberating. He did not want to stay too long. The trains to suburbia were erratic, with long hold-ups and diversions. Lots of the track had been targeted by the German Air Force. Stanley did not relish the idea of sitting in a stationary train if the raids started. He would have one more drink, then go home.

'Give us a tot o' whisky, Florrie, 'e's not well at all!' Mrs Morgan said.

'There we are, luv. I hope he's better tomorrow.'

'Takes 'im days ter pull round a bit. Dicky 'eart the 'orspital told 'im. 'E's never been right since we lorst our lad.'

'Never mind, luv. He'll be okay. Mind how you go.'

'Yeah, I've gotta be careful meself. Nearly went down a "sender" crossin' the Street. It's me bloody knees. Keep givin' way they do.'

'You shouldn't have come out. Julie wouldn't have minded popping over for you.'

'I would 'ave asked 'er, but she 'ad ter go out. I do 'ope she gets back afore it gets blackout.'

'Night, Mrs Morgan.'

'Night, Florrie.'

Stanley had allowed the conversation to drift over him, until Julie's name was mentioned. He felt the vibration as Mrs Morgan closed the off-sales door behind her, and he took his back off the partition. He sat up straight. Julie had not wanted to be taken out that evening, and now she was out somewhere. It was strange, he thought. Had the man in the pub contacted her? Perhaps she was going to meet him. What did it mean? Stanley did not order the other drink. Instead, he walked out into the dusk, his mind turning over the possibilities. He felt ashamed of the thoughts that raced through his head; he walked on, not realising the direction he was taking. He ignored the few cheery 'hellos', lost in suspicion.

The huge, imposing mass of Tower Bridge loomed up in front of him, the white stonework standing out against the blue-black clouds. The lone, tall figure of a City policeman stood motionless on the centre span of the bridge, his hands clasped behind his back. The policeman gave Stanley a quick glance then resumed his downriver gaze, motionless except for his thumbs that twirled over each other behind his back.

Stanley walked on to the bridge and stopped to look down at the black, cold water. A snub-nosed little tug chugged through the centre of the river, passing between the twin bastions. It tooted twice, a spurt of steam emitting from the whistle on the funnel each time it sounded. The toot was answered by a booming, bass sound from a cargo ship at anchor. A hawser dropped over its side and splashed down into the river. The tug turned in its own length and made for the towline. The cargo ship was no doubt anxious to get out from the Pool on the evening tide, down to the estuary, and obscurity. The tug fussed and snorted, eager to assist, and the ship eased away from the quayside, slowly and deliberately.

Stanley turned back to re-cross the swirling river, his mouth set firm. He walked slowly towards the Tooley Street junction, not able to cast out the terrible thoughts that plagued him. He should have been more firm, more aware of Julie's needs. He should have insisted that she went with him, instead of staying at the Morgans'. He had been wrong to try to bury her past for her. Her need was for him to listen and to understand. His reluctance to talk to her had been his downfall, and now it was too late. He slowed down his pace, cursing his prejudgement of her. God! If only he knew where she was, who she was with, why she should slip out to keep an appointment. He cursed his thoughts again. How easy it was to think the worst. She may have gone out for some air. To do what he was doing right this minute. That was it! She wanted to be alone with her thoughts. To walk in the quiet evening and think.

The tram stopped at the junction and the conductor jumped down. He pulled on the lever and the points clanked into place. As the tram started off, the conductor jumped nimbly aboard. The rattling contraption slowly took the right-hand turn and she saw him; the heavy, sure step, the broad back, and the distinctive gait. Julie jumped up and pulled hard on the bell string. The tram eased up as the driver automatically shut off the power handle.

'Silly little mare,' shouted the conductor, but Julie neither heard nor cared. She ran across the road and turned the corner. Stanley was some way ahead, his long stride taking him away from her. Julie ran faster, and Stanley heard her steps. He turned and saw her, his eyes lighting up and his face splitting in a huge grin. The girl ran to him, her arms outstretched.

Stanley swept her up into his bear-like grasp, her body crushed to him, her face buried in his heaving chest. They embraced, without asking for reasons, not realising the improbability of their paths crossing at that time. They hugged. Julie cried and Stanley grinned, his flushed face resembling a harvest moon.

'Take me home with you, Stanley darling, I need you so much.'

Chapter Twenty

By the end of the second week of nightly, non-stop bombing, the folk of Conner Street were utterly exhausted. The ritualistic ordeal began with the air-raid siren screaming out its warning, drawing the people out of their homes and into the dark caverns of concrete. The people came and sat in the evil-smelling place of refuge, and whispered together beneath a dim electric lamp. They waited for the worst, nervously conditioned by the awful wailing.

It was inevitable that some character would give the siren a more appropriate name, and that name was borrowed from one of the Fletcher sisters. It was Tom Carter who renamed the siren 'Moaning Minnie', and he told his wife that the only difference between the two noises was that Minnie Fletcher made the most. Tom Carter swore that the old spinster kept up the racket longer than the siren, and it would have been a good idea, so he maintained, to have tied Minnie to the top of the police station and let her give the warning.

The Fletcher sisters had both been jilted early in life, or so the story went, and were now quite content to live with their memories and a profusion of stuffed birds and china ornaments. They were happy to clean daily the china and glass domes that covered the birds, or rather Maud was. Minnie was the task mistress, watching out for any speck of dust that the more timid Maud overlooked. Minnie would tut, and give her sister a scathing look, then Maud would go over her cleaning to Minnie's satisfaction. The younger Maud was totally dominated by the elder, and at times harshly treated. Minnie was a stern-faced woman with dark piercing eyes, while Maud had a hooked nose and soft, sleepy eyes. The dreamy Maud was quite content to submit to Minnie's domination and the elder took advantage.

The day started very early for the spinsters, and Maud would begin her tasks by polishing the brass fire-tongs and stand. Then with loving care she would gently wipe and polish the many little china ornaments and glass trinkets. It was then the turn of the stuffed birds to receive the younger sister's attentions. The birds were glued onto wooden perches and housed beneath thin glass domes. The glass covers glistened brilliantly from the stroking of Maud's duster, but Minnie would still tut-tut and remove an imaginary speck of dust that irritated her. Maud merely sighed, and carried on dusting and polishing.

After Maud had prepared the midday meal and they had eaten in their grossly over-adorned parlour, the sisters parted company. Minnie went upstairs, and Maud took her nap in the hard leather-bound chair. Minnie did not sleep. She spent the afternoons at the upstairs window, looking down on the passing folk, and sometimes calling out in her high-pitched voice to a young lad below, 'Come 'ere, boy!' and the lad obeyed.

It was the custom among the lads in Conner Street that on no account was Minnie Fletcher to be ignored. Many times a youngster would half-slide, half-creep past Minnie's window, hoping to avoid having to run errands for the frightening old lady, and sometimes the strategy worked. When the old woman called out however, the lad would pick up the thrown message and run to the shops. It was usual for Minnie to wrap her shopping list around a half-crown, and woe betide the lad who did not bring back the correct change. Minnie would scream out a tirade of abuse at the terrified lad then send him back to the shops. It was something that all the youngsters of Conner Street dreaded, bringing back the wrong change.

Minnie Fletcher knew which lad to select for her errands, and she hovered in the upstairs window like a bird of prey, waiting and watching. She owed her success to her sister Maud, for the dreamy-eyed woman had inadvertantly terrified one of the lads and from then on the sisters had become witches to the more impressionable youngsters. Minnie's bidding was invariably done, and the lads weaved tales around the strange happenings at number 10.

Young Joey Solomon started it off. 'The one wiv the funny nose was talkin' to 'er parrot an' it dropped dead! Honest it did, I see'd it.'

'Cor! Did she put a spell on it?'

'Yeah. Mumbled somefing, an' it plonked down wiv its eyes still all starey.'

'Cor! What did she do then?'

'She didn't bury it like me dad done when our rabbit died. She got glue an' stuck it back on its pole.'

'Cor! I fink she's a witch or somefink.'

Joey nodded. 'My dad said they're both spinsters.'

'Wot's spinsters?'

'Spinsters is worster den witches. Spinsters can fly ter der moon, an' turn people inter frogs an' fings.'

'Cor!' said the little lad, who was even younger than Joey's six years.

Not being conversant with the skills of the taxidermist, and not daring to risk being turned into frogs or worse, the lads did Minnie's bidding.

Joey's impressionable young friend went home and that night he dreamt about terrible spinsters. He awoke screaming out their names and his mother shook her head, mystified.

The lads of Conner Street suffered Minnie's commands, and even bragged about it. If the errands were quickly done, and the change was correct, and if Minnie Fletcher had not needed to scold her sister too much that day, the lad received a silver threepenny bit for his troubles.

'Cor, did Minnie der witch give it yer?'

'Yus, an' I see'd 'Arold.'

'Who's 'e?'

''Arold's 'er parrot. Talks to it she does, and it stares at 'er.'

'Cor.'

The older children often played 'tin-can Tommy' in the Street and if the game happened to be beneath Minnie's window, the participants of the game received the sharp end of Minnie's tongue. The verbal explosion was such that her neighbours winced noticeably from the old spinster's vibrating tonsils. Tom Carter wilted from one verbal exchange with Minnie. It concerned his son Reg, and it all started when Tom found out that his lad had been sent across the Tower Road for errands. The final result was that Tom Carter discovered a new name for the air-raid siren.

It became 'Moaning Minnie'.

It was Saturday night, and two weeks after the first bombing raid. As usual 'Moaning Minnie' wailed, and the shelter quickly filled up.

Ada Dawkins stayed in her bed that night. She had a heavy chill and was running a temperature. Poor Bobbie sat by her bed and refused to budge. He had his box of treasures with him, which he placed on the foot of Ada's bed.

'Bobbie, it's no good you sittin' there. I'll be okay. Now get yerself orf down the shelter.'

'I stop 'ere, Ada. Bobbie look after Ada.'

Bobbie's landlady sighed and shook her head. It was no use arguing with the idiot. Ada could see by the set of his mouth that his mind was made up.

'Well if yer gonna stay, don't sit there starin' at that box. Put the kettle on, we'll 'ave a cuppa,' Ada croaked.

Granny Flint did not go to the shelter either. She was too exhausted to leave her home, and Lizzie Brown sat with her. Jack Davis too remained obstinate and sat nightly in his front parlour, protected from flying glass by the planks of wood nailed to the outside of his windows. The Fletcher sisters said that they would not be seen dead in the shelter, or rather Minnie said. The Morgans, Frank and Mabel, had stopped at home for the past couple of nights. Frank had been feeling ill. Tonight, however, the couple had decided to go to the shelter. The bombing seemed to be getting worse and Mabel was worried. It seemed that even the vibration from the guns in the local park was threatening to bring their little house down around their ears. Mabel packed Frank's medicines and a blanket to put around his shoulders and left early to get a seat in the already cramped and overcrowded shelter.

As the siren wailed, and the guns opened up, the china crockery rattled on Granny Flint's dresser and a spoon tinkled against a medicine bottle.

'Is them bombs I can 'ear?' asked Granny Flint, and Lizzie reassured her. 'Only guns, Granny.'

The barrage continued and the sound of aircraft became louder. The bomb run had started. The drone became a roar as the planes wheeled and turned above. The whistle and clatter of falling bombs and the explosions that shook the small homes in Conner Street were getting nearer. Each bang was louder than the previous, and each explosion shook the homes more severely. Jack Davis cursed the Germans and put his cap on.

Granny Flint was snoring, and Bobbie and Ada looked up at the ceiling, half expecting a bomb to come through the plaster. Flashes lit the Street and something fell through the Carters' roof. A fire started in the bedroom upstairs.

'Quick lads, it's an incendiary! Get the sand!' Bob Bowman shouted.

Men ran from the safety of the shelter. The warden crashed through the Carters' front door, his momentum carrying him halfway up the stairs. Men followed him, each one holding a bag of sand. The bedroom was ablaze, and lying on the bed was a silver tube, burning with a phospheric glow. The smoke was choking the men as they dumped the sand onto the bomb. Joe Harper threw a chair through the window and the bed was thrown out onto the pavement below.

Shrapnel fell, and another incendiary hit the cobbles, bounced along the Street and stopped outside the Flannagans' home. The silver tube did not flare, but white smoke was pouring out from near the fins. Hoppy Dyke did not stop to get a sandbag. He darted across the Street and grabbed the incendiary by the fins. As he was momentarily bent over it, the device exploded in flames. Hoppy screamed in agony as a sheet of white hot fire ran up between his legs melting his flesh and setting his clothes alight. Men close behind him ran up and quickly doused the flames. Hoppy lay in a heap by the Flannagans' door, moaning pitifully, only half-conscious. They strapped his legs together and carried him gently into the Flannagans' passage. Wheezy Morris took off his coat and laid it beneath Hoppy's head. The lower half of the cripple's body was soaked in blood and sand and his club foot was twisted at a grotesque angle. Wheezy went out into the Street and vomited against the wall. Men ran back from the Carters' house and someone sent for Bob Bowman.

'The telephone at the post!' he shouted. 'I'll phone fer an

ambulance.' The warden jumped on his rusty bike and pedalled desperately along the glass-strewn turning. Half a mile along the Tower Road stood the Wardens' post, reinforced with sandbags at the entrance. Inside, two ashen-faced men wearing steel helmets dealt with constant messages. 'I've got another one 'ere, Fred. The bloody picture palace is alight. Two bodies by the door!'

Bob Bowman charged in. 'Quick get an ambulance ter Conner Street! We've got a bad 'un! Poor bastard's 'ad 'is legs burnt off 'im!'

'Christ! They're all out, Bob. Even got the emergency cars runnin' ragged.'

'Well, get someone there quick as yer can, or 'e's gonna die!' shouted Conner Street's warden.

Two men stayed with Hoppy, and the rest went back into the shelter entrance. A shell cone bounced along the turning and slithered down to the men's feet. Joe Harper noticed Skipper by the shelter door.

'C'mon, Pop, let's get yer inside, there's not much you can do.'

Skipper protested but Joe gently led him by the arm into the dark, stuffy interior. Rosie saw her husband's blackened face.

'You okay, luv?'

'Fine. Don't worry, we'll be all right. Keep yer eye on Skipper.'

The old seaman was grumbling. 'Treatin' me like a child. I'm as good as any of yer.'

''Ave a rest, Pop. Come out later,' whispered Joe.

The old seaman sat down heavily by the door and Joe returned to his post.

The guns were sounding off and overhead searchlights pencilled the night sky with their white lances. The bomb run was beginning again. A loud clatter echoed along the Street and an oil bomb hit the leather factory. Within seconds the factory was a burning hulk. Chunks of flaring debris dropped down over the wall onto the roofs in Tanners Alley. Fires started along the pretty cottages, and the factory wall fell outwards into the alley. The few inhabitants who were still in their homes managed to clamber over their back gardens and along the waste ground to Kent Road.

The Carters' home next to the factory was set alight once more, and the roof fell in. One of the men ran to get the firemen, and Tom Carter had to be restrained from trying to enter his fiercely burning house.

'Gawd Almighty! All we've ever 'ad is in there, Joe.'

The signalman had his big arms wrapped around the sobbing docker. 'It's not true, son. Everyfink yer got that really matters is in the shelter. Yer wife an' kids. That's all that matters right now.'

Tom Carter relaxed and Joe Harper allowed the man to break away from his grasp.

A battered car pulled up at the Flannagans' house and two men quickly untied a stretcher from the roof of the makeshift ambulance. Hoppy was carried out and gently placed onto the car. He had ceased moaning, and now lay very still. As the ambulance car pulled out of the turning, an explosion ripped out some shop-fronts along the Tower Road. The car rocked to one side, swerved around a fallen lamppost and continued on its way.

High above dockland, a parachute billowed out and fell gently earthwards. On the end of the silk cords hung a wicked-looking object. The parachute almost cleared the Street, then sailed back. Down it fell, directly above the shelter. The intense heat from the burning leather factory caused the chute to rise up and drift. Once clear of the upward current of air it started to fall again. Directly below was the row of little houses that stretched from the shelter to the Kent Road. The drifting landmine went through the Morgans' roof exploding instantly. The row of houses collapsed and the Morgans' clock stopped at half-past midnight.

As the landmine fell to earth the folk in the shelter were trying to get some sleep. One little child whispered to its mother, 'Mum, can I go 'ome?'

'You are 'ome, luv, go back ter sleep.'

On another bench sat the Solomon boys with their mother. Joey leaned his head against his mother's arm and dozed fitfully. The rest of the Solomon family stared ahead. Rachel Solomon was a proud woman. Her shoulders were square and upright. Her raven coloured hair was pulled across her head, plaited in a thick rope that came down to the middle of her back. Bernard Solomon her husband worked at the fire station as a controller. That night, as the counters and tiny marker flags closed in around Conner Street, he worried more than ever. A messenger pedalled in, and a new counter was placed directly on Conner Street. Bernard Solomon turned deathly white and answered the phone for the umpteenth time.

As the bomb exploded the shelter seemed to lift up. Dust fell from the roof and the lights went out. There was no warning. No clatter or scream from the falling bomb. The explosion violently surprised everyone. People stood up in panic and trampled over some of the younger children sleeping on makeshift beds between the rows of benches. Men were knocked off their feet, and in a tremendous swirl the blast tore off the shelter doors, sucking them out into the Street. A huge chunk of concrete fell over the entrance, bringing down a pile of earth with it. The shelter entrance was sealed. A smell of gas drifted across to the men who were picking themselves up. Water from a ruptured main poured along the Street. The water seemed to absorb the gas vapour, and it started to run down the sloping entrance to where the pile of rubble lay.

'Quick! Gi' us an 'and!' Joe cried, grabbing a shattered bench.

The men levered away at the concrete.

'It's no good, we'll 'ave ter get some of the dirt away!' the warden shouted out.

Wheezy Morris clambered up to the top of the pile, his slight frame squeezing into the gap near the roof. Working like a scratching dog, he gradually made some space. Another figure ran down to help the men. He was dressed in a dust-covered black suit and wore a steel helmet. A white collar stood out against the flames and flashes. Reverend Leslie Weston did not have time to pray to his chief as he battled away with the men.

At last, the concrete slab was prised away and cool air rushed into the shelter. Someone inside had found the emergency oil lamp and lit it. Reverend Weston poked his head and shoulders into the hole.

'It's all right, folks. You are safe. Shall we all offer up a short prayer?'

'Cor blimey!' exclaimed Mrs Jenkins. 'Wot d'jer fink we've all bin doin' all night!'

With the oil lamp held high the Conner Street folk bowed their heads.

'Holy Father, we thank you for our deliverance . . . ' began the reverend.

The light from the oil lamp shone down on a still figure near the door. Rosie Harper's hand went quickly to her mouth. She eased herself towards the figure. A small blue mark had appeared on Skipper's temple. His clay pipe, held between his stiff fingers was pointed towards the floor.

'From the valley of the shadow of . . .'

The prayer was halted by Rosie's scream.

'Skipper! Talk to me, Skipper!' screamed Rosie, pulling on the old seaman's shoulders. Skipper's body toppled over and fell down between the benches.

Emmie Jones and Bridie rushed to comfort the sobbing woman, and the reverend squeezed through the small gap. Outside it had become quiet. The bombers had left and the guns were silenced. The white-collared man knelt down and administered the last rites to Skipper, his mumbled words resonating around the cavern.

The hush was broken only by a tiny voice that said, 'Mummy, why is that man asleep?'

The mother's tears dripped down on the fair hair of her child.

''Cos 'e's tired, darlin'. 'E's very tired.'

At number 4, Ada Dawkins was twisting and turning in her bed. Bobbie's head was drooping, and at each gun report he jerked back. The explosion brought most of the ceiling crashing down on to Ada's bed. The window frame fell in, showering broken glass everywhere. Both Ada and Bobbie were cut about the hands and face. Bobbie was whimpering at the foot of the bed, his cut hands still holding on tightly to his box of treasures.

A voice called out, 'You all right up there?' The tread of heavy feet sounded on the stairs and big Albert Conlin barged in.

'Gawd, Ada! The bleedin' Street's a right mess. Yer better get dressed, there's big cracks along yer wall, the bloody lot might cave in any minute.'

Ada pointed to the washstand. 'Give us that towel, Albert. Pour some cold water on it.'

Disregarding her own cuts, Ada bathed Bobbie's face. The cuts were not deep, but the blood ran down in lines along the idiot's white features.

''Elp 'im down the stairs, Al. I'll be down in a few minutes.'

Albert Conlin stepped back into the Street, the idiot by his side. The smell of cordite hung in the air, and high in the heavens cold stars twinkled down. Albert could feel Bobbie's arm shaking as he gently steered him towards the shelter.

Bob Bowman had organised the men into groups and they were sent to check on the rest of the Conner Street folk who were not in the shelter. Men came running up to Albert Conlin. 'Are they all right?'

'Few cuts. Nuffink serious. This poor bleeder's in a state o' shock,' he replied.

Jack Davis was okay, but old Granny Flint was in a bad way. Lizzie Brown was trying to comfort her. Granny was unhurt but the blast had smashed the windows and broken almost everything in the old lady's home. The shock of it all had caused her to go into a fit. Her lips were blue and she shook uncontrollably. One of the men ran to try to get the doctor in Kent Road. Doctor Mason usually got very drunk after his evening surgery and was very rarely to be tempted out at night.

Tom Carter and Patrick Flannagan, who had rushed home from his night-shift when he heard of the Conner Street explosion, went to check on the Fletcher spinsters. The front door of number 10 was hanging from one hinge. All the windows were shattered, and the interior was a terrible mess. Thousands of pieces of china and glass ornaments lay broken around the room. The glass domes were also broken into small pieces. Poor Harold had fallen from his perch again and lay in a stiff position on the dresser. The two men called out and faint voices answered them.

'Where are yer?' cried out Patrick.

'Under the stairs,' answered Minnie in a strangely quiet voice.

'C'mon out, it's all right,' said Tom Carter.

The two old spinsters appeared from beneath the stairs, their clothes covered in dust. Maud was sobbing, but Minnie had a stern look. 'If them ornaments are damaged I'll . . .' she started, but Patrick interrupted.

'Never mind the bloody ornaments as long as you've been spared, ladies.'

The two women suffered the destruction with differing reactions. Maud cried bitterly; her lifetime's work of cleaning and polishing the pieces of china and glass had ended on that Saturday night. Minnie, on the other hand, stared stone-faced.

'Shut yer snivellin', Maud. Don't let them see yer cryin'.'

Maud caught sight of the stuffed parrot lying on the dresser. 'Oh Harold, poor Harold,' she sobbed, clutching the bird to her.

'Stop it, Maud, stop it this minute,' shouted Minnie, giving Patrick a despairing glance.

'C'mon, luv, let's get yer down the shelter. It ain't safe ter stay 'ere.'

Maud shook off Patrick's attempts to coax her from her shattered home. 'Poor Harold,' she cried.

'Well bring the bloody parrot with yer,' shouted Patrick.

The fire at the leather factory had been brought under control. The flames were still licking up from the ruins, and everywhere the Street was littered with broken glass and rubble. Fire hoses ran along the turning, but the exhausted firemen were taking a breather. The night sky was red with fires, and the dust pall over Conner Street glowed with a pink tinge.

The men watched the approaching figures with sad eyes. They walked slowly, with Patrick Flannagan holding the sobbing Maud Fletcher's arm. Maud held the dust-covered parrot like a child, close to her body. Minnie scorned the assistance of Tom Carter. She walked proud and upright. Behind them came Bobbie, a pathetic figure, his face still blood-stained. Big Albert Conlin walked beside him, talking to him in a quiet voice. Jack Davis had been persuaded to leave his damaged home and was already at the shelter gates, talking to the men.

'The bastards 'ave finally done it. They've got our Street,' he said in a choked voice. 'More'n forty years I've lived 'ere. Brought me kids up 'ere an' lost the ole lady while I lived 'ere. Gawd Almighty, the bastards ain't gonna get away wiv this. You wait. You'll see. We'll give 'em back double, mark my words.'

Someone handed Jack Davis a small, flat metal flask. He put it up to his lips and took a swig. The men had started to gather round at the shelter gates. It had gone very quiet. Footsteps could be heard running in the Tower Road end of the turning. The runner appeared from around the corner and stopped breathless at the shelter gates. Two haunted looking eyes stared out from a blackened face. He pointed to the bend of the Street.

'They got the Eagle!'

Around the elbow of Conner Street, and up on the corner, another bomb had fallen during the height of the raid. It had narrowly missed the Eagle but hit a gas main. The explosion had brought down the little pub and below, down in the cellar, two bodies lay side by side. The pathetic heap of rubble still exuded whiffs of smoke, and as the men from the Street reached the place of the tragedy, they saw a strange sight. From the heap of stones and timbers a marker stuck out of the ruins. It was the wooden pub-sign.

Bob Bowman pulled some of the eager volunteers back, saying, 'If they're still alive, too many pairs of feet treading over the top of 'em won't 'elp much. Just stand by, we'll call yer if need be.'

The warden, Joe Harper and Patrick Flannagan started to remove some large timbers. Bob Bowman beckoned to Harry

Smith and Arthur Jones to help with the smoking joists. Gently they eased away the timber and some of the larger stones and bricks. The progress was slow and hard. The rest of the men stood silent and white faced. In the middle of the pile of rubble Arthur Jones was reaching for a chunk of stone when a disconnected timber joist fell on his hand. 'Christ! Get it orf!' shouted the docker.

The men who waited rushed to help. They heaved on the timber, and Arthur was finally freed. He sat down, ashen-faced, clutching his crushed hand. Someone produced a bottle of iodine and bandages. Arthur Jones nearly passed out as the contents of the bottle were poured over his wound. While the first-aider was bandaging Arthur's hand the men made progress. They had removed enough debris for Wheezy Morris to squeeze down into the cellar. He disappeared like a ferret going into a rabbit warren, only to emerge again almost immediately. His shocked face said it all. Bob and Joe hauled him out and Wheezy vomited into the gutter.

'Crushed! Pair of 'em! 'Oldin' 'ands they are!' he spluttered.

Joe Harper sat down heavily on a timber joist. He mopped his forehead with a red handkerchief. 'Bloody shame. First young Dyke, an' poor old Skipper, an' now Florrie an' John. They've done it proper ternight,' he said bitterly. 'Wiped out good people, an' finished orf our Street.'

The survivors of the night's bombing stood around the ruins of the little pub, half-reluctant to leave. Joe Harper stood up and walked away down the Street. He looked up at the cold, white stars and at the eerie reflection of the fires. He saw the broken, shattered turning and he choked back tears. As he turned the corner he could see the pathetic little group of homeless folk who stood by the shelter gates. Anger boiled up within him as he crossed the Street and entered his home.

Chapter Twenty-One

The stars were blanketed by the smoke-laden sky. The first dawn light crept into the heavens, mercifully changing the blood-red night into an orange-coloured day. The all-clear had sounded, yet still the Conner Street folk did not leave the shelter area. Some people were emerging from the stuffy interior, rubbing their eyes in total disbelief. They stared hard through red-rimmed lids at the desolation around them. They stared pityingly at the few dust-caked homeless who sat on makeshift seats at the shelter gates. Empty, ragged cameos of utter despair and complete dejection, the folk from within sorrowed with the rest.

Already a small band of volunteers was arriving. A mobile canteen with steam coming from inside was parked opposite the shelter. Tea was being issued in large mugs, biscuits were being passed around, and a few cheery words from the Salvation Army ladies and WVS workers helped to muffle the shock of the night. Scalding hot mugs were clasped in shaking hands and tears dripped into the steam. Bowed heads reached down to the hot tea, as though their hands could not be trusted to bring up the mug to their lips. The drink helped to steady their jagged nerves and some folk were smiling their thanks. Bobbie Wilkins sat slumped on an upturned dustbin. He was shaking violently and big Albert Conlin stood by his side, his large arm around the idiot's shoulders. Albert's other arm was crooked towards his face, a steaming mug clenched in a massive fist.

The morning was strangely cold, the wind rising sharply. The northerly gusts blew over the glowing embers that once was the leather factory, and warmed as they swirled along the Street. The winds carried the sweet, sickly smell of scorched, charred leather and brick dust. The flurries whipped up dust and rattled at the loosely-hanging doors. It took the remaining pieces of glass from shattered frames and whipped off loose slates from insanely leaning roofs. Smoke curled in the sky and in the Street the growing group of red-eyed people stared. They were witnessing the end of their Street; for some of them the Street that they were born in, set up home in, and had hoped to die in.

The wind dislodged a door from its broken hinge and it clattered on to the pavement. Bobbie jumped in fright but Albert Conlin reassured him, 'It's okay, son, drink your tea.'

Bobbie bent his head and sipped noisily. Ada Dawkins sat by his side, her hair covered in white dust. Next to her sat the Fletcher sisters: Minnie, proud and upright; Maud, head bowed, her hands clasping her coat tightly around her frail body. Occasionally Maud would peer furtively beneath the folds of her wrap and smile sweetly to herself. Harold must be kept warm, she mused, and gathered her coat tightly against her. Minnie gave her sister a sideways glance and pursed her lips. God knows what will happen to her if she's ever left alone, she thought. One thing is certain, that flea-bag of a stuffed parrot will have to go. Better wait though. Let her get over the shock of the bombing. For the moment there was other pressing business to be taken care of. Minnie looked around her and spotted a likely candidate.

'Young man,' she shouted, and the young man jumped. 'Will you help me? I've got some things to gather together.' The virago stormed off, her recruited vassal trailing in her wake.

The Conner Street folk were beginning to overcome the initial terror of the destruction around them. The first shock that numbed their senses and made their blood turn to ice was now quite dull, and the stranger shock of deliverance was refracted into cold fury at the German Air Force and the German race as a whole. Tears of anger welled up in the eyes of the Conner Street folk, and rolled down Ada Dawkins's face.

'The bastards. They've finished our Street. I 'ope the tykes rot in 'ell, an' that whoreson 'Itler dies an 'orrible deaf.'

Bobbie stared at Ada, his eyes reading the anger, but his befuddled brain unable to grasp the reasons for the things that were happening around him. He sat hunched in the cold early morning, his grease-stained cap pulled down around his ears and his old tattered coat buttoned up incorrectly against the wind.

Bob Bowman came up to the group, his dust-covered tunic flapping open. 'All this side of the Street's gone. The roofs are all ready ter cave in. There's not 'ardly a stick o' furniture werf savin'.' He sat down heavily on the kerbside, his feet in the gutter. The events of the night had left him utterly exhausted. He remembered that only last week he had pleaded with his wife Grace to go to the shelter with Brenda instead of their preferred refuge under the stairs. If he had not been so persistent they would both be dead by now. The cold sensation of the closeness of death, in trembling fingers of ice that gripped his vitals, made the warden shudder violently. He held his head in cupped hands and closed his eyes.

Joe Harper saw the tired figure sitting there in the gutter and felt a wave of pity. The warden had taken on the job and had assumed the responsibility for the Street. He had never spared himself since the blitz had started. Each night he had organised the men and regularly patrolled the turning. He had stopped the squabbles in the shelter and made sure that the old folk were looked after. He had hardly slept in the two weeks of non-stop bombing, and the exhaustion was evident.

'You okay, Bob?'

The warden looked up at Joe Harper through red-rimmed eyes. He did not answer but nodded faintly, then resumed his sad looking position.

Rosie Harper had emerged from inside the shelter with Bridie holding her arm. Rosie held a handkerchief to her face and sobbed loudly. Behind Bridie came her brood: Maureen, who carried the baby, and the twins, Sheena and Sally. Patrick junior held the two-year-old Terry's hand and Terry was struggling to get himself free. The Flannagans walked up the shelter path onto the Street, to be met by Patrick.

'It's no good, you can't go in,' the Irishman said quietly.

Bridie looked at him. 'I've got to! There's the children to feed, and the baby's bottle . . .'

'I tell you it's no good. The gas is off, an' the ceiling's all over the floor. I tell you it's not safe.'

Bridie started to cry. 'Holy Mary, Mother of God, what am I to do?'

Patrick held his hands up to the heavens, and one of the volunteer women came over. 'Don't worry, my dear, we can get the bottle made up in the mobile, then we'll get you to the rest centre.'

Bridie sniffed her thanks, and Terry started to cry. Maureen handed the baby to her mother and then comforted her young brother.

'If you stop cryin' Pat'll give you some of 'is marbles, won't you, Pat?'

'Nope.'

'Yes you will,' asserted Maureen, and Patrick junior appealed to his father. Patrick shook a fist at him and the boy reluctantly fished out two coloured marbles. Terry took the gift and tried to put them into his mouth. Maureen sighed the way she'd seen her mother do on such occasions, and slapped his wrist. Terry threw the marbles into the gutter and started crying again. Patrick junior tried to retrieve them from the broken glass and debris, but his sister hauled him away. The twins laughed at Patrick junior, and he kicked out. It looked like the Flannagans were starting a war of their own when, suddenly, Bobbie fell off the dustbin. The tears turned to laughter at the idiot's misfortune and the war was forgotten. Bobbie picked himself up and proceeded to dust his tattered coat, a sheepish grin spreading over his grimy features, and Ada Dawkins shook her head in despair.

The early morning wind was getting up, with the promise of a cold spell in the northerly gusts. A figure appeared in the Kent Road end of the turning, walking briskly towards the shelter, and from the other end of the Street the local policeman, pushing his bicycle around the debris, picked his way to the group of homeless folk. PC Smith stopped by the shelter gates and bent down to remove his cycle-clips. His face was red from his exertions and his eyes were watering.

'We've got ter get 'em all in the centre, Bob. No good 'em 'angin' around 'ere.'

The Street warden had got up from the kerb and was resuming his usual role of Conner Street's guardian. He cast a worried glance over the milling group and started to get the exodus under way. The other newcomer to the group was in conversation with Joe Harper and the Irishman.

'I've roused 'im, bloody ole goat. Pissed as a pudden 'e was. I told 'im, get yerself round ter Granny or I'll send some o' the boys along ter see yer.'

Nan Roberts was listening to the conversation. 'Who's 'e talkin' about?' she asked of Betty Smith.

'Why that there Doctor Mason. Poor old Granny Flint's 'ad a fit. 'E went ter get 'im. Looks like 'e's put the fear o' God inter the drunken ole bastard,' Betty Smith said with venom.

Nan Roberts nodded her agreement. ''E was a good doctor once. Saved my Bert's life 'e did. Ole Doctor Moore was treatin' 'im fer indigestion. Bloody great ulcer 'e 'ad.'

'I grant yer, 'e was a good doctor years ago, till the booze got 'old of 'im,' admitted Betty Smith.

The messenger was talking, his thumbs tucked through his braces. 'Couldn't rouse 'im at first. 'Ad ter pour a jug o' cold water over 'im. Soon woke 'im up it did. Should 'ave 'eard 'im goin' orf. Anyway, when I told 'im I'd get the lads round if 'e didn't 'urry up, 'e soon changed 'is tune.'

The exodus had started. Women with young children were helped on to the back of a battered old removal van that had somehow been found by one of the volunteers. The driver sat glumly in the cab while Bob Bowman and the red-faced PC Smith sorted out the passengers. Bridie Flannagan was helped up on to the van with her brood. The Solomon boys with their raven-haired mother were next, then little Ernie Jacobs and his large mother, who found difficulty in climbing aboard. The operation was expedited with the helping hand, or rather shoulder, of Patrick Flannagan, who was rewarded with an icy stare from an ungrateful Mrs Jacobs.

'C'mon now, folks,' urged Bob Bowman, 'let's get yer in the warm.'

The mums with their young children waited patiently.

'Don't worry, folks, we'll send the van back,' announced the warden.

The driver looked even more glum and he slumped over the wheel.

It was one thing to be working on Sunday morning, but to have to make a return trip to the Street on what was supposed to be a day of rest irked the employee of Watson's Cartage Contractors. He mused over his bleak chances of a drink before closing time and his face took on a scowl.

While the loading was taking place, the swaying figure of Doctor Mason appeared in the Street. He carried a small black bag in his hand, and blinked his bloodshot eyes as he picked his way gingerly through the debris-strewn turning. The medic's hair was dishevelled from his impromptu cold shower, his blue nose twitched, and his unshaven chin moved from side to side. He cursed the war, the young popinjay who nearly drowned him, and the old lady for having the temerity to throw a fit at such an inconvenient hour. God! he thought, how he needed a drink. He could feel his tongue swelling and he swallowed with difficulty. Perhaps old Granny Flint would have a tot of the good stuff lying around! He quickened his pace and almost fell through the front door of his patient, which was suspended from one hinge, with the iron knocker broken in half. As he picked his way along the passage, the voice of Lizzie Brown rang out, 'We're in 'ere!'

The doctor entered the tiny bedroom at the back of the house, and saw the pale figure of Granny Flint propped up against a pile of pillows. Lizzie Brown and her friend Emmie sat at the old lady's side; Lizzie stroking the patient's bony hand.

Doctor Mason realised that the possibility of obtaining a drink in the present circumstances was nil. Better get the examination over with as soon as possible, he thought, opening his black bag and fumbling for the thermometer. He finally found it and wiped the biscuit crumbs from the glass. The doctor's attempts to lower the mercury were unsuccessful, for after two shakes, he dropped the instrument under the bed.

Lizzie and Emmie looked at each other, and Granny Flint opened one eye. The bleary-eyed doctor got down on all fours and searched among the plaster and broken glass, under the chunks of window-frame, and around the old lady's chamber pot. Finally the thermometer was recovered and wiped on the sleeve of the medic's coat.

'Can you hear me?' croaked Doctor Clarence Mason, holding Granny Flint's chin between thumb and forefinger. The old lady opened one eye, decided she didn't like what she saw and immediately shut her eye again. It was going to be hopeless to take the woman's temperature, especially with her pursing those lips so tightly. Better settle for the pulse, he thought. This proved to be more of a success, except for the fact that the hands of Doctor Mason's pocket-watch seemed to be spinning round at a terrific rate. When the hands slowed down, and the doctor regained his control over his vision, he realised that he had forgotten the count. Never mind, he thought, let's do the heart bit. The stethoscope is here somewhere, sure it went into the bag. He fumbled around among the bottles of pills, biscuit crumbs, and grimy prescription pads.

Lizzie Brown got impatient. 'You lookin' fer yer sounders? They're in yer pocket. I can see 'em stickin' out.'

Doctor Mason almost got the earpiece of the stethoscope rammed up one nostril, but finally found both ears.

Granny Flint opened one eye again and decided there and then that she didn't fancy being prodded with a cold sounder. 'Tell 'im ter breave on it first,' she hissed at Lizzie, who grinned widely. It was the first words the old lady had uttered since the bomb fell. Emmie patted the old lady's hand, and the doctor completed his exacting examination. One thing puzzled the man. He couldn't be sure whether or not the rushing sound was coming from Granny's chest. He had experienced a similar sound inside his head ever since the cold water episode. It was becoming very confusing. The doctor extended his white-coated tongue, then meaningfully licked his dry lips. The meaning was lost on the ladies of Conner Street, and the venerable Doctor Mason clicked his tongue in an irritable fashion as he removed the prescription pad from his black bag.

'Give her two, night and morning. She'll be running around in a couple of days.'

Granny Flint did not intend running anywhere, and what was more, she didn't care for the black bag resting upon her bunion.

'Oi, yer bleedin' bag's on me foot,' she yelped.

The doctor mumbled his apologies and stepped to the foot of Granny's bed to retrieve the bag. The movement of his foot caught the handle of the chamber pot, and it spilled over. The medic raised his bleary eyes to the plasterless ceiling and cursed all chamber pots. The cold, wet feeling in his right shoe made him even more irritable and he made for the door. Some plaster trickled down from the shattered ceiling and found its way down the considerable gap between Doctor Mason's collar and neck and he left as quickly as his shaky legs could propel him.

Out in the Street, the evacuation was well under way. The van had left for the rest centre at the Tanners School. Some of the menfolk had formed a patrol in the Street against possible looters, and the rest of them were coming back later. Bob Bowman was already organising the men into a recovery team. Everything of value, anything that could be saved was piled outside the shattered homes. The heap did not look very impressive: a broken armchair, a rickety wardrobe, and an even more rickety table. Here and there along the devastated turning appeared a small bundle of bedding, a few worthless but priceless heirlooms, and the odd timepiece. There was a table outside Ada Dawkins's home. On the table stood a faded photograph in a glassless frame. A tall guardsman stared down the Street, as though waiting for his Ada.

Those of the homeless who did not hitch a ride on the van had decided to walk to the rest centre. It was situated in a back street off the far end of the Tower Road, and the band of volunteers had some of their group making the old school hall a little more accommodating. The children's benches were spaced out to section off areas. The tea urn was steaming, and hot soup stood in a large stewpot above a simmering gas flame. There were blankets piled neatly on the benches, and clean, crisp towels, with a small bar of white soap beside each towel. Around the walls were the efforts of the schoolchildren. Water colours of bright yellow suns, and deep blue skies. Black-haired men, and red-haired women with scarlet lips. There were also paintings of less translatable ideas; strange fits of colour, and nightmarish brush-work that reflected the troubled minds of the young.

The morning wore on, and the van had returned to load up the treasures of Conner Street. Carefully, with due reverence, the vases and the clocks were placed on the bedding bales. The wardrobes and tables, the washstands and the tallboys were packed on the van until there was no more room. The motor growled into life and the irritable driver crashed in the gear. Slowly the van moved off down the Street. Over the bricks and rubble, crunching the glass beneath its tyres, the vanload of treasures went on its way to the warehouse for the homeless. There the furniture, the bric-a-brac and timepieces would join the huge pile of belongings, to remain until the lucky folk reclaimed their treasures, or until the firebombs destroyed them.

It was quiet, almost too quiet on that fateful Sunday morning, a war-time Sabbath when the church bells could not ring, when the rag-and-bone man ceased to call, when the ice-cream vendor and the winkle stall did not appear at the corner of Conner Street. No more could the Eagle open its doors, defying the German Air Force to take away what was an age-old custom; to walk through the doors of a public house on the stroke of twelve noon on a Sabbath, to order a glass of beer, and to dwell on the events of the week. To sit in the company of one's own and to smell the dampness of the bar, the tang of ale on wood from the overfull pints that dripped on the polished counter and imbued the air with the smell of hops and wax. The silver-blue smoke of Nosegay and Goldflake. To sit in the bar and drink in the company of the docker, the carman and the coster. To dwell with one's kin, in a sharply-creased serge suit and highly polished boots. The white silk scarf that twirled around braces, and the loud checked cap, worn at a cocky angle. To pick up a pint glass with work-scarred hands, and to toast one's neighbour. To hell and beyond to the foe, and welcome to the folk of dockland, was once the message as the doors swung open. There would be no welcome this Sunday to the shuffling few; the Conner Street coalman and the dockers, the Irishman, and other grim-faced characters as they stood in silence, looking at the pile of rubble.

Down the Street, the drama continued. Granny Flint would not allow herself to be persuaded out of her wrecked house. Lizzie Brown pleaded with her, and Emmie Jones remonstrated with her, but to no avail. It was an hour since the doctor had left, and the two helpers had only just managed to get Granny dressed. The old lady sat in the cane chair beside her bed and pursed her lips.

'It's no bleedin' good. The ole cow won't move,' hissed Lizzie.

Emmie shook her head in despair. 'Well she can't stop 'ere. There's no water, no gas, an' the bleedin' roof don't look none too good. If we don't get 'er round the rest centre, she's gonna 'ave anuvver one o' them there turns.'

'Keep yer eye on 'er, Em. I'll 'ave a word wiv Bob,' Lizzie said.

As Lizzie ducked under the hanging front door, she spotted the Street warden talking to Joe Harper. The men were standing by the shelter gates, and they looked over in Lizzie's direction.

''Ow's the old gal, Liz?' asked Bob.

'Bright as a new pin. Trouble is, we can't get 'er out o' the place. She just won't budge,' Lizzie moaned, hands spread to the sky.

Bob Bowman's face was serious. 'Give us a few minutes, Liz. We're expectin' the 'earse for poor ole Skipper any time now. Soon's 'e's bin I'll see what I can do.'

Almost as soon as the warden had uttered the words, a van turned the corner and pulled up outside the shelter gates and two men got out. Joe Harper waved them in the direction of the cavern which contained the body of his old friend.

Lizzie looked hard at the plain grey van with whitened rear windows, and then at Bob Bowman. 'Never seen an 'earse like that before. Must o' bin a few poor bastards copped it last night.'

The two men appeared with the stretchered body carried between them. Expressionless and casual, the men slid the stretcher into the rear of the van and banged the doors shut. Lizzie Brown's face suddenly brightened and she winked at the warden. ''Ere, mate, where yer takin' the ole chap to?'

'Got a mortuary set up in the Drill Hall,' answered the doleful driver.

'Ain't that near the Tanners School?' Lizzie enquired.

'Just round the corner,' said the driver.

Lizzie took the man's arm and steered him away from the rear of the hearse.

Minutes later, Granny Flint came out of her house, with Emmie and Lizzie both holding on to her. The warden and Joe had removed the hanging door and Granny Flint strode through the opening like a queen. There was a look of serenity upon her aged face and a sweet smile on her lips. Eagerly she made her way to the hearse and allowed herself to be placed beside the driver. Emmie squeezed in beside her, and the driver's mate got into the back of the van beside the body of Skipper.

As the van drove slowly away around the corner Joe looked at Lizzie with a puzzled frown. 'What made the ole gal change 'er mind, Liz?'

Lizzie Brown put her hands under her apron and grinned a toothless smile. 'I just told 'er the Lord Mayor o' London sent a special moter car for 'er. I told 'er it was 'cos she was ninety terday.'

'Well I'll be,' gasped Joe, and the warden laughed aloud.

'Is it really 'er birfday?' asked Bob.

'Gawd knows,' grinned Liz. 'She finks it is, that's all that matters.'

'Well, I 'ope she don't find out she's bin in an 'earse. If she ever does, your life won't be worf livin',' chuckled the warden.

Joe Harper swallowed hard and stared down at his feet.

'Ter tell yer the trufe, I don't fink she will mind,' Liz said quietly. 'She always 'ad a soft spot for the ole chap. She won't mind sharin' 'is last ride.'

Chapter Twenty-Two

Early on Sunday morning, Stanley Nathan was awakened by the local police and told that his shop had been extensively damaged by blast during the night.

He and Julie arrived at London Bridge Station at lunchtime and walked the mile or so to Tower Road. The extent of the night's bombing was apparent as they neared Conner Street. Tower Road itself was closed to traffic as there were at least two large bomb craters that spread across the road from pavement to pavement. Workmen had already sealed off the fractured gas main, and other men were busy boarding up the damaged shop fronts.

Tower Road curved slightly, then straightened out for its last half-mile to the junction with Kent Road. The lovers picked their way carefully through the curve and came face to face with a horrifying sight. Every shop had been damaged, every roof had shed tiles, and every inch of the pavement was strewn with broken glass, bricks and rubble. Just short of Conner Street was a large crater, caused by the gas explosion. The ruins of the Eagle spread out to the lip of the hole and some of the large timbers had ended up standing upright in the concavity, like giant markers. The smell of destruction was all around the two as they walked slowly, unbelieving, up to the entrance of the Street. Burnt wood mingled with brick-dust. A sickly sweet smell of cordite and gas fumes lingered in the air, and from the ruins of the Eagle came an aroma of sour beer.

A lorry was pulling slowly out of the turning. It turned left to dodge the crater and then drove along to Kent Road. Stanley and Julie saw the battered pieces of furniture piled up on the lorry and tied with rope. The two men sat holding on tightly to the swaying load as the vehicle bounced and shuddered over the debris-littered roadway. The Street warden was replacing a rope that had been stretched across the turning and he greeted the two with a solemn face.

Julie did not need to be told that the Bradens were dead. She could see that no one would have survived beneath the ruins of the pub. Her nails bit into Stanley's arm as Bob Bowman recounted the events of the night. Her eyes glazed with tears and the warden's features swam before her as she listened. She tried to speak but the words stuck in her throat. Two of the people she really cared for and loved were dead. Florrie had been like a mother to her, and helped her when she most needed it, and now she was gone. John too had always treated her with kindness and understanding, even though he himself was often muddled and confused. Julie sobbed loudly and buried her head into Stanley's chest. The shopkeeper gently stroked her hair and held her close. There was nothing he could think of to say that would ease her pain. He knew only that time could heal the hurt, and he steered her away from the ruins and into the silent Street.

The two walked reverently along the turning, Stanley holding Julie's arm tightly. Slightly behind them, the tall, stooping figure of the warden moved in their wake, like an unwilling guide whose job it was to point out the ugly results of the past few hours. Bob Bowman felt he should walk with them. It was his Street and the responsibility still weighed heavily on his shoulders. As they passed the burned-out leather factory and turned the corner Bob kicked a piece of brick from the pavement in a futile gesture.

Stanley did not know why he steered Julie into the Street. He thought about it as they came up to the flattened row of houses. It seemed to him that they had to look at it for the last time. The old backstreets of the East End were disappearing with the relentless bombing.

The day was cold and damp as the two slowly and painfully made their way along the damaged Tower Road. Julie wanted to talk to the Conner Street folk. She felt the need to be with them, to share their sorrow and compassion, and almost without thinking they wended their way towards the rest centre. They went to meet their friends, refugees from a place of chaos and confusion.

Only a few houses at the Tower Road end of the devastated little backstreet were still habitable, and even in these the water and gas had been turned off. A water main had been damaged in the Tower Road and the gas works along Kent Road had sustained a direct hit during the night. No roast meals were cooked in the area on that cold Sunday. Emergency water tankers were moving around the backstreets dealing out one bucket of water to each person. For the kids it meant that they had to go without a wash, which did not seem to trouble them too much. As for lighting, kerosene lamps were brought out, cleaned and trimmed, then placed in the small parlours in preparation for the coming darkness.

Conner Street on that cold Sunday afternoon seemed to have become a graveyard, quiet, devoid of life. The adjoining Tanners Alley was desolated, hideous in silence. The wall of the leather factory had fallen into the cobbled path, and the damage caused by the heat of the fire had left the cottages blackened and shell-like. Gone were the autumn flowers, gone were the dainty window shutters and the little window boxes, and gone too were the inhabitants, who had made their escape over the back gardens. Very few of them had left their homes for the shelter the previous night, but the caprices of Providence had dealt kindly with them, and everyone who lived in the once pretty alley was safe.

One thing remained the same, although it now seemed to lean a fraction more from the perpendicular. The Crimean cannon had heard the rumble of war once again and now bore a new scar on its iron carcass, a deep indentation caused by a bomb fragment. It had been warmed again, not by the speeding ball-shot through its core but by the terrible searing heat of the factory fire. Now in the cold, dull afternoon, the Crimean cannon that had changed into a hitching post cooled. Northerly winds whistled around it and gusted along the Street, creating eerie sounds in and about the forsaken homes, as though lamenting the departed.

In the old school hall, the refugees from Conner Street ate their Sunday lunch and then resumed their places on the low benches. They felt the enormity of the night's events now, and they sat hunched, with few words passing between them. The children in their innocence were more vociferous as they sat in a group at one end of the hall.

One of the refugees was missing. Wheezy had slipped out early that afternoon to visit his pal, Hoppy Dyke. Hoppy lay propped up against a mound of pillows in a small converted storeroom. Guy's Hospital was full of blitz casualties; the less severely injured were resting in corridors, or in any odd corner that could accommodate them. They lay quiet and shocked, drugged against the pain and sleeping fitfully. Wheezy gave one or two of the casualties a cheery wave as he followed the nurse's directions to the storeroom. He found his friend and pulled up a chair at the bedside. An iron frame beneath the bedclothes kept the linen away from Hoppy's burnt legs, and by the bed, covered with a white cloth, was an instrument trolley. Wheezy looked hard at Hoppy, hardly recognising him. The casualty from Conner Street was wincing with pain, his face drained of colour, and he looked much older than his years.

''Ow's it goin', mate?' Wheezy asked cheerfully.

Hoppy's face screwed up in pain. 'Bloody legs are givin' me 'ell.'

Wheezy lifted the white cloth from the trolley and peered beneath. 'Wot's this, yer dinner?'

Hoppy screwed up his face again and his eyes closed for a second or two. Wheezy now sitting by the bed felt at a loss for words. He looked up at the ceiling and around the windowless room. A nurse appeared and went over to the bed opposite. She leant across the patient and listened to his breathing for a few moments before taking his pulse. Wheezy's lecherous eyes never left the nurse until she disappeared from the room. The white of her thighs above the black stockings had aroused him and he turned to Hoppy. 'Did yer see that, mate? Cor! I bet yer get an eyeful in 'ere!'

The patient's singed legs sent their painful ciphers along his nervous system and he grimaced.

''Ere, yer ain't burnt yer ole plonker, 'ave yer?' Wheezy asked suddenly.

This time Hoppy managed a weak grin. 'It's only singed, fank Gawd.'

The pretty nurse appeared again and walked up to Hoppy's bed. She placed a thermometer in his mouth and took his wrist, looking at a watch that was pinned to her apron front. Wheezy watched until the nurse was finished, then he gave her a crooked smile. The reply was a cold stare from the nurse as she walked from the room.

'Cor! I bet they drive yer mad in 'ere,' Wheezy said, screwing up his face for effect.

The pain was getting worse and Wheezy's conversation irked the patient. He wanted Wheezy to leave and the nurse to hurry up with his painkiller.

'Never mind. Give it a couple o' days an' you'll be up an' at 'em, mate,' Wheezy went on.

Hoppy managed a tired grin. His eyes closed again and he bit his lip. The nurse walked over to the bed and looked down at Wheezy. 'I'm afraid it's time to go,' she said coldly. 'He must get some sleep now.'

The swirling fog seemed to be getting worse as Wheezy Morris made his way back to the rest centre. The early evening was cold and damp, with condensation glistening on the cobbled streets. If it gets any worse they won't be coming tonight, he thought, and he whistled tunelessly as he reached the centre, crossed the deserted playground, and entered the stuffy interior.

It was tea-time at the Tanners School Rest Centre, and Granny Flint was causing a minor stir. 'It's no good, I can't eat yer bleedin' cake. It's stone 'ard I tell yer.'

The volunteer gave Granny Flint a forced smile and persisted with the cake.

Granny Flint pulled a face. 'Now listen 'ere. I ain't eatin' that lump o' brick yer call cake, so there. An' I tell yer somefing else. I ain't drinkin' that bloody cocoa, 'cos I don't like cocoa, so put that in yer pipe an' smoke it.'

Seeing that it was hopeless to persist, the helper left Granny Flint.

The rest of the women of the Street sat around Granny, their faces tired and strained, but their spirits still high.

'Wiv that fog comin' down outside, I reckon we'll get a rest from the bastards ternight,' said Lizzie Brown.

'As long as that wind don't get up,' said Emmie.

'Well I don't know about you lot, but I'm stoppin' 'ere ternight. I couldn't face that shelter again, not after seein' poor ole Skipper's face as 'e lay there,' Nan Roberts joined in.

Mrs Wallace got up and beckoned her ailing husband to follow. 'Well we're goin' back ter the shelter, ain't we, luv?'

George Wallace coughed loudly and nodded.

As the couple got to the door, Mrs Wallace turned and looked at Nan Roberts. 'Yer know the old sayin', lightnin' don't strike the same place twice.'

Granny Flint gave out a wicked chuckle. 'I didn't know it was lightnin' wot knocked our 'ouses down.'

The Wallaces left the centre, the women's laughter ringing in their ears.

Lizzie Brown watched them leave and turned to Granny Flint. 'Granny, you're a wicked ole lady,' she said with a sly grin.

Granny Flint shrugged her shoulders and the women laughed, except for Emmie Jones. She wiped a tear from her eye and sat with her head bowed.

'Cheer up, Emm, it could be worse,' said Lizzie.

Emmie looked at Lizzie Brown and the tears started to fall. 'Gawd, Liz, you make me so mad sometimes. We've lost our 'omes, an' we've lost good neighbours, an' wot's more the bastards will be back ternight.'

The women went quiet, and Granny Flint started to doze.

Lizzie Brown looked at the little group for a while, then got up and stood before them, hands on hips. 'You lot make me sick, sittin' there as though it was the end of everyfing. We're alive, ain't we? The Almighty smiled on most of us last night. We're warm, an' dry, ain't we?'

The group looked at Lizzie in silence.

'Well, ain't we?' Lizzie said more loudly.

The women nodded.

'When I say fings could be worse I mean it,' Lizzie went on. 'Just imagine that door openin' an' that ole tyke o' mine strollin' in. Yes, my ole luvs, fings could be worse.'

The evening wore on and the fog swirled around the school building. From the interior, sounds of a harmonica and singing drifted out into the haze. A sudden breeze caught a sweet wrapper and sent it across the school playground. The wind freshened, and above an early star winked down. The fog was clearing.

Epilogue

A high flying jet plane was tracing a thin line across the azure sky. The sun was climbing and there was just a ghost of a breeze. June flowers were blooming in the public garden as the old man walked slowly along the gravel path. He stopped once or twice to admire the gardener's efforts and to rest his tired and aching legs. He leaned heavily on a stout walking-stick, for his arthritis had been paining him of late. Today, however, he felt much better. The prospect of an early summer cheered him and it would certainly help his stiffening joints.

The public garden allowed a short cut to the Bargee, which was only a few minutes from the park exit. If he had timed it right they would just be opening by the time he reached there. The old man usually left his ground floor bedsit at ten thirty am and stopped to buy a morning paper and tobacco at the corner shop. Weather permitting, the old man's journey to the Bargee was a daily occurrence. The riverside pub was the popular haunt of managers from local firms, and more than one contract had been finalised in the little saloon bar. Tourists as well found the Bargee on their itinerary, and the pub's manager and his wife had by now become quite used to appearing in the tourists' family snapshots, usually taken on the pub's veranda overlooking the Thames.

That veranda was the old man's destination, and he liked to get there before the lunchtime flow of impatient, harassed businessmen. On this particular morning, with the heat already rising up from the gravel path, the prospect of a pint of bitter made him lick his lips. As he left the garden the old man turned to his right then walked a few yards before crossing the street. Since the wharves had closed there was not much traffic using the riverside route through dockland. The only vehicles he encountered were a slow-cruising police car and the milk float that whined along on its way back to the depot. At the entrance to the pub the old man leant on the wall and glanced up at the clock face on the tower of St Mary's Church. The hour hand pointed to the six and had been in that position since the Blitz, when a bomb had blown the minute hand away and shattered the clock's mechanism. Still leaning against the wall the old man pulled up his sleeve to look at his thick wristwatch and realised that he hadn't wound it lately. Must get one of those new-fangled watches that don't need winding, he promised himself.

The sound of sliding bolts came from inside the pub and the door swung back.

''Ello, Bob. You're bright an' early this mornin'.' The speaker was a pretty young girl who served behind the bar. Her hair was fair and cascaded over her eyes as she bent down to fasten the door back.

'Nice mornin'. Gonna be a scorcher, mark my words,' Bob commented as he walked into the pub.

The girl trotted in behind him and walked around the counter. She adjusted her yellow smock, then waited while Bob Bowman went through his usual ritual. First he doffed his greasy cap and stuffed it into his coat pocket. Then he hooked his walking-stick over the back of a bar chair, his clenched fist placed on the bar counter for support. Next he took a handful of silver from his pocket and dropped the coins in a heap in front of the girl. Molly Wright smiled and counted out the price of a pint less ten pence. While she was pulling on the bar pump Bob looked around him. There was only one other person in the saloon bar, a young man who was filling up the cigarette machine.

'There yer go, Bob,' Molly said as she placed a foaming pint of beer at his elbow. Conner Street's ex-warden took a long swig from the glass and then put it back on the counter. He pulled out a large red spotted handkerchief from his coat pocket and shook it furiously before wiping it across his mouth. He gasped and burped loudly, his face still flushed from the effort of his walk.

'Cor I needed that,' he gasped as he wiped his watery blue eyes on his handkerchief.

Molly leaned on the counter facing him, her large brown eyes looking at him fondly. 'Where yer goin', Bob, on the veranda?' she asked.

'Yus, I reckon I will. A bit o' sea air will do me ole chest good,' Bob replied, with a grin spreading over his bony features.

Molly followed him out on to the veranda and placed the pint of beer by his hand. Bob settled himself and proceeded to fill his pipe.

Molly sat on the edge of the table facing him. From her position she could see into the bar. 'The river looks calm, Bob. It's 'ardly movin'.'

The old man squinted up his eyes and looked upriver to the distant Tower Bridge. 'Tide's on the turn. Looks calm I grant yer, but them currents is bloody treacherous. If yer fell in yer'd be swept downriver quick as lightnin'.'

The cigarette man popped his head around the door and winked at Molly. 'All done. See yer next week, babe.'

Molly bared her white teeth in a forced grin, then pulled a face at the disappearing figure.

The gesture was lost on Bob. He was scanning the river, his eyes narrow slits. He noticed that a few of the wharves were coming back to life. Here and there a pane of glass replaced a loophole, and a few brightly coloured window boxes had appeared, suspended over the water.

Molly followed his gaze as she sat with her arms folded over her small breasts. 'We're getting quite a few new customers in lately. Some of 'em are dressed real funny. Lovely people they are though. Ever so friendly.'

Bob Bowman took another swig from his glass. 'I've seen a few changes on that river, girl. I was only a pup when I started workin' in the docks, an' I packed up in '65. Took me severance I did. I'm eighty come August, please Gawd.'

Molly smiled at him. 'Well you don't look a day over sixty, Bob.'

Bob snorted. 'Go on wiv yer, yer cheeky little mare.'

Molly Wright ignored his remark. 'Can I get yer a refill before the crush starts?'

'One more. I gotta bit of a dry froat, luv.'

While the barmaid was filling Bob's glass a customer came in. He was elderly and straight-backed. Molly served him a Guinness then carried Bob's drink out on to the veranda. 'Mr Fred'ricks 'as just come in,' she said.

The old man pulled a face. ''Im. Bloody ole moaner. What wiv 'im an' that Miss Cavendish. Right pair o' neighbours they are.'

Molly frowned, and Bob continued, ''E's bin complainin' about me geraniums. Said they gave orf a smell o' cat's piss. I tell yer. If them flowers do smell it's 'is bloody ole tom cat wot's done it.'

Molly watched him take a sip from the glass, her eyes wide and smiling.

'There's 'er. Scatty mare.' Bob snorted.

'Who?'

'Why, ole Miss Bloody Cavendish. She reckons they're spyin' on 'er.'

'Who is?'

'Why the council. Told me last week. Said they're peepin' in 'er letter-box.'

'No.'

''S'right. Told me they're watchin' ter see if she takes in men friends.'

'Really?'

'Sure as I'm sittin' 'ere. Sure as Gawd made little apples. Bloody 'ell, who in their right mind would fancy ole Miss Cavendish?'

Molly laughed heartily. 'Bob, you are a one. If your Brenda could 'ear yer carryin' on like that she'd 'ave somethin' ter say.'

Bob Bowman looked up at Molly. 'That reminds me. Brenda an' Joe are coming up ter take me out fer a drink come Saturday. I s'pose they'll tell me all about their new 'ouse.'

Molly's eyes became sad, and she looked at the old man fondly. 'Didn't yer want ter go ter Sevenoaks wiv 'em, Bob?'

'O' course I didn't. I like it 'ere better. I've got me flowers an' me privicy. Can't ask fer much more, can yer?'

Molly noticed that some customers had walked in. She excused herself and Bob was left alone with his thoughts.

Presently a tall stranger walked out on to the veranda. He was broad-shouldered and wore a sand-coloured suit. Around his neck hung a large camera, and he carried a small bag with the letters TWA stamped on the side. For a time he stood looking at the river.

Bob followed his gaze. A lone sculler was battling against the ebbing tide, and a pleasure boat was passing under Tower Bridge, heading in their direction. Apart from the two craft the river was empty.

The American started to take some snapshots, his camera clicking and whirring. When he was satisfied with his efforts, the American sat down facing Bob Bowman and gave him a friendly grin. 'That's some river, isn't it?'

The old man wanted very much to tell the tall man about the river. His river: the ships moored at anchor, awaiting a berth, the tugs hauling clusters of laden barges up into the Pool, the cranes, dipping and swinging over the quays, the shouts of the river men, the laughter and the curses. Instead he bit his tongue and said simply, 'It's pretty quiet terday, mate.'